About

Candace 'Candy' Havens is a best selling and award-winning author. She is a two-time *RITA*, Write Touch Reader and Holt Medallion finalist. She is also the winner of the Barbara Wilson award. Candy is a nationally syndicated entertainment columnist for *FYI Television*. A veteran journalist she has interviewed just about everyone in Hollywood and you can hear Candy weekly on New Country 96.3 KSCS in the Dallas Fort Worth Area.

Maisey Yates is the *New York Times* bestselling author of over one hundred romance novels. An avid knitter with a dangerous yarn addiction and an aversion to housework, Maisey lives with her husband and three kids in rural Oregon. She believes the trek she makes to her coffee maker each morning is a true example of her pioneer spirit. Find out more about Maisey's books on her website: maiseyyates.com, or find her on Facebook, Instagram or TikTok by searching her name.

Jessica Lemmon is a former job-hopper who resides in Ohio with her husband and rescue dogs. She holds a degree in graphic design currently gathering dust in an impressive frame. When she's not writing emotionally charged stories, she spends her time drawing, drinking coffee, and laughing with friends. Her motto is 'read for fun', and she believes we should all do more of what makes us happy. Learn more about her books at jessicalemmon.com

Fake Dating:
Tempted at Christmas

CANDACE HAVENS

MAISEY YATES

JESSICA LEMMON

MILLS & BOON

First Published in Great Britain 2024
by Mills & Boon, an imprint of HarperCollins*Publishers* Ltd,
1 London Bridge Street, London, SE1 9GF

www.harpercollins.co.uk

HarperCollins*Publishers*
Macken House, 39/40 Mayor Street Upper,
Dublin 1, D01 C9W8, Ireland

ISBN: 978-0-263-39665-2

MIX
Paper | Supporting
responsible forestry
FSC™ C007454

This book contains FSC™ certified paper and other controlled sources to ensure responsible forest management.

For more information visit: www.harpercollins.co.uk/green

Printed and Bound in the UK using 100% Renewable Electricity
at CPI Group (UK) Ltd, Croydon, CR0 4YY

CHRISTMAS WITH
THE MARINE

CANDACE HAVENS

This book is dedicated to the Blaze readers.
Thank you for all of your support.

1

Marine Major Ben Hawthorne had served three tours in the Middle East. He'd survived being shot and a near-fatal helicopter crash. But this… This was beyond his capabilities. This is what happened when people gambled.

They ended up in giant toy stores in the Barbie aisle, trying to find the right one for a six-year-old orphan.

He'd rather go on another tour. Not that he didn't want the child to have her toy, it was just difficult. There were so many. Doctor ones and scientists, and an underwater one. And they came in all sizes. But all the child had listed was "Barbie." And Ben had lost a bet with his friends, so he was on his own buying more than one hundred gifts for the Toys for Tots program.

And he'd do it. As a kid, he'd lived through more than one Christmas without much under the tree. He understood how it felt to wake up with next to nothing there, not that it had bothered him much back then. He'd tried to make sure his little sister always had at least a couple of toys, even if they weren't exactly what she wanted. Seeing that smile of hers was something he'd sorely missed while being out of the country for the past ten years.

So he felt a lot of responsibility to get this right. That was one of the reasons he hadn't thrown much of a fit when he'd lost the bet.

Still, a Barbie was not his forte. GI Joe maybe, even Superman, but these dolls were beyond him.

"Hey, are you okay?" He glanced down to see a pair of light blue eyes staring back at him. They reminded him of the color of the sky on a clear day and were framed by a heart-shaped face and beautiful long strawberry-blond hair.

"What?"

Well, that was cool. Beautiful woman talking. Pay attention.

"You keep looking at the list and then the shelf. Do you need help? Are you buying something for your daughter?"

Her voice was soft and she didn't have a drawl like most of the people who lived in Corpus Christi. Even a lot of the guys on the base where he taught had a Texas accent. He'd grown used to it.

"Do you work here?" Of course she didn't work here. She was dressed in an expensive leather jacket and jeans and carrying one of those purses that probably cost more than his truck. The last woman he'd dated had treated that same kind of purse like it was her child. She'd definitely liked the purse more than she had him.

This lady laughed and heat warmed his lower regions. *Come on*, he told himself, *she's trying to help you.*

"No, but thanks to my twin nieces I'm well versed in everything Barbie. If you tell me a bit more about the little girl, I can probably help you."

She was beautiful, but more than that, he was desperate. If she could just point him in the right direction, he'd be her love slave for life.

Where the heck did that come from? *Dude, chill.*

He handed her the list. "It says she wants to be a vet when she grows up," he said. "Each kid has a short, one-line description about them."

Her eyebrow went up as she scanned the page. He pointed to the name of Jolie, the little girl in question. "She also likes puppies."

"This is a long list of kids. Your family must be huge." She frowned as her chin dropped and then she flipped to the next page and then the next. "There's more than fifty names here."

"Oh, no." He laughed. "I kind of lost a bet and I'm having to get the gifts for the Toys for Tots program. I'm from the Marine base." He pulled the other list out of his back pocket. "I also have a list of elderly patients from a nursing home facility who also need gifts." It was the last time he'd be playing poker with his friends Brody and Matt. They'd been in charge of the Christmas event, and now it was all on him.

"Wow. That must have been some bet."

He grunted. "Yep. Anyway, we have a fund everyone on the base donates to throughout the year, and then the first week of December we try to buy as many items as the money allows."

"This, my friend, is your lucky day." She grinned again, and then actually winked one of those beautiful blue eyes. It did all kinds of crazy things to his body.

Funny, he was thinking the same thing—about it being his lucky day. He'd practically been sent an angel for his very own Christmas present. He cleared his throat. "How's that?"

"Well, I happen to be a professional shopper."

His brows drew together. "So you like to shop?"

"More than that, it's my business. I shop for busy professionals. That's why I'm here. On the hunt for a few gifts for a CEO's kids."

"Wait. People pay you to shop for them?"

She smirked. "Yes. It's a *real* profession, and I do just fine, thank you."

He'd offended her, and held up his hands in surrender. "Sorry. I've just never heard of anything like that. But it's cool. I didn't mean to insult you. I'm the guy standing here staring at a million dolls without a clue what to do."

She shrugged. "I'm used to the attitude. My family feels that way about my chosen profession. Since you're doing this for charity, and I think it's sweet you're taking this so seriously, trying to find the right gift for each child, I'll help for free."

"Oh, I don't mind paying for your services." That sounded really wrong. A woman walked past them and gave them a dirty look. "I mean, uh, I'd be grateful. So much so that I'll pay the fee."

She started laughing. "Sweet. But you can't afford me."

Another woman walked by, yanking her kids along, giving them more dirty looks. They would get arrested if they kept this up.

"Before we get thrown out, maybe I should hurry up and say thanks. And can I buy you dinner, at least?"

She laughed nervously. "Hmm. We'll see." She held out her hand. "I'm Ainsley Garrett."

He shook her hand and her skin was so smooth. "I'm Ben Hawthorne, and thanks again."

"Go get two more carts. I'll start on your list."

Two hours and six carts of toys later, he had everything he was supposed to buy. He and one of the store clerks were piling the bags in the back of his SUV when Ainsley walked out carrying a couple of large bags of her own.

"Hey," he called to her and waved. "I really would like to thank you. Let me take you to dinner."

"It isn't necessary. Besides, I have plans." And just like that she shot him down. Figured. Someone as beautiful as she was wouldn't be alone. But at least he'd tried.

"Okay, but I feel guilty about not paying you for your time."

"No worries. It was fun."

If she said so. Even though the toys were for a good cause, shopping gave him a headache.

She turned and walked away, and he wanted to say something. Pull her back into his orbit. Even though he understood she was way out of his league—from her designer shoes to those sunglasses perched on top of her head—he was sad their time together was up.

Pathetic. Yeah, but it had been a long time since he'd met a woman like her. Maybe never. He hadn't seen a ring, but she might have a boyfriend or be engaged, and he didn't poach.

He'd seen too many of his fellow Marines cheated on by lonely spouses left back home. So he was wary of that sort of thing. And it was one of many reasons he wasn't big on long-term anything. He was married to his job and planned to stay that way for the fore-seeable future.

He turned to finish helping the clerk with the last of the bags.

"Hey," she said.

He glanced back.

"So, do you have to wrap all those gifts by yourself?"

Shoot. He hadn't even thought of that. He pinched the bridge of his nose. "Man, that didn't even occur to me." It was the truth. He'd have to buy paper, and he was the world's worst gift-wrapper, not that he'd done it that often. A few times, he'd sent things home while he was overseas, but he never wrapped them.

"Give me your phone."

Was she giving him her phone number? Things were looking up.

She typed into his phone and then handed it back to him. It was an address.

Even better.

"Tomorrow, meet me there at twelve forty-five. The drill team is holding their annual craft fair."

"Drill team?" What was she talking about?

"They have a gift-wrapping service. For a dollar donation per gift they'll wrap it and do a beautiful job."

"Thank you. I'll definitely do that. Wait? Did you say meet you there?"

She nodded. "Yes. Give me your list for the nursing home."

He pulled the paper out of his back pocket. She perused it again.

"What's your budget?"

"We have eleven hundred dollars, but I was going to add a little more if we needed it."

"I think that should be plenty. I'll pick these gifts up for you and meet you at the high school tomorrow. See ya."

"Hold on. Don't you need money for the gifts?"

"Not yet. You can give it to me tomorrow. How gullible are you giving your money to a stranger?"

"You just helped me buy a couple thousand dollars' worth of toys for children. I'm pretty sure I can trust you." She didn't bother to turn around.

What kind of person went and bought all those gifts without taking the cash?

Look on the bright side, he told himself, at least you'll see her the next day. That idea for the gift wrapping was awesome. The whirlwind that was Ainsley had saved him. Again.

"Thanks," he said belatedly. But it was to air. He hadn't even seen where she'd gone.

Hmm. She was so beautiful and kind. Hard combination to find sometimes.

But so out of his league.

Yes, she was. And he had a feeling she was going to fuel a whole lot of fantasies for a while.

Yep. Enjoy your dreams. Since that was about the only way a guy like him was going to get a woman like her.

AS HARD AS SHE tried not to, Ainsley stole a look in her rearview mirror at Ben. That man was too gorgeous for words with his muscles, chiseled jaw and close-cut Marine haircut. Her mouth had gone dry when she'd seen the big muscled man in a uniform searching for dolls, of all things. He'd been so serious, trying to find the right gifts for kids, as if he was on the mission of a lifetime. He'd been so enthusiastic about making sure those children had a great Christmas that it had been contagious. It had been the most fun she'd had in a really long time.

He had a heart.

It was something she was pretty sure had been missing from the last three guys she'd dated, two of whom her parents had picked out for her. She'd never trust them again. The men they pointed out to her were all narcissistic jerks, every one of them. And she couldn't imagine any of them, losing a bet or not, shopping for gifts for a bunch of kids and the elderly.

That tugged at her in a way she couldn't ignore.

No. No more men. The next two years I'll be focused on growing my business.

Ben lifted his arms to close the back of his SUV and his shirt pulled loose from his jeans. Those abs.

Chiseled was the only word that came to mind. Like they'd been carved in stone.

She sucked in a breath.

Oh, my. She fanned herself and waited for him to pull out of the parking lot before backing out her hybrid. That was a M-A-N.

Though it had been work she'd had a good time today. She and Ben had laughed as they questioned some of the toys' characteristics. Like a doll that pooped, and one that had the creepiest voice as it called for its mama. It made them both shiver, and then chuckle out loud.

After they'd picked up the gifts for the girls on the list, they'd been to the aisle with all the Matchbox cars.

"I bet you had a ton of these when you were a kid," she'd said.

He'd held one of the sports cars with reverence. "No..." His voice had been a whisper and then he'd frowned. And that's when she'd noticed he didn't have a lot of experience with toys...at all. Everything seemed new to him.

What kind of childhood had he had?

It made her feel selfish because she'd never wanted for anything. Ever. She'd wanted to ask him about his past, but it didn't seem right. And she had the sense that it might make him sad. They only had a few hours together and she hadn't wanted to ruin it.

It also felt good to help someone in need. Okay, she did that every day. Her job gave her the greatest joy, as she helped her clients find the perfect gifts for their loved ones, employees and friends. But making kids and old people happy—that was a different level of giving.

Her phone rang. "Accept call," she said.

"Hello?" Bebe said. Her trusty partner's British accent came through loud and clear. Ainsley wasn't sure what she'd do without her best friend—the woman was a master scheduler and kept their finances in order. She also wasn't afraid to talk to a client about a bill, which was something that made Ainsley really uncomfortable. Talking about money always did. Bebe had started as an assistant, but had quickly become her partner in crime.

"Are you there?"

"I'm here," she said as she left the parking lot, her mind still on the Marine. "And, yes, I know I'm running late. I got caught up doing some charity work. I'll drop Bob's presents off for you to wrap, and then I'll head out to Clinical South." The head administrator wanted to discuss gifts for the staff, and for any of the patients who would be stuck in the facility over the holidays.

This really was their busiest time of year and she'd spent too much of her packed schedule helping the hot guy.

"That's why I'm calling. They actually pushed you to tomorrow. I've been trying to call for the last hour. Did you leave your phone in the car again?"

No. She'd been distracted by the glorious man in uniform.

"I didn't hear it ring."

"I swear I'm going to put 'The Imperial March' on

your phone so you hear when I call. Anyway, Craig Price at CIM wants to meet with you about gifts for his staff. He had a four o'clock open. Can I tell them you'll be there?"

She sighed. Craig was an ex. One of the several narcissists she'd dated, though he hadn't been as bad as some of the others. He was married to his job, though, and when he thought it was okay to go six months between calling for dates, they parted ways. But his technology company, CIM, had over four hundred employees—that was a pretty tidy commission for her company.

But Craig. *Ugh.*

"I know he's a prat, but that commission pays the mortgage for a year. I'd go, but I'm meeting with the Funky Monkey folks at three. They have a bunch of new merchandise they're bringing by."

"I wish we could switch," she said. She loved the boutique called Funky Monkey more than just about any other. The owner, Amy, was one of the most creative people she'd ever met.

"I promise to nab something shiny for you. Craig specifically asked for you. Maybe he wants to apologize for being such a fool. And hello, we promised ourselves a Christmas bonus this year if we made our goals, and we're so very close."

She had a point. And this was business. In the two years she'd been operating, she'd had to handle much worse. Some of her wealthiest clients, a few of whom were her parents' friends, felt entitled and had to be treated that way. Even after she'd grown up around that sort of wealth, their attitudes chewed at her gut. But she wasn't dumb. The client was always right. Even if they were jerks sometimes. Well, as long as they paid their bills.

"Yep. You're right. Yes, I can do four. Do you have suggestions? Did they give you a budget?"

"Yes, on both counts. His assistant gave me the rundown on what type of gifts and how much they wanted to spend for each level from the board on down."

Ainsley did love it when they were organized. "Okay, good. That makes our job easier. Can you print out the ideas and put a book together for me?"

They did most of their presentations on a laptop or tablet, but clients liked to have something they could hold in their hands and peruse. It was a trick she'd learned early on. Folks tended to buy more when they could feel the pages. Weird, but true.

"Already working on it."

"And that, my friend, is why I love you best."

"Yes, luv, remember that when it's time for my raise." Ainsley smiled. Bebe could give herself a raise whenever she wanted, although they would discuss it first, as they did everything.

"Yes, ma'am. Okay, so I'll see you in a bit."

That's what she needed—a reminder of what was most important. Her work. This was their most important time of the year. The last thing she wanted to deal with was a distraction.

Especially a hot Marine.

She took another deep breath.

A very hot, sexy Marine.

2

THE HIGH SCHOOL cafeteria buzzed with activity. And it was loud. Really loud. Ben wasn't a huge fan of big crowds or noise, but this was for a good cause. There were booths with everything from wooden toys to homemade candles to miniature Christmas trees. He'd never seen anything like it.

"Explain to me again why we're here and not watching the game? It's almost the end of football season," Matt complained.

"I bought the toys, you guys have to help me haul them in to get them wrapped." It would have taken him thirty trips from the car and back without his friends.

He searched the throng of people for the pretty blonde, but he didn't see her. Dang if he hadn't thought about her all night.

Jake grinned and tightened his grip on the bags he was carrying. It was as if his buddy could read his thoughts.

Mari, Brody's wife and mother of his child, bustled up next to him.

"I think it's sweet that you're doing this," Mari said to Ben. "You're helping the Toys for Tots program *and* the fund-raiser for the drill team. You're my hero."

Brody cleared his throat. "I thought I was your hero."

"Oh, honey, always. Always." She kissed him, and Ben had to look away. Sometimes their intimacy bothered him. He wasn't sure why. Maybe because he'd never been that close to another person. He'd dated a lot of women, but none that made him feel the way that Brody talked about his wife. And his friend Matt was a goner, as well, with his fiancée, Chelly. His buddies were so wrapped up in their women, and Ben just didn't get it.

He was attracted to the women he dated, but his interest waned after a short while. The guys on the base where he taught helicopter maintenance classes, tested the machines and helped out with training missions called him Casanova because he had a different girl every week.

There was one woman he definitely wanted to spend time with, but he had a feeling she was far beyond his reach.

It took a few minutes but they finally found the booth set up for gift wrapping. It was staffed by a bunch of young girls, with ponytails, in stretch pants and T-shirts that read Dance with Me.

"You want us to wrap how many?" one of the young girls asked. She had her hair piled so high on her head it almost added another foot.

She gave him a once-over, and it was all he could do not to laugh. Where was Ainsley?

"Yes, and I'll donate two dollars a package, which is a dollar more than you guys usually ask for," Ben said. Even at this young age, money talked.

The girl's smile grew, and then a woman came up behind her. She held out her hand. "Hi, I'm Coach Kaylie. That's very generous of you. May I ask who these toys are for? There are a lot of them." She didn't look much older than the girl giving him a tough time.

"Toys for Tots," Jake said, as he patted Ben on the back. "Our boy here picked them all out, but we need help wrapping them."

"Terrific," Kaylie said. "That's so kind that you're doing this for kids. Of course we'll help you. And we really appreciate the donation. We're trying to get to three different dance competitions this year, so every penny counts." She batted her eyelashes at Jake.

This time Ben did chuckle. Jake had that effect on women. Never failed.

"Wonderful," a woman's voice said. He glanced down to see Ainsley. She was here, and she looked every bit as beautiful as she had the day before. He'd been sure his imagination had been playing tricks on him.

Today, she wore jeans and boots that came up to her knees. But it was the tight white sweater that nearly did him in. Her body was the stuff of fantasies. His fantasies.

Once again he found himself clearing his throat, and he positioned the bag he was carrying so no one would see the sudden tent in his pants.

Crap. Sad puppies. Old, crinkly people. He had to think of something that was not the beautiful woman beside him.

"Hi," he said. *Well, that was brilliant.*

She beamed up at him. "I've brought the rest of your gifts. Got them first thing this morning. Since they're for the nursing home, I asked the girls to put them in bags with tissue so it would be easier for those arthritic hands to open," she said sweetly. "They should be just about finished with those."

"You really do think of everything."

"Part of the job."

"Oh," Kaylie said. "This is the guy you were talking about?"

"Yes," Ainsley, said waving a hand to the group of kids wrapping at the tables behind the coach. There was now a bunch of boys, as well. "I'm glad you picked up some more volunteers."

"Yeah, I never seem to have a hard time getting the football and basketball teams to help out the dancers. Though, keeping a constant eye on them isn't always the easiest." Kaylie laughed. "We should be done in about thirty minutes with the seniors' gifts, and we'll need a few hours for the tots."

Brody groaned behind him.

"It's okay, guys, if you want to go on home." He turned back to Kaylie. "Can some of those players help me load the truck later?"

"Absolutely," she said.

"I'll stay," Jake offered. "I don't mind volunteering

if you need help," he said to Kaylie. "I'm not much good at wrapping, but I'm good at other things."

Kaylie and Ainsley both roared with laughter.

"What?" Jake asked innocently. "I meant I can keep an eye on the players to make sure they aren't trying to put the moves on these lovely young ladies."

The dancers giggled and whispered to one another.

"I might take you up on that," Kaylie said. "You two," she called out, pointing to Ainsley and Ben, "go look around and come back in a couple of hours. We'll have everything ready."

"That sounds like a good plan," Brody said. "I'm going to search for Mari. Make sure she doesn't need help with anything. Matt, I can give you a ride back."

They waved goodbye and then left.

Ainsley crooked her arm through his. "Come on, Marine. I'll buy you lunch and we can check out the booths. I have a few homemade gifts on my list. I might find them here."

He'd walk across hot coals to spend a little time with her, so he could easily handle the loud noise of the craft fair a little longer. "Only if you let me buy," he said.

"Sure. If you really want to."

"Hey, you've donated a lot of time and like I said, I owe you a meal at the very least."

"Whatever. Come on."

He thought they'd head back to the parking lot. He planned on taking her somewhere nice. Instead, she pulled him through a maze of booths to reach the other end of the cafeteria.

"Hold up, you want to eat here?"

"Yes," she said. "This booth has the best chili pies."

She walked up to the window. "Who made the chili today?" she asked the elderly woman manning the cash box.

"Frank," the woman replied. "He doesn't let anyone else touch it. Doesn't want to ruin his reputation. What can I get for you?"

"You are in for a treat," Ainsley said to Ben. "Frank is an award-winning chili star. His daughter, Amber, is on the drill team. He's pretty much the best thing about coming to the craft fair."

She turned to the woman. "We need two chili pies and a Coke. And what do you want to drink?" she said to him.

"Water is good." He didn't drink a lot of soda. He tried to avoid sugar and he was careful about what he ate, too. Not that he had a lot of choice when he was deployed. You ate what the mess hall gave you or what was in your pack. But when he was stateside he ate fresh food whenever he could. He'd learned to cook when he was kid. It'd helped out his mom because she had to work so much of the time.

"You okay?" Ainsley was handing him a bottle of water.

"What? Yeah. Sorry. I've never had a chili pie."

"No way. Fritos and chili and cheese. Best things ever. Are you some kind of health nut? Is that how you have that hot bod?" Her eyes flashed as if she'd realized what she'd just said.

"You think I'm hot?"

"Marine, everyone here thinks you're hot."

A grin spread across his face. "Uh, thanks. But I don't think everyone's looking at me, I have a feeling all eyes are on you. How could they not be? You're gorgeous."

She snorted. "You're so polite."

"You don't know how beautiful you are, do you?"

She shrugged. "Don't really think about it. Let's go sit. Can't believe I'm hanging out with a chili pie virgin. This is going to be fun."

He nearly tripped when she said the word *virgin*. He picked up their drinks, so she could grab the cardboard containers with their food. The chili didn't smell too bad, and he was hungry. She led him to an orange table with matching plastic chairs. Been a long time since he'd eaten in a high school cafeteria.

"Make sure you get some Fritos in that first bite. It's the salty mixed with the chili spices that makes it worthy of worship."

He did what she'd told him and it was...good. Really good. "I had no idea corn chips could taste like this."

"I know, right? So amazing." She took a swig of her drink. "How long have you been in the Marines?"

"Joined up the week I graduated from high school. Best way I could think of to take care of my mom and little sister. It was decent pay, and I didn't have to worry about living expenses so I could send them just about everything I made."

She blinked and he wasn't sure if those were tears in her eyes.

"Did I say something to upset you?"

"No. Not at all. You risked your life when you were nothing but a kid to take care of your family?"

"Yeah. And I'll admit, it seemed cool at the time. Fighting for my country. But I had no idea what I was getting into. Still, I wouldn't trade being a Marine for anything."

She blinked again.

"Are you okay?" he asked.

"Yep. I've just never met a selfless man before. You're an anomaly."

Her compliment made him laugh.

"I don't know about that. Maybe you just haven't met the right guys."

"True that." She wiped some chili from the corner of her mouth with a paper napkin. "I'm so impressed that even that young you were looking after your people. Wow, when I was eighteen, I was an idiot. Partying in college and making bad choices." She rolled her eyes. "Really bad choices."

He chuckled. "Well, if I'd had the opportunity, I probably would have made worse choices, another reason why my mom didn't fuss too much when I went off to boot camp. She knew I needed the discipline. I was never a bad kid, but I didn't always make the smart choices, especially in high school. My grades were low." Of course, a lot of that had to do with being tired from working sometimes as many as two jobs after school. There wasn't anything he wouldn't do to help his family.

It had taken his mom challenging the principal in

front of the school board before they finally gave him some grace. His mom was a lot of great things, and fierce was one of them. Never in his life had he won an argument with her, and the principal had learned that the hard way.

"Still," she said, "it took me another four years before I figured out what I wanted to do. And another year after that before I finally had the guts to do it. What you do is heroic and dangerous. It takes a special type of person to do that job. To run toward the scary when everyone else is running away."

"We don't really think about it that way." He wanted to find out more about her, and he'd never been comfortable talking about himself. "I'm curious how you make money shopping for people."

She blanched.

Shoot. He'd done it again. "No, no. I mean, I think it's a cool job. And I'm curious about how it works. Oh, and that reminds me." He pulled out a wad of cash. "How much do I owe you?"

"You can pay me later. I have receipts for you in my car. I was able to get some of the stuff donated when I told them what it was for, so I bought twice as much. I hope that's okay. Maybe these elderly people might enjoy getting more than one gift. It's small stuff, mostly, to make their lives more comfortable. Only spent a little over half your budget and that's with the wrapping. I'll have to look at the receipts but it was right around six hundred."

"You are good at this. We can donate the rest to

the charity. Are you sure I can't compensate you in some way?"

She shook her head. "Nope. And to answer your question, I usually get a commission. A negotiated percentage of the whole budget. A lot of what I do is for corporate clients. Finding the perfect gifts for their staff or for guests they have coming in, or finding giveaways for trade shows. We have a whole division for that last thing, and by division, I mean that's mostly what my partner, Bebe, handles, where she finds promotional swag for different companies."

He swallowed the last bit of chili. "That's interesting. I didn't even know a business like that existed."

She put down her fork. "Yeah, my grandmother actually helped me figure it out."

"Did she have the same kind of business?"

"Oh, no. She's a retired professor who lives in Ireland now. But she's always had a knack for finding the perfect gifts for people. Like an intuitiveness for knowing what's wanted. I sort of inherited it from her. I know that sounds weird, but I get this gut feeling for what's right for folks. And after college, I wasn't quite sure what to do with that awesome philosophy degree I had."

"Wow. I didn't see that one coming," he said honestly. He figured an MBA or something.

"What? I can spout Plato and Charles Hartshorne with the best of them."

"I know the first, never heard of the second."

"Trust me, most people haven't. But about two months after I graduated, I was working as a personal shopper at Neiman Marcus in Dallas. I really wasn't qualified to do anything else. I was promoted three times in six months. Grandma said I should take what I was best at and apply it to my career goals. 'But never work for the man.' Did I mention Grandma is a bit of a hippie, much to the chagrin of my mom, her daughter?

"Anyhoo, I took some business classes and decided to open my own personal-shopping service. There are a lot of them in Dallas and the competition is stiff. But there wasn't here in Corpus, so I came home and... Wow, I'm telling you my life story." She rolled her eyes.

"Nah, I'm intrigued. And your grandma sounds supersmart and practical."

"She's brilliant. Taught at Oxford. Still lives over there. She's my favorite philosopher."

"Ah, and it comes full circle. Oxford? Wow. That's pretty fancy." All this info made him even more curious about Ainsley. She was intelligent and beautiful, a dangerous combination. He could sit here all afternoon listening to her talk.

That had never happened before.

She nodded. "So I guess you didn't mind the chili pie, after all?"

He held up the empty container. "One of the best things I've eaten in a while. Who is this Frank guy?"

"He owns a barbeque place out by the beach, Duley's, which is named after his dad. They've been around a long time. And his ribs are even better than his chili."

"Maybe I could take you there some time?"

"I don't know. We'll see."

"You keep saying that. Do you have a thing about not dating guys in the military or something?"

Her head popped up. "A thing? No. Should I? And who says I want to date you?"

She had him there. He sounded like a jerk. "Sorry, I—"

She reached out and touched his arm. "I'm messing with you. Your face. That was classic. But I'm going to be straight with you. I'm focused on my career. I'm really not looking to date anyone right now. I don't have a lot of luck with guys, and I find them kind of self-centered. Not that you would be. But…if you want someone to hang out with today, I'm your girl. Want to come shopping with me?"

"Uh, sure?"

The way she talked—so fast—it took him a minute to catch up.

"And for the record," he said, clearing his throat, "I'm not looking to date, either. I simply wanted to thank you for helping me."

She chewed on her lip as she eyed him. "Okay. So," she began and waved to the empty containers, "we've had our meal. We should be good. You still want to hang out?"

He shrugged. With this one, it was probably best to play it cool. She didn't want to date. Well, he'd been honest when he said that wasn't his thing. His teaching at the base was keeping him busy, and besides, he didn't do relationships.

But he definitely wanted to spend more time with her.

"I'm yours for the afternoon," he told her.

And a small voice inside said "and more," if she wanted.

3

BEN WAS SNIFFING some homemade candles at a booth, and Ainsley could not keep from staring at him. She had to stop ogling poor Ben, or he was going to get the wrong idea. But everything about him… Heck, she'd never been so attracted to a man. Never in her life had she believed in pheromones but it had to be something like that.

That and he had one of the most jaw-dropping examples of the male body she'd ever seen. Oh, and the fact he was sweet. Taking care of his mom and sister. Putting his life on the line for them, and his country.

A heart-stopping combo if ever there was one.

How many times do I have to tell myself no more men?

He glanced back and shot her one of his devastating smiles.

At least a hundred.

"My mom might like this vanilla one. Do you think giving her something like this would be a good Christmas gift?"

She nodded and smiled. "Everyone loves candles," she said.

"What else is on your list?" he asked her.

Right. Stay on task.

"I have gifts for two executives I need to pick up. The client wanted something homemade but nice. Classy. Wood sculptures or pens. There's a man here who crafts things out of old bourbon barrels. I usually buy him out. Those are popular gifts for men and women."

Her phone played Ozzie Osbourne's "Crazy Train." It was the ringtone for her sister, Megan.

"Just a second," Ainsley said.

"Help!" Megan yelled before Ainsley could even say hello.

"Megan, breathe." Her sister was a bit of a drama queen in all things, but she loved her. She was the only person who made worse choices when it came to men than Ainsley did.

"Sorry. I'm freaking out. The bachelor auction is tonight, and," she gasped and sniffled, "two of our guys had to cancel because they have the flu. I swear, if they're faking I will kill them both. Dead."

Ainsley thought to downplay the situation and scoffed, "It's fine, Megan. So you have a couple less bachelors. No biggie."

"Yes, biggie. It's for charity. I promised twenty of the hottest guys in Corpus. What am I doing to do with eighteen? And those guys were my big tickets, the two that backed out. My end-of-show wow factors."

"What?" Sometimes Megan talked in riddles.

"My moneymakers. They were going to push us over the top. I so wanted to beat Stephanie at her own game. She's been talking behind my back about how she was so much more organized last year. And it's true. But still. I want to win. And by win, I mean I want the children's cancer fund to make a ton of money. The most money ever."

Ainsley smiled. "You want to stick it to Stephanie in the worst way. Be honest."

"Yes. Okay. Fine. But the only way to do that is to get the most donations for these guys, right? So, it's a win-win, if I can make it happen. But I can't do that without some hot studly studs."

Her sister always had a way with words. "So call your friends. You know hundreds of guys." Megan went through men faster than she did shoes, and she really loved shoes.

Her sister sighed. "Yeah, unfortunately, I do. I've called in all the favors I could. A lot of my friends already donated the silent auction prizes. They don't like the idea of being in front of a bunch of drunk women trying to buy them."

"I can't imagine why." Ainsley had never liked these types of events for that reason. Even though the guys were doing it out of the goodness of their hearts, she always felt it was kind of humiliating. The whole objectifying them, and then there was the women pawing after them on the dance floor. No, she couldn't imagine why.

"Please," Megan begged. "You know everyone. Surely you can scrounge up a couple of super good-looking guys. I'll owe. Like, my life. Please don't make me beg more."

Ainsley glanced up to find Ben watching her intently. No. She couldn't. He wouldn't. But if ever there was a big moneymaker, it was him.

"Hold on." She put her phone on mute and gave him her best smile.

"What are you and Jake doing tonight?"

"I'D RATHER BE in the middle of a war zone with insurgents ready to take me down," Jake said, messing with his tie for the fiftieth time. Ben and Jake were both dressed in penguin suits for the charity auction. This was the worst idea in the history of ideas. That's what he got for giving in to a pretty face.

"Right there with you, brother."

When Ainsley had smiled that big, hopeful smile at him, he couldn't say no. Heck, he'd probably have done just about anything to spend time with her.

But this. Well, it was definitely beyond the call of duty. Ainsley had talked about kids with cancer, and that was all it took. He couldn't say no. And he'd coerced Jake into doing it with him by telling him not just about the charity, but that there would be hot women who wanted his body.

Jake seemed a lot more comfortable with that idea than Ben. He liked things quiet, without so many people. This would be mayhem. The sound of voices was growing louder and louder. The night had begun with free champagne and light appetizers since, as Megan had explained, "We like the women to be slightly tipsy because they spend more."

Ben didn't think that was a nice way to do things, but it was for the kids, which was what he kept telling himself. They'd just finished the video showing why the research needed to be done. There were some sniffles on the other side of the curtains.

"Sorry, ladies. That video gets me every time," the announcer said. "But now, let's turn up the music and have some fun." The announcer went on to explain how the women could bid.

His gut twisted. One by one the guys went and strutted their stuff. The screams grew louder every time. When the bidding began for the first guy, Ben never wanted to retreat more than he did right then.

"We're Marines. We can do this," Ben said, more to convince himself than anything.

Jake turned to face him.

"Oorah," they said together and high-fived. The other remaining bachelors laughed and shook their heads. They were pretty nice guys—had to be to do something like this.

"I bet I pull in twice as much as you," Jake said. This is what they did—challenged each other. They'd been on two tours together and humor was the one way they all dealt with the horror.

Ben grunted. "Only if they like their side of beef with a hunk of cheese," he said. "This," Ben said as he patted his abs, "is the real deal."

They both grinned. It was bravado, nothing more.

There was one more to go before it would be Jake's

turn. And then Ben was last. Ainsley had told him it was a prime spot, but man, he was feeling the pressure. Each bachelor was pulling in more than the next. The last guy had made two thousand for the charity.

The noise went up a couple of decibels and he and Jake peeked around the curtain. They were in a large hotel ballroom that had been set up for the event, with lots of tables and chairs, and a stage, or rather…a runway. It was a fancy affair with crystal chandeliers, gilt centerpieces and lots of pink and white flowers. Everyone was dressed up. None of the women were as beautiful as Ainsley, who wore a white gown that fit her curves. Her hair was up and she looked like a royal princess or an A-list movie star.

Damn, he couldn't' stop looking at her. She wasn't even paying attention to the guys, but was glancing down at her phone. And then, as if she sensed him, she met his eyes and gave him a little smile. And she winked. He loved it when she did that. Like they were in on their own little secret.

"So out of your league," Jake said when he figured out where Ben had been watching. Ainsley was sitting at a table, dead center.

"Yep," Ben said. The music volume went up a bit more, as did the screams. The noise was getting to him. This happened sometimes. He backed away from the curtain and bent over to put his hands on his thighs, drawing in deep breaths. He concentrated on his breathing like his therapist had taught him.

"Hey." Jake patted his shoulder. "It's just a bunch of crazy tipsy women. I was kidding. It's going to be okay.

It really isn't much different than the country bar we were at a few weeks ago. Remember all those women when we joined their line dance? At least, maybe these women won't puke beer on your shoes."

There was that. He'd had to toss out his favorite pair of cowboy boots because there was no coming back from that.

Ben hated this weakness. Nothing had ever bothered him until that last tour. They'd spent twenty-four hours holed up in a camp where they were hit with mortar after mortar. He'd been working maintenance on a downed Black Hawk. And they were only getting out when the chopper was fixed. Problem was, he didn't have the parts he needed. It took every mechanical brain cell he had to figure out how to create something makeshift to get them to safety.

And it wasn't as if he hadn't done that sort of thing hundreds of times. They were always in some hot zone. Always under pressure. But that one hit him. It was the noise. The constant *boom boom boom* of the electronic music.

"Oh, no," Jake said.

"What?" Ben glanced up to find his friend loosening up and cracking his neck like he was getting ready to go into the ring with a prizefighter.

"You're on," Megan said to Jake. Ainsley's sister was the reason they were there. She'd needed help, and Ainsley had turned to him. And with that smile.

"Good luck, dude," Ben said as he straightened and then high-fived his friend. "You got this."

The noise level rose even louder. Ben pushed it

away, focused on his breathing. He wouldn't disappoint Ainsley or her sister. All he had to do was walk to the end of the stage, stand there and wait for someone to say "sold," and he was done.

"Five thousand!" he heard a woman shout.

What the...? A date with Jake brought in five thousand dollars?

Ben had been hoping for maybe five hundred for himself. He'd even offered to give Ainsley two hundred and fifty if the bids didn't go up for him. She'd kept telling him that he had nothing to worry about, but there was no way he would bring in that kind of big money.

Ben popped his jaw. This was nuts. He was a confident guy. He'd never had problems with being appealing to women, and this was for charity. He was going to have fun.

Sure. Keep telling yourself that, buddy.

"Okay, ladies, we've got another treat for you," the announcer said. "Ben is a Marine, working on the base here in our lovely hometown. We hear he's great with his hands, and that his abs—well, are to *d-i-e* for. Ladies, let's welcome Ben."

The women cheered.

Ben laughed. Yep. He could do this. Raise the most money for those kids. He wouldn't be outdone by Jake. He didn't care if he had to strip to do it.

In fact... He quickly undid his shirt buttons and held his tie in his hand. When the curtain opened he tossed the bow tie out to the audience.

The screeching reached an all-time high, but he

forced a smile and walked to the end of the stage. His eyes found Ainsley, and his smile widened.

More screeching, but he wasn't really listening anymore. She was smiling back, and then she winked at him and mouthed something. He had no idea what she'd said, but he nodded as if he did.

Then she made a motion to pull his shirt open a little and to turn around in a circle. She was doing a twirly thing with her fingers.

It's for charity. He kept repeating the mantra to himself.

"Oh, my, we did not disappoint. Look at those abs, ladies. Those are scrumptious! And that tattoo. Does anyone have a fan? Now, can I get—" The announcer was interrupted.

"Two thousand," a woman shouted. Ben ripped his eyes away from Ainsley and gave the woman a little wave.

Whew. At least he wouldn't be some loser who didn't bring in any cash.

"Thirty-five hundred," another woman said.

All right, then. Things were looking up. Ben shook his head and laughed, then gave that lady an even bigger wave.

And so it went on. A few seconds later they were up to six thousand.

"Everyone wants to take home a Marine. We hear they never let a woman down."

"Ten thousand dollars," a woman at Ainsley's table shouted, as she stood up and waved her paddle. She was probably in her late thirties.

There was a huge gasp. Then clapping.

Ben wasn't sure he heard her right.

"That's ten thousand going once, twice and sold! That's table one, paddle thirty-five. And that's it, ladies. The table monitors will be by to take your checks and credit cards. Please don't forget to visit our silent auction next door. If you didn't get some time with your favorite bachelor, bid on that trip to Fiji. A tropical vacation will get your mind off your troubles. And those raffle tickets for the Audi are still available. That thing is definitely going home with one of you tonight."

Ben exited to the left, where the rest of the bachelors had gone.

"You put us all to shame," one of them said. He was a doctor or something like that, and had been one of the first guys to be bid on.

"Nah," Ben told him. "They'd just had more to drink by the time they came to me."

The guys laughed.

"Speaking of our bachelors—gentleman, can you come back out onto the stage?" the announcer asked.

"Hey, guys, I need you to line up on stage again," Megan said.

There was some groaning, but they did what she asked. Ben buttoned his shirt and tucked it back in. Megan handed him his jacket. "Thanks for what you did," she said as he followed the other men.

They were back on stage, the lights beating down on them. "Gentleman, we could not have done this without you. Let's give them a hand!"

There was a lot of clapping and plenty of wolf whistles.

"Take a bow, bachelors."

They all gave awkward bows and then high-fived each other.

"Okay, ladies. Once you've paid for your bachelor, an escort will bring him to your table. Don't forget our silent auction, it closes in an hour. I know I said that, but the hunkiness on the stage makes us all forget our own names. We'll be announcing the winners in only two hours."

"Whew. Glad that part's over," Ben said.

"Me, too. Did you see who bid on me?" Jake asked.

"Nah. Wasn't watching."

"It was the CO's daughter-slash-niece's table."

"Clarissa?"

"Yep," Jake said.

Ben couldn't help but laugh. He'd had to take Clarissa to a couple of events for the CO. She was a wild one. They'd actually become pretty good friends because he didn't put up with her drama. The CO thought she was a handful, but the truth was, she was confused about what was important in life. All she really wanted was to find the right guy. Even, as she'd told him, if she had to date a couple of hundred to find him.

She might have something there. There weren't many people who could get along with someone like her. He wasn't attracted to her, which was probably why the CO had stuck him on babysitting duty for a few weeks.

"Good luck with that," Ben said.

Everyone knew the CO's daughter-slash-niece was

way off-limits. That was unless you wanted to be stationed in Antarctica.

"Hey, handsome," Ainsley said from behind him. "You were fantastic up there."

He turned and nearly bumped into her, she was so close. His hands rested on her forearms to steady himself. Her soft skin made him think of touching more of her and...

Focus.

"Thanks for getting that woman to bid for me, but that was a lot of money."

She laughed, the sound sending heat through his body. "We actually bid on you as a table. So you don't have one date tonight, you have ten."

Wow. "How does that work? I thought I was supposed to take someone on a date or something."

"Sorry, Megan and I should have clarified it for you sooner. Actually, the dates should happen tonight, here at the event. Takes the pressure off the guys having to plan something else. The bachelor basically dines with the lady that bid on him, dances a bit and that's it.

"But some of the higher bidders did it as a table. So the guy, like you, has to hang out at the table, dance a little, if you want to with us, and then you're done."

Well, that was a relief. He'd been worried about taking some woman he didn't know out on a date, especially someone from this crowd where money didn't seem to be a problem for a lot of them. He'd been wondering if Ainsley might come from money, given the fancy gown she wore and the fact that her sister was covered in diamonds. At least, they sparkled like real diamonds. Maybe it was costume jewelry. But then, he'd remembered how Ainsley had been dressed at the toy store, and even her casual look at the craft fair was pretty classy.

"Is it the same way with my table?" Jake asked.

"Yes, they also bid as a table."

Jake blew out a deep breath. "Saved."

The guys shared a look.

"What is that about?" Ainsley asked.

Ben shrugged. "Our boss's daughter is the one who was doing all the bidding. She can be a, um, handful."

"You said it, brother," Jake said. "So she has to share. That's a good thing. What I do not need right now is the CO ridin' my butt. You guys have fun."

"So, let's get you to the table. I'm your official escort." She tucked her arm through his. "Oh." She stopped and opened her hand. "I tracked down your tie. I promised Sandy—she caught it—that you'd dance with her later."

"Thanks."

A few minutes after that, Ainsley made the introductions. "And this is my mom, Carol. She's the one who jumped up to bid on you."

"Mom?" He frowned. "You can't be old enough to have a daughter of Ainsley's age and Megan's."

Her mom's hand fluttered against her chest. "From the look on your face, I almost believe you mean that," she said. "Either way, you made my night. Maybe even my month." The women all whooped.

"I do mean it," he said seriously. "I thought you

might be late thirties when you were bidding. Now I see where Ainsley gets her beauty from. It's very nice to meet you, ma'am."

He shook her hand.

"Yes, you are something special," her mother said. "Thank you for helping out Megan tonight. You and your friend were kind to show up at the last minute like that."

"You're welcome. That was a lot of money, though."

She waved a hand. "Oh, hon, don't worry about it. The women at this table were more than willing to keep you out of Steph Montgomery's hands. That was the table that kept trying to outbid us. I couldn't let that happen. She and her mother, well, it's tacky but they weren't winning this round."

"That's right," Megan chimed in. She'd come up behind her mother and was giving her a hug. "Thank you. We doubled what they did last year. I know you had a lot to do with that. You and your friends. And they're telling me that the bids on the auction items are already so high that we may even triple."

Her mother turned to kiss her daughter's cheek. "Our pleasure, dear. By the time that video finished, we were all in tears. That was brilliant of you, showing it at the beginning of the fund-raiser to get those purse strings loose."

Megan squeezed her mom. "I learned from the best."

Mother and daughter shared a smile. They must have done a lot of charity events together. All the women seemed very comfortable with one another. And he hadn't lied about Ainsley's mom—she was a beauty. The diamonds around her neck sparkled brilliantly. He was betting the necklace could pay for a house, or maybe two. Once again it hit him that Ainsley came from all of this. And here, he didn't even have a couch.

"We should probably feed him so he has the energy to dance," Ainsley suggested. "They've set up a buffet so we can grab some food before the music begins."

Crud. The dancing. "Uh, just so you ladies know, I'm not exactly the world's best dancer. I haven't actually broken any toes, but I've come close," he admitted honestly.

"You'll be fine," Ainsley assured him. Then she stood on her tiptoes and kissed his cheek. "You really are amazing for doing this," she whispered.

For that he would have done anything. The kiss was like a slow burn on his cheek, spreading through his nerves like wildfire. All the anxiety he'd felt earlier in the night fled.

"Anything for—" He'd almost said *you.* Would that scare her off altogether? She'd said more than once she didn't want anything serious. In fact, neither did he, so it was best if he kept this light. "The kids. Anything for the kids."

"Such a good guy," Ainsley said. "Let's get some food in you. You're going to need all your energy tonight."

It was how she said it that made him do a double take.

They were a few steps ahead of the others.

She smiled but didn't look at him. "Those abs were impressive. I might like a little alone time with them."

"So are you saying you want to touch them?" He'd always been direct and wasn't into games.

"Yep, all over."

He laughed. "Well, at least you're honest. What happened to not wanting to date?"

"I didn't say anything about a date. I just want to run my hands across those abs more than I want to breathe."

He nearly tripped.

"It's bad for me to objectify you," she said. "But those abs mixed with that big heart of yours is kind of my kryptonite. Just sayin'."

"Ainsley, you can objectify me all you want. Over and over again."

She sucked in a breath and fanned herself. "Marine, you cannot say things like that. I might melt into a puddle at your feet."

His mind flashed to her down on her knees in front of him. *No. No. No.* He had to get that out of his head. She was just flirting and having some fun.

"Hey, Ainsley, stop hogging the Marine," Megan called to them.

"Yeah," a chorus said behind them.

Then there were gales of laughter.

"Your ladies await," Ainsley told him and made a show of curtseying. Then she waved her arm in a regal manner to the rest of the women from the table.

He'd play the gentleman and make them all feel like they'd gotten their money's worth.

But there was only one lady he was interested in.

And he couldn't wait for her to touch his abs.

4

AINSLEY HAD WAITED patiently for more than two hours for her turn to dance with the Marine. Her mother's friends had helped pay for the privilege to have him at their table, but they were all a bit too handsy for her comfort.

Not that she should in any way feel possessive.

But she did.

Right now he was dancing with Sara Reyes, who was batting her eyelashes at him. The woman was her mother's age.

"If looks could murder," Megan said beside her.

"Shut it."

Megan laughed. "I thought you'd just met him."

"I did. I told you, at the toy store."

"Yep, but I've never seen you look at a guy like that. Ever. Not even Joe What's-His-Name when you were twelve and Mom took you to his concert."

Joe What's-His-Name had nothing on Ben. She hadn't been lying about his abs. When he came out from that curtain with his shirt unbuttoned, she'd squirmed in her seat along with every other woman in the place. Ripped. That's what he was. And there was a tattoo over his heart she was dying to explore.

Her body warmed again just thinking about it.

Fingers snapped in front of her face. "You do have it bad," Megan said.

Her sister had the most annoying habit of interrupting her fantasies tonight. First, on the way to dinner, and now this.

"What? I was thinking about work."

Her sister snorted. "Maybe workin' it. But that face…" She did a dismissive finger wave, clearly to tease Ainsley. "It's most definitely not thinking about work. He's so thoughtful. And one of the most gorgeous creatures I've ever seen. He keeps stealing glances at you like he wants to eat you up. I say go for it. Have a good time."

That's all it could be. She was sticking to her guns when it came to men, especially right now. While her parents might want her to marry and settle down, that wasn't a part of her plan. Not for a long time. It didn't matter how many men they paraded in front of her, or forced her to sit with at dinner. Their manipulation wouldn't work. They thought they were doing what was right—finding her a man who could take care of her—but she could take care of herself.

"I'm not interested. I keep telling you that," Ainsley said resolutely. "My business takes up my days, nights and weekends. We're doing really well. He's a nice guy who did us a big favor tonight. Leave it alone, okay?"

Then she gave her sister the glare. The one that said *if you push any harder, I'll tell Mom and Dad on you*.

Her sister held up her hands in surrender. "Fine. Fine. But just be straight with him. Tell him that you want to hang out, nothing serious. I bet he'd go for it. And from what he said about teaching and being a helicopter pilot, it sounds like he's kind of busy, too.

"He was saying they sometimes leave at a moment's notice for training exercises all over the world. This could be great. You don't have to marry the guy, although I'd love to see Dad's face with that one. Can you imagine? He'd probably have a coronary. I'll be honest. If you aren't interested in that Marine, I am. I'd be all over him like—"

"Megan!"

"Yeah, you aren't possessive at all," her sister teased.

"What's so funny?" Ben asked, approaching them.

"Girl stuff," Megan replied quickly. Ainsley was grateful for her sister's vague answer. She prayed he hadn't heard their conversation.

"Would you like to dance?" he said to Ainsley. The poor guy had been on his feet for two hours straight, wobbling through two-steps and waltzes, and a few fast dances with the other women at the table. He always seemed attentive and incredibly kind.

The way he treated others, it was like an aphrodisiac to her. Who needed oysters when Ben was in the house?

He was one heck of a hot guy. "Absolutely, but why don't you sit down for a little bit and rest. We've kept you running all night."

"I'm good. Besides, this kind of running is a lot easier than the obstacle courses on base. Afraid I'll step on your toes?" He moved by her mother's chair so she didn't have to twist around. And then he held out his hand.

"Not at all. I've been watching you all night. I've danced with a lot worse." She took his hand and then stood.

It was a slow number, thankfully.

As they hit the dance floor, he pulled her close and she put her arms around his neck. His went around her waist. With everyone else, he'd been quite formal. She liked that he treated her differently. Special.

"Been waiting for this since I got here tonight," he said. "Holding you like this."

She tipped back her head so she could see his eyes. She was five-seven and he had at least a good six inches on her.

"I said it earlier, but you've been such a champ. Every woman at that table has a thing for you, including my own mother. She keeps talking about you to her friends, about how you saved the day."

He chuckled. "How about you? Do you have a *thing* for me?"

She shook her head and he frowned.

"No. I mean, I do," she answered. "I mean… Oh, I'm making a mess of this. I told you what my life is like. I don't have time to have a *thing* for anyone. My schedule is insane. Crazy busy."

He shrugged. "This is how you let guys like me

down easy, right? I get it. You're out of my league. It's okay."

"No, you're not. If anything, the opposite is true. I just don't want to lead you on or set up some kind of expectation. And so we're clear, I want you. I just probably shouldn't."

"I told you before, I'm okay with getting to know each other. No pressure."

She smiled. "Guys always say that, and then they wonder why I'm not available twenty-four seven. I mean, I know I'm projecting. But the last couple of guys I dated—you're nothing like them. I get it. But I don't want to set up any false expectations. I pretty much live for my next appointment. Tonight is a luxury I don't normally allow myself. But it's for a good cause, and I've made some excellent networking contacts. Plus, we helped the kids, so it's all good."

"Uh, I don't have any expectations," he said. His brows drew together. "I simply want to spend some time with you. Maybe where we aren't in a store, or in a fancy ballroom with two hundred very loud women."

She'd noticed that he'd rub his temples now and then. Did he have a headache? Was the noise getting to him?

"Are you okay?" She was worried that maybe he'd been suffering all night and she hadn't been aware.

"What? Why would you ask that?"

"You were rubbing your head earlier. And Megan told me she was worried you were having a panic attack before you came out, but then you strutted down that catwalk like you owned the place, so she figured that maybe you were just preparing."

He pulled her tighter, and she liked feeling him pressing into her. She liked it a lot. "I'm fine. Sometimes noise gets to me a little. It's not that big of a deal. Though, I could have used some ibuprofen a couple of hours ago."

Oh, no. He didn't feel well.

The noise, between the music and the chatter, had been deafening most of the night. Poor guy. And he'd acted like it wasn't an issue.

"Would you like to take a break? I know somewhere we could go and it's quiet."

He raised an eyebrow. "What about your mom and her friends?"

"The party is dying down. They'll be fine." She hadn't lied. Most of the attendees were gathering their things. "If it makes you feel better, we can go say a quick goodbye. I'll tell them I'm the one with the headache and you're taking me home. What they don't know is home is a lot closer than they think. In less than five minutes, it will be superquiet and I also have something for your head."

He let go of her immediately. "Really? A couple of aspirin or something and even twenty minutes of quiet and I'll be good as new. That's a great plan. Let's do that."

This time she was the one who chuckled.

They said their goodbyes quickly, although she felt like her mom might have held on a little too long when she'd hugged Ben, but soon after they were headed out of the ballroom.

He started to lead her to the front of the lobby, but she grabbed his hand.

"This way," she said, pulling him to the elevator.

He frowned again. "I thought we were leaving."

"No, I said I wanted you to take me home and I promised you quiet. I always get a room the night of this event in case I drink a little too much. So tonight, home is on the top floor of this hotel. Come on. We can raid the minibar. Dinner seems like a million years ago and I'm starving."

She had no idea what she was doing or why she was taking him up to her hotel room.

Right. You have no idea. Okay, so alone time didn't sound like the worst idea in the world. And maybe her sister's words about having a good time were sinking it. This guy wasn't like anyone she'd ever dated. He'd even told her that he had no expectations.

And I really want to know more about that tattoo on his chest.

"You're okay with this, right? Going up to my room?"

He didn't argue, just followed her onto the elevator. A couple women joined them and gave her knowing looks. She didn't care.

She was taking her sister's advice and was about to get happy with a hot Marine, or at the very least, kiss one.

The warmth coursing through her body didn't lie, though. It was looking forward to so much more.

5

THE ROOM HAD floor-to-ceiling windows that looked out on the beach. Ben walked onto the balcony to listen to the calming waves. He was curious if he'd missed some kind of signal because Ainsley was all over the place with them. One minute she was talking about touching his abs—which he was, for the record, perfectly fine with—and the next she was telling him how she didn't want to get involved with anyone. That she didn't have time to date.

And then she'd invited him to her room. So he could have some peace and quiet and raid the minibar.

Ben was more than a little confused. Usually he kept things pretty simple with women. They had a good time, slept together and then that was that.

With Ainsley, well, it was complicated.

But he did welcome the quiet. He was embarrassed that Megan had told her about his breathing exercises backstage. That was something no one, except some of his closest friends, knew about. The waves were a lot more relaxing than the sounds in the ballroom and his shoulders felt like they'd dropped at least an inch, maybe two.

Inhaling the salty air, he closed his eyes.

Heaven. This thing with Ainsley, whatever it was— he'd let her lead the way. Maybe she was just as confused as he was. Given how she'd acted in the elevator, he had a feeling she wasn't in the habit of asking guys to her room.

He heard the faucet in the bathroom turn on. She'd gathered some clothes and gone into the bathroom to change.

He remembered he was supposed to be finding them drinks in the minibar, which was better stocked than most of his friends' kitchens.

Certainly better stocked that his. He'd moved into his apartment right before Thanksgiving. Then they'd been sent to Germany for a training mission. And since he was hardly ever at home, except to sleep, he hadn't done anything with it, or bought much food. It was the first place of his own. For years he'd been living on base, or military housing, but he'd always had roommates. He preferred sending his money home to help out.

But last year, his mom had finished her nursing degree and had a great job. She refused to take his money, though she allowed him to contribute to his sister's college fund. She was also paying him back for the house he'd bought them a few years ago.

He didn't need the money, so he put it in savings with the hope that some day he might settle down and get a place of his own. But that was a few years away. He had his eyes on making colonel, so he had to focus on the Marine Corps for now.

"You were drinking champagne—do you want that or something else?" he asked Ainsley, who was still in the bathroom.

"What do you want?"

You. But he didn't want to sound cheesy or scare her off. Maybe she really was just being nice and giving him some peace and quiet before he headed out.

"I was going to stick with water since I have to drive home in a bit." He'd already had a couple of whiskeys. That was his rule. Two drinks and done. He never had liked the feeling of being drunk or out of control. Plus, he had enough trouble with headaches, so the last thing he needed was a hangover.

"Oh, uh…" She sounded unsure about something.

"What?"

She opened the door and stepped forward. She was wearing little flannel shorts and a long-sleeve pink T-shirt that came down to her hips. He turned around and headed back to the minibar, pretending to be interested in the contents.

No question, the woman was beautiful.

Those legs. He so wanted them wrapped around his waist.

"I thought we might hang out a little. I'm hungry again. I was going to order room service."

Food and hanging out. Well, if that's what she wanted to do, he was game. And there was never a time he couldn't eat.

"I could go for some protein. Do they have a late-night omelet or something?" He shut the fridge door. But when he turned he found her staring at his chest.

He glanced down at his shirt. Had he spilled something?

"I don't do this," she said, and then she bit her bottom lip. She was nervous.

"You're going to have to explain what *this* is, because I'm not really clear on why I'm here," he said honestly. Though her look was telling him something that he wasn't sure she was ready to say. "I'm a pretty straightforward guy. Just tell me what you want, Ainsley. Tell me why I'm here."

She fisted the bottom of her shirt, and then took a deep breath. "I don't just have sex with guys, usually. I, um, I have to know them, uh, you. But you're different. I want to be superclear about this. *This* is simply fun. Okay. Just fun."

"Got it. You don't normally have sex with a guy in a hotel room, someone you've recently met, but you want to with me?"

She nodded. "You know, I'm a confident woman. So I don't understand why this is so tough for me. Do you want to have sex with me? I mean, we were flirting—"

His mouth was on hers before she could finish the next word. She tasted of mint, and he had to have more. He backed up against the wall and she leaned hard into him, her breasts pushing into his chest.

Her tongue warred with his, and when he slid his hands over her butt and brought her against his hardness, she let out a sweet little moan.

The woman was supremely sexy.

It was tough, but he broke off the kiss and lifted his head. "How does this feel?"

She blinked and then glanced back at his hand on her ass.

She nodded. "This feels good. Amazing. Spectacular. More. If this is our one night of fun, I want us to make the most of it. I need you to touch me almost more than I need to breathe." Her hand caressed his chest through his shirt. "Give me more, Marine. Much, much more."

"Unbutton my shirt, Ainsley." She wanted quid pro quo, he'd give it to her. Though her touch might be more than he could take. He was already so hard.

She gave him a fake salute and did what he'd asked. Then she pushed the shirt off his shoulders and he let it hit the floor.

She traced the Semper Fi tattoo with her finger. He'd had it for years, the first thing he'd done after boot camp. The same boot camp that nearly killed him. When he'd finished the intense training, he felt as if he could do anything. He also felt as if he'd found a home. He was faithful to the Corps through and through.

"Now you," he said, and he lifted the hem of her T-shirt. She was naked underneath. "More beautiful than I could have imagined," he told her. His thumbs gently teased the tightening buds.

"So are you," she said, her hands gliding up his torso. Then she kissed him. The sensation of her mouth on his, combined with the feeling of her nails lightly brushing his stomach... Well, he very nearly lost it.

Her hands moved lower, caressing him, and he hissed in a breath.

As much as he hated to, he gently took her wrists and put her hands on his shoulders.

"If this is going to last more than five minutes, I need you to keep your hands up here," he said, tapping his shoulders, before kissing her again.

She ground her pelvis against him, which wasn't helping him maintain his control. She needed a release and he was going to give it to her.

He rubbed her intimately, her shorts still on, but she quickly seized his hand and slipped it inside underneath them.

Well, okay then.

When his fingers found her slick heat, she groaned. At his tender touch, her body shook. Closer and closer still, she was reaching for that sweet release. Harder and faster, he aroused her; she now rode his fingers as if her life depended on it. He opened his eyes to watch hers glaze over.

"Ben," she whispered. "There. Yes. Right there." He increased the pressure and soon she was chanting his name. Her body was so responsive, it made him want her even more. He wasn't even sure that was possible.

She writhed and repeated his name, her cry sounded, her pleasure peaked. He waited for her breathing to calm—he had a feeling if he let go of her, she would fall. Remembering what she'd said about being a puddle, he smiled.

He walked her over to the bed and carefully laid her on it. It was high off the floor, which was perfect.

Soon, he was out of his pants, but not before retrieving a foil packet from his pocket. Marines were always prepared.

Leaning next to her, he caressed her cheek and kissed her lips, her cheek…

"Ben, I need you." She raised her arms and opened them, welcoming him.

The trust she showed him was an aphrodisiac if ever there was one. A man could get lost in those beautiful green eyes of hers.

After putting on the condom, he spread her legs and wrapped one around his waist, the other he left down. He slid his tip into her.

She shifted, and used her leg for traction, easing him farther inside her, moaning as she did.

He couldn't help but smile. He pulled out and then pushed back in gently.

She bucked against him. "I need you, Ben. Fast," she said. "Please."

That confident woman he first met, the one who seemed to own the world was back. She was no longer hesitant, and he found it attractive. Oh, yeah, he was going to give her whatever she wanted.

He pumped into her strongly each time and picked up speed, biting his cheek as she lifted that other leg and locked her feet behind him. She was fisting the sheets, and from how she tightened around him, he knew her climax was close. He put a thumb on her clit and she arched off the bed. He'd barely rubbed it before she was quaking around him, her muscles squeezing him. It only took him a few strokes and he came hard.

He collapsed over her, careful to catch himself on his forearms so he didn't land his full weight on her. He kissed her as they rode the final waves together.

She touched his cheek lightly with her fingers. "That was fun," she said huskily.

"Yep." He wasn't sure how she could speak. His mind wasn't quite back on planet Earth. "Fun."

She kissed him. "I think we should do it again."

He chuckled.

"I mean, if you want to. And not right this second. I need food. But then. Then I want to do it again."

"Yes," he told her, though it was more of a mumble. "Again," he said.

"Good. Good. I'm craving waffles," she said, as she dropped kisses along his chest, lingering at his tattoo.

He didn't eat food like waffles. He was careful about what he put in his body, but he wasn't about to tell her that. She was so sweet, and hot, and sexy.

They talked about nothing and everything. A half hour later their food arrived and they discovered creative ways to eat it off of one another.

And then she said two words—"More, please." And he was lost in her again.

Insatiable, that's what he was when it came to her. But this one night was it. They'd both been clear about that, but as she climaxed around him for the third time, a truth became apparent.

He was in big, big trouble.

6

"Luv, you've been staring at that same screen for a half hour. The CEO from Wilson's will be here in twenty minutes." Bebe's voice broke through the haze that was her thoughts. Dang her. All morning Ainsley had tried to think of something other than her night of heaven with Ben. But—

"Ainsley! Bloody hell." She glanced up to find Bebe shouting from the door frame.

"How do you know I wasn't working?"

Her friend rolled her eyes. "People who are working make clickety clack sounds with their keyboard. Usually your constant rattle on the keys drives me bonkers. But today, you keep sighing and then nothing. Are you going to tell me what happened this weekend? You've been acting weird ever since you walked in the door. And what's with the gutted look?"

Was she gutted? Maybe. She shook her head. No one, as far as she was concerned, would ever know what happened with her and Ben. It was a special night she was going to keep in her fantasies, probably for the rest of her life. They'd made love three times and her body still felt the effects, a wonderful soreness that she didn't want to forget.

Even though she had to. That was it. They weren't even repeating that night. If only she could get the image of the hot Marine out of her head.

He'd had to leave before it was light out; he needed to get to the base, and she was still mad because she'd barely been able to open her eyes when he was gone. He'd whispered something but she couldn't remember the words.

She'd pay big money to know what he'd said.

When she'd opened her eyes finally, he was no longer there. She'd wanted to make love to him one more time. Just to get him out of her system.

Yep. That's why.

Bebe cleared her throat.

She glanced up at her friend. "I'm on it, okay? You know how I am when I'm working on those creative problems. Sometimes I stare off into space. Go make the coffee or something, already."

Bebe quirked an eyebrow.

Cranky. "Sorry. Sorry. I'll make the coffee."

Her friend smiled. "Don't worry about it. I'm just giving you a hard time. I already know about your midnight shag with the handsome Marine."

"What?" Her hands flew out and nearly knocked over her coffee cup.

"Well, technically, I didn't know. I guessed, but you just gave it away." She held up a newspaper. There was a picture of her dancing with Ben with the headline Military Men Break Charity Records.

Kill. Me. Now. What would Ben think of that photo? She hoped he didn't mind being in the paper or linked to her. Sometimes she forgot about the fact that some people were interested in her life just because her parents were wealthy. But the story really did seem to be more about the charity. At least there was that.

"So we danced."

"Yes. And then what? You must have been snogging the heck out of that Marine," Bebe said. "Look at how he's staring at you, like he could never get enough of you. Whew. That's some heat, luv.

"*And* you've been starry-eyed all morning. So this is what you're like when you get some good sex! Quiet, and introspective. Those aren't two words I'd ever use to describe you. Maybe it should happen more often. Should I call the Marine for another session? He might be better than meditation or even yoga."

"Shut it." What if he'd seen the photo? Would he be embarrassed? And her expression wasn't much better than his. What had she been thinking right then? Because she looked like she was ready to rip her clothes off and have him… Well, she sort of, in a way, had been thinking exactly that.

No. No. Don't go there. He'd been doing her sister a favor and now here was his picture. No doubt it was online, as well. Would he get in trouble with his boss? He'd mentioned a couple of times how the officers were expected to lead by example and she didn't know what he might think about ending up on the social pages. A big part of her was too chicken to even text him to ask.

"Hmm. You are smitten. Fifteen minutes until one of our best clients arrives. You might want to at least look at your presentation, which I did just email to you. I think you'll like the gifts I picked out for the executive level."

"Bebe?"

Her friend turned back. "Yes?"

"I really do love you best."

Her friend and business partner grinned.

Ainsley downloaded the presentation and sure enough, her friend had outdone herself.

Her phone dinged, and she glanced down to see Ben's name flash across the screen.

Her pulse quickened and she might have gasped a little.

OMG. She hadn't expected to hear from him again. They'd both agreed. She reached down to swipe across the screen, but stopped.

There were voices in the outer office. Shoot.

Ben would have to wait. Even though reading his text was the only thing she wanted to do. This was why she couldn't do relationships, or fun in general. Life was too busy and she had to put all of her energy into her business. Spending hours mooning over some guy was not the best route to being productive.

That settled it.

Leaving her phone on the desk, she gathered her laptop and headed into the conference room of the old house where she and Bebe worked. She lived upstairs, and the bottom of the Georgian home was where she did business. The conference room had actually once been the front parlor. She'd inherited the house and had planned at first to use it as a rental, but when she moved back to Corpus from Dallas, she and Bebe fixed up the downstairs for their offices.

They'd kept the original style, but freshened up the place. It didn't have the opulence of any of her parents' houses, but that was one of the reasons she liked it here. This house felt like a home, not some museum where you couldn't put your feet up. Straightening her shoulders, she didn't bother glancing back at her phone. Even though she really wanted to.

It was strange that Mr. Wilson wanted to meet here at the office, but who was she to question him? Saved her the drive to downtown, since her house was in one of the quaint neighborhoods near the beach.

She pasted a smile on her face and entered the conference room. When he stood to shake her hand, the smile became real.

Mr. Cam Wilson III was wearing board shorts and a T-shirt with flip-flops. Not exactly his usual Armani.

"The waves up today?" she asked.

"Yes, as a matter of fact they are. Packery Channel Beach is reporting five-foot swells—not so big, but bigger than usual." He clapped his hands together. "We have twenty minutes. Show me what you got."

And this was what it was all about. Her business and the clients who depended on her.

"Five minutes, and I'll have you out of here. Wait until you see what we've come up with." Thank goodness for Bebe. Maybe she really should talk to her friend about giving her a raise. She'd saved her today.

She'd get through this.

And then she was going to read the message Ben had sent, even though she really, really shouldn't.

AN HOUR LATER, she was in her car, still not sure what to do about Ben's text or where she was going. He'd texted I need an emergency gift. Can you help me out? Call me. Please.

It was business. She had to call him back, right? This was dumb. And he spelled all the words out. She liked it when people did that in a text. Half the time she struggled to know what people were trying to say. Megan only used emojis. Ainsley had yet to figure out what ice-cream cones, flowers and clowns stood for in a conversation.

Just call him.

She pulled into a grocery store parking lot because she didn't trust herself to drive, but before she could push the call button, her mother's number flashed across the screen.

"Hey, Mom."

"Hello, my lovely child. Where are you?"

"Heading to a client meeting." She was worried her mom would keep her on the phone for a while; technically, she was picking up lunch because she'd been so rude to Bebe about the coffee earlier and the guilt was still weighing on her. And she needed to get away from the knowing looks from her friend. Bebe shared Ainsley's intuitive nature, which was good for their business, but bad when Ainsley was trying to hide something from her friend.

"Oh, I was hoping we could have lunch before I head back to San Antonio to meet your father and some friends for dinner." Her parents had pretty much moved their base of operations to San Antonio two years before she'd graduated college, though her mom was in Corpus Christi at least once a month for a charity function or to visit friends. And they'd kept their house on Ocean Drive in Corpus. The monstrosity sat empty most of the time.

"Sorry. Crazy day ahead. It's my—"

"Busiest time of year. I know, dear. Are you going to be coming up for your father's football party this weekend? I can't remember which game it is. Anyway, he had some people he would like you to meet."

That was code. By people, she meant eligible bachelors. Ones who were well pedigreed, and probably boring, or really narcissistic jerks. She never liked to generalize, but the men her parents thought appropriate would never be her type.

If she had a type. Which she didn't. But if she did, it might be Ben.

No. Not Ben. Why couldn't she get it together? It wasn't as if she'd never had sex before—just not like that.

"Ainsley? Did you hit a bad cell area?"

She had to stop thinking about him. "No, I'm here. Was just checking my phone. Sorry, no can do. Busy, busy this weekend." That wasn't a lie. Her parents, or more specifically, her father, didn't see her business as something relevant. He thought it was more of a hobby for her. Her father didn't understand why she couldn't drop everything when he expected her to be around.

"How about the Christmas party? You're not going to disappoint us, are you? The whole family will be there, and won't your busy season be over by then?"

Not exactly. The last few hours before the holidays were insane. Last year, they were still dropping off presents at midnight on Christmas Eve, mainly for men who had somehow forgot to buy a gift for their significant others. How did you forget your partner? It didn't say a whole lot about marriage.

There was no getting out of her parents' holiday party, though. It was a family tradition, and they always had their big family get-together the next day. That part she liked. The party, not so much. Despite the decorations, drinking and general merriment, it always seemed a bunch of people trying to kiss up to her parents.

"Of course, wouldn't miss." And she'd already made plans with Bebe to hire some part-time staff to help them with the last-minute deliveries.

"Lovely. I'll tell your father you can meet his friends then. Bye, darling girl."

"Bye, mom."

Oh, well. Maybe she could find a date for that party. That would show her dad. She'd never understood why he raised her and her sister to be decisive, independent women, and then he wanted to pair them off with the nearest available bachelors. Correction, the nearest available well-connected and usually shallow bachelors.

She loved her dad, but she was tired of the game he'd been playing the last two years.

A plan began to form in her brain.

She couldn't. No. It was so very wrong.

Oh, but she was so going to do it.

7

Ben had made a deal, and he always kept his word. As he pulled up in front of Ainsley's office, he couldn't for the life of him figure out why his palms were sweaty. She was kind and beautiful and there was no reason for him to be nervous.

She'd offered to get some gifts together for him to pick out for the CO. All the officers had chipped in, and because he'd lost that original bet, he was still having to find presents for several events they had. Two more and he was done. But the next one was the CO's annual holiday party on Friday night. The whole platoon had been invited, and that was when the officers gave the CO their gift.

He'd wanted to ask Ainsley to the party, but she'd made it clear Saturday had been a one-and-done kind of night.

The problem for him was he wasn't done. It was hard for him to concentrate while at work. At odd times during the day he'd wonder what she was doing. And then at night, yeah, he couldn't think about that, either. No way he was going into her house thinking about the constant hard-on he'd had after their fun on Saturday night.

He could do this.

He double-checked the address on his phone, and then glanced up at the two-story house. It was white brick with shuttered windows and a large porch across the front. The door was painted a dark blue, the same color as the shutters. It was fancier than he'd expected. Her business must have been doing very well. Or maybe she shared the place with several other businesses.

She answered on the first knock. And darn if she wasn't the freshest thing he'd seen all day. Her hair was piled on top of her head. She didn't have a bit of makeup on, and she was dressed in a tight red skirt and white blouse, and was wearing glasses.

A librarian fantasy sprung to life in his head. He wasn't sure he'd ever fantasized about a librarian before, but Ainsley did those sorts of things to him. All the time.

"Oh, it's you," she said, frowning. "You're early."

Not exactly the welcome he'd hoped for. Well, that settled it. She wasn't interested in anything but business. And not the going-to-bed business he'd had on the brain for the last two days.

She glanced down at her phone. "Nope, I'm running late. Sorry about that. Come on in."

He followed her into the foyer, where there was a stairway to the left. "This is your business?"

"The downstairs is. The upstairs is where I live. Let's go into my office." Her black high heels clacked along the hard floor, and he remembered those legs being wrapped around him.

Dude. You've got to stop that! "It's very nice," he said, trying to act normal. What was wrong with him? So she lived in a nice house. Didn't matter. He was here to find something for the CO's gift, and then he was gone.

"I have some executive items for you to see. You mentioned your CO likes golf, which makes this a whole lot easier. One of my dad's companies makes all kinds of golf accoutrements. He has some new products that are going to be out in the spring catalog, but I have several of them. And then I have other gifts that might work if you don't feel like those are appropriate."

"You live upstairs?"

She turned and smiled at him. "Yes. Cuts down on the commute time in a major way. The house was kind of dated when I got it, so Bebe and I fixed it up."

"Bebe?" Why was he only asking questions? Because she was so strikingly beautiful he couldn't think straight.

"Oh, I keep forgetting she wasn't at the auction the other night. She was visiting her mom in Fort Worth. She's my business partner and best friend. She started out as my assistant but we soon learned she was really good with the finances. Way better than me about budgets and making sure we got paid.

"She is also great with the clients, so we both do a little bit of everything. About six months after she started, I asked her to become a partner. We say that means half the headaches are hers. And I'm rambling. I tend to do that when you're around."

Good, he made her nervous, so maybe it wasn't just him.

He followed her into her office. It was girly, with soft blue-gray walls and mostly white everything else. But it was classy, it fit her. There were pink flowers on her desk. And touches of pink around the room.

"You like pink?" Wow. He had to stop with the twenty questions, but he couldn't. Seeing where she worked, well, he wanted to know more about her.

"Yes. It's bright and happy. And I know, it's a little girl's color to most people. But I love it. For me it's a neutral. It goes with so much."

"It's my sister's favorite color. She's seventeen, and she's liked it, hmm, I'm pretty sure since birth."

Ainsley pointed to a side table. It was painted white like her desk. "Well, I promise you'll find no pink in the gifts I picked out for your boss." Right. This was about business.

She showed him a variety of products, including a putting machine that seemed tailor-made for the CO's office.

"Choosing was easier than I thought it would be," he said when they were done. He was disappointed because now it was time for him to leave.

"I'll get it wrapped and to you before your event, when did you say it was?"

"Friday." This was the perfect opportunity for him to ask her to go with him.

"Okay. Friday. Great. No problem," she said. "Will that be cash?"

He paid for the gift, and then put his wallet back in his pocket along with the receipt.

"Guess I should go," he said.

"Oh. If that's what you want, sure." She acted like maybe she didn't want him to leave.

This woman was the queen of mixed messages.

"There was something—" They'd said the same words at the same time.

And then there was a bit of nervous laughter.

"You go," he said.

She shook her head. "No. Go ahead. What did you want to ask?"

"Right. Like I said, the CO's party is Friday night. And I was wondering…"

"Yes?"

"If maybe you could help me find a date? I get that it's kind of last-minute. But I don't know that many people in town. And…"

"You want me to *find* you a date?" Her face fell. She was upset.

Wait. What did he say? *Find him a date.* Not what he meant.

Retreat. Retreat.

He'd just had sex with her on Saturday night. "I wanted to ask you," he said quickly. "That came out wrong. Not what I meant to say. I meant, I'm trying to find a date. I know you said you weren't interested in seeing me again. I think your words were 'one and done.'"

"Yes. That is what I said." She chewed on her bottom lip. He had the urge to kiss it.

No. Focus.

"And it would be as friends because, as I explained the other night, I don't really date. I'm concentrating on my career. But if I show up alone, I'm going to get stuck with the CO's niece. You know her, Clarissa. She's nice but she—"

"I'll do it," she said quickly.

Well, okay. That was great. There wasn't anyone he wanted to be with more than Ainsley. And she hadn't punched him for the idiotic comment about her finding him a date, so there was that.

"I'll go with you. You know, as friends… To help you out. But I need you to do me a favor on the twenty-third. Do you have plans then? It involves going to San Antonio for an event."

He was still wrapping his head around the fact that she was willing to go with him to the CO's party. Well, she was doing it to give him a hand, but he wasn't about to say no to spending even more time with her. "What day was that again?"

"The day before Christmas Eve."

"Oh, I was going to Austin to see my mom and my sister for the holidays," he said. It was true. He hadn't been home for Christmas in years, and he'd promised his mom he wouldn't miss it.

Ainsley's face fell again, and she leaned back on her desk. "That's okay. I'll still help with your thing."

"Nah, you're being a champ about the CO's party. It's the least I can do to help you in return. As long as

I can leave sometime that night to get to my Mom's for Christmas Eve morning, I'm good. It's only an hour away from San Antonio, so it shouldn't be a huge deal."

She gave him one of those devastating smiles. But there was something else there. Maybe relief? "So, what's going on that night?"

"Well, um, it's my parents' Christmas party. They throw it every year."

He wasn't following. If it was her family, why would she bother having him there?

"And you need a date because…? I mean, I don't mind, but you ought to look in the mirror. You could have any guy you wanted."

She gave an unladylike snort. "You're sweet. My parents use a party like this, or pretty much any time I'm home, to put eligible bachelors in front of me. And I'm about to be a lot more honest than I should."

"Okay," he said, curious as to where she was going with this.

"My dad has terrible taste in men when it comes to finding a mate for me. Like, the worst. I don't know why he can't see that these men are mostly narcissistic jerks, maybe because he can be a bit of one himself. Don't get me wrong, I love him. He's my dad.

"But everything is about him. He has it in his head that I have to marry so I'm taken care of. What he doesn't understand is that isn't what I want. I can take care of myself. If I ever get married, and that's a big *if*, I will marry for love. Not a bank account. Or invitations to galas and the Riviera. Shoot. I did it again with the rambling. Sorry. I'm frustrated with my parents right now."

"You're still so young, I don't understand why they'd want to marry you off." He wasn't going to explore the reasons why every time she talked about being with someone else, he wanted to punch something. They weren't dating. He needed to get his head straight.

She shrugged. "It's that protective instinct, I guess. Dad started off poor, never had enough to eat when he was a kid. When it comes to his daughters, he's always wanted to make sure we're taken care of. But what he doesn't see is I'm a lot like him. I'm making my own way in the world. I don't need someone to take care of me."

"Isn't that what marriage is, taking care of each other?"

She pulled the pins out of her hair and then put it back up. He wished she'd leave it down. He wanted to wind his fingers through it and kiss her again.

"Yes. But, I mean, my mom is always trying to please my dad. And a lot of the guys I've dated expect me to drop everything for them. If ever I'm crazy enough to say 'I do,' it will be to someone who sees me as a full and equal person in the relationship."

"How is taking me to the Christmas party going to help you with your dad? I'm not wealthy. Your dad will see right through that." No way could he compete with the kind of guys she was talking about. And he was curious about her dad. It was obvious she was used to money. He'd seen that at the charity event the other night. Just how rich were these people? Not that it mattered to him, but it did make him wonder.

"If I show up with you, you're an officer in the military and respectable. A Marine, which automatically makes you superbrave, and we already know my mom likes you. With you there, my dad won't keep questioning me on when I'm going to settle down. The parade of men will stop, at least, maybe for that one night. Then I can go on avoiding them for another year. It's terrible, but part of the reason I don't go see my parents as much as I should is every time we're together, they have a guy they want me to meet. And I have to go to this party and I do enjoy being with my family the next day."

"I don't mind helping you, but you're a successful businesswoman, a grown, adult person. I mean, you can do whatever you want."

"Right? And when I'm ready to settle down, I will. I make my dad out to sound like an ogre. He's not. He's old-fashioned. For some reason, to him, marriage means I'll be safe. Protected. But I'm perfectly happy to take care of myself, thank you very much."

She was. But he understood where her dad was coming from. If he was honest, he was pretty protective of his mom and sister. What didn't make sense to him was that he also felt protective of Ainsley. He had no right to those kinds of feelings. They barely knew one another. "I haven't been around you for long, but you do seem smart and capable."

"Sorry for ranting. By doing this, you will help me out. No matter how capable I seem, every year it's the same thing. I'll even throw in finding gifts for your mom and sister. What do you say?"

He stuck out his hand to shake hers. "Buying for them is tough. Deal."

She wrapped her fingers around his, and the heat nearly scorched him.

They both stood there, staring at their hands.

"I should go," he said.

"Sure. Thanks for agreeing to my plan."

This was getting awkward. "No, I'm the one who's grateful. And the gift you found for the CO is going to save my butt."

There was another long pause, and they both stared down at their hands again, letting go when they realized they were still connected.

"I was going to order pizza," she said. "It's weird eating a whole pizza by myself."

She wanted him to stay.

"Sure. Um, pizza's great." Again, it was something he didn't normally eat.

"You don't eat pizza, do you? Or chili pies. You're a health nut. And here I thought you were pretty much Mr. Perfect."

He chuckled. "Being healthy makes me less than perfect? Not that I consider myself that."

"Oh, no. As far as I can tell, you're perfect. But I happen to have the worst eating habits ever. I admit it, I'm a fan of junk food."

He nodded. "I don't judge. But I have to be careful about what I put in my body. Part of it's for the job, but there are other reasons."

She cocked her head. "It obviously works for you. Those abs made the kid's cancer fund a good ten thousand, but can I ask what the other reasons are?"

He followed her past the staircase and down a hallway.

"My dad died when I was twelve from a heart attack. He was in his late thirties and had seemed healthy, but they learned too late that his arteries were clogged." He wasn't sure why he was telling her all of this. "When he died it was really hard on my mom. She'd been staying home with me and my little sister, who was only two months old. He was a chef in Austin."

She stopped so abruptly he almost ran in to her. Then she turned and gave him a hug. "That's so sad. I'm sorry for your mom. Did you have other family around to help?" She let go before he could even wrap his arms around her.

But he wanted to.

"Not really. Her family was in Wisconsin, and she never talked about them much. It was a long time ago," he said. Thinking about the past didn't do any good. It had been rough. At twelve, he'd become the primary carer for his sister so his mom could work. When he was old enough, he'd had odd jobs sweeping up, or cleaning out houses that had been abandoned for one of his dad's friends to flip.

They'd made it through, and that was all that mattered. Taking on that responsibility so young had helped make him who he was, and he was okay with that.

She stepped through an open doorway and into a

large kitchen, so large his whole apartment would fit in it. There were creamy white cabinets and stainless-steel appliances. The stove alone was probably a few months' pay for him.

"This is—"

"Ginormous," she said. "This was the one part of the house that had already been remodeled before I moved in. They knocked out a bedroom down here to create the extra space. It's maybe a bit over-the-top, but I like it. I just wished I knew how to cook because it's definitely a chef's kitchen."

"So cooking isn't your thing? Is that the reason you eat the way you do?" he asked.

She shrugged. "That, and when we were growing up my dad was into fitness. He still is. He's obsessed with the body being a temple and all that. Believes that a healthy body and mind are what led to his success. So I grew up on green beans and brussels sprouts. It's childish, but my bad food habits are probably a late reaction to that. Do you know how to cook?"

"It's in my genes. At least, that's what my mom says. When my mom got a job and was gone for long hours, she did her best to prepare what she could ahead of time, but a lot of the meals were left to me. At the start, a lot of the food came from cans. It was easy to fix, but I got tired of that kind of quick.

"And my sister was superpicky. Finding stuff she liked was hard, and we didn't have money to waste. I wound up spending less time on the sports channels and more on the cooking ones. I learned to cook off the Food Network."

At first, it had seemed like another unfair chore, but then he'd discovered cooking was relaxing. He could lose himself in creating dinners for his family, and he didn't even worry about all the stuff he was missing out on, like the football team or track.

Ainsley shook her head. "I admire that you did that when you were so young. I can't believe you were taking care of your sister when you were still a kid yourself. It's like when we were talking about what you did right after high school—I was such a spoiled brat in comparison. I was probably more worried about boy bands and wearing the right jeans."

He laughed and she joined in.

He tried to be jealous, but he couldn't. That was just sweet.

"Yep. I worshipped a bunch of those groups. I used to spend the majority of my days on fan boards just praying they'd show up and post something. It's sad, but true. For the record, they never did. And they never showed up on my doorstep, which I just knew if they understood how much I loved them, they would have."

Okay, maybe he was feeling a little jealous right then. "Their loss."

She slapped a hand on the counter. "Exactly. That's what I think."

"Funny. I never had a crush like that when I was young. Though, maybe when I was in high school. My sophomore English teacher, Dr. Hatcher, believed in me. She's the reason I love books. She could see I needed some extra help so she made me read out loud to her—and by made, I mean, I sat in her classroom during lunch every day. At first I hated her for making me miss my one free period during the day. But I loved the book. It was *To Kill a Mockingbird*. And after that one, I read *Catcher in the Rye*. And then she introduced me to fantasy and sci-fi novels and I was hooked."

"That's such a great story. I was lucky. I was a total nerd who loved school. And I had so many great teachers, except for Mr. Brown. He was my geometry teacher. Ugh. Triangles still make me cry. But the rest of my teachers, I just loved them."

"They do make a difference to a lot of lives. Dr. Hatcher did to mine. Books were how I kind of lost myself in other worlds." It had been one of the biggest blessings of his life.

"So, do you actually have food in that Sub-Zero?" He pointed to the gigantic fridge. "Maybe I could cook us something that doesn't involve artery-clogging pizza dough."

She waved a hand toward the appliance. "We keep it stocked, or Bebe does. She's like you—with the exception of the occasional sweet, she eats pretty healthy. You're welcome to take a look. And if you don't see anything, I can order from a different place."

He opened the fridge door. He found chicken, lemons and minced garlic in a jar. "I've got this," he said. "Can you maybe make a salad?"

"If you're asking if I can chop stuff without cutting off my fingers, probably."

After showing her how to cut vegetables so she never had to worry about her beautiful long fingers again, he went to work.

A half hour later the kitchen smelled of lemon and garlic.

"True story—if ever you get tired of the Marines, you could so be a chef. Your mom was right." She took her last bite of chicken. "This was better than any restaurant meal I've had in a long time."

He chuckled. "I was worried I might be rusty, since it's been a while."

Her eyebrows drew together. "Why?"

"I've been living on base most of my career, so I eat what's in the mess hall. They've made a better effort of trying to provide better, healthier food. Same as when we're deployed, although, depending where we are the choices can be restrictive for obvious reasons. So I haven't cooked much. I only moved into my own place last month and we've been away doing training exercises for most of that time. To be honest, my fridge doesn't have much more than the makings for protein shakes and grilled veggies."

She leaned her elbows on the breakfast bar. "I haven't wanted to be too nosy, but what exactly do you do? You fix helicopters, but you can also fly them?"

"I'm a pilot and I also teach pilots how to do maintenance on their aircraft as well as what to do in extreme situations. On the base, I'm a senior staff officer of the squadron. But we do things a bit differently here in Corpus."

"What do you mean?"

"We share the base with the Navy. We're a special squad. All of us do a bunch of different things. We're support staff for other branches of the military, as well as the Marines. What I teach specifically is emergency mechanics while in the field. So if the navigation goes out, or something is wrong with the fuel tank and the squad has to land in the middle of nowhere, they can maybe fix the problem and get out of there."

"That's impressive. You're pretty *and* smart—such a dangerous combination," she said.

He batted his eyelashes and did fluttery fingers on his cheeks. His sister used to do it while singing Disney songs at the top of her lungs. "You think I'm pretty?"

"And I forgot funny." She was nearly bent over laughing at him.

She straightened and tried to be serious. "Thank you for dinner. I can't remember the last time I had such a good time." Her hand landed on his chest and the heat seared through him. He took her hand in his and kissed her knuckles. There was a connection, and while they might dance around it, there was no denying it.

"I'm not much for games," he said as he let go of her hand. She didn't pull away—in fact, she twisted her fist in his shirt. "And I'm not much one for pretending."

She leaned into him then, lifting her face until their eyes locked. "What do you mean?" Her words were barely a whisper.

"I want you."

"I want you, too."

"Then I'm giving you three choices. Take off your clothes right now so I can bend you over this breakfast bar and make love to you. Show me where your bedroom is so I can make love to you there. Or I'll sit in that comfy living room chair and you can straddle me."

She blinked.

"Pick one."

Her tongue teased her top lip. She glanced at the breakfast bar, and then back at him.

"Here is good."

8

"STRIP," HE ORDERED. They were in the middle of the kitchen and he wanted her. Here and now. Never in her life had she been more turned on. This night was so much better than she could have ever imagined. He was hot *and* he cooked.

Cooked her. She was heating from the inside out, and couldn't get her clothes off fast enough.

"Someone might walk in," she said, but unbuttoned her blouse anyway. She wasn't about to let this moment pass by.

"Do you have a lot of clients show up at seven thirty at night? Ones who just walk in the front door?"

He had a point.

"Right. You're so smart, as well as built." She tossed the shirt over one of the bar stools.

"That's the second time tonight you've said something like that. I almost think you might want me for my body," he said as he pulled his T-shirt over his head.

Wow. She hadn't imagined those abs. They were as perfect as she remembered.

"Like I said, here is good." She reached back and unzipped her skirt. It dropped to the floor. His eyes traveled down her body, and his look sent a delicious shiver through her.

Thank the universe she had the foresight to wear decent lingerie. The azure bra-and-thong set had been a last-minute addition to her wardrobe.

She started to step out of the red Louboutins, but he held up a hand. "Leave those on."

"Um, okay. But only if you start stripping, as well." She pointed to his jeans. "More than the shirt."

He smiled and her body actually shook.

"I was hoping you might do that for me," he said.

He didn't have to ask twice. Her hands were on his belt, zipper and, soon, on his erection. No wonder she was still delightfully sore from the other night. He was so hard and his cock had hit all the right spots.

Before he could say a word, she kneeled down and began sucking him. She couldn't resist, especially considering the pleasure he'd given her after the auction. That and she really wanted him in her mouth.

His cock twitched.

He moaned and then whispered her name. His pleasure was unmistakable.

She glanced up to find him watching her and the look in his eyes made her body tremble.

She teased him with her tongue and then teased just the tip of his erection.

"Ainsley." He said her name as if it required all

of his control. As she increased the tempo, they hit a rhythm and she enjoyed every moan, every bit of his praise and encouragement. Suddenly, he pulled out and reached down for her to help her up.

"Lean over the bar," he whispered in her ear. She smiled and turned her back to him, heard the rip of the foil package.

His hand caressed the length of her spine. Then those fingers found her heat. She was ready for him, but he found that same spot, the one that only took a few strokes before she was shuddering and crying out.

Never had sex been this good for her. Mind-bendingly good. The kind that made her worry he may have ruined any other man's chance with her.

Before she could catch her breath from the orgasm, he pumped his cock into her. His fingers found her clit. He caressed, and teased, and all the time thrust harder and faster until she forgot to breathe.

It was pure, glorious sensation. And when his other hand squeezed her breast, causing her to groan again, she couldn't seem to find the words.

"So good," he said, as if speaking for her. She held on as tightly as she could, overcome by the sheer outright bliss she was experiencing. This was so much more than she'd ever felt before. Thanks to Ben. He was a gifted lover, a good guy, honorable, kind…something she didn't want to think too much about.

"You are perfection," he murmured in her ear. "Like you were made for me."

She couldn't agree more and pushed her ass out to meet him, to feel his thrusts deeper. The orgasm came then, sure and swift, with black dots swimming in her vision and every muscle tingling with satisfaction.

"Yes," he said, and didn't stop. His thrusts were strong, relentless. She was going to come again. It was too much, too—and then she was lost. He lifted her chin back toward him and he kissed her with such passion.

As he came, he moaned her name. The syllables vibrated through her. And never in her life had she felt so fulfilled. So wanted and cherished.

They stayed like that for a few moments as he trailed kisses along her neck and then her shoulder and down her spine.

She then turned around so that she could kiss him. "So sexy," he said against her lips. "I could barely hold on."

She pressed her mouth to his and then broke away. "I say you held on just fine. But maybe don't let go of me anytime soon because there's a good chance my legs aren't going to work. You seem to do that. I'm thinking you give new meaning to the phrase *weak in the knees*."

He smiled and she beamed right back at him.

"I should probably help you do the dishes," he said.

Dishes? Who could even think about dishes? This Marine had some stamina. She tilted her head toward his. "You cooked, and um…gave me the best orgasms of my life. Well, you did that on Saturday as well, so not to worry, I can handle the dishes."

"Hey! What are you doing in the kitchen? I didn't think you even knew where it was. It's weird. The house smells like real food. Food that hasn't been burned," Bebe called out from the hallway.

Ainsley stammered, her mouth refusing to work.

"I was at the store, and thought I'd drop off some snacks. Don't freak out, I bought fruit. You should try it sometime."

"No," Ainsley yelled.

"Ains, you've got to get some vitamins in you somehow."

"No," Ainsley yelled again as Bebe entered the kitchen. She did a full stop just as Ben unceremoniously tucked Ainsley behind him.

"I was trying to say don't come in here right now. I'm—"

"Bloody brilliant. You're shagging the Marine in the kitchen," Bebe said. "About time you had some sex. What do you know? Miracles do happen." Then she plopped the groceries on the counter and walked out.

"Uh," Ainsley finally said. "Sorry."

"What for? That chest of his is the best thing I've seen in years," Bebe shouted from the hallway. "Good choice, luv. Excellent choice. I'll see you tomorrow. Don't forget to put the almond milk in the fridge. And I'll lock the front door so you don't get any other visitors tonight. Toodles."

The front door slammed and Ainsley stood there mortified.

He turned to face her. "So I'm guessing that was Bebe?" He had a big smile on his face. The tension eased from her shoulders.

"I'm so sorry about that."

"Why? Funniest thing that's happened to me in a long time. It's not often I get caught with my pants down." And he did—still had his pants around his ankles. Thank goodness the bar hid the rest of his body, or her best friend would have seen a whole lot more than his chest.

"I'm never going to hear the end of this," she said as she wrapped her arms around his neck. "She's going to throw innuendos at me for the next week, maybe month. Heck, probably for a year."

He leaned back. "Are you embarrassed by me?"

She frowned. What was he talking about? "You? Of course not. You're the best thing ever. It's the situation of having been caught in my own kitchen with a man. I haven't dated in over a year."

"That's a long time." He pushed her curls behind her ear. Her hair must have fallen down. She probably looked like an unmitigated mess.

"Yep. Right now, it's business first, which is why I told you about my no-dating policy. And then, of course, I asked you to be my date. So you probably think I'm crazy."

"Not even close," he said and kissed her cheek. "Trust me on that. I need to clean up, but then I have a fun idea about how to do the dishes. You up for it?"

She loved how he didn't care that her best friend had caught them at it, or technically post at it, in the kitchen.

"Oh, I'm up for whatever you've got, Marine."

THE WOMAN WAS ADDICTIVE and that brought him up short. And she hadn't lied about being up for whatever he desired. She was as open a lover as she was a human being. He'd never met anyone like her.

They were in her bed watching Fallon. Well, he was watching. She'd dozed off after their escapades in the shower. Her bedroom wasn't as girly as he'd expected. The walls were chocolate-brown, the trim and furnishings white. Except for some pink flowers in a vase on one of the nightstands, that was it for frills. She'd said she liked to keep things minimal where she slept so there were less distractions.

But sleep wasn't in the cards for him, not with her next to him. She might be the best distraction he'd ever come across. The sex was... Well, he thought he'd known what great sex was. But with her, it was more.

And they couldn't do it again. They'd talked about that on Saturday. This was a fluke. A one-off.

The last thing he needed was a girlfriend. Between his duties as a major and all the extra work he was creating for the incoming crew of new grunts, he was busier than he'd ever been.

They'd joked after the shower that maybe they had this lust out of their system.

She snuggled into him. He had to go. Needed his space, to clear his head. He couldn't think when she was around.

"Hey," he whispered as he kissed her cheek. "I need to go home. I've got to be on base at oh-four hundred."

She blinked her eyes open. "You can stay," she said sleepily. "It's okay with me."

"Thanks, but I have to get ready for work in the morning. I wasn't planning on staying even this long."

She sat up and blinked again. "Oh, sorry. Sure, you should go. I didn't mean to keep you."

He'd hurt her feelings. Even sleepy she was apologizing for what had happened. That was something he definitely didn't want. What they'd shared was great. But that had to be it.

He chuckled. "Ainsley, I wanted to be here. This was amazing tonight. I just… Well, you understand better than anyone about work priorities." He felt a bit like a jerk. But he did have reports to finish, and he needed space. Otherwise he might say something he'd regret. Like, they should do this every night…

Yep, definitely time to go.

"I'll walk you to the door."

She'd need to lock the door behind him, so he nodded.

When they were downstairs, he kissed her. And it was hard to lift his head and pull away.

"Hey," she said and grabbed his belt loop. "Anytime you want to come over and cook for me, I'm good with that." Then she gave him one of her smiles.

"Is that so," he said, wondering if she meant what he was thinking.

"Yep. You know, so you don't have to eat alone or anything." She wanted to spend more time with him. Interesting.

He was beginning to speak Ainsley.

"You said earlier that you were hoping we'd gotten this," he said to her and pointed between them, "out of our systems."

"Is it?" she asked. "Out of your system?" She glanced away, as if she didn't want to hear his answer.

"No." He wouldn't lie to her. "How about you?"

She shook her head, and then grinned. "So we keep it simple, right? Friends with benefits. We'll be each other's plus one at a couple of events, but that doesn't mean we can't also have a little fun, right?"

For some reason, and he knew he should, there was no way he'd argue with her logic.

"How about tomorrow night? I'll make us something good."

"That sounds like a plan. And by good, you probably mean healthy. But when you cook, it's better. Maybe I won't mind so much." She yawned.

"I better go." He kissed her cheek and then headed out. He waited on the porch until he heard the lock turn.

It wasn't long before he was back at his place, and he flipped on the light. The stark contrast between Ainsley's place and his home hit him like a slap on the face. He basically had a recliner in the living room, and a bed in the bedroom. An old, beat-up dresser he'd had when he was kid was the only other piece of furniture he owned.

It wasn't as if he couldn't buy more things. He'd planned on it, but he didn't mind the sparseness. Still, it was a far cry from her house. He'd never be able to invite her over.

And there it was again, him wanting what he shouldn't—couldn't—want. Even though she'd made it clear that they'd keep things simple. They were merely helping each other out. That was it. Okay, along with the best sex he'd ever had in his life.

It was dangerous for him to think about more. Not that he wanted to. He was as married to his career as she was to hers. And he really wasn't sure he'd fit into her world. That reminded him, he wanted to look up her dad.

He pulled out his phone and typed in Ainsley's name. There were tons of photos of her at parties and galas. And then her father's name and his bio.

The dude wasn't just rich, he had an empire. He owned sporting goods stores, restaurants and an oil company.

Ben scratched his head. That confirmed it. No way would he ever be the type of man who could hold on to Ainsley. She wasn't just out of his league, she was out of his universe.

So, he was going to appreciate their fun. And after Christmas, well, they'd both be moving on.

And he was going to keep on pretending that wouldn't bug the heck out of him.

He wasn't going to sleep anytime soon, so he grabbed his laptop and took it to bed. After finishing his last report, he turned off the light and stared at the ceiling, thinking about Ainsley and her curves.

When his phone rang, he sat up straight. Years of training had him instantly alert.

"Yeah?" he grunted into the phone.

"Dude, open your door," Jake said.

His feet were on the ground before he even thought about it.

When he opened his door, Jake stumbled forward, looking and smelling pretty rank.

"What happened to you?"

"Don't want to talk about it. Please tell me you have coffee. I've got to sober up before going back to base, because the CO will make my life a misery if I show up drunk."

True. He took in his friend's rumpled appearance, and then checked the time on his phone. Three in the morning—they had to be at the base in an hour.

There was a cut on his right eye.

"Did you get in a fight?" His friend was more a lover than a fighter, although he could hold his own if need be.

"Man, you wouldn't believe me if I told you."

Ben headed to his kitchen and pulled out the coffee. "Try me."

"So, remember that dance teacher from the other day?"

He tried to remember her name but couldn't. "Yeah, you were going out with her tonight. Did she punch you in the eye?"

Jake leveled him with a stare.

"Fine, so what happened?"

"Turns out she had a boyfriend. Well, technically they were taking a break. Guy shows up at the restaurant. Punches me in the face, and then proposes. Who does that?"

He coughed to hold back the laugh because Jake was so serious. He also wanted to hear the story. His friend was right, this was something else.

"No clue. A jerk?"

"That's what I was thinking. I was ready to punch him back when she grabbed my arm. Begged me not to, and then told him yes. That she'd marry him."

"Wow."

"The whole time I'm thinking, why does she want to marry this violent jerk who just punched my face? She tells me she's really sorry, but she loves him. She just wasn't sure he loved her. Then she hopped up into his arms, and he carried her out of there. All kinds of messed up. I'm telling you, I probably dodged a bullet with that one. What a night."

Ben couldn't hold back. "You do know how to pick 'em."

He grabbed some ice, and then threw it in a plastic bag and handed it to his friend. "That will help with the swelling. So what happened once they left?"

Jake leaned on the breakfast bar, clearly dead on his feet. "Dude, you have got to get some furniture."

"Go sit in the recliner. I'll bring you the coffee."

"I paid for dinner, and then headed to the bar a block away from here. Tried callin' you but you didn't answer. Nine beers later, I decided maybe walking was better than driving."

Well, at least there was that.

By the time the coffee was ready, Jake was asleep in the chair.

Ben decided to let him sleep for twenty minutes while he showered and changed.

This was why he didn't date or get serious about women. It wasn't only about work. He didn't need the drama. The "why didn't you call me or text me?" messages. Having to make plans that would impress. Jake provided the perfect reminder of why it was probably best to keep things simple with Ainsley.

It wouldn't do for him to think they could ever be anything more than friends with benefits. Albeit very good benefits.

He needed to make that clear the next time they were together.

9

AINSLEY WAS LATE. Ben tried not to think about it. He forced himself to focus on Brody's story about putting something together for the baby's nursery, but he was bored. And a little worried. She had texted him about an hour ago apologizing for running behind. She'd had an emergency situation with a client, but said she'd be there soon.

He'd told her to just show up when she could, but now he was wondering if she would arrive at all. And that had to be okay, because she was doing him the favor. There was one problem, though—she had the CO's gift.

He was about to text her again, when there was a commotion at the door. He glanced over the crowd to see long, feminine arms holding a gigantic present wrapped in gold, with a big red bow in the doorway.

"Excuse me, guys," he said to the little group around him. "That's Ainsley. I'll be right back."

"I can't wait to meet her," Matt's wife, Chelly, said. "Mari says she's gorgeous."

Clarissa beat him to the door. *Great.* Who knew what the brat would say.

"Wait, you're here for Ben?" Clarissa asked as he stepped up to the door. He took the heavy package from Ainsley and then blew out a breath.

She wore a red dress that fit her figure perfectly. It had crisscross wide bands across her chest, and then flared out at her tiny waist. And she wore the red shoes from the other night.

"When people talk about stealing their breath, they're looking at you," he said honestly.

Her cheeks turned a deep shake of pink. He wanted to ask her to go back to her place and beg her to take him to bed. But he had to remember where he was.

"Thanks," she said. "I'm sorry I'm so late. I actually had to drive up to San Antonio to get the gift. It didn't arrive today like it was supposed to. Some mix-up at dad's office. And then I got stuck in traffic. But I'm here."

"So, I was the problem client," he said.

She smiled. "Yes. But I didn't want to worry you."

"I'm sorry you had to go through all of that for me. We could have picked another gift."

"Oh, no. It's fine." This time the smile didn't quite reach her eyes. He didn't know her well, but something had happened today that bothered her.

"I understand you're really busy and that was four hours out of your day that you probably didn't have to spare."

"Maybe you should let her come inside," Clarissa said. "That Chanel dress is terrific and it looks like it might rain." He stepped back so Ainsley could come in. The back of her dress swooped down, exposing most of her beautiful back. He shifted the present to hide just how much that turned him on.

"I remember you from the charity event. Wasn't your sister in charge of that?" Clarissa asked.

"She was the chair, yes. Hi, I'm Ainsley."

"Clarissa." They shook hands. Then she glanced over at him. "Looks like you're dating up," she said.

That woman. She was right, but you didn't make those sorts of comments in public. She had no filter, which inevitably made everyone uncomfortable at some point. He'd talked to her about it numerous times. He was one of the few people whom she actually listened to.

Occasionally.

"Clarissa!" he said. "Just because you think it, doesn't mean you should say it."

She rolled her eyes. "Whatever, Mr. Polite Manners. I simply meant that she's pretty and rich. You could do worse."

He sighed.

Ainsley was laughing, and this time the sound was genuine. "Thanks," she said. "But if anyone is dating up, it's me. This guy." She squeezed his arm. "Best man I have ever known. I'm definitely the lucky one. And he cooks. What kind of guy looks like him and can cook? I feel like I've won the lottery."

She sounded genuine. That gave him a sense of pride—that she enjoyed spending time with him. From what he'd heard about her dating past, she'd been connected with a fair number of jerks.

Before Clarissa could say something else controversial, Ben broke in and said, "Let me put the CO's gift by the tree, and then I have some people I'd like you to meet."

She waved goodbye to Clarissa and followed him. The house was very modern and stark, much like the CO. He preferred things to be neat, ordered. Most Marines did, but he took it to the extreme. The best part was the view that looked out onto the beach.

After dropping off the present, he introduced Ainsley to his friends.

"So where did you two disappear to the other night?" Jake asked.

The guy had not given him a break for leaving him the night of the auction. He'd been so caught up in Ainsley that he'd forgotten that Jake had hitched a ride with him to the hotel.

"Dude, I told you she wasn't feeling good so I took her home," Ben explained, trying to stop the conversation before it went much further. He didn't want everyone knowing his and Ainsley's business.

Before Jake could mention that he had to take a cab to Ben's house to pick up his truck, Ben whisked her away...and right into the CO.

"Sir," he said.

The CO smiled. "Welcome. So, who's this, Major?"

"Sir, I'd like to introduce you to my date, Ainsley Garrett."

The CO held out his hand and shook hers. "Are you having a good time?" he asked her.

"Yes, thank you. It's nice to put names and faces together. Ben's been talking about everyone."

The CO shot him a glance. "He has? I hope it's been all good."

She laughed and nodded. "Absolutely. It's fascinating what you are doing on the base. Certainly, he doesn't tell me everything. But it's interesting that your squad is working with other branches of the military."

"Have you told her all of our secrets?" The CO smiled as he said it.

"No, sir. She's just a good listener."

"Clarissa tells me that your dad is Ed Garrett."

Her smile disappeared. "Yes, he is."

"We've been in a few charity golf tournaments together. Known him for years. In fact, I was going to hit him up for that new putting prototype he was talking about the last time he was here."

Ben glanced at Ainsley and did an inner hallelujah. That was the first gift she'd shown him. She was very good at what she did.

She smiled. "Hmm. Call it a guess, but I have a feeling that when you open your present from your staff, you're going to be very happy."

The CO's eyes rounded. "Really?"

"It was Ben who asked if we could get one for you. And it's hard for me to tell him no. I drove to San Antonio today to pick it up from the factory."

"Good call, Ben. Come on. Let's open it," the CO

said. Never had he seen the CO behave this way. He was like a little kid.

They all shared a laugh together.

"Excellent suggestion," he said to Ainsley as they followed his commanding officer across the crowded living room. "And thanks for giving me all the credit, which you deserve. This might keep him off my ass for a day, maybe even a whole week."

He slipped an arm around her shoulders.

"It's my pleasure," she said. But she didn't smile this time. Something was bugging her.

Ten minutes later, much to the chagrin of Clarissa, they had the new putting machine set up in the middle of the party. All the guys were trying it out.

"You did good," Ben said. "I've never seen him this happy or relaxed. The guys and I owe you."

She frowned. "It's no problem." But it didn't look like it.

"What's wrong?" He was genuinely concerned. In the short time he'd known her, he'd never seen her do anything but smile.

She shook her head. "Nothing. Sorry. Just thinking about today. We can talk about it later."

He glanced around and noticed everyone was focused on the CO's new toy. "Want to grab some air? The deck is covered, and he has a great view from there."

She twisted her lips and glanced nervously through the windows. "If that's what you want."

What was going on?

The rain had stopped, but the wind had picked up.

He took off his jacket and put it over her shoulders. "Thanks," she said.

"You want to tell me why you're upset? I really am sorry about you having to take so much time to get the CO's present." They might be just friends, but he wanted to help if he could.

"No. Because this is nice. The party is great. Your friends are fun. I like the way you covered with Jake. Thanks for that. It's been a long day, and I want to focus on what's going on right now. Nothing else matters."

So there was something.

"I wish you would go ahead and tell me whatever it is that's bothering you. I know this is temporary, but I don't want secrets between us. Did you meet someone else? It's okay if you're having a hard time telling me."

He wasn't sure where that had come from, but it would explain why she was acting so uneasy. But his gut churned and maybe he didn't want to admit how much the idea unsettled him. *A lot.*

She sighed and leaned her hands on the railing. "No. It's complicated. I told you that I had to go to San Antonio to pick up the gift because the shipped one wasn't going to arrive on time. I'm not sure what happened with that. We ordered it in plenty of time and, hello, it's only an hour away. And after what's occurred with my dad, I'm not so sure he didn't have something to do with it."

"I really appreciate that you did that. I know how busy you are."

She nodded. "One of the main reasons I was late…

Dad insisted I have lunch at the club with him. And, of course, being my dad, he had this guy he wanted me to meet. I felt…weird. Like I was cheating on you. I mean, I know all of this is supposed to be temporary. We only met a short time ago. But I really like you a lot. And it just seemed wrong being there with him."

Dang if Ben didn't feel like throwing his arms around her. Okay. This was supposed to be casual, easy, but the truth was the last few days he'd been thinking maybe they should look at spending more time together. He wasn't exactly sure what *more* was, but he couldn't get her out of his head, and he had a feeling that wasn't going to change anytime soon.

"I like you, too," he said. "But it's not like you initiated the date, right? And even if you did, I'd have to accept that. We aren't really dating." It was hard for him to say, he realized.

"Yes, but I should have anticipated my dad doing that. And what bothered me the most was it did very much feel like I was cheating on you. I can't, that's… I'm just so confused. This thing between you and me, we're having fun, right?"

"Absolutely."

"But it feels, I'm not sure how to explain it exactly. I almost wanted to call you from the table and say, 'Hey, I had no idea this was going to happen. This guy is pretty much a blockhead. I'll be back as soon as possible.'"

He chuckled. "I get it," he said. And he did. They'd only spent a short time together, but they'd spent every night since Monday in her bed. Whether they wanted to be or not, they were connected. "If it makes things any better, I'm as confused about what's going on between us as you are. But in a good way."

She glanced up at him. "Really?"

He nodded, and then he turned so he could wrap his arms around her. "This thing between us is kind of intense."

"Kind of?" she asked.

He smiled. "Okay, it just is. So we see it through, right? Neither of us has much experience with relationships, or at least long-term ones. We don't have the time to maintain them. But we hang out, enjoy each other and see where it goes. Deal?"

"It's an exclusive deal, right?"

He thought for a minute, trying to figure out what she meant. "As in we only date each other as long as we're together?"

"Yes."

He shrugged. "I kind of thought that was implied."

Then she hit him with one of her devastating smiles. "Good," she said. "I was about to read the riot act to Clarissa. See how she kept looking at you like she wanted to eat you up? The only person who can look at you that way is me. Got it?"

Smiling, she poked his chest with her finger.

He smiled back.

"Wow. Who knew Ainsley could get jealous? I kind of like this side of you."

"That woman rubs me the wrong way," she said as she wrapped her arms around his waist. It was crazy how she fit him so well.

"She does that to a lot of people. You don't have to worry about her. I'm more worried about these surprise dates your dad keeps setting you up on. Now every time you go to San Antonio, I'm going to wonder."

She sighed. "You don't have to worry, either. You already know how I feel about all of that. And today, that guy, Todd, I think he was blindsided, as well. I doubt he had a clue what my dad was up to until I got there. He thought he was there to talk about a business venture. I felt bad for him. But he was a blockhead. He was nice to me, but only when my dad was looking. Not a very genuine type of person, to put it frankly.

"Have I mentioned my dad has really bad taste in men, when it comes to picking out one for me? Fortunately, that was the last time, until the Christmas party in a few weeks, that I'll see my dad. I now have the world's best excuse and I'm really good at using it. Work is crazy! Which reminds me, I'll be late tomorrow night. We're wrapping all the presents for Clinical South."

"At the house?"

"Yep."

"I could make you and Bebe dinner? I'm the world's worst wrapper, but I can provide sustenance."

She kissed his chin. "You're the best. As you find out more about my family, you'll see I'm not like them in a few ways. They love me and I love them. But I've felt like an outsider at times. Like I don't belong or I'm playing a part. That world isn't who I am. I'm just a girl who runs a business, and is into a really hot guy."

He squeezed her tight. "And I'm just a Marine. I'm

kind of a 'take me like I am' dude. But if you can deal with that, I can deal with the fact that your dad might not see me as a prime candidate for his daughter. I won't fit in that world, either."

"That's funny. Clarissa commented about my dress. But it didn't even register who made it. You told me the other night that you liked the color red, and I wanted to wear it for you."

This woman was special, truly. "Ainsley, you were wearing red the other night when I said that. I love any color you're in."

"You say the sweetest things," she said. "Oh, I actually do have a favor to ask you."

"Name it. I'm yours."

"Be careful with that," she said and winked at him. He loved when she did that. "This is more physical."

He couldn't help his smile. "Even better. I've proven getting physical is my specialty."

She giggled. "You are so bad. That's not what I mean."

He pretended to frown, and she rolled her eyes.

"When I was looking for ribbon earlier today," she said, "I found a box of Christmas lights and holiday lawn ornaments I'd forgotten about. I love having things all done up and festive, so I was wondering if you might put up the lights and decorate outside for me? I'd do it, but I'm afraid of heights. Bordering on 'having a breakdown' fear of heights."

Right. Well, the last thing she needed to be was on a two-story ladder. "I'd be happy to do it. I've got the

Toys for Tots drive in the morning, but if the weather clears I can do it tomorrow afternoon or Sunday."

"You are my favorite person," she said and then her lips were on his. Kissing her was nothing but sunshine. He couldn't get enough.

He lifted his head just as thunder hit. She jumped a little and he held her tighter.

"Are you cold?"

"Are you kidding? Every time you touch me I feel the heat. I've never—"

His lips were on hers before she could finish speaking. That heat burned within him, as well. The storm raged around them, but they were lost in their own world.

"Hey, Major, you know how the CO feels about PDA," Brody said.

She jumped away and then giggled. "You scared me," she said.

Their quiet alone time was over. They both turned to look at Brody. Ben's frown was for real.

"We're just talking about putting Christmas lights up on the house. Uh, Ainsley's house," Ben explained. There was no way to salvage the situation. They'd been caught.

"Hmm. That's interesting that you can still talk when your lips were together like that. Hey, I have an idea. If you help me with my lights," Brody said, "I'll help with yours. I had to buy new ones because suddenly Mari doesn't like all white, now she wants blue on everything. I can't keep up with her. She's nesting, and by nesting I mean she decides she wants something and then it's up to me to make it happen."

They all laughed. "Better not let her hear you say that," Ben warned.

"Say what?" Mari asked from behind Brody. "Step aside, Marine, I need some air. Look at that storm." She went to the railing and gulped in the fresh gulf air. "It's stuffy in there. Oh, hey, Ainsley. I didn't know you were here."

"Good to see you again," Ainsley said and let go of Ben so she could shake hands with Mari.

"Same here. That dress is gorgeous. Chanel, right? So amazing. Man, makes me miss my waist." Mari patted her pregnant belly, which was twice the size as it had been at the high school craft fair. Though Ben knew better than to say anything like that.

"Oh, you look gorgeous," Ainsley said. "Pregnant women have the most beautiful skin and hair. Even in the dim light out here you're radiant."

Brody came up, put his hands on Mari's shoulders and kissed her cheek. "She's the most beautiful woman I've ever seen."

Mari sighed. "And that's why I keep him around. Never mind that he had to help me put my shoes on tonight because my belly is so fat I can't see my feet anymore."

"Just more of you to love, baby," Brody said.

Some good-natured teasing ensued.

"We're saved, honey," Brody said. "Ben's agreed to help me with the Christmas lights if I return the favor and help with Ainsley's house."

"Oh, that's nice of you guys. I worry about him out there on the ladder by himself. He won't let me be his assistant."

"No way," Brody said. "You're getting nowhere close to a ladder, even if it's only to hold it."

"No prob," Ben said. "Happy to help out."

"Toasts are about to begin," Jake called to them from the patio doorway. "I should have known you guys would all be here making out."

"Jake!" Mari said. "We're talking about holiday lights. Would you like to help the guys tomorrow?"

Jake's jaw dropped as he realized he'd just walked into a trap. "Uh, I'm busy?"

"Too late," Mari said. "Brody will text you the details. Once you finish at my house, you're going to give a hand to Ainsley with hers."

"Fun times. Does anyone ever say no to you?" Jake asked Mari.

"Nope," she said. "And you're not going to start. I'm pregnant, so it's totally against the law to even think about saying no."

Everyone roared with laughter.

They traipsed back inside, but Ben claimed Ainsley's hand before they joined the others. They'd been interrupted. Well, technically, their kiss had been. It was a strange night, and he needed to make sure she was okay.

"We're good, right?"

She stood on her tiptoes and kissed him. "We're great," she said. "We'll be even better when you get me home and out of this dress."

Ben hissed out a breath. "You can't say things like that to me, especially in public." He pulled her against him so she could feel his erection. She wiggled into him.

"This is work, Marine, and you should probably be responsible and mingle. But I really wouldn't mind if in twenty minutes or so we said our goodbyes." She slipped her arms around him. "This dress is suddenly feeling way too tight. I can't breathe. I might be feeling faint. How are you feeling?" She slipped her hand between them, rubbing up and down his cock.

Yes. Yes. Yes. This was happening.

Desire crowded out any rational thoughts in his head. He couldn't think, period. They had to go. Like yesterday. "Goodbyes be damned. We're leaving."

"But my car," she protested, laughing. "I can't leave it here. That would look bad for both of us." The wind was whipping her hair. And the dress outlined her curves.

"Give me your keys." He sounded like he was ordering one of his students to do something. "Please. Sorry. Those words came out of your mouth and now I can't think about anything else."

She kissed him again and handed him the keys.

He leaned his head inside the doorway, noticing the party was in full swing. "Brody," he said because he was the closest.

"Yeah?"

Ben held out the keys. "Jake has to get Ainsley's car to my place. I'll pick it up tomorrow. Tell him he owes me. He owes me like ten times over."

Brody frowned. "Okay, what's up?"

Crud. He wasn't expecting an inquisition. "Uh, she's got a work thing, so I'm taking her home."

Brody glanced at Ainsley, no doubt noticing her flushed face, and then gave him a knowing look. "Right. She has a migraine. Got it."

They both smiled.

"You're a good friend," Ben told him.

"Yep, remember that tomorrow afternoon when you're at the top of that ladder sticking lights on my house."

Ben didn't care about tomorrow. All he wanted was to get Ainsley naked as quickly as possible.

10

BEN WOULDN'T LET her peek at what he'd been up to outside. She'd heard the guys laughing and thanks to him putting something in the Crock-Pot, the whole house smelled like yummy food.

She was starving.

They'd made love most of the night. She couldn't get enough of him. Then he'd brought her breakfast in bed. She kept trying to find ways to surprise him, or do little things for him, as well.

Like giving him a massage, but then that had turned into something for her because they'd ended up in the tub and wow. Yep. That had definitely turned into something for her.

"You two look serious," Bebe said as she finished up the last of the wrapping. The drill team had done most of the patients' gifts, but she and Bebe had wrapped the gifts for the staff and executive board for Clinical South.

"I told you. We're just having some fun." She couldn't

help the sly smile slipping across her face. Something had happened the night before. It wasn't just sex anymore. They'd made love, and it was intense.

Every time she thought about the way Ben looked at her as he came, tingles spread throughout her body. It was as if he'd committed to her in that moment, and she'd liked it…a lot.

"Right. The kind of fun where he's here every night. Cooks for you and puts Christmas lights on a two-story house for you. Where he stares at you as if you were the most beautiful woman in the world. The kind of attention that most women only dream of."

"Yep. That kind of fun," she said sheepishly. "We can't call it anything else. We're both being honest about putting our careers first right now. He wants to make Colonel sooner than expected. Did you know he made Major about six years ahead of time? He's such a hard worker and a good leader. Mari was telling me that Brody can't say enough nice things about him. It scares me that he's almost too perfect, and what experience do I have with that? None."

"Not that I have a lot of experience, either, with great relationships," Bebe said, "but I'm pretty sure love doesn't stick to a timetable."

"Love?" The word caught in her throat. She took a swig of water before she choked. "Oh. No. It's not serious like that. I mean, shoot. We've only just met, or rather, it's only been a week."

Bebe waved the scissors dismissively in the air. "Yes, love. Again, not really speaking from experience, however, you have to know that whatever you call it, it's special. Do you feel the same about him as you have the last ten men you've dated?"

When she put it like that, it made Ainsley think. "You're scaring me. Don't go there. I'm not joking. You'll freak me out. Why do people always have to put labels on things? Fun. It's just some serious fun."

Bebe gave a dramatic sigh. "It shouldn't scare you. If anything, you should be grateful and running toward the light."

Ainsley snorted. "This isn't some *Wuthering Heights* drama. Yes, it's something new for me. A man who puts me before his needs. Who supports my career. Wants the best for me. But I'm not rushing anywhere. I won't get tied up with any guy."

"Tied up. Hmm." The humor in Bebe's eyes was plain to see. "Tied up by the Marine? Interesting. I bet you're one present he'd definitely like to unwrap."

He already had. Many. Many. Many times. "Oh, stop it." Ainsley threw a bow at her. "Don't ruin this for me. Let me live in the bubble, at least until Christmas."

Bebe frowned. "What happens at Christmas?"

"We put an expiration date on the whole idea. But then, last night… Well, it's confusing. I'm just not counting on this being long-term."

"Nonsense. Do you actually believe what you're spouting? You can't schedule love or expect it to be there when you do want it."

"Ugh. It's not love!" She very nearly screamed the word.

"Ainsley?" Ben called for her.

Shoot. She hoped he hadn't heard her. "Shut it. And behave." She pointed a finger at her friend.

Bebe made the universal sign for a zipper over the mouth. Not that it would stop her.

"In the conference room," she called to him. "What's up?"

"Ready for your surprise?" he asked.

Bebe stood and made an explicit back-and-forth motion with her hips like she was having carnal relations with the curtains.

"You're insane," Ainsley hissed.

Then they both laughed.

"Yes," Ainsley said and rushed to find him. "I can't wait. I'm so excited." She caught up to him in the front entry.

He rubbed his hands together, clearly happy with himself. "Just so you know, Ains, I might have gone a little crazy. My engineering brain took over, but it'll be easy for you to use."

Now she was nervous. Her neighborhood had rules, and if he'd gone too crazy she'd probably get cited. If he'd put Rudolph in her yard or one of those giant blow-up Christmas ornaments, they were going to have to have a chat. And he'd been so sweet. She didn't want to disappoint him.

But she also didn't want to get fined by the home-owners' association.

She and Bebe followed him to the front yard. Jake was there, putting a ladder into his truck. "Thanks for helping out," she told him.

"No prob," Jake said. "We actually had some fun.

And it was interesting to see the way Ben's mind worked."

"How so?" Ainsley asked.

"Ben can do anything with a bunch of wires and some electricity. He's a magician. Wait until you see."

They all talked about how smart Ben was, not that she'd seen anything to the contrary. But he wasn't a showoff about it. They'd talked about books, the world, music, politics, but he was never a snob about anything.

"What happened to Brody?" she asked.

"Mari called, so he headed home. She's due any day, so it's better if she isn't alone a lot of the time. And she was hungry. I swear, I had no idea a person could eat so much."

"I guess it's true about eating for two," Ainsley said. Still, she believed Mari was gorgeous. "I hope she's doing okay."

Jake shrugged. "Brody didn't seem too worried. He's like a mother hen around her. So if he's not worried, I'm sure she's fine."

"Are you ready?" Ben asked. He was on the porch now, holding an iPad.

She nodded, curious to see what they'd been doing all afternoon.

He handed her the iPad. "I made it easy for you. All you have to do is push the button on this app. Go on, just push the button and you'll see."

It was silly, but her hand was shaking a little.

She did as he asked and then gasped. It was beautiful. He'd used white lights to outline the architecture of the house. The rooflines and windows, as well as the columns. They'd even wrapped the chimneys. Wreaths had been hung over each of the windows. It was simple and beautiful, like something out of a winter wonderland. It couldn't have been more perfect for the home if she'd designed it herself.

"I love it." She turned and threw her arms around him, squeezing him tight. "Amazing. It's everything. I can't even thank you."

On each side of the porch he'd put two Christmas trees with matching lights. It was a scene from a postcard. All they needed was some snow and it would be Norman Rockwell worthy.

Not that snow was a possibility in Corpus, unless it was the fake kind.

"I'm glad you like it," Ben said, looking relieved. He'd been worried she wouldn't like it? Oh, that made her heart beat even faster.

"I was kind of afraid it might be too much. But we were having a blast. The lights go off automatically at midnight. Or you can turn them off with the iPad. And they come back on at seven p.m. It gets darker in the winter. That way, you don't have to worry about it. I know how busy you are."

"Ben." She brushed her fingers across his cheek. "I'm so happy. You totally got me and what I wanted. You really are a true hero. But with wires, like Jake said."

"Jake, perhaps we should leave these two alone," Bebe said. "This looks like it could get X-rated soon."

"Shh," Jake said. "Let's just tiptoe away."

"Relax, guys." Ben turned her so they were both

facing the house. "I promised Mari we'd drive by their place later so you can see her blue lights. We used part of the white ones Brody had bought to finish off the roofline. He said there's no need to pay him since I helped him out. You've got a very big house."

"I can't believe all the work you put into this, and you did it in a few hours. It's wonderful," she said, starting to sniffle. *I will not cry. I will not cry. I will not cry.* It was all the kindness that was getting to her. It was one of the reasons she loved her business so much because it was focused on giving.

But Ben had given her the greatest gift. And he always talked about how busy *she* was, but he worked just as hard, and often more hours. A couple of times she'd caught him doing work on his laptop when he thought she was asleep, and he was up and at the base in the morning before she'd even thought about waking up.

"I don't think anyone has ever done something this nice for me." She hugged him.

He pushed her hair behind her ear. That was his thing, and every time he did it, she fell a little bit harder.

This man gave her all the feels.

"This was a new one for me. I've never had a house with Christmas lights. When I was growing up we lived in apartments. I got Mom the house a couple of years ago, but I can't remember if she decorates. Like I said, it's been a long time since I've been home for the holidays."

"You bought your mom a house?"

He shrugged. "I thought I told you that. She's paying me back. I don't want her to, though she insists now that she's got a good-paying job as a charge nurse. Anyway, I like doing things for you." His voice grew husky and then he stepped back.

He'd bought his mother a house. And this was his first time home for Christmas. It made her want to bake him cookies and put up a tree. Hmm, maybe not the baking. She was dangerous in the kitchen. But the tree—definitely. She was so taking him to buy a tree. And maybe one for her place, too.

She'd meant to ask him about his apartment. If maybe he wanted her to come there sometime.

"Jake wanted to put a giant plastic Santa on the roof, but I drew the line there."

She laughed. "Thank you for that."

"Hey," Jake said, jumping in. "There's nothing wrong with Santa. Santa's a classy touch."

"Yeah, dude, if you say so." Ben grinned. "Jake did have a good idea for later, that is, if you have time."

"I thought we were eating dinner?"

"After that," Ben said. "I know you aren't a fan of heights, but we thought it might be in keeping with the season to go and look at Christmas lights."

She frowned. "I'm confused. Why would I have to be afraid of heights for that?"

"We want to take you and Bebe up in one of the Apaches. I've got to get some flight time in this weekend, and it might be fun. Bebe, what do you say?"

Helicopter. Big sigh. She'd been in one in Hawaii, but it hadn't been her favorite experience. In fact, it was one of the reasons she hated flying in general. She did it, but she wasn't a fan.

On the other hand, Ben seemed so excited and she didn't want to disappoint him. And there was the fact that this was his work and he wanted to show it to her. Yup. That was just plain sweet.

Suck it up. She hugged him again to delay her answer. *Just say yes.* But she couldn't quite form the words. Sweat trickled down her back.

"I don't know about Blondie. She's not a fan of flying, but I'm in," Bebe said. "I've never been in a helicopter and certainly not a military one. Sounds like fun to me. And Christmassy. All these lights make me a little homesick for London."

Her mouth opened, but still the *yes* wouldn't come out. Ainsley usually considered herself brave. She wasn't afraid of anything—with the exception of helicopters. Planes, she could shut the window shade and pretend she was in a safe tiny capsule. But with helicopters there were windows everywhere.

"I promise, we'll make it a smooth ride," Ben said. "You won't even realize we're in the air. The weather is perfect, not too windy or cold. And we'll be up for maybe forty-five minutes max. Come on."

She squeezed him hard. "Okay." He was so happy and she didn't want to be the buzzkill.

That's when she realized she'd do anything for him just to see that smile.

The thought scared her. It was a slippery slope if she wasn't careful. She refused to be like her mom sometimes, giving in to her dad's whims. But Ben had done so much for her, she wouldn't let him down.

Not tonight. Relationships were about compromises. And she refused to be ruled by fear.

"It'll be a blast." She didn't think she sounded very convincing.

He gave her another one of those smiles. Mmm-hmm, she'd do just about anything to make him happy. And that might be scarier than the promise of any helicopter ride.

AINSLEY WAS NERVOUS. That much was obvious. He hadn't realized just how bad her fear of heights was. As they ascended, she squeezed her hands so tight, her knuckles were white.

He was beginning to wonder if maybe they should have eaten after their little excursion.

"I swear, it will be the smoothest ride you've ever had," he said over the headset.

Her eyes were clamped shut, but she nodded. *Dang.* He'd hoped this would be enjoyable for her.

"Woo-hoo. This is bloody brilliant," Bebe said from the backseat. The Brit and Jake had been giving each other a hard time, but their bluster was all an act. They were getting along great.

"Any time you want to go back, just say the word," he told Ainsley. "I can get my hours in tomorrow."

"No." She coughed and then cleared her throat. "It's fine. Really."

He grinned. "Might be easier for you to see the lights if you open your eyes." He held the copter low over the gulf so she could see the lights all across town. He'd never seen anything like it.

He watched as she peeked with one eye open and then the other.

"Oh," she said. "That's cool. I mean the rotor blade thingies are kind of loud, but it doesn't even feel like we're moving."

He laughed. "I'm holding us steady right now, but I've been taking it slow, and at this altitude with no wind, no issues."

She glanced out at the scene ahead. "It's so-o-oo pretty. I'm glad you made me come."

"So what happened to make you afraid of flying? I know you've traveled the world. You're maybe the only person who's been to more places than I have."

"Travel was my means of escape. I spent a lot of time with my professor grandmother, studying different cultures during her summers off from college.

"The last time I took a helicopter ride was in Hawaii three summers ago. When we went over one of the volcanos, something happened. We dipped down low and just when I thought we would crash, the pilot pulled the helicopter back up. But I was pretty green by then, and that pilot was lucky I didn't puke on his shoes."

"You don't have to worry about that with this one," Jake said, pointing at Ben. "He's one of our best pilots, and if we were going to crash you're in the safest hands possible."

Ainsley's hands balled into fists again.

"No crashing tonight," Ben promised. "No wind

shears, which is probably what happened in Hawaii." He shot a glare to Jake.

His friend shrugged and mouthed, *I'm sorry, man.*

"We won't have any air currents or volcanos to worry about," Ben assured her. "We're good. Ainsley, you know I won't steer you wrong." He meant those words on all levels, though he wasn't sure if she was hearing anything at the moment. She still seemed panic-stricken.

"You can let go of your hands, Ains, and maybe breathe a little before you pass out."

"I feel so dumb," she said. "People do this all the time."

"Not really," he told her. "It's a different kind of flying experience. And it takes a bit of getting used to. You should see some of the grunts on their first flights. Nervous as all get out. But the more you do it, the easier it gets. At least that's how it is most of the time."

"Thanks for being so patient," she said.

He caught her watching his hands work the controls, so he explained what he was doing. Her shoulders dropped and her breathing was finally normal.

He inched the bird forward, slowing as they flew over the beach houses and into town. He circled downtown and then took them back to the base.

As he was landing, a big smile lit up her face. "That was way better than the last time," she said. "I might want to do that again. And I'm so proud of you. You've been doing this a long time, sure, but it's one thing to know what someone does, and it's quite another to actually see it in action. And then I was thinking, wow, you do this under fire, with unbelievable stress because it's life and death. You're incredible."

He laughed. "I don't know about that. I've had a lot of good training, and the team I'm a part of is second to none." Once he landed the copter, he jumped out and went around to open the door so the others could exit. He helped Ainsley and Bebe. Jake could handle himself.

"Did you like it, Bebe?" When they'd been up in the air and he'd glanced back to ask Jake a question, he noticed his friend's hand on top of hers. He wondered what that was about. Hopefully, Jake was just keeping her calm, though Bebe didn't seem to have a problem flying. The last thing he wanted was his best friend upsetting Ainsley's business partner and closest friend. Jake was a "love 'em and leave 'em" kind of guy.

Then again, that's the way Ben would have described himself until a few weeks ago. It was weird having someone he felt so connected to, who'd been there for him. Made him nervous in a way, as if he had something to lose. Strange how it was so hard to even think about what his life had been like before he'd met Ainsley.

He wasn't even sure if he could do more, meaning, formalize their relationship. Although he'd sort of been watching Brody for that. What his friend and Mari had was about as strong as it came. Pretty much looked like they put each other first. That was the trick. His job, which was still important to him, had always been the focus of his life. But now, he could see how maybe it would be possible to put someone else ahead of all that.

After checking on a couple of maintenance issues, and making sure the paperwork was in order, he headed out to the truck, where his friends had said they would wait for him.

As he neared, Ainsley was watching him from inside the cab. There was a smile on her face, but something else in her eyes, something he couldn't quite define.

He stepped up into the truck. He was about to turn on the ignition when she reached for his hand. Leaning across the console, he kissed her. They were lost in each other for a good two minutes, before something niggled in the back of his brain.

They had an audience. He reluctantly pulled away, surprised neither Bebe nor Jake had said anything.

He glanced over his shoulder, and that's when he noticed that Jake and Bebe weren't there.

"Hey, where did they go?"

Ainsley grinned and shook her head. "You just now noticed?"

"My eyes were on you, babe."

"Good answer, Marine. Jake said he had one of his motorcycles here and asked if she wanted to go for a ride. It's some kind of British one and she was all excited about it. Also, I think she might be a little sweet on Jake. He's not hard to look at."

They were passing the guardhouse, and Ben stepped on the brake. "You think Jake's hot?" He wasn't sure how he felt about that.

"Settle down. No one is as hot as you. But Bebe was doing her thing."

"What thing is that?"

"She gave him a hard time, and then she got quiet. That means she might like him. Though, with her, it's hard to tell sometimes. She can be a real ballbuster, but she's also one of the kindest human beings I know. I've never had a better friend. And she's like you in the sense that she's not dazzled by the fact that my family has money."

Ben turned the truck onto the main road leading to the highway. "I'm not sure I should say this, but Jake's not really, uh, boyfriend material."

She laughed. "Way to throw your friend under a bus. Listen, she's not looking for Mr. Right. She just wants Mr. Right Now. She's not the settling-down type, either. But she usually goes for supersmart nerdy guys."

Ben shrugged. "Well, he might be pretty, but he's not stupid. Jake actually designs a lot of the drills and almost every component of the combat exercises."

"Hmm. You wouldn't get that from a conversation with him." She slapped her hand over her mouth. "Wow. I'm so sorry. I didn't mean that the way it came out. He just doesn't seem to take life too seriously. He's always making jokes and teasing."

She was right. Jake wasn't one to brag about how bright or capable he was, unless it was with the team and they were offering some kind of challenge.

"Promise me if something happens between them, it won't affect us."

They were pulling up in front of her house. The Christmas lights were on and he was pretty proud of himself.

"It won't," she said. "Bebe's a big girl and after what happened with Jake last week, I'd think he'd be a little gun-shy when it comes to women."

"Ains, you can't keep a good Marine down. And Jake's a great Marine. Might have been good for him to get taken down a peg or two. I'm not sure I've ever heard of a woman turning him down."

"You coming inside?" She gave him a shy smile.

"You've had a long workday. Are you sure you aren't too tired?"

She pursed her lips as if she was thinking. "I was earlier, but after watching you fly… I could use a little extracurricular activity."

"Like volleyball? Or maybe badminton?"

"Um. No. Not what I had in mind," she said.

"How about football? Or maybe you want to play Monopoly?"

He could do this all night.

"Not even close. But if you come in—" she winked "—I'll show you some really fun things to play with, or some really fun plays. Your choice."

He couldn't help but laugh. "Done."

AINSLEY WAS FALLING HARD, and it frightened her. She watched him sleep, his arm around her waist as if he needed that connection. Had to be touching her when they slept. She loved it.

Things were so easy with Ben. And the sex, well,

she'd never experienced anything like it. Once again, it felt like every time they were together they moved up the level of intensity.

The old saying that passion burns out fast worried her. But even scarier was the idea that it might burn out for him long before it did for her. Everything was moving too fast.

How can I feel this way about a guy I met just a week ago?

Didn't matter how. It had happened. Bebe's mentioning the word *love* freaked her out in so many ways. But was this what love was? Being so caught up in someone that it hurt when they were away?

The thing was, he seemed to be just as into her as she was into him. He was beyond generous...and kind...and...

He was too good to be true was what he was. They'd even talked about their pasts. He said he didn't date a girl more than once, maybe twice. What was that about? And what was it about her that made him stick around?

It wasn't as if she didn't believe in herself. She did. But he was Adonis material. So rugged...so hot.

When he'd mentioned that he usually didn't make it past the first date with someone, she'd wanted to ask him about their relationship. She wasn't needy, but maybe she could use some kind of assurance, and, in a way, he'd given it to her the night of the CO's party. They were exclusive.

For now.

And the fact was, they were good together. Living in the moment. That was important.

"What's making you frown?" Ben's voice was deep and husky. He reached out and cupped the side of her face, and she kissed his palm.

No way would she tell him the truth. "Not frowning, just thinking about all the things I need to do tomorrow."

He rubbed his thumb across her lips and she sucked it.

"You're making me think about all the things I want to do to you," he said, before his lips replaced his thumb. Their tongues tangled.

Yes, this. She melded into him, their bodies already comfortable with one another.

This was all she needed. All her worries disappeared as his hands slid down her body, caressed her hips, her thighs and then slid between her legs.

She was more than ready for him. Even before he found the tiny nub and used the right amount of pressure, waves of pleasure overwhelmed her. Her body reveled in each new sensation. She arched, panting, moving as he brought her to the edge again.

Then there was the tear of a wrapper, and he was settling her on top of him, guiding her down his length, his powerful hands on her hips.

Bending back, she put her hands on his thighs and rocked up and down his shaft, setting the pace, loving every thrust.

He tugged her forward, toward him. "I want to see your face," he said. "Come with me."

He pumped deep within her, the motion hitting that same sweet spot he'd found, and her body tightened before trembling with orgasm.

"Ainsley, only Ainsley," he groaned, as he pulsed inside of her.

Yes. She was most definitely his.

11

EARLY THE NEXT MORNING, Ben met Jake at the airfield. They were getting in their flight hours before the big training exercises next week. The grunts would have their final exams and then graduate from the program—at least, those who passed would. But his friend Brody was pretty good at making sure everyone did well on the course.

He'd become a different guy after meeting Mari. Calmer, and more centered in a way he hadn't been before. And definitely friendlier. Before Mari, Brody had been a real hard-ass and few people could tolerate being in a room with him. But she'd brought out a hugely positive side to his character and personality.

Ben understood that. In a way, even though he was busier than ever, he felt more centered with Ainsley around. He looked forward to their time together, and in the mornings, waking up with her wrapped around him. It was good, so much so it was hard to think about anything but Ainsley.

Yet why was she hanging with him? He just didn't get it. After their discussion the other night, he'd done more research. He felt like a fraud checking up on her family, but she'd made such a big deal of how she wasn't like them at times, he had to know more.

Turned out "filthy rich" was a real thing. Her dad had started with nothing, and now he was one of the top fifty wealthiest men in the world. *The world.* From a business point of view, he had his hands in everything.

There had been pictures of Ainsley at debutante balls, and in tabloids on beaches in tropical locations. She was pretty in her teens, but she'd grown into a beauty. It was interesting that in all the pictures where there had been guys, even if she'd been linked to them in the copy, she stood apart. No kissing or even hugging.

It was weird that she had all of that and yet she seemed so unaffected by it. Not seemed—she was. They had a lot in common, from a strong work ethic, to believing in making the world a better place by giving back. She maybe did it on a slightly grander scale, but they did share that.

And being with her was easy. Never in his life had he found someone he could talk to about anything, but Ainsley fit the bill. They'd discussed…everything. From future plans for their careers, to favorite cartoons to family pets.

He grinned at that. She had definite opinions about cats versus dogs.

And then there was the sex. Heck if he'd ever had better than the night before. When he woke up, he'd watched her for a few minutes. Her teeth had worried her lip like she did when she was nervous about something. He had a feeling she was thinking about their relationship. Knew it in his gut, and as a Marine, trusting his gut was important.

He couldn't find the right words to tell her, so he had to show her how he felt. When their eyes had met as she orgasmed, and then her heat squeezed him tight, never in his life had he felt so strongly, so passionately for a woman. One woman, and only one.

He'd meant the words he'd said. *Only Ainsley.* He couldn't imagine feeling that way, whatever way that was, about another woman.

They were good. No, they were great. No idea what might happen in the future, but he was along for however long the ride lasted. He knew she was, too.

"Dude?" Fingers snapped in front of his face. "Earth to Ben. You in there?"

He'd been standing next to his truck in a daze. Thinking about Ainsley. He did that way too much lately.

"It's the same training maneuvers we've been doing for weeks," Jake said. "Are you nervous? You've got this, bro. What am I saying, you taught the rest of us how to do most of the maneuvers. Even came up with the fight roll. The Navy scrubs are still talking about that piece of awesomeness. No one is as good as you when it comes to this stuff."

"Had no idea I had a one-man fan club," he joked. "Nah. I appreciate your faith in me, but I wasn't thinking about that." The words slipped out before he realized what he was saying. Jake was smart, and there would be no getting around his admission.

"So, is it Ainsley?" And there it was. "That was a pretty serious look, dude. You guys seemed fine last night. Once you got her over the initial shock of flying, she was fine. Was she mad about me taking Bebe? It was the Brit's idea. Kind of. I told her about the bike. She said she loved them, so yeah."

The last thing he wanted to talk to Jake about was his love life. "Things are good, thanks. So what happened with you and the Brit last night?"

Jake frowned. "I drove her home on the bike. End of story."

"Huh?"

"What?" Jake asked. "I guess she wasn't feeling it. Didn't invite me inside. We talked for a little bit, and then she said 'Toodles,' or whatever it was, and that was it. The end. The whole night I'd been getting a different vibe, but maybe she changed her mind."

"Got no idea. She's a sweetheart, though. Very protective of Ainsley," Ben said, which was true.

"Yeah. A looker, as well. Kind of crazy with the pink-striped hair and the tattoos, but beautiful."

So he thought she was pretty. It was odd that Jake didn't get that far with her, especially since Ainsley had said Bebe might be into Jake. Ainsley seemed to be intuitive when it came to people. It was one of the reasons she was so good at her job.

But Ben wasn't sure what to think. Most days he just felt lucky to be able to make Ainsley happy.

And he liked doing that—making her happy. Ex-

cept for his mom and sister, he'd never been so preoccupied with taking care of someone. Well, not taking
care of, just wanting her to have what she needed. She'd
get mad if she heard him say that she needed taking
care of.

"Man, you really do have it bad," Jake said, waving his hands.

Jake would never let this go. He'd zoned out again.

"What are you talking about?"

"You're in love with her, aren't you?"

Ben coughed. "I don't know what you're talking
about. We're just having fun. Like you said, end of
story. Besides, what would I even know about that?
Love. We're both married to our jobs, you know how
it is."

"Right," Jake said. "Well, I'd like to stay alive if you
don't mind. Today isn't the joyride we had last night.
So, head in the game, Marine."

Head in the game.

Focus was important today.

And he absolutely was not in love with Ainsley.
They'd only met a week ago. Besides, he didn't do love.
Wasn't even sure if he knew what it was.

Yep. That was his story and he was sticking to it.

Ainsley stepped out of her car and that's when she
looked down.

"Shoot." She had two different shoes on. This had
to stop. Business was booming and her head was in
the clouds constantly thinking about Ben.

The man was so handsome and wonderful. And his body, he…

Focus! You have two different shoes on and you have to meet one of your top clients in four—she glanced at her watch—*make that two minutes.*

She only had one option. She pulled her yoga toe slippers out of her workout bag.

Whatever.

They were bright green, but at least they matched. Better than having one navy Manolo and a black Louboutin.

What was I thinking? That was the problem, she wasn't. She'd been all dreamy-eyed and still high on her orgasmic bliss from the night before.

And now she was meeting with one of her biggest clients wearing yoga slippers.

So professional. This wasn't junior high, where she'd doodle a boy's name on her binder with hearts and flowers. She didn't have time for this crap. Didn't have time for relationships and…who was she kidding?

Ever since she'd seen Ben standing in that toy aisle, she'd been a goner.

Great. Just great.

She quickly loaded up the dolly with the boxes of presents wrapped over the weekend. Normally, Bebe hired a courier service to deliver the gifts, but Craig had wanted to speak with her.

"Ha, maybe if he sees me in these completely inappropriate shoes he'll think twice about hitting on me again." With this guy, she always walked a fine line of letting him think she thought he was cute, but making it clear that she never dated clients. It was one of her most important rules. To which, he often reminded her, they *had* dated.

Arg.

After waving hello to the receptionist, she pushed the dolly with the presents to Craig's office. He wanted to store everything there until the company Christmas party, where he could play Santa—minus the red hat and beard—and dole out the gifts.

Be nice.

It was tough. They had gone out together before she started her business, and she quickly discovered that he was as bad as any of the men she'd been out with, but he was really good at hiding it.

And the only reason he wanted to be the one to give out the presents? So that he looked nice.

Because he really wasn't.

He was ruthless, and even mean, at times. There were bosses, people who liked to make themselves feel important. And then there were leaders, people who made those around them believe in themselves. If ever she was the owner of a large company like this, she would want to be the latter. To be a colleague, someone who wasn't afraid of the hard work or getting in there when things were tough.

That was one of the reasons she and Bebe kept things tight with the company. They sometimes hired extra staff, but for the most part they did everything themselves. She could always count on Bebe, and Bebe could absolutely always count on her.

Although, this might be the last holiday for that.

Even Bebe, the hardest worker Ainsley had ever met and the keeper of the budget, had said they should consider hiring at least a few part-time regular staff to help with deliveries and shopping.

But Craig. He was one of those guys who wanted to always be the most important guy in the room. She bet his employees hated him, which to her was a true judge of his character.

Yep. Definitely not her type.

Before she could get to the door, it opened and the man of the hour waved her in. "You can set those boxes in the corner," he said as she shut the door.

Any other person would have offered to help with the boxes. Not Craig. He stood there and watched as she lifted the heavy boxes off the dolly.

An image of Ben fixing her hot chocolate leaped to mind. He was always ready to lend a hand, or help out whenever she needed. He'd been such a blessing since they'd met.

"Okay, I think that's it," she said. "All of your executive gifts are there. The staff gifts will be delivered later this afternoon by the courier. Bebe checked and everything is on the truck, so you should be good."

"Great." He leaned back on his desk and crossed his legs at the ankle. He was a handsome man in an Armani suit, but his attitude made him ugly to her. He had no soul. "So I was talking to your dad the other day."

Here it comes. Why were these guys always talking to her dad? She glanced down at the dolly so he couldn't see her roll her eyes. "Um. Great. So I've got a busy day, if you'll excuse me."

"He was telling me about the family Christmas party. They didn't feel right inviting me last year, since we'd broken up the year before. But now, you know, I was hoping that wouldn't be an issue."

Ugh. What kind of person invited himself to a party where he wasn't wanted?

Craig.

"I'm not sure what you want me to say."

"I was hoping I could come as your date. Your father said you weren't seeing anyone."

She shrugged and pasted a smile on her face. "Sorry. Dad's wrong, and doesn't always listen. I am dating someone. I have for some time now. It's very serious, so I'm not sure what Dad was thinking when he told you that."

He cleared his throat and folded his arms across his chest. *Crud, if I lose this account because I couldn't be nice for ten minutes, Bebe is going to kill me.*

"I did mention it to my dad, but you know how he is. He's so busy he forgets. If you want to come to the party, that's fine. But I have a date, uh, thanks anyway."

"Who?" The man was just rude. He was trying to trip her up.

"Does it matter?"

He just stared at her.

"His name is Major Ben Hawthorne. He's a Marine helicopter pilot and basically the most amazing man I've ever met. We're exclusive and have been for some time." Okay, it was only since the weekend, but that was definitely some time.

"Oh." His face was scrunched up as if he was confused and her words did not compute. "I thought Marines were ground troops—since when do they fly helicopters?"

Oh, wow. He thinks I'm lying. I hate this guy.

"They have pilots and navigators, and also provide support for other branches of the military. You can look it up. They share services with the Naval airbase here."

"Huh."

Maybe she'd made it through that thick skull of his. "Thanks again for using our service, Craig. Let us know if you need anything else. Have a nice day." And with that, she took the empty dolly and strode out in her yoga shoes, feeling proud of herself.

So what that she was a bit too infatuated with Ben? Still, thinking about him would have to be relegated to certain times of the day. Like between the hours of eight and ten o'clock at night or something.

Her phone rang, and she pulled it out of her skirt pocket. It was her mother calling.

Not today. She just couldn't deal. Her mom and Megan had been texting since early in the morning. They wanted her to come up to San Antonio a day early before the party for some event.

But she already had plans with Ben. She'd sent them a text letting them know that she had a prior commitment. They just didn't listen.

Ever.

Maybe I should get a new phone and I won't tell my family the number. Never mind that this number was on all of her business cards.

She called the office.

"Thank God it's you and not your mother. She won't stop calling. I almost took her head off the last time."

Ainsley couldn't help but smile. "She's a nuisance, no argument there. Sorry, but I needed a buffer. I'm trying to avoid them until at least, I don't know, Sunday?"

"What's going on?"

Even though her friend couldn't see her, she shrugged. "Dad's trying to get me in town a day early, probably to meet more awful eligible guys. Anyway, I have plans. Told them that many times. Just help me. I don't care what you say. Make them stop."

Bebe cackled. "I bet Megan told them you were dating the Marine."

Ainsley slid into her car and slammed the door. Then she banged her head on the steering wheel. "No. Please. I've been trying to keep that news in a protective bubble. You know them. They won't mean to, but they'll destroy this. They don't like it when I'm happy. And I'm really, really happy right now."

And there it was. She was giddy almost. Couldn't wait to see him that night. That was wrong. She didn't need a man. She was a strong, smart woman.

But damn if she didn't want him.

Bebe laughed again. "Girl, you know they want what's best for you. But I admit, they can be some dysfunctional twits at times. I thought your mother liked Ben."

She sighed. "In theory. She certainly likes what he represents. Honor, duty, loyalty. Oh, yeah, and he's super-handsome. But you know how my dad is. He can be such a snob when it comes to how much someone makes. Net worth, stock portfolio...those things don't matter to me at all. But my dad just doesn't see it the same way. I was hoping to take Ben to the party and let Dad meet him. I mean, Ben's terrific. How could my dad not like him? They could even talk fishing and sports, and all that stuff."

"Kiddo, maybe that's exactly how it will be."

Ainsley gave an unladylike snort. "Right. Because my dad's so open and accepting of people. I do, I love my dad, but seriously. And you'd think my dad, since he came from nothing, would respect a guy like Ben. But he's just so…ugh. You know."

"Well, you won't know until you talk to your dad."

"I tried to at lunch the other day, but it was difficult since he brought me a date to the club. Oh, I don't know what to do. They have to stop trying to interfere in my love life."

Bebe cleared her throat. "They can't do that unless you let them."

Hmm. Wasn't that the truth?

Bebe had a point. It was time for Ainsley to set her dad straight. "You're right. I'll drop off the Wilsons' gifts and then call the house."

They hung up and she turned on the car. She breathed deeply several times and did a neck roll. As she was about to drive away, her phone dinged.

The message was from her sister.

She swiped it open to read the text.

Dad won Business Mag's Man of the Year award. Banquet Dec. 22, NYC. Private jet. Please call Mom to confirm.

That was a huge award. One of the most prestigious in the country. She was proud of her dad.

But why now? She sighed.

Because the universe really doesn't like you.

She didn't want to disappoint Ben by backing out of accompanying him to his CO's next event, but this was Man of the Year.

He'd understand.

Yep. Hopefully.

Then why did she feel so guilty?

12

BEN HUNG THE Santa suit in his closet and smiled. It had been a good afternoon. They'd given out the last of the Toys for Tots gifts at the community center. The kids had been so wide-eyed and happy, even to get the smallest gift. And it hadn't made him sad or got him thinking about when he was a kid and the fact that the holidays had felt like a time of hardship, not one of joy.

But he couldn't say that anymore.

The joy of making the kids' dreams for a fun Christmas come true had made all the shopping and running around worth it.

And it was because of those kids that he'd met Ainsley, who had done the majority of the work. He wished she'd been there. She would have enjoyed it as much as he did.

Of course, the best part was Brody, Jake and Matt dressed in elf uniforms. Chelly, Matt's wife, and Mari, Brody's wife, had both decided that Ben needed some elves to help out Santa. Elves with pointy-toed shoes and red tights and cute green outfits.

Those pictures would give Ben something to smile about for years to come. And if ever he lost another bet, he'd be happy to share said photos with the world.

He glanced at his phone, half hoping Ainsley had called. There was a part of him, a part he wasn't too proud of, that was disappointed by the fact she chose her family over him.

Dumb. He understood why she had to go. This was a huge deal for her dad. He was being honored by one of the top business magazines out there. With a big gala being held in New York, of course she had to be there.

All he had tonight was the Christmas party at the officers' club. Not quite the same level of fancy. And his brain understood why Ainsley had opted for the other event. There was no contest.

Right. Family came first.

In fact, he'd been the one to push her out the door so she could make the flight in time to meet up with the company jet.

The company jet. That was still a bit mind-bending to him that she came from so much wealth. But he'd never met a more adjusted, beautiful soul.

And he had to admit that it was sweet that she'd whined how much she didn't want to go, that the officers' party was really more her style. And she'd picked out the perfect sapphire dress to wear.

She even modeled it for him. And then he'd made love to her, the dress hiked up over her beautiful ass.

She'd watched him in the bathroom mirror as he took her from behind and didn't stop until her orgasm hit.

Yep, neither of them was likely to forget last night. He had another hard-on just thinking about it.

Picking his phone up, he dialed her number. It went straight to voice mail. No surprise. The plane was probably still in the air.

"Hey," he said. "I wanted to make sure you made it safe. I miss you. Just shoot me a text when you can." And then he hung up before he said something stupid, like "I love you."

Because he still wasn't sure what this connection was between them. All he knew was she'd been gone for only twelve hours and he felt as if she'd taken a part of his heart with her.

Jake's words about him having it bad were making more and more sense. But he wasn't about to admit that truth to himself or anyone else. They needed time. And they had to get through the party at her parents' house the next night. *One thing at a time.*

After his shower, he heard his phone ringing in the bedroom and ran for it, not even bothering to check to see who it was.

"Hello?"

"Hey," said Jake.

It was all he could do not to sigh. "What's up?"

"Don't sound so excited. I was wondering if you could be my DD tonight. You don't drink and you read the invite. If you have more than one drink, you have to take the shuttle service. Lame. Anyway, I'd rather you be my shuttle service. Can you pick me up?"

He wouldn't mind, except he'd been planning on exiting as early as possible. "Sure. But I'm not going to stay too long. It's already been a long day."

"You don't get to complain," Jake chuckled. "I swear if you ever show any of those photos, I will come after those you love. That's a promise."

"Don't make threats to the people you want to drive your drunk backside home. I'll leave you there with Clarissa."

His friend coughed. "No. Sorry, man."

"That's what I thought. I'll be there in about fifteen."

He was putting his dress blues on when his phone rang again. This time it was his mom. Everyone but the one person he wanted to talk to the most was calling him today.

"Hey, hon. We're so excited. I can't believe we get to see you in a couple of days."

"I'm looking forward to it," he said.

"We're making some special treats for you," his sister chimed in over the speakerphone. "Mom's been cooking for three days."

"Remember, I have that party tomorrow night. It may run late, but I promise to be there early on Christmas Eve. And I've got five days of leave." He was hoping maybe Ainsley could come up to meet them while he was in Austin.

But he hadn't had the courage to broach the subject with her yet. They'd also been busy, and with her having to leave town so fast, there hadn't been time.

"Hey, I'm getting ready for the officers' party and

I've got to pick up my friend. I'll call you guys soon. Okay?"

They hung up.

Two hours later, Ben was ready to leave the party. The party itself wasn't that bad. It was smaller than the gathering at the CO's house, with only the officers on his team. But he was missing Ainsley something fierce. Brody and Mari, Matt and Chelly were all so tight. And without Ainsley at his side, he couldn't help it, he felt left out.

As soon as he thought about her for the millionth time that night, his phone vibrated in his pocket. He stepped away from the team to take the call outside.

"Hey," he said. "Is everything okay?"

"It's so good to hear your voice," Ainsley said. "My phone died, and I'd forgot to turn it back on after it charged. Sorry I missed your call."

"Don't worry about it. How's everything going there?"

She sighed. "Okay. I'm freezing. I'm an idiot and didn't think about how cold it would be so far north. Did I bring a coat? And before you answer, that's a rhetorical question. It's in the single digits. I wish you were here to keep me warm. And sane. I've been staying away a lot and forgot what my family can be like sometimes." She laughed, but he could hear the stress in her voice.

"I'm wishing I was there to keep you warm, too. Was your flight all right? I know how much you love to fly."

"Honestly, I slept through most of it. That's the easiest way to deal with my folks. Oh, no."

"What?"

"My sister's waving me in. I'll have to—"

"Ben? Why are you out here? We're about to do the buffet dinner. My uncle was wondering where you were," Clarissa said.

He nodded and held up a finger indicating he'd be there in a minute.

"Who was that?" Ainsley asked.

"Just Clarissa."

"Is she there alone? Is she hitting on you? Oh, wow, I sound like a jealous witch. I'd say I'm sorry, but I'm not. I should be there to protect you from her."

He laughed. "Everything's cool. My head is so full of you these days, I can't think about anyone else. I don't even see other women anymore. Jake's been making fun of me. She was just telling me they're about to serve the food, which is good news. After that, I'll be able to go. Well, if I can get Jake out the door. I'm his designated driver."

"Aw, on the you can only think about me part. I'm the same way about you."

"Go ahead and do your thing, and I'll do mine. I don't want you to miss anything."

"I would feel better if you were here holding me."

"Yep. Feeling the same exact thing here," he said. "But I'll see you tomorrow night, right?"

She sighed. "That seems like forever."

He smiled. She really did miss him. "It is. But call me tonight when you get home."

"Okay. It'll be late, though."

"Wake me up. I like it when you wake me up."

"Ben?"

"Yes."

"I, uh, being away from you is harder than I thought it would be and it's only been a day."

His grin widened. "With you on that, babe. With you on that."

She laughed, and it warmed his heart. "Good. Good. I was worried it was just me. And now I sound pathetic and maybe a little lovesick."

He chuckled with her. "Again, with you on that."

"Bye," she said.

He said the same and hung up. And couldn't wipe the stupid smile off his face if he'd wanted to.

Sure, she might come from one of the wealthiest families in the world, but she was his Ainsley.

And that made him happy.

CLARISSA WAS THERE. Probably digging her nails into Ben's arm, while Ainsley sat here, listening to some of the most boring speeches ever. Her dad's award was the last of the evening. And she shouldn't have been so selfish, but she wanted to be with Ben badly.

It had caught her off guard how much she missed him. She seriously missed him, deep in her soul. And yet she'd spent most of her life trying not to get attached to men. Always keeping things light with the guys she dated.

She never knew if they liked her for her, or for her pop's money. In the end it was usually the latter. The breakup had always been easy, too, because she'd never wanted to be serious.

Until Ben.

Just hearing him on the phone settled the raw nerves she'd been experiencing all day. Her family tied her up in knots. Sad, but true. Last night with Ben had been special. That look in his eyes as he made love to her, yeah, that would be seared on her soul for a lifetime.

Maybe this was it. The real thing. The one thing she'd been avoiding until she had her career on track.

But the business was doing well, really well. Bebe had things handled with the last of the deliveries. They'd stocked up on last-minute gifts. Those calls would continue to come in through Christmas Eve. But things were great.

They'd be hiring new part-time staff after the New Year. They already had several trade shows in the works. All sides of the business were doing well.

So maybe it was time to have a life. A full and re-warding one, not just a professional one. Over the past few days she'd come to realize that she'd used her business as an excuse to separate herself from having a personal life.

That changed when she'd met Ben. He'd shown her that she could work hard and have a very rich and kind of wonderful life. And even though she spent too much time thinking of Ben, she'd managed her busiest time of year while starting a relationship with him.

She kept flip-flopping back and forth as to whether this was a good thing or not, but most of the flipping had to do with the fact that she was scared. Really scared he'd hurt her because at some point, she'd have lost herself in him and what he wanted.

It was funny. Neither of them wanted something serious. They'd just been having fun.

And yet, here they were. Well, he was there with flirty Clarissa. But she'd be back with her Ben soon.

Applause rose up around them. Her dad was walking to the stage.

"Almost done," Megan said from beside her. "My face hurts from the fake smiling."

"Mine, too," she said. Though Ainsley had been smiling for a totally different reason. Thinking about Ben.

Her dad thanked his family, who were always there for him, even when he was gone for weeks and months at a time in those early years. He talked about why, even though he had businesses all over the world, he stayed in south Texas. It was home. It was a little different than his usual spiel, and there was something earnest in his demeanor.

She was so used to her dad owning every room he walked into. He was bigger than life, bossy to a fault, but she and her sister had never doubted that he loved them. Even though he wasn't around much when they were younger, he'd made a point to be there for the important moments, from pictures for prom to swim meets. Now that she thought about it, her mom and dad had always been up in her business.

Sometimes she wished she had a family who didn't care so much. Dumb. But true.

As her dad returned to their table, everyone stood again. There were lots of pats on the back. And a little less than an hour later, they were back on the jet.

She wanted to tell her dad about Ben, maybe prepare him a little.

"I haven't seen your dad this happy in a long time," Todd, the guy her dad had brought to their lunch at the club, said as he sat down next to her.

What is he doing here? And what would he know about her father? This was supposed to be a family-only trip.

"Yes, he should be. That's quite the honor," she said. "I don't mean to be rude, but I didn't realize—I mean, most of the people here are family, or people I've known my whole life. I had the feeling that you and dad hadn't known each other that long."

He shrugged. "For a couple of years. We were in a meeting when he got the call, and he asked me to join him. Is that a problem?"

"No, I was just curious."

"I think he hoped maybe you and I would have a chance to talk again. You were preoccupied the day we met."

One of her eyebrows rose. She couldn't help it. "No, I was busy. And to be honest, I wasn't, and I'm still not interested. I'm dating someone."

He held up his hands as if in surrender. "I heard about the Marine. Your father is hoping it's just a phase you're going through."

Why did they have to be on a plane right now? All

she wanted to do was punch this jerk in the face and then run as fast as she could.

And wait? Her dad knew. That meant he couldn't know the whole truth about Ben, because she was the only one who did.

I'm going to kill Megan.

"Yeah. Not a phase. Serious relationship with one of the best men I've ever known. A man who is not you. If you'll excuse me, I need to speak to my dad."

She rose, but just then the pilot called for everyone to take their seats as they were about to hit turbulence. She took one as far away from Todd as she could.

By the time they landed, she was so mad she wasn't sure she could speak to her dad. It ate at her that he'd heard she was in a relationship with Ben, and was still trying to pawn men off on her.

She wouldn't confront him even though she was on edge. She didn't want to spoil his special night.

Tomorrow would be soon enough to set the record straight. If the Marine wanted her, well, she was ready to take that leap. Not into marriage. But to whatever the next step in their relationship might be.

And her family would get on board or else. She was done letting them walk all over her.

When the limo finally pulled up in front her parents' home in San Antonio, it was nearly two in the morning and she was wiped. Still, a promise was a promise.

She texted Ben as she headed upstairs. We're back. Miss you.

Call me when you get in bed, he texted back. He'd

answered quickly and she wondered if he was still out with his friends.

Ok

She washed her face and changed. Then she crawled into bed and hit the FaceTime button to call him. She wanted to see his face.

"Hey, gorgeous," he said as he yawned.

"Did I wake you up with the text?" she asked.

He nodded. "You know I'm a light sleeper, but I wanted you to wake me up, remember? So how was tonight? I bet you're exhausted."

She smiled. "It was fine. Really great for my dad. There was a lot of turbulence on the way home. You're so much better at finding me calmer weather." In more ways than one.

"You sure you're okay?"

"Yeah…I'm just really tired. I might have a tough time going to sleep without you holding me."

"Or you holding me," he said.

"Would it be really needy if I asked you to keep the phone line open so I can go to sleep looking at you?" she asked. Praying that he didn't think she was some kind of lost soul who couldn't live without him for a night.

He chuckled and then gave her one of his best smiles. The kind that sent instant heat to her core. "I was thinking the same thing."

She lifted up and positioned the phone on the pillow so that she could look straight at it when lying down.

"We're lame, right?"

"Yep. Babe, but we're lame together." They both laughed.

"So how was the officers' party?"

"Okay. The food wasn't too bad, though. And Jake didn't puke in my car, which happened a few months ago and I'm never going to let him forget it. That reminds me, I have something to show you."

A picture flashed up on the screen of Matt, Jake and Brody in elf outfits. For a full minute she laughed so hard her stomach hurt.

"That might be one of the funniest things I've ever seen. How did you get them to do that?"

He explained about his friends' wives playing a little joke on the guys. Then he switched to a picture of him in a Santa suit.

"I bet the kids went crazy," she said.

"I actually had a lot of fun."

"It wasn't too loud?" She'd been worried with the way noise bothered him that it might be tough. It was one of the many reasons she'd wanted to be there for him.

"It was at first, but then, those kids were so happy, I didn't think about the noise, or the fact that they wanted to hug me. It was just pure joy."

"I'm so mad I had to miss it. I love kids, and I would have paid big money to see you in that suit in person. Maybe you can wear it for me sometime?"

He grinned.

"What time will you be here later?" she asked.

"I needed to talk to you about that."

For a minute, she panicked. If he couldn't come, she'd have to make an excuse that she was needed for work because she could not face this party without him. Maybe that made her weak, but she needed Ben.

"O-kay," she said carefully. "What's up?" She tried to be cheerful so he wouldn't see her abject fear at the thought of being at her parents' party without a date.

"I might be an hour or so late getting there."

Whew.

"They had to move the graduation ceremonies to oh sixteen—I mean four p.m. We don't have that many grunts, but the ceremony is important and then there's a reception. I have an arrangement with Brody, that if we're not done by six, I sneak out and he'll cover for me. I've had to do it three times for him so he could make doctor's appointments with Mari. We've got a system."

That might actually be better. It would give her time to talk to her dad. She didn't want him to make Ben feel uncomfortable in any way. "That's fine. The good thing is we're only a short drive away."

"True. I thought about showing up tonight and waiting for you. But I can't miss that graduation and besides, it might have come across strangely. 'Hello, Mr. Garrett, I know I'm supposed to meet you tomorrow night, but I have a difficult time sleeping without your daughter. And by difficult, I mean hard.'"

Then he flashed the camera down his body to his cock, which had tented his pajama bottoms. She hissed in a breath at the sight, as warmth tingled through her to her toes. He was stunning. And she needed him.

"You should do something about that."

He laughed. "I will once we hang up."

"No, I mean now," she said. "Show me. Touch your-self—I want to watch." He brought the camera back up to his face.

"I will if you will," he said. His voice had dropped to that husky tone.

"Deal," she said.

13

MOSTLY, BEN ENJOYED the graduation ceremonies. He understood the work the grunts had put in and it was a joyous time after a lot of blood, sweat and tears. But today all he could think about was Ainsley. He wanted to see her.

She'd texted him a couple of times already, and he knew she was anxious. So was he. Meeting her parents was nothing short of fear-inducing and he'd been in a lot of scary situations.

Finally, after two hours in traffic, he pulled up on what he thought was the right road.

This can't be it.

Ben stretched his neck out of the truck to look past the iron gate that had been left open for the line of cars pulling through. He'd thought she said the event was at her parents' home. Glancing down at his phone, he double-checked the numbers and then looked back at the address carved in the stone wall.

Yep, this was the place. As he moved farther along

the long drive and the house came into view, he blew out a long whistle.

Home sweet hotel.

She was rich. He'd known that in theory. But he hadn't been expecting this. The house was bigger than some makeshift bases he'd stayed at, and that was not an exaggeration.

This kind of rich was something that didn't seem to be within the realm of possibility. It was one thing to read about it and look at pictures, but quite another to have it hit you hard in the face. The collar of his dress blues grew tight around his neck. It took a lot to make his palms sweat, but they were damp against the steering wheel.

No way he'd fit in here. All those insecurities about being a kid from a modest one-parent household—and a struggling one parent at that—flooded his mind.

Her dad would see right through him.

He could text her. Tell her that his mom was upset he wasn't already in Austin, which was true. Mom had called earlier and told him that if helping a woman was so important, he should bring her home to meet his mother.

He'd promised to see what he could do, but explained that Christmas was a big deal to her family. That this party was important to her, and he wanted to be there for her.

He glanced up again and took a deep breath.

The monstrosity of a house made of stone and glass leered back at him, reminding him just how naive he could be sometimes, even after everything he'd been through.

No wonder her father was trying to find her a rich husband—somebody who would fit easily into this world, know what to expect. Ben didn't measure up.

Feeling protective toward Ainsley was something he could understand. But this—he just couldn't wrap his mind around it.

His phone buzzed. He answered without looking. "Hello."

"Where are you?" she asked. The anxiousness in her voice brought him back to earth. She was upset. "I swear if Dad introduces me to one more of his young associates I'm going to scream. Loud. I'm not saying that to make you jealous. I don't think he believes you are real. That's the only thing I can figure. I will start screaming soon, and then my mom's going to be really embarrassed and I'll probably end up on the gossip pages as they haul me out in a white coat with those funny arms. I'm…weak. I guess. I don't know. But I can't take it anymore. Tell me not to go crazy and run through the party screaming 'I have date. I have a date. I have a date.'"

The idea of her father pushing other men on her was not sitting well with Ben. Even if part of him understood why.

That should be me.

No, it shouldn't.

He would never be able to live up to her expectations. She might be okay with giving up the rich life for a little while, but he wasn't sure she'd turn her back on it for good.

"Ben, I need you." And there it was—the whole reason he was here. "Please."

"Ains, did you forget to tell me something?"

"You're wearing your dress blues, right? You look so hot in those. I'm going to have to keep my eye on you the whole time around these women. Wait, did I type the address wrong? I'm always transposing numbers. It's the one with the big iron gate."

"And even bigger house. This looks more like a museum than where someone lives."

"Whew. You're here. Thank goodness. I was so, oh, the 'forgot to tell you' part. But you knew about my dad," she said.

"Knowing and seeing are two different things."

"I'll meet you outside. We can chat. I really want this evening to be good—for both of us."

And so he promised himself that no matter how he felt, he would fake it for her.

At least for tonight.

True to her word, as he pulled up to the valet, she was there on the steps. Dressed in a dark blue gown that matched his uniform, with her hair in curls on top of her head, she looked like a princess.

She was a princess.

He handed his keys and a ten-dollar bill to the valet. "No, sir, we aren't allowed to take tips," the valet said.

"Keep it," he said. "It's not a tip. It's a 'sorry it's not a Mercedes or a Ferarri' gift."

The kid laughed. "It's the truck I want. No gift needed. And it's American-made. Oorah."

"Oorah. You're all right, kid," Ben said.

They fist-bumped, and then he climbed the steps to Ainsley, who was twisting her hands nervously. There were others coming up behind him, but she hugged him and then tugged his hand. "Come on inside, I promise we'll talk before I introduce you to everyone."

He nodded.

Inside, the foyer was a rotunda with painted ceilings and a chandelier the size of a small car. She pulled him to the left and into a private room. When she flipped on a light, he saw it was a study with a large desk.

Wrapping her arms around his neck, she gave him a quick peck on the jaw, and then rubbed away her lipstick mark with her thumb.

"You're probably mad, but to be honest I just didn't think about how the place looks. You'd asked about my house in Corpus and I kind of skirted around the fact that I'd inherited it from one of my great aunts. But I don't tell people who my parents are for a good reason. I don't want them to possibly like me because of this." She waved a hand toward the expensive-looking painting on the wall.

"I get that, but you could have given me a heads-up before I got here. I thought maybe I was in the wrong place. Yes, I figured out who your dad was, but still, I was surprised. This is— You're so normal."

"Yes. Exactly. To you, I'm normal. That's what I want. I never know who likes me for who I am. My whole life has been that way. I'm not some poor little rich girl, but I've had situations where I was friends with people because their parents told them to make nice with me for some lucrative business reason. That's this world…sometimes. But it isn't who I am."

He couldn't even imagine what that must be like, people coming after you with agendas. Never knowing if those closest to you were really folks you could trust.

One of the things he liked best about being a Marine was even though they didn't always agree or necessarily get along, his team had each other's backs. No matter what, they were there for one another. Ainsley didn't have a lot of that. At least, until she met him.

"Those guys I was telling you about? It isn't about love or even attraction. It's about mergers and acquisitions. That is not a life I choose for myself. If I ever decide to spend my life with someone, it will be for love. And it won't matter what they do or how much money either of us has."

She took his hands in hers and clasped them between their chests. "Tell me you understand."

He nodded again. "I do. It's just a lot to take in, Ains."

She gave him a nervous smile. "It is. I get that. I do. But we're good, right? What we have is real. That's what I'm holding on to tonight. The rest of this, it doesn't matter, okay? It's one night in fantasyland. And then we get to go back to our regular lives. Please, don't be mad. Please. I thought we would be driving together and I had this big plan to explain about what you were going to see. There aren't any pics of the house in the media because dad doesn't want to advertise for security reasons.

"That's partly why when they moved here, I stayed in Corpus. I just didn't want to be a part of this. I'm grateful, don't get me wrong. I've had a lot of amazing opportunities, and a good life. But I told you before, this was never me. It was just the situation I was born into."

How could he blame her? It wasn't her fault her father was a billionaire several times over. She was right. He didn't exactly announce how he'd grown up when they first met. Not that it was that bad, but it was a far cry from this.

"I forgot to tell you something," he said as he drew her hands to his lips and kissed her knuckles.

"What?" she asked hesitantly.

"You're the most beautiful woman I've ever seen."

She blessed him with one of her angelic smiles and then blinked really fast as though she was trying to keep her tears at bay.

"I'm sorry I gave you a hard time. I thought I was prepared, but it was a shock. I'm good now. We're good."

"You're the most honorable, handsome man I've ever met." Then she kissed him, and he pushed away all his troubles and the fact that she was so rich.

When she backed away, they were both breathing heavy.

"You ready for this?" She cocked her head toward the study door.

He chuckled. "After that kiss, I need a second."

She laughed with him. "So I'll give you a tour. We might as well start here. This is my dad's study. He never uses it. He's got his own man cave in the back of the house with his televisions, pool table and a bar. I'll take you back there in a bit.

"It's where he does most of his business these days. Mom likes having him around, and he's never been one for sitting behind a desk. He's always moving, always doing. And, uh, I just want you to know that I talk a lot about my mom and dad but they're good people. Still, I'm not really sure what to expect. But they've loved me. They've given me an incredible life. It's just, you know, they drive me nuts. The way parents can do sometimes."

He'd been through several tours, and nearly died twice. He could do this.

I'm a Marine.

Funny how that statement meant so much to him. When he first started at boot camp, he'd hated it. It wasn't until his first tour when he helped save some kids from a village that was being bombed that he realized he was making a difference. And that's when he changed. The Marines became his life. A brotherhood.

A bunch of rich people were nothing. He'd faced much worse. And he was his own man.

As he and Ainsley left the study, a man with almost white hair was coming in through the front door. His skin was tanned leather, but it was the blue eyes just like Ainsley's that made him recognizable. He stared directly at Ben.

"Dad, what are you doing?" Ainsley sounded upset. Ben couldn't see her face since she was just a step in front of him.

"I was looking for you. One of the caterers said they'd seen you with someone in a uniform. I'm guessing that's you," her father said. His eyes never left Ben.

"Yes, sir. I just arrived."

Her father glanced to the study door and then back to them. "Why are you hiding in my study?"

"Dad! We weren't hiding. We were talking. I kind of forgot to tell him about…well, everything. He'd met mom, but…" She was fumbling with her words. She hardly ever did that.

"It's nice to meet you, sir." He stuck out his hand and the other man shook it. "I wasn't aware that Ainsley came from such a wealthy family. She's so accomplished and such a savvy businesswoman, I assumed what she had, she had earned."

She turned to Ben. "I did earn it," she said, an eyebrow going up.

Ben shook his head. Great first impression. *Not.* "Not what I meant. Of course you earned it. You're one of the smartest people I've ever met."

"That's better." Ainsley pretended to be perturbed, but clearly she'd liked his save.

Her father started laughing. "So this is the Marine you've been talking about?"

"No. I just invited some random Marine to our Christmas party because that's how I roll, Dad."

"Always with the snappy comeback," her father said.

"It's nice to meet you, Major. Welcome to our Christmas party."

"Thank you, sir."

"Why were you looking for me?" Ainsley asked.

Her dad frowned. "Had someone I wanted you to meet, but it can wait."

Probably another one of the rich dudes he wanted her to marry.

"Maybe you can convince my lovely daughter to give up this fool business of hers and help me run one of my companies," he said.

Ainsley stiffened in front of him. A direct attack probably wouldn't be the best course of action—especially since this was her dad.

"I'm not sure what you mean, sir. I've found her to be incredibly talented and intuitive in her business. She comes highly recommended by her clients. I was reading some of the reviews about her company after she agreed to help me, and she never has less than five stars. I've always been so impressed with her. You must be really proud."

Her father raised an eyebrow and acted like he was about to say something and then stopped himself. "Why don't you introduce the Major around to our guests?"

"That's where we were headed," she said. And pulled him away quickly. "Well, that happened," she laughed nervously. "At least he didn't catch us kissing."

"Kind of felt like he did," Ben said as she guided him to a larger room on the other side of the big rotunda.

"I know, right? I felt like I'd been caught making out in the closet with Tommy Williams."

Ben froze, and then started laughing. "Did you really?"

"Yes. He promised to teach me how to French kiss. We were thirteen. Turned out he didn't know what he was doing and he slobbered all over my face and I threw up on him. Dad heard me, and jerked open the door and I'll never forget the look on his face. He was so fierce and then he almost fell over laughing. I'd never been so mortified."

Ben laughed even harder.

"You two are having way too much fun for this particular party," her sister, Megan, said as she came up to join them.

"I was telling him about Tommy Williams."

Megan smiled. "I swear every time I see him he turns and goes the other way. She definitely made an impression that has lasted a lifetime."

"Did that happen here?"

"Oh, no. It was at the Corpus house on Ocean Drive. Haven't you taken him over there?" Megan asked. "You guys have been dating a few weeks. You should have been using that hot tub. Best view of the gulf is from there."

They had another house on Ocean Drive? Nothing there was less than a couple of million. This was nuts.

"We've both been really busy," Ainsley interjected quickly. "And mom closed up the house last time she was there. Speaking of Mom, we'd better go find her.

If she discovers that I didn't bring you right over to say hello, she'll be mad."

They left Megan and started toward another room crowded with guests. "Thank you," Ainsley said to him, "for earlier, with my dad. He just doesn't get what I do."

"Maybe you should explain it to him the way you did me the first time we met."

He always wanted to kiss her, especially now, but he didn't. This wasn't the time or place for a PDA. "I've tried. He was upset when I got a philosophy degree and then didn't go into law or apply to study for an MBA. It wasn't what he wanted."

"That's crazy. You're incredibly successful. It's his problem, not yours. You have to live your own life."

She squeezed his arm. "You truly are amazing," she said. "I know people use that word all the time but I can't figure out a better way to describe you. Seems like you always know the right things to say. And I don't care about admitting that I needed you with me tonight. I need a man who stands beside me."

That's what he had to focus on. She cared for him, and he was good for her. Didn't matter what her father thought. Well, it did. But she was her own person and could think for herself.

They could sort the rest of the mess out later.

"I feel the same about you, and have from the first moment I met you."

She smiled and the stress from the encounter with her dad seemed to have dissipated.

By the time they made it to the ballroom—yes, they

had a ballroom in their house—he'd met well over sixty people. The uniform was something different to the crowd. He could tell from the surprised looks as they passed through the room. They'd eye him up and down, glance at Ainsley and then smile.

They were polite and respectful. Many even thanked him for his service. A number of them couldn't tell what branch of the military he was from, but he was used to that.

But they couldn't hide their curiosity. Who was the guy in uniform with Ainsley, daughter of one of the richest men in the country? The question was easy to see on their faces.

He had nothing to prove to these people, but at the same time he wanted to be good enough for Ainsley.

Even though he was pretty sure he wasn't.

"There they are," her mother said, as they approached. He still couldn't believe how young Ainsley's mom looked.

"Ma'am, it's good to see you again."

"'Ma'am.' I love that. Always so polite. I was delighted when Ainsley told me she was bringing you." Her mother crooked her arm in Ben's. "So, are you having fun?"

He smiled at her. "I just arrived—" he glanced down at his watch "—but yes, I'm always happy when Ainsley is around."

"Good answer. My daughter tells me that you've been busy with charity duties, helping children and the elderly."

He looked over at Ainsley, but she shrugged and smiled.

"Yes, we've had a couple of events for Toys for Tots. My base also works with nursing homes in the area. A lot of my team members are away from home, and some of the old folks don't get a lot of visitors. So we take them gifts and visit with them."

They were surrounded by a group of women, who all said "Awwww" in unison.

"I told you he was a keeper," her mother said.

"Mom. Please."

"What?" Her mother smiled. "Strong, handsome and does good work in the community. You could do worse."

Ainsley rolled her eyes. "Ben, please forgive my mom. I'm not sure what she's up to, but we may need to have a talk about what's appropriate and what isn't."

"There's no reason to apologize," he said. "She's right. You could do worse."

Everyone laughed around them.

Her mother patted his back. "You kids have a good time. Ainsley, you should take him on a tour of the house and find him some food. Big strapping man like him needs to be fed often."

Once again, Ainsley pulled him in a different direction. "We could just hide in my room until it's over," she said.

"Now there's an idea."

"Trust me, if I could we'd be up there. My mom and dad tend to have extra radar at these events. If Megan and I try to sneak off they always find us. Like Dad with the study. It's weird. Anyway. I do want to show you the house."

He had a feeling that in a house like this, her dad probably had an app on his phone that kept in touch with everything. Oh, and he'd counted at least ten rented security types in suits with earpieces since he'd arrived.

"I'm curious about something," he said.

"What?" They were going down what was the main staircase after seeing so many bedrooms that he'd lost count.

"Why doesn't your dad have full-time security watching your house? It's all sort of hitting me, but you do need to be protected at all times. Kidnappers, anyone, could use you as a pawn. He should have an entire team following you around," Ben said seriously. The more he thought about it, the more worried he felt. She ran all over Corpus by herself. She could have been nabbed at any time.

She sighed. "My house has a security system. And when I went away to college, I don't know. The media quit following me. I was the boring one. And then when my family moved here, I stayed in Corpus. No one really cares there. It isn't a small town, but it kind of is. It's the one place I don't feel like I have to worry."

He guessed she was right, since he'd never really heard of her until they'd met. She was good at keeping her private life private. The only time he'd seen her picture in the paper had been after the bachelor auction, and she'd been with him.

They finished the tour and he bet they'd covered about thirty thousand feet.

"I saved the best for last," she said. "Well, the pool and kitchen outside are actually my favorite. But this room is a close second."

They stepped into a room that had just about every arcade game from the eighties one could imagine. *Centipede*, *Tron*—they were all there. When he was a kid he'd been invited to a couple of birthday parties that weren't much different than this. Okay, with the exception of the marble floors, massive bar with every kind of liquor and pristine machines.

"It's too much, right?" She grinned. "I love *Centipede*. Dad had to unplug it for a while when I was in the eighth grade so I'd get all my homework done. He told me it was broken. I was so gullible back then. I came in and saw him playing it one day, and I was so mad."

"Your dad plays these games?"

She nodded. "He started installing the machines in convenience stores when he was still in high school. Then he bought his own machines to go into bigger retail places like arcades and movie theaters. Then he invested that money, and well, if you looked on Google you know the rest."

"He really is a self-made man."

"Yes, which is why I don't understand why he keeps pushing these shallow, good-for-nothing twits—that's what Bebe calls them—on me."

"I'm pretty sure it's a dad thing," he said, honestly. "I haven't known you that long and I feel pretty protective of you, even though I don't have any right to.

And he is your father. He thinks he knows what's best for you."

She paused with a hand on her hip. "You feel protective of me? That's really sweet."

He put an arm around her shoulder and pulled her into him. He never tired of her scent. For of the rest of his life when he smelled vanilla, he'd think of her. "I want what's best for you, too, and I'm pretty sure that's where your dad's head is at."

"Maybe. But it's annoying the way he does it. Your way, however, is superhot." She kissed him, and he couldn't stop himself. He only stepped back when he heard voices coming down the hall. She once again wiped the lipstick from his face.

"I'm going to the ladies' room. I'll be back in a sec," she said. "Or maybe meet me in the kitchen? I could also use a snack, and I don't want to try to maneuver through the crowds at the buffet tables. And while I'm a horrible cook, my mom knows how to hire some great caterers. We always have excellent food."

"Sure. I'll meet you in the kitchen, if I can remember how to get there."

They shared a laugh. She turned to walk away, but then glanced back. "It's the second hallway on the left, go all the way to the end."

He was glad she clarified because even though he had a head for maps and directions, the house was massive.

Before he could get very far, her father rounded the corner. This time he wasn't smiling. "Is Ainsley with you?"

"No," he said. "She's—"

"Good," her father said. "Look, son. I'm sure you're a nice guy and a brave soul. What you young people do, it's admirable. But I think you know it's not going to work between the two of you."

The man was direct, he'd give him that. "Ainsley and I are friends," he said. "I'm not sure what you mean."

"I think you do," her father repeated. "You have a solid record. I had one of my staff check you out. And you do seem like a good man. But you aren't the right one for my daughter."

Hitting him is not an option.

Ben had never considered himself a violent man, not without provocation. But he was tempted.

High road. He had to take it. "The great thing about Ainsley is she has her feet on the ground and makes smart choices. I believe she's able to decide who she wants to be friends with, and perhaps is a better judge of character than most. You could perhaps learn a lesson or two from her, instead of trying to push her to accept any *Fortune* 500 CEO that crosses your path. You could perhaps listen to what it is she wants. You raised her to be an incredibly thoughtful and brilliant human being. You should be proud.

"To your point, if I'm good enough for your daughter, I never said I was. But she's absolutely the best thing that's ever happened to me. Now if you'll excuse me."

He had to leave before her father had a chance to

say something else, because Ben wasn't sure how much longer he could hold on to his temper.

He didn't run, but it was definitely a fast walk down the hall. Head spinning, he stopped at the entry to the busy kitchen. Caterers were going at warp speed. He didn't see Ainsley.

About to go in search of her, he heard her voice. "I told you no." She was annoyed.

"Why are you so prickly? You know your dad wants us together," some guy said.

Seriously, did the universe want him to get arrested at this party? He forced himself to stay where he was. Ainsley could handle herself.

"What my dad wants and what I do are two very different things," she said. "And I told you on the plane last night, I'm dating someone."

"Yeah, your dad said he wouldn't be around long. Come on. No way that guy is going to give you what you really need."

That was it. He couldn't take anymore.

Ainsley was shaking her head as he walked up behind the guy.

But the man shook his head right back. This guy was disrespecting her wishes.

"I don't know who you are but I promise you I've got her needs covered," Ben said. Okay, that came out wrong.

Ainsley rolled her eyes.

The guy turned around and glanced up at Ben.

"Go ahead," Ben said. "Say something."

The guy just stared at him. "It's going to take more

than some tough guy to take care of Ainsley the way she expects."

"Oh, hey, I'm standing right here. And for the record, I don't need any man. I don't need anyone to take care of me. Todd, you have to give it up because you and me are never going to happen."

"You heard her, Todd. Trust that you're not the kind of man she needs."

"And you are? She's just getting her hands dirty with you. I know what's best for her."

Ben might have growled at that point. "I'm going to suggest you leave now, Todd. And never say she doesn't know what's best. That woman is smarter, funnier, more thoughtful than most people, and she doesn't need some two-timer like you trying to make her think otherwise. That's right, I saw you twenty minutes ago with your hand up some brunette's dress. So get lost before I rearrange your face. That's what we tough guys do, ya know."

"He's serious," she said to Todd, shoving him quickly into the next room. "I suggest you leave before the tough guy throws you off the property. You and I need to talk," she said to Ben.

Fine, he had it coming. But he'd had to set the jerk straight.

Ben shook his head. Stupid. That was really stupid what he'd done. But he was frustrated, feeling so out of place. And her dad was right, he'd never fit in. He couldn't kiss up like these people. It just wasn't in his nature.

"Ainsley, I…"

She held up a hand to cut him off. "Wait until we are at the beach." *Crap.* She was really mad. He'd never before heard that edge in her voice.

He shouldn't have engaged. But he was tired of her father and Todd treating him like less than he was. He'd gotten rid of the chip on his shoulder the second day of boot camp. Yep, he came from poor, but he'd made something of himself. And he was proud.

But her father's words tore at him. Was he really not the right guy for her? And it wasn't about taking care of her. She could do that herself. True, he couldn't always be there for her. He was a career Marine. If she wanted something more permanent, and she'd hinted she did, this was never going to work.

How would she deal with him possibly being on the other side of the world? And it could happen. Maybe her dad was right, but not about the money. Everything was good for them, but they'd spent nearly every day together since they'd met. That wasn't how it would be when he was on tour. And he could be deployed at any time.

He followed her out to the pool area. There were a few people, and she pulled him off down a path that eventually led to the beach.

"I'm sorry," he said, knowing he had to apologize. "It's no excuse, but your dad said a few things to me, and then I walked up on you talking to that guy. And you'd said it was only family last night. But that guy was on the plane with you."

Dang. He hadn't meant to say that. What was wrong with him?

She blew out a breath and then took off her heels. "I can just imagine what my dad said. I should apologize for him. I like to think he has my best interests at heart, as you said, but I'm tired of this. All the fighting."

That was a knock.

"What do you mean?" he asked, carefully.

She tossed the shoes to the ground. "I don't need a man to protect me or take care of me. I thought we'd covered this. I can handle it, remember? If you see me as some damsel in distress, then move along. Please. I'm beginning to think you are all the same."

"You're lumping me in with those creeps you've dated?"

"No," she said. "Not really. But I'm mad. I don't need you to fight my battles. I was doing just fine with Todd."

"Right, that's why even though you told him no last night, he was in front of your face again today. You know, on the plane you said was just for family, and now he was back for more."

"Ben! I don't know why Todd of all people was a part of my dad's special night. He invited him, not me. And they're both acting like fools. My dad can push all he wants, I'm not going to change my mind because I don't care about his money. Or his protection. I'm good. Really good. All. By. Myself."

"Got it." Ben figured this was as good a time as any, even though what he was about to say tore at his gut. "You're an amazing woman, Ainsley. Beautiful and talented. You don't need anyone, especially a grunt like me."

"Wait. What?"

"It's probably best if we say our goodbyes before this goes any further." As he said the words, he wanted to call himself a liar. If they went on, it would only be tougher on the both of them. And he wasn't at all sure he could live in her world. He'd have a hard time standing by watching jerks like what's-his-face trying to make a move on her. And he'd always be wondering who her father was trying to set her up with next.

She'd been facing the water, but now she turned to him. "So, what? You're breaking up with me? The first time we actually disagree?"

Stay strong. This was for her. "It's not that. Just tonight showed me how different we are. I'm not the proper guy for you. What's going to happen when I'm deployed for six months or even a year? Your dad is going to keep throwing men at you. And I'm always going to wonder. Always. 'Is she being faithful?' Do you have any idea how many military come home to find their spouses, significant others with other people? We're just a mistake waiting to happen."

"No. You're serious right now?" A tear slid down her cheek.

He pretended he didn't care.

"Well, yep. It'd be best for us to cut our losses before this gets much more serious." He shrugged. "I care about you, Ainsley. I want you to be happy."

She picked up a shoe and threw it at him, but he ducked before it hit him.

"You have a dumb way of showing it, you know? A

really dumb way. Don't you think I've thought about what it might be like when you go on a mission?

"I'm not an idiot. It's scary to consider what could happen to you. Frightens me half to death. But if you're brave enough to go, then I would have to be brave enough to stay here and wait for you. I would have been.

"But you're right, Ben. You don't deserve me. That you think I would cheat on you because you were away—what kind of person does that make me? Have you met me? I should be with someone way better than a jerk who believes I'd be one of those 'out of sight, out of mind' types. I thought… Doesn't matter." There were more tears running down her face, and he felt ashamed.

He reached out for her, but she shook her head.

"Bye, Ben. You can go now. I thought I needed you. I was wrong."

Then she ran to the house and left him on the beach with a broken heart.

But it was for the best. For the both of them.

Yeah, you keep telling yourself that.

14

AINSLEY GRABBED AN open bottle of champagne before running up the back stairs to her room.

What had just happened?

Ben had broken up with her. Or she'd broken up with him? It happened so fast she wasn't sure. The whole night was a mess.

Whatever her father had said, well, he'd done a number on Ben for sure. But it didn't matter. She thought… no, she believed Ben was the kind of guy who wouldn't care what anyone else said or thought.

She slammed the door to her bedroom, and then went into the bathroom and sat on the counter. After chugging half the bottle of champagne, she burped very loud twice and took several deep breaths.

How could Ben think those things? And she'd never seen him act like…what? A jealous boyfriend?

Rats. That's exactly what he looked like when he walked up on her and Todd.

True. That jerk had been kind of handsy, but still.

Ben didn't have to get all protective of her. That would just give Todd more ammunition for her father.

But Ben's look of fury at Todd was burned into her brain. And how would she have felt if some woman was pawing him? And talking about getting married?

Double rats. She took another swig of the champagne. But Ben was the one who said she wouldn't be faithful and wait for him.

He was kind of right about the waiting, but not in the way he believed. She'd been thinking about his career aspirations. He'd told her more than once he wanted to make Colonel, and she'd done research. That meant probably a lot of moves to different bases. More tours of duty. But she had plans for that. Plans she hadn't shared with him because she didn't want to scare him off. For him to know she was thinking about their future.

Well, not anymore.

Good riddance, Ben.

The tears fell in great trails down her face.

We couldn't even handle one fight. One fight and he's gone.

"Whoa," Bebe said. "What's gone on here?" Her friend crossed the bathroom, took the toilet paper roll off the holder and brought it to her.

Ainsley sniffed. "When did you get here?"

"About five minutes ago. Just in time to see him storm off without even a hello. I asked him where you were and he said he had no idea. That you left him. Did you?"

"I left him on the beach, but I think he's the one who left me first." She chugged more of the bottle.

"Hey, slow down. He didn't seem like a guy who broke up with a girl. Are you sure? Because he was visibly upset."

She sat the bottle on the counter. "I don't know. Everything was out of control tonight. I think I ruined it."

Bebe eyed her up and down. "Maybe you should tell me exactly what happened."

IT WAS LATE AND Ben worried about waking up his mom and sister. There was a light coming from one of the windows of the little three-bedroom bungalow, so someone was still awake. He texted his sister.

Doodle, you awake?

She texted back. Yep.

Turn off the alarm and unlock the door. I don't want to disturb Mom.

He grabbed his duffel, and then he waited on the front porch for the door to open.

Amy, his little sister, threw her arms around him so hard, she nearly took them both to the ground. "I thought you were at some fancy party and weren't coming until tomorrow."

"Change of plans," he said, as he walked with her wrapped around him into the house. "Couldn't wait to see you guys and the party ended earlier than expected."

"Liar," his mother said from the living room.

He dropped his bag in the entry, and then peeled his sister off of him. Mom was standing up with her arms out. "That look on your face says something different. You aren't happy."

He frowned. "What? I told you earlier in the week that I couldn't wait to see you guys. I missed you." He gave her a long hug. She always smelled like roses. Home.

"I thought you were bringing your new girlfriend to meet us," she said. "Are you hiding her in the car?"

His mother was tenacious when it came to the truth. It's one of the reasons he hardly ever lied as a kid. She had a sixth sense that way, always said it was a mother's intuition. Other kids got away with stuff, he never did. Even though she had to be gone a lot between her two jobs, and then her job and school when he was older, she always seemed to know.

"She has family stuff," he said, which was true. "I told you they spend the holidays together, like us."

Mom held his face in her hands and studied him. "I'm here when you're ready to talk about it, Ben."

"Did you bring presents?" his sister asked.

"Amy!" his mother said. "Don't be rude. He's your brother and his being here is all the present we need."

He stepped back just in time to see his sister roll her eyes.

"Yeah, yeah. But did you bring any presents?"

He playfully socked her shoulder. "Yes. But technically it isn't even Christmas Eve yet, so no snooping. And you're seventeen now, haven't you grown out of the whole present thing?"

"Did you hit your head or something? You're never too old for presents." Amy clapped her hands and hopped up and down.

He'd missed this. Just being with his family. It made him stronger. His new position at the base had kept him busy, and he was trying to get his hours of flight time in on the weekends. He put an arm around both of them. Family. This was what mattered.

"I made a batch of banana bread and some cinnamon tea. And before you say something, the bread is made with whole wheat flour."

He laughed. His mom was one of the few people who normally didn't give him grief about his diet. She understood why he took care of himself.

"Sounds good."

She led the way into the kitchen, which did smell like fresh bread. He sat at the breakfast bar next to his sister and watched as his mom busied herself pulling everything together.

He'd offer to help, but he knew better. She liked to dote on him whenever he'd been away for long periods of time, said she felt guilty for all the years she'd had to work and wasn't there for him. But she was wrong. She'd always been there for him in the ways that mattered. She'd loved him, and made him a responsible human being. His shoulders dropped a few inches and he relaxed for the first time in several hours.

These were his people. It only hit harder how out of his element he'd been at the Garretts'.

"So tell us what been going on," his mother encouraged as she handed him a plate of bread and a cup of tea.

His shoulders immediately tensed again. "What about you'll be there when I'm ready to talk?" He really didn't want to discuss it. In some ways, he still hadn't wrapped his mind around the fact that he'd broken up with her, even if he did think it was for the best. The not knowing, the snap deployments—she could have it so much easier than that. Although…it meant she wouldn't be his girlfriend, let alone his wife.

And there wasn't anything he wanted more than having Ainsley as his wife. It was something he hadn't realized until he was halfway between San Antonio and Austin. It just wasn't in the cards. She might be angry with him, but he wasn't wrong about some of what he'd said. He didn't want her worrying and waiting for months at a time. It wasn't fair.

His mother crossed her arms and gave him the stare.

"Fine. We were at the big party her parents were throwing. Let's just say the Garrett house was the size of a small mountain. Not quite the Driskill in downtown Austin, but pretty darn big. But it made it clear to me that Ainsley and I come from two different worlds. Then her dad keeps throwing these rich guys at her. She was talking to one of them and I found out they'd been on a plane together the night before, when I thought it was supposed to be only family. Nothing happened between them. I know it didn't. She does not like the guy.

But it just hit me wrong. That it's never going to work. And I decided it was time for me to go. End of story."

"Did you give her a chance to tell her side of things?" His mother handed his sister a plate of bread and a cup of tea.

Amy was watching him and his mother as if they were playing a tennis match. "Shouldn't she be in bed?" he asked.

"It's Christmas holidays, and you're trying to change the subject," Mom said.

"What more was there for her and I to discuss? When I tell you these people are rich, I mean billions. Her dad is one of the wealthiest men in the country. I was helping her through the holiday season as a friend, and she was helping me.

"I thought maybe we had something, but we were both caught up in… I don't know. Obviously, I was confused because I kept thinking maybe she was the one. But after what her dad said, and then what I over-heard…yeah. The guy was a jerk, but he had a point. She's not cut out for the life I have. It's done. Can we please talk about something else?"

"Wait," Doodle said. "You just decided the way it was going to be for the both of you? Did she say she felt the same? That she didn't want to be with you? I've never had a boyfriend, mainly because Mom won't let me date until I'm thirty, but maybe if you really like her, you should have fought for her? Or at least maybe not taken off so fast. Maybe she just got mad, because it sounds like you were being really dumb and mean. But she might be over it."

"You're too young to understand." He paused to take a bite of bread. "It wasn't like that." But it sort of was. "Doodle, it's more complicated than that. We… It's… I figured that I'd be more of a problem for her, than someone who was helping. Her dad made it very clear that I wasn't the sort of man he wanted for his daughter. And I'm not the kind of man who is going to make the woman he loves choose between her family and him."

"What kind of man is that?" his mom asked. Her chin jutted out, which meant he was about to get an ear-ful. "Honest, brave, kind, loving and caring. That kind of man? Because if her father has a problem with that kind of man, I might just have to go kick his backside."

"Mom!" he and Doodle said together.

"Oh, all right, all right. But I hate to see you like this, Ben. It's clear you're not okay with how you left things tonight."

He gave a quick nod.

"Look, son. I'm not going to get involved in your romantic life. It's not my place. But when you talked about this girl, there was something in your voice I haven't heard in a long, long time. You were happy. And if someone made me that happy, well, I might think about fighting for that. Your sister makes a valid point." She gave Amy a big, wide smile.

They didn't get it. "I appreciate that. Look, it's been a long day, and I'm pretty tired."

"You know where your room is," his mom said.

He stood.

"Ben, wait." His mother rose from her chair and gripped his hand. "You're one of the most courageous men I've ever known. You have been since you were a boy. And you, as a Marine, know you never leave a man behind. I just want to make sure you aren't doing that with Ainsley, in a sense, because—and maybe this is just my interpretation—it sounds like you deserted her when she needed you the most."

It was the first time anyone had said her name, and it was a punch to the gut. Had he left her behind? No. *No.* It wasn't like that. She was better off without him. She should be with people who were like her.

It wasn't until he was in his old bedroom and had stared at the ceiling for two hours that it came to him. The tears in her eyes. The hurt that was there in her tight mouth and flushed cheeks. He didn't believe in her. It wasn't the other way around.

Not once had she ever given him an indication that she didn't believe in him. In fact, she'd done nothing but support him. Been there for him.

While he talked a good game, when push came to shove, he'd left at the first hint of trouble.

She hadn't done anything wrong.

But he'd been a first-rate jerk.

15

THE MORNING AFTER the party, Ainsley sat at brunch in her parents' dining room, a knot the size of Texas twisting her belly.

She'd spent most of the night crying. She didn't cry. Well, maybe at Hallmark commercials and only the mushy ones with kids or animals.

But this hurt. Ben had left her alone at a time when she'd admitted to him it was the last thing she wanted. Something had happened to set him off, before the whole Todd fiasco. It had to be what her dad had said. Whatever it was, it had changed everything. His eyes… Never in her life had she seen someone more tormented, as if she'd reached in and ripped out his heart.

And he'd been so dismissive, like leaving her wasn't that big of a deal.

But had it been an act? She had this terrible feeling that he hurt her because he was trying to protect her in some way. She kept trying to remember his words, but when she thought about him saying she would cheat on him, fresh tears came.

Bile rose in the back of her throat.

"Ainsley, are you hungover?" Her sister's question penetrated her haze. "And dang, girl, you look bad. I don't remember you drinking that much."

Conversation stopped around the table and everyone stared. There were a mixture of aunts, uncles and cousins, along with members of her immediate family. This brunch was a tradition. One she no longer wanted to be a part of.

My heart is dead and I lost the only guy I've ever loved. Probably the only guy I'm ever going to love.

"No," she said.

"No, you aren't hungover? Because you might have a fever or something. Your eyes are really red," Megan went on.

Leave it to her sister to poke and prod. "Let it go," she muttered under her breath. Then she shoved away from the table, crystal falling and china rattling.

"Ainsley, what is wrong with you?" her mother admonished.

"She's sick or grumpy or…something," her sister said.

"I'm none of those things. I'm…" *Heartbroken, sad and, okay, maybe a little angry.*

"Should I call Dr.—"

"I'm not sick, okay? I'm sad. I'm upset about the way Ben left last night. He didn't deserve to be treated that way, Dad." She stared at her father. "He couldn't get away fast enough. Said things I'm not sure I believe or that he believed, but…it hurts. I've never hurt like this." She stood in the middle of the dining room with tears streaming down her face.

"It's just as well he's gone, Ainsley. He's not our kind of people," her father said.

That was it. "What kind of people is that, Dad? The Todd Rightner kind? The man you secretly set me up with on Thursday night? Want to know what kind of man he is, Dad? He likes to hurt women. Only gets his kicks a certain way. Not really my thing. Pain. Yep. Not into it."

Her dad's jaw dropped. *Good*. "Oh, and Mike Anton? He's a crook. Been siphoning cash off the books for years. Wake up, Dad. You need to start reading between the lines sometimes, keep your ears open. That's right. Deal with that."

"Ainsley!"

"What, Mom? You know it's true. You know what kind of *people* Ben is, Dad? Hardworking, kind and caring. He's been looking after his family since he was twelve years old. Twelve. He puts his life in danger for his country every day. He's smart and funny and he treats me like a queen. He adores me, and wants the best for me. He believes in me. Or at least he did until he met you. And though it kills me to say this, Dad, I don't blame him. You're right, we aren't his kind of people. Brave. Wonderful, exceptional people. And that makes me sad for us."

Then she turned on her heel and left. In the grand foyer, she stood there, circling. She had to get out of the house. More than anything she wanted to talk to Ben. But maybe they needed more time. She had to sort through her feelings, and she had to be strong and sane when she faced him again. And she was really far from either of those traits right now.

After grabbing a few things from her room, she headed downstairs to find her sister on the landing.

"Not in the mood," she said.

Her sister took her keys out of her hand. "I know. I'll drive, since you're too upset. I mean brava telling off Pops, but you're a mess."

She sighed. Her sister was faster and fitter—there would be no getting the keys from her without a fight. "Fine. But do not talk to me."

"Okay. Got it. No speaking. But just so you know, I'll drive you home and Mom can send a car for me later. I'm sorry about before. I was just giving you a hard time. I thought you were hiding Ben in your room, and I couldn't help but tease in front of the parentals."

It wasn't her sister's fault her life was a wreck. "It's okay."

Her sister unlocked the car and five minutes later they were on the highway. "About the 'no talking' thing," her sister said. "Yeah. That's not going to hold up. You need to tell me what Ben said. And did you know that Bebe punched that dopey Todd last night? What was that all about?"

Bebe punched Todd. Ainsley started laughing hysterically. And then it all came out. Everything that had happened.

Megan exited the highway and then pulled into the parking lot of a Cracker Barrel. When they were kids, it was the only place they ever wanted to go when her grandma was visiting from England, much to the chagrin of their parents.

"This requires pancakes." Megan turned off the car.

"I'm not hungry."

"Yes, but I am. I skipped breakfast to drive you home."

Ainsley sighed, but followed her inside the restaurant.

Once they were inside, the smell was irresistible. They ordered pecan pancakes and hot chocolate. When they were done, her sister blew out a breath.

"So, I didn't hear the conversation, but I saw Ben alone with Dad. They were both pretty serious-looking. And then I followed Ben. I don't know exactly what he heard, but he'd been listening to you and Todd for a bit before he walked in. I thought for sure Ben was going to start yelling at him, and then you hauled Ben out to the beach, and I didn't keep following because you had that scary look on your face. By the way, I might have accidentally spilled red wine all over Todd's jacket. Right after Bebe punched him. I didn't know why she was so mad, I just figured it had something to do with you after the thing in the hallway."

"He deserves all of that and so much more. Why does Dad think he's a good choice over Ben? I can't see the logic. Money doesn't necessarily make someone a decent human being. Surely, Dad, who came from nothing, would understand that?"

Megan shrugged.

"I don't blame Ben. He must hate me. There's a good chance something he heard Todd say was what broke the camel's back. That's where all the stuff started about him believing I wouldn't wait for him while he was away." First her dad and then… It was silly, but she could see how he might think he was doing them both a favor by letting her go.

It was all a big misunderstanding.

Idiot. Well, they'd both been so ready to believe the worst.

"I have to talk to him. No wonder. It all makes sense. Why he left like that."

She rubbed her temples. "And who knows what Dad said to Ben. I'm not sure I can forgive him for this."

Her sister shrugged. "Dad loves you, and that's hard to see right now, but he means well. He just wants to make sure you're taken care of. He didn't have the kind of security we do. And, I'm the last person to take up for Dad, but he doesn't mean to hurt you. He wants you to be comfortable and settled. But he goes about it in the worst way."

Ainsley held up a hand. "Enough. Hurry up and eat. I've got to find out exactly where Ben is so I can go apologize. That is, if he'll even speak to me. What a mess."

Her phone dinged and she pulled her cell out of her bag. "It's him."

But it wasn't.

The text said This is Ben's sister, Amy. I thought you would want to know. He's at the VA Medical Center fourth floor in South Austin. Hurry.

No. No. No. Tears burned and ran onto her cheeks. Ben was hurt or sick.

Her sister grabbed the phone and then threw two twenties on the table. "Come on," Megan said, lifting her up by the elbow and dragging her out. "We've got to go. Now."

No longer did Ainsley care if Ben forgave her, or if he couldn't get past her crazy family.

She just wanted him to be alive and okay.

Please, God, let him be okay. Please.

16

BEN COULDN'T HELP but notice there was a loud commotion outside the door of the hospital room. People were screaming, and the noise was giving him an instant headache.

"He's here, I'll show you. See, fourth floor. The Austin VA? We're at the VA." The voice sounded so much like Ainsley's that Ben thought he might be hallucinating.

He handed the Christmas gift to the Sergeant he'd been visiting and smiled. Maybe his mind was playing tricks on him. He hadn't slept very well.

"Please," the woman wailed. She was definitely upset. He felt for the poor families who had loved ones here. It was awful being in a hospital, but especially during the holidays.

"Ma'am, if you don't calm down, I'm going to have to ask you to leave. We have to keep things quiet on this floor. You're going to upset the patients."

"Please." The woman was sobbing. It really did sound like Ainsley, but why would she be here?

"Excuse me. I'll be back in a minute," he said to the man.

Ben poked his head out of the room.

There she was at the desk, dressed in a rumpled sweater and worn-out jeans, and no makeup. He'd never seen a more beautiful woman.

He turned back to the guy he'd been talking to. "I'm awake, right? You hear her, too?"

The guy chuckled. "Maybe you should have them check you out while you're here. But yes, I hear her."

"Good. Good. That's the woman I love and she's here. Why is she here?"

The guy shrugged. "Maybe you should ask her?"

The nurse was staring at Ainsley as if she had two heads.

"I'm telling you, we don't have a patient by that name."

"Ainsley," he called out to her, his voice a coarse whisper. "What are you doing here?"

Her head snapped to the right. "Ben!" She ran to him, wrapping her arms around him and squeezing tight. He patted her back, breathing in the vanilla scent that followed her everywhere.

Then she started patting him down. And lifting his arms as if she was looking for something. "Are you okay? I got the message from your sister. I thought maybe you'd been in a wreck or something."

"What message? I'm fine."

She backed up, rubbing the tears away with the heels of her hands. "She said you were here."

"I am, I'm visiting vets. It's Christmas Eve, I told you. I always do this when I'm home. Not that I've been home much the last several years."

"But I thought…"

And then it clicked for him. She'd thought he'd been hurt.

"I'm going to kill Doodle. And now I know what happened to my phone. I couldn't find it when I left this morning. Brat has it at the house. I'm so sorry. I'm fine. I don't know why she did that. She shouldn't have made you worry."

Ainsley half coughed, half laughed. "I don't care. You're okay. I was so scared." She hiccupped. "After everything…"

He moved toward her. But she took a step back. "You left me. I mean, I ran away. But you left me before that. Those things you said…" She chewed on her bottom lip.

And he had. Abandoned her. The one thing he'd promised he'd never do.

"I understand if you don't ever want to see me again. My family, namely my dad, is going to regret whatever it was that he said to you. Believe me, he'll get an earful when I see him again. But I wanted you to know, I love you. Nothing happened with Todd. It couldn't. I love you."

She loved him. *Him.* Even after he'd been so foolish.

"I'm sorry," he said, taking a step toward her. This

time she didn't move away. "Do you think you can forgive me?"

She shook her head. "I need you to tell me the truth. What happened? Why did you say those things? You left, but I think we pieced it together. My dad, well, being himself probably was the trigger. I couldn't figure out why all of a sudden, after defending me all night, you changed so drastically."

He started to speak, but she kept talking. She did that when she was nervous. He wanted to smile, but he bit the inside of his cheek. She loved him, and this was her way of venting. Of working it out. And he'd let her.

"I told him off, by the way. Just so you know. But you didn't believe in me. And that's something." She paused and glanced left and right, as if she'd forgotten they were in public. "We have to talk about that. I do love you, Ben. Did I already say that? I know you don't think I'm strong enough to be yours—I am, though. I'm strong enough." Tears streamed down her face.

And that's why he should have stayed. Deep down, he knew she was. "I was a coward," he said. "I didn't want to believe with everything you have that you could love someone like me. I can never give you all of that, Ainsley. The mansions or fancy cars. But I love you more than life. I will spend eternity trying to show you just how much, but I'm always going to be just me."

She leaned forward and fisted her hands in his shirt. "You're so dumb, and yes, I realize that's a mean word, but I can't come up with a better one," she said, grinning. "I meant what I told you last night. I know who I am and what I'm capable of, and I can take care of myself. I know that you know that. That you respect that.

"I didn't ask you for anything. Except to be there for me when I needed you, and I will always do the same for you."

"You are the most gorgeous, intelligent, funny woman I've ever met," he said. "Every time I see you, my heart thumps hard in my chest. I have a feeling that's never going away. I can't stop thinking about you."

She beamed. "You're sounding smarter all the time, Marine."

"I deserve that. It was wrong of me to leave last night. Your dad was telling me I wasn't good enough, and then that guy said you... I knew better."

"You left me with *them*."

"We're not all bad," Megan said, as she came down the hall. "So he's alive? And wearing a Santa suit. I'm so glad I didn't miss this."

"Shhh, Megan. Ben is apologizing to me. He's telling me how much he loves me. And that he's never, ever going to leave me. Isn't that right, Ben? Well, you will have to leave to save people and tackle important missions. But you're never going to leave me here." She pointed to her heart. "Right?"

He smiled. "That's one-hundred-percent right. And for the record, I was coming to see you tonight. I'd even called in the troops to help me rappel over that wall at your parents' house. I was betting your dad wouldn't let me in the front gate. I know you don't need rescuing, but I was coming for you just the same."

"You were?"

"He was," one of the nurses said. "So this is Ainsley?"

"Yes, Mom. This is Ainsley."

"Did you apologize?" His mom was smiling.

"I'm working on it. We keep getting interrupted."

Ainsley turned toward his mother. "It's very nice to meet you, ma'am. I apologize for causing a scene. There was a bit of a mix-up, and I thought Ben had been injured."

"I heard," his mother said. "My daughter is going to be grounded for quite possibly the rest of her life. I apologize for her behavior."

Ainsley smiled, but it was a little wobbly and he realized she still wasn't quite over the hurt. He had a lot of making up to do.

"Don't be too hard on her, please," Ainsley said. "She's the one who's gotten us back together."

She turned back to Ben. "Actually, I'll be grateful forever to Amy."

This woman is the one. How could he have let her go? Never again.

"Ainsley, no matter what happens from here on out, I love you. Nothing is ever going to change that." He took her hands in his. "I promise."

"You don't make promises very easily," she said.

"I promise to always love you with everything that I am."

"I promise to do the same."

They stood there staring at one another, as Megan started a chant. "Kiss. Kiss. Kiss," sounded out around them.

"I know you don't like PDAs, but if you don't kiss

me, I might die," she said. "Right here. On the fourth floor of the VA hospital."

"Can't have that," he said, as he swooped in and captured her lips with his. Cheers went up, but he was lost in her.

He poured everything into the kiss, a promise of a future and of the happiness he wanted with her. And she gave it all right back to him.

"Merry Christmas," he whispered against her lips.

"Christmas with my Marine. Best present ever," she said.

"Oorah," he shouted and swung her around in his arms. But she had it wrong.

She was the best present ever.

Epilogue

One year later...

"I DO," BEN SAID. It was done. The woman of his dreams was his. She'd just pledged a lifetime of love to him on the beach in front of their friends and family. Life was good.

No. It was great.

"You may kiss the—"

He didn't hear what the CO said after that. His lips were on his wife's. Ainsley smiled when they came up for air. "I love you," she whispered.

"I love you more," he said, and then he showed her with his kiss.

There were wolf whistles and clapping.

"Get a room, you two. Shagging comes later," Bebe, the maid of honor, said.

He lifted his head.

"I present to you the happy couple," the CO announced.

He and Ainsley began their walk down the aisle. His

mom was smiling, and Ainsley's mom and dad were clapping and crying.

After Ainsley had told him off, her father had not said another cross word about Ben and Ainsley, and he'd also given them his blessing. That was good, since they were inseparable.

Brody and Matt were his best men, with Chelly and Mari a few rows back, holding their babies. He and Ainsley weren't quite ready for that, although they had no problem practicing.

He and Ainsley made it to the flowered arbor and headed for where the reception was going to be held at her parents' Corpus house. Pictures would be done after they greeted their guests. But Ben didn't mind about the formalities. With Ainsley by his side, he was happy. So very happy.

Hours later, they were in bed at her house, preferring to wait on the honeymoon until after the holidays and her busiest season were over. "That was the best wedding ever," she said, as she turned to him and brushed her fingers along his cheek.

His body hardened at her touch. His cock was always at attention when she was around. They'd been together a year, and the passion was no less than the first time they'd made love. It had only grown stronger, as had their bond.

"I agree. And Jake's face when he caught the garter, that was priceless."

She chuckled. "I swear the CO ducked. But you're right, poor Jake. He looked a little sick there for a minute."

Ben's heart felt so full—his wife was the most beautiful woman he'd ever seen. Even tonight in the moonlight, her soft features called to him. He slid a hand down her hips and then lower.

"I love you, Ainsley. More than I ever thought possible. You're it for me. Forever and always."

She looked so pleased. "I love it when you say things like that." They both smiled. "I feel the same. And I keep wondering if this is as good as it's going to get?"

His fingers caressed her core, and she whimpered. He'd never get tired of that sound.

Her expression turned teasing and she shoved him onto his back. "But it just keeps getting better," she said, as she moved over top of him. Her heat against his cock was almost more than he could stand. He'd been wanting to make love to her for the last week. But she'd insisted they wait.

Torture.

She slipped off the long, sexy silk shirt she'd worn to bed without any bottoms. He liked her like that and she knew it. Her pert breasts, with nipples so tight, were ripe for his touch. She wiggled against his cock and he couldn't take it anymore.

He flipped her onto her back and she was giggling as he brought her ankles up to his shoulders, and then slipped inside her.

"We waited a really long time for this," he said, kissing her smooth skin. "I promise I'll make it count."

"Oh, I'll take that bet," she said, and she stroked his chest, his shoulders, his back and lower. She stared into his eyes, and it spurred him on. Faster and harder he thrust, until she was laughing, and moaning, and bucking against him, heading for the edge of control. Watching her, knowing he was giving her this pleasure—it was all he could do to hold on.

And then they were coming together, riding the wave, their bodies becoming one for those few seconds of bliss. "My Marine," she said. Her smile was soft and her eyes shone with happiness. He loved seeing her like this.

"And you're mine, gorgeous. All mine."

* * * * *

CLAIM ME, COWBOY

MAISEY YATES

For Jackie Ashenden, my conflict guru and dear friend. Without you, my books would take a heck of a lot longer to write, and my life would be a heck of a lot more boring. Thank you for everything. Always.

November 1, 2017
LOOKING FOR A WIFE—

Wealthy bachelor, 34, looking for a wife. Never married, no children. Needs a partner who can attend business and social events around the world. Must be willing to move to Copper Ridge, Oregon. Perks include: travel, an allowance, residence in several multimillion-dollar homes.

November 5, 2017
LOOKING FOR AN UNSUITABLE WIFE—

Wealthy bachelor, 34, irritated, looking for a woman to pretend to be my fiancée in order to teach my meddling father a lesson. Need a partner who is rough around the edges. Must be willing to come to Copper Ridge, Oregon, for at least thirty days. Generous compensation provided.

One

"No. You do not need to *send pics*."

Joshua Grayson looked out the window of his office and did not feel the kind of calm he ought to feel.

He'd moved back to Copper Ridge six months ago from Seattle, happily trading in a man-made, rectangular skyline for the natural curve of the mountains.

Not the best thing for an architect to feel, perhaps. But he spent his working hours dealing in design, in business. Numbers. Black, white and the bottom line. There was something about looking out at the mountains that restarted him.

That, and getting on the back of a horse. Riding from one end of the property to the other. The wind blocking out every other sound except hoofbeats on the earth.

Right now, he doubted anything would decrease

the tension he was feeling from dealing with the fall-out of his father's ridiculous ad. Another attempt by the old man to make Joshua live the life his father wanted him to.

The only kind of life his father considered success-ful: a wife, children.

He couldn't understand why Joshua didn't want the same.

No. That kind of life was for another man, one with another past and another future. It was not for Joshua. And that was why he was going to teach his father a lesson.

But not with Brindy, who wanted to send him self-ies with "no filter."

The sound she made in response to his refusal was so petulant he almost laughed.

"But your ad said…"

"That," he said, "was not my ad. Goodbye."

He wasn't responsible for the ad in a national paper asking for a wife, till death do them part. But an unsuitable, temporary wife? Yes. That had been his ad.

He was done with his father's machinations. No matter how well-meaning they were. He was tired of tripping over daughters of "old friends" at family gatherings. Tired of dodging women who had been set on him like hounds at a fox hunt.

He was going to win the game. Once and for all. And the woman he hoped would be his trump card was on her way.

His first respondent to his counter ad—Danielle Kelly—was twenty-two, which suited his purposes nicely. His dad would think she was too young, and frankly, Joshua also thought she was too young. He didn't get off on that kind of thing.

He understood why some men did. A tight body was hot. But in his experience, the younger the woman, the less in touch with her sensuality she was and he didn't have the patience for that.

He didn't have the patience for this either, but here he was. The sooner he got this farce over with, the sooner he could go back to his real life.

The doorbell rang and he stood up behind his desk. She was here. And she was—he checked his watch—late.

A half smile curved his lips.

Perfect.

He took the stairs two at a time. He was impatient to meet his temporary bride. Impatient to get this plan started so it could end.

He strode across the entryway and jerked the door open. And froze.

The woman standing on his porch was small. And young, just as he'd expected, but… She wore no makeup, which made her look like a damned teenager. Her features were fine and pointed; her dark brown hair hung lank beneath a ragged beanie that looked like it was in the process of unraveling while it sat on her head.

He didn't bother to linger over the rest of the details—her threadbare sweater with too-long sleeves, her tragic skinny jeans—because he was stopped, immobilized really, by the tiny bundle in her arms.

A baby.

His prospective bride had come with a baby.

Well, hell.

* * *

She really hoped he wasn't a serial killer. Well, *hoped* was an anemic word for what she was feeling. Particularly considering the possibility was a valid concern.

What idiot put an ad in the paper looking for a temporary wife?

Though, she supposed the bigger question was: What idiot responded to an ad in the paper looking for a temporary wife?

This idiot, apparently.

It took Danielle a moment to realize she was staring directly at the center of a broad, muscular male chest. She had to raise her head slightly to see his face. He was just so…tall. And handsome.

And she was confused.

She hadn't imagined that a man who put an ad in the paper for a fake fiancée might be attractive. Another anemic word. *Attractive.* This man wasn't simply *attractive*…

He was… Well, he was unreal.

Broad shouldered, muscular, with stubble on his square jaw adding a roughness to features that might have otherwise been considered pretty.

"Please don't tell me you're Danielle Kelly," he said, crossing his arms over that previously noted broad chest.

"I am. Were you expecting someone else? Of course, I suppose you could be. I bet I'm not the only person who responded to your ad, strange though it was. The mention of compensation was pretty tempting. Although, I might point out that in the future maybe you should space your appointments further apart."

"You have a baby," he said, stating the obvious.

Danielle looked down at the bundle in her arms. "Yes."

"You didn't mention that in our email correspondence."

"Of course not. I thought it would make it too easy for you to turn me away."

He laughed, somewhat reluctantly, a muscle in his jaw twitching. "Well, you're right about that."

"But now I'm here. And I don't have the gas money to get back home. Also, you said you wanted unsuitable." She spread one arm wide, keeping Riley clutched firmly in her other arm. "I would say that I'm pretty unsuitable."

She could imagine the picture she made. Her hideous, patchwork car parked in the background. Maroon with lighter patches of red and a door that was green, since it had been replaced after some accident that had happened before the car had come into her possession. Then there was her. In all her faded glory. She was hungry, and she knew she'd lost a lot of weight over the past few weeks, which had taken her frame from slim to downright pointy. The circles under her eyes were so dark she almost looked like she'd been punched.

She considered the baby a perfect accessory. She had that new baby sallowness they never told you about when they talked about the miracle of life.

She curled her toes inside her boots, one of them going through a hole at the end of her sock. She frowned. "Anyway, I figured I presented a pretty poor picture of a fiancée for a businessman such as yourself. Don't you agree?"

The corners of his lips tightened further. "The baby."

"Yes?"

"You expect it to live here?"

She made an exasperated noise. "No. I expect him to live in the car while I party it up in your fancy-pants house."

"A baby wasn't part of the deal."

"What do you care? Your email said it's only through Christmas. Can you imagine telling your father that you've elected to marry Portland hipster trash and she comes with a baby? I mean, it's going to be incredibly awkward, but ultimately kind of funny."

"Come in," he said, his expression no less taciturn as he stood to the side and allowed her entry into his magnificent home.

She clutched Riley even more tightly to her chest as she wandered inside, looking up at the high ceiling, the incredible floor-to-ceiling windows that offered an unparalleled mountain view. As cities went, Portland was all right. The air was pretty clean, and once you got away from the high-rise buildings, you could see past the iron and steel to the nature beyond.

But this view... This was something else entirely.

She looked down at the floor, taking a surprised step to the side when she realized she was standing on glass. And that underneath the glass was a small, slow-moving stream. Startlingly clear, rocks visible beneath the surface of the water. Also, fish.

She looked up to see him staring at her. "My sister's work," he said. "She's the hottest new architect on the scene. Incredible, considering she's only in her early twenties. And a woman, breaking serious barriers in the industry."

"That sounds like an excerpt from a magazine article."

He laughed. "It might be. Since I write the press releases about Faith. That's what I do. PR for our firm, which has expanded recently. Not just design, but construction. And as you can see, Faith's work is highly specialized, and it's extremely coveted."

A small prickle of…something worked its way under her skin. She couldn't imagine being so successful at such a young age. Of course, Joshua and his sister must have come from money. You couldn't build something like this if you hadn't.

Danielle was in her early twenties and didn't even have a checking account, much less a successful business.

All of that had to change. It had to change for Riley.

He was why she was here, after all.

Truly, nothing else could have spurred her to answer the ad. She had lived in poverty all of her life. But Riley deserved better. He deserved stability. And he certainly didn't deserve to wind up in foster care just because she couldn't get herself together.

"So," she said, cautiously stepping off the glass tile. "Tell me more about this situation. And exactly what you expect."

She wanted him to lay it all out. Wanted to hear the terms and conditions he hadn't shared over email. She was prepared to walk away if it was something she couldn't handle. And if he wasn't willing to take no for an answer? Well, she had a knife in her boot.

"My father placed an ad in a national paper saying I was looking for a wife. You can imagine my surprise when I began getting responses before I had ever seen the ad. My father is well-meaning, Ms. Kelly, and he's willing to do anything to make his children's lives better. However, what he perceives as perfection can only come one way. He doesn't think all of this can possibly make me happy." Joshua looked up, seeming to indicate the beautiful house and view around them. "He's wrong. However, he won't take no for an answer, and I want to teach him a lesson."

"By making him think he won?"

"Kind of. That's where you come in. As I said, he can only see things from his perspective. From his point of view, a wife will stay at home and massage my feet while I work to bring in income. He wants someone traditional. Someone soft and biddable." He looked her over. "I imagine you are none of those things."

"Yeah. Not so much." The life she had lived didn't leave room for that kind of softness.

"And you are right. He isn't going to love that you come with a baby. In fact, he'll probably think you're a gold digger."

"I am a gold digger," she said. "If you weren't offering money, I wouldn't be here. I need money, Mr. Grayson, not a fiancé."

"Call me Joshua," he said. "Come with me."

She followed him as he walked through the entryway, through the living area—which looked like something out of a magazine that she had flipped through at the doctor's office once—and into the kitchen.

The kitchen made her jaw drop. Everything was so shiny. Stainless steel surrounded by touches of wood. A strange clash of modern and rustic that seemed to work.

Danielle had never been in a place where so much work had gone into the details. Before Riley, when she had still been living with her mother, the home decor had included plastic flowers shoved into some kind of strange green Styrofoam and a rug in the kitchen that was actually a towel laid across a spot in the linoleum that had been worn through.

"You will live here for the duration of our arrangement. You will attend family gatherings and work events with me."

"Aren't you worried about me being unsuitable for your work arrangements too?"

"Not really. People who do business with us are fascinated by the nontraditional. As I mentioned earlier, my sister, Faith, is something of a pioneer in her field."

"Great," Danielle said, giving him a thumbs-up. "I'm glad to be a nontraditional asset to you."

"Whether or not you're happy with it isn't really my concern. I mean, I'm paying you, so you don't need to be happy."

She frowned. "Well, I don't want to be unhappy. That's the other thing. We have to discuss…terms and stuff. I don't know what all you think you're going to get out of me, but I'm not here to have sex with you. I'm just here to pose as your fiancée. Like the ad said."

The expression on his face was so disdainful it was almost funny. Almost. It didn't quite ascend to funny because it punched her in the ego. "I think I can control myself, Ms. Kelly."

"If I can call you Joshua, then you can call me Danielle," she said.

"Noted."

The way he said it made her think he wasn't necessarily going to comply with her wishes just because she had made them known. He was difficult. No wonder he didn't have an actual woman hanging around willing to marry him. She should have known there was something wrong with him. Because he was rich and kind of disgustingly handsome. His father shouldn't have had to put an ad in the paper to find Joshua a woman.

He should be able to snap his fingers and have them come running.

That sent another shiver of disquiet over her. Yeah, maybe she should listen to those shivers… But the compensation. She needed the compensation.

"What am I going to do…with the rest of my time?"

"Stay here," he said, as though that were the most obvious thing in the world. As though the idea of her rotting away up here in his mansion wasn't weird at all. "And you have that baby. I assume it takes up a lot of your time?"

"He. Riley. And yes, he does take up a lot of time. He's a baby. That's kind of their thing." He didn't respond to that. "You know. Helpless, requiring every single one of their physical and emotional needs to be met by another person. Clearly you don't know."

Something in his face hardened. "No."

"Well, this place is big enough you shouldn't have to ever find out."

"I keep strange hours," he said. "I have to work with offices overseas, and I need to be available to speak to them on the phone, which means I only sleep for a couple of hours at a time. I also spend a lot of time outdoors."

Looking at him, that last statement actually made sense. Yes, he had the bearing of an uptight business-man, but he was wearing a T-shirt and jeans. He was also the kind of physically fit that didn't look like it had come from a gym, not that she was an expert on men or their physiques.

"What's the catch?" she asked.

Nothing in life came this easy—she knew that for certain. She was waiting for the other shoe to drop. Waiting for him to lead her down to the dungeon and show her where he kept his torture pit.

"There is no catch. This is what happens when a man with a perverse sense of humor and too much money decides to teach his father a lesson."

"So basically I live in this beautiful house, I wear your ring, I meet your family, I behave abominably and then I get paid?"

"That is the agreement, Ms. Kelly."

"What if I steal your silverware?"

He chuckled. "Then I still win. If you take off in the dead of night, you don't get your money, and I have the benefit of saying to my father that because of his ad I ended up with a con woman and then got my heart broken."

He really had thought of everything. She supposed there was a reason he was successful.

"So do we… Is this happening?"

"There will be papers for you to sign, but yes. It

is." Any uncertainty he'd seemed to feel because of Riley was gone now.

He reached into the pocket of his jeans and pulled out a small, velvet box. He opened it, revealing a diamond ring so beautiful, so big, it bordered on obscene.

This was the moment. This was the moment when he would say he actually needed her to spend the day wandering around dressed as a teddy bear or something.

But that moment didn't come either. Instead, he took the ring out of the box and held it out to her. "Give me your hand."

She complied. She complied before she gave her body permission to. She didn't know what she expected. For him to get down on one knee? For him to slide the ring onto her fourth finger? He did neither. Instead, he dropped the gem into her palm.

She curled her fingers around it, an electric shock moving through her system as she realized she was probably holding more money in her hand right now than she could ever hope to earn over the course of her lifetime.

Well, no, that wasn't true. Because she was about to earn enough money over the next month to take care of herself and Riley forever. To make sure she got permanent custody of him.

Her life had been so hard, a constant series of moves and increasingly unsavory *uncles* her mother brought in and out of their lives. Hunger, cold, fear, uncertainty…

She wasn't going to let Riley suffer the same fate. No, she was going to make sure her half brother was protected. This agreement, even if Joshua did ultimately want her to walk around dressed like a sexy teddy bear, was a small price to pay for Riley's future.

"Yes," she said, testing the weight of the ring. "It is."

Two

As Joshua followed Danielle down the hall, he regretted not having a live-in housekeeper. An elderly British woman would come in handy at a time like this. She would probably find Danielle and her baby to be absolutely delightful. He, on the other hand, did not.

No, on the contrary, he felt invaded. Which was stupid. Because he had signed on for this. Though, he had signed on for it only after he had seen his father's ad. After he had decided the old man needed to be taught a lesson once and for all about meddling in Joshua's life.

It didn't matter that his father had a soft heart or that he was coming from a good place. No, what mattered was the fact that Joshua was tired of being hounded every holiday, every time he went to dinner

with his parents, about the possibility of him starting a family.

It wasn't going to happen.

At one time, he'd thought that would be his future.
Had been looking forward to it. But the people who
said it was better to have loved and lost than never to
have loved at all clearly hadn't *caused* the loss.

He was happy enough now to be alone. And when
he didn't want to be alone, he called a woman, had
her come spend a few hours in his bed—or in the
back of his truck, he wasn't particular. Love was not
on his agenda.

"This is a big house," she said.

Danielle sounded vaguely judgmental, which
seemed wrong, all things considered. Sure, he was
the guy who had paid a woman to pose as his temporary fiancée. And sure, he was the man who lived in
a house that had more square footage than he generally walked through in a day, but she was the one who
had responded to an ad placed by a complete stranger
looking for a temporary fiancée. So, all things considered, he didn't feel like she had a lot of room to judge.

"Yes, it is."

"Why? I mean, you live here alone, right?"

"Because size matters," he said, ignoring the shifting, whimpering sound of the baby in her arms.

"Right," she said, her tone dry. "I've lived in apartment buildings that were smaller than this."

He stopped walking, then he turned to face her.
"Am I supposed to feel something about that? Feel
sorry for you? Feel bad about the fact that I live in
a big house? Because trust me, I started humbly

enough. I choose to live differently than my parents. Because I can. Because I earned it."

"Oh, I see. In that case, I suppose I earned my dire straits."

"I don't know your life, Danielle. More important, I don't want to know it." He realized that was the first time he had used her first name. He didn't much care.

"Great. Same goes. Except I'm going to be living in your house, so I'm going to definitely...infer some things about your life. And that might give rise to conversations like this one. And if you're going to be assuming things about me, then you should be prepared for me to respond in kind."

"I don't have to do any such thing. As far as I'm concerned, I'm the employer, you're the employee. That means if I want to talk to you about the emotional scars of my childhood, you had better lie back on my couch and listen. Conversely, if I do not want to hear about any of the scars of yours, I don't have to. All I have to do is throw money at you until you stop talking."

"Wow. It's seriously the job offer I've been waiting for my entire life. Talking I'm pretty good at. And I don't do a great job of shutting up. That means I would be getting money thrown at me for a long, long time."

"Don't test me, Ms. Kelly," he said, reverting back to her last name, because he really didn't want to know about her childhood or what brought her here. Didn't want to wonder about her past. Didn't want to wonder about her adulthood either. Who the father of her baby was. What kind of situation she was in. It wasn't his business, and he didn't care.

"Don't test me, Ms. Kelly," she said, in what he assumed was supposed to be a facsimile of his voice.

"Really?" he asked.

"What? You can't honestly expect to operate at this level of extreme douchiness and not get called to the carpet on it."

"I expect that I can do whatever I want, since I'm paying you to be here."

"You don't want me to dress up as a teddy bear and vacuum, do you?"

"What?"

She shifted her weight, moving the baby over to one hip and spreading the other arm wide. "Hey, man, some people are into that. They like stuffed animals. Or rather, they like people dressed as stuffed animals."

"I don't."

"That's a relief."

"I like women," he said. "Dressed as women. Or rather, undressed, generally."

"I'm not judging. Your dad put an ad in the paper for some reason. Clearly he really wants you to be married."

"Yes. Well, he doesn't understand that not everybody needs to live the life that he does. He was happy with a family and a farmhouse. But none of the rest of us feel that way, and there's nothing wrong with that."

"So none of you are married?"

"One of us is. The only brother that actually wanted a farmhouse too." He paused in front of the door at the end of the hall. He was glad he had decided to set this room aside for the woman who answered the ad. He hadn't known she would come with a baby in tow, but the fact that she had meant he really, really wanted her out of earshot.

"Is this it?" she asked.

"Yes," he said, pushing the door open.

When she looked inside the bedroom, her jaw dropped, and Joshua couldn't deny that he took a small amount of satisfaction in her reaction. She looked... Well, she looked amazed. Like somebody standing in front of a great work of art. Except it was just a bedroom. Rather a grand one, he had to admit, down to the details.

There was a large bed fashioned out of natural, twisted pieces of wood with polished support beams that ran from floor to ceiling and retained the natural shape they'd had in the woods but glowed from the stain that had been applied to them. The bed made the whole room look like a magical forest. A little bit fanciful for him. His own bedroom had been left more Spartan. But, clearly, Danielle was enchanted.

And he shouldn't care.

"I've definitely lived in apartments that were smaller than this room," she said, wrapping both arms around the baby and turning in a circle. "This is... Is that a loft? Like a reading loft?" She was gazing up at the mezzanine designed to look as though it was nestled in the tree branches.

"I don't know." He figured it was probably more of a sex loft. But then, if he slept in a room with a loft, obviously he would have sex in it. That was what creative surfaces were for, in his opinion.

"It reminds me of something we had when I was in first grade." A crease appeared between her eyebrows. "I mean, not me as in at our house, but in

my first-grade classroom at school. The teacher really loved books. And she liked for us all to read. So
we were able to lie around the classroom anywhere
we wanted with a book and—" She abruptly stopped
talking, as though she realized exactly what she was
doing. "Never mind. You think it's boring. Anyway,
I'm going to use it for a reading loft."

"Dress like a teddy bear in it, for all I care," he
responded.

"That's your thing, not mine."

"Do you have any bags in the car that I can get
for you?"

She looked genuinely stunned. "You don't have to
get anything for me."

It struck him that she thought he was being nice.
He didn't consider the offer particularly nice. It was
just what his father had drilled into him from the time
he was a boy. If there was a woman and she had a
heavy thing to transport, you were no kind of man if
you didn't offer to do the transporting.

"I don't mind."

"It's just one bag," she said.

That shocked him. She was a woman. A woman
with a baby. He was pretty sure most mothers traveled with enough luggage to fill a caravan. "Just one
bag." He had to confirm that.

"Yes," she returned. "Baggage is another thing entirely. But in terms of bags, yeah, we travel light."

"Let me get it." He turned and walked out of the
room, frustrated when he heard her footsteps behind
him. "I said I would get it."

"You don't need to," she said, following him persis-
tently down the stairs and out toward the front door.

"My car is locked," she added, and he ignored her as he continued to walk across the driveway to the maroon monstrosity parked there.

He shot her a sideways glance, then looked down at the car door. It hung a little bit crooked, and he lifted up on it hard enough to push it straight, then he jerked it open. "Not well."

"You're the worst," she said, scowling.

He reached into the back seat and saw one thread-bare duffel bag, which had to be the bag she was talking about. The fabric strap was dingy, and he had a feeling it used to be powder blue. The zipper was broken and there were four safety pins holding the end of the bulging bag together. All in all, it looked completely impractical.

"Empty all the contents out of this tonight. In the morning, I'm going to use it to fuel a bonfire."

"It's the only bag I have."

"I'll buy you a new one."

"It better be in addition to the fee that I'm getting," she said, her expression stubborn. "I mean it. If I incur a loss because of you, you better cover it."

"You have my word that if anything needs to be purchased in order for you to fit in with your surroundings, or in order for me to avoid contracting scabies, it will be bankrolled by me."

"I don't have scabies," she said, looking fierce.

"I didn't say you did. I implied that your gym bag might."

"Well," she said, her cheeks turning red, "it doesn't. It's clean. I'm clean."

He heaved the bag over his shoulder and led the way back to the house, Danielle trailing behind him like an angry wood nymph. That was what she reminded him of, he decided. All pointed angles and spiky intensity. And a supernaturally wicked glare that he could feel boring into the center of his back. Right between his shoulder blades.

This was not a woman who intimidated easily, if at all.

He supposed that was signal enough that he should make an attempt to handle her with care. Not because she needed it, but because clearly nobody had ever made the attempt before. But he didn't know how. And he was paying her an awful lot to put up with him as he was.

And she had brought a baby into his house.

"You're going to need some supplies," he said, frowning. Because he abruptly realized what it meant that she had brought a baby into his house. The bedroom he had installed her in was only meant for one. And there was no way—barring the unlikely reality that she was related to Mary Poppins in some way— that her ratty old bag contained the supplies required to keep both a baby and herself in the kind of comfort that normal human beings expected.

"What kind of supplies?"

He moved quickly through the house, and she scurried behind him, attempting to match his steps. They walked back into the bedroom and he flung the bag on the ground.

"A bed for the baby. Beyond that, I don't know what they require."

She shot him a deadly glare, then bent down and unzipped the bag, pulling out a bottle and a can of formula. She tossed both onto the bed, then reached back into the bag and grabbed a blanket. She spread it out on the floor, then set the baby in the center of it.

Then she straightened, spreading her arms wide and slapping her hands back down on her thighs. "Well, this is more than we've had for a long time. And yeah, I guess it would be nice to have nursery stuff. But I've never had it. Riley and I have been doing just fine on our own." She looked down, picking at some dirt beneath her fingernail. "Or I guess we haven't been *fine*. If we had, I wouldn't have responded to your ad. But I don't need more than what I have. Not now. Once you pay me? Well, I'm going to buy a house. I'm going to change things for us. But until then, it doesn't matter."

He frowned. "What about Riley's father? Surely he should be paying you some kind of support."

"Right. Like I have any idea who he is." He must have made some kind of facial expression that seemed judgmental, because her face colored and her eyebrows lowered. "I mean, I don't know how to get in touch with him. It's not like he left contact details. And I sincerely doubt he left his real name."

"I'll call our office assistant, Poppy. She'll probably know what you need." Technically, Poppy was his brother Isaiah's assistant, but she often handled whatever Joshua or Faith needed, as well. Poppy would arrange it so that various supplies were overnighted to the house.

"Seriously. Don't do anything… You don't need to do anything."

"I'm supposed to convince my parents that I'm marrying you," he said, his tone hard. "I don't think they're going to believe I'm allowing my fiancée to live out of one duffel bag. No. Everything will have to be outfitted so that it looks legitimate. Consider it a bonus to your salary."

She tilted her chin upward, her eyes glittering. "Okay, I will."

He had halfway expected her to argue, but he wasn't sure why. She was here for her own material gain. Why would she reduce it? "Good." He nodded once. "You probably won't see much of me. I'll be working a lot. We are going to have dinner with my parents in a couple of days. Until then, the house and the property are yours to explore. This is your house too. For the time being."

He wasn't being particularly generous. It was just that he didn't want to answer questions, or deal with her being tentative about where she might and might not be allowed to go. He just wanted to install her and the baby in this room and forget about them until he needed them as convenient props.

"Really?" Her natural suspicion was shining through again.

"I'm a very busy man, Ms. Kelly," he said. "I'm not going to be babysitting. Either the child or you."

And with that, he turned and left her alone.

Three

Danielle had slept fitfully last night. And, of course, she hadn't actually left her room once she had been put there. But early the next morning there had been a delivery. And the signature they had asked for was hers. And then the packages had started to come in, like a Christmas parade without the wrapping.

Teams of men carried the boxes up the stairs. They had assembled a crib, a chair, and then unpacked various baby accoutrements that Danielle hadn't even known existed. How could she? She certainly hadn't expected to end up caring for a baby.

When her mother had breezed back into her life alone and pregnant—after Danielle had experienced just two carefree years where she had her own space and wasn't caring for anyone—Danielle had put all of her focus into caring for the other woman. Into arranging state health insurance so the prenatal care and hospital bill for the delivery wouldn't deter her mother from actually taking care of herself and the baby.

And then, when her mother had abandoned Danielle and Riley…that was when Danielle had realized her brother was likely going to be her responsibility. She had involved Child Services not long after that.

There had been two choices. Either Riley could go into foster care or Danielle could take some appropriate parenting classes and become a temporary guardian.

So she had.

But she had been struggling to keep their heads above water, and it was too close to the way she had grown up. She wanted more than that for Riley. Wanted more than that for both of them. Now it wasn't just her. It was him. And a part-time job as a cashier had never been all that lucrative. But with Riley to take care of, and her mother completely out of the picture, staying afloat on a cashier's pay was impossible.

She had done her best trading babysitting time with a woman in her building who also had a baby and nobody else to depend on. But inevitably there were schedule clashes, and after missing a few too many shifts, Danielle had lost her job.

Which was when she had gotten her first warning from Child Services.

Well, she had a job now.

And, apparently, a full nursery.

Joshua was refreshingly nowhere to be seen, which made dealing with her new circumstances much easier. Without him looming over her, being in his house felt a lot like being in the world's fanciest vacation rental. At least, the fanciest vacation rental she could imagine.

She had a baby monitor in her pocket, one that would allow her to hear when Riley woke up. A baby monitor that provided her with more freedom than she'd had since Riley had been born. But, she supposed, in her old apartment a monitor would have been a moot point considering there wasn't anywhere she could go and not hear the baby cry.

But in this massive house, having Riley take his nap in the bedroom—in the new crib, his first crib—would have meant she couldn't have also run down to the kitchen to grab snacks. But she had the baby monitor. A baby monitor that vibrated. Which meant she could also listen to music.

She had the same ancient MP3 player her mother had given her for her sixteenth birthday years ago, but Danielle had learned early to hold on to everything she had, because she didn't know when something else would come along. And in the case of frills like her MP3 player, nothing else had ever come along.

Of course, that meant her music was as old as her technology. But really, music hadn't been as good since she was sixteen anyway.

She shook her hips slightly, walking through the kitchen, singing about how what didn't kill her would only make her stronger. Digging through cabinets, she came up with a package of Pop-Tarts. *Pop-Tarts!*

Her mother had never bought those. They were too expensive. And while Danielle had definitely indulged herself when she had moved out, that hadn't lasted. Because they were too expensive.

Joshua had strawberry. And some kind of mixed

berry with bright blue frosting. She decided she would eat one of each to ascertain which was best.

Then she decided to eat one more of each. She hadn't realized how hungry she was. She had a feeling the hunger wasn't a new development. She had a feeling she had been hungry for days. Weeks even.

Suddenly, sitting on the plush couch in his living area, shoving toaster pastries into her mouth, she felt a whole lot like crying in relief. Because she and Riley were warm; they were safe. And there was hope. Finally, an end point in sight to the long, slow grind of poverty she had existed in for her entire life.

It seemed too good to be true, really. That she had managed to jump ahead in her life like this. That she was really managing to get herself out of that hole without prostituting herself.

Okay, so some people might argue this agreement with Joshua *was* prostituting herself, a little bit. But it wasn't like she was going to have sex with him.

She nearly choked on her Pop-Tart at the thought. And she lingered a little too long on what it might be like to get close to a man like Joshua. To any man, really. The way her mother had behaved all of her life had put Danielle off men. Or, more specifically, she supposed it was the way men had behaved toward Danielle's mother that had put her off.

As far as Danielle could tell, relationships were a whole lot of exposing yourself to pain, deciding you were going to depend on somebody and then having that person leave you high and dry.

No, thank you.

But she supposed she could see how somebody might lose their mind enough to take that risk. Especially when the person responsible for the mind loss had eyes that were blue like Joshua's. She leaned back against the couch, her hand falling slack, the Pop-Tart dangling from her fingertips.

Yesterday there had been the faint shadow of golden stubble across that strong face and jaw, his eyes glittering with irritation. Which she supposed shouldn't be a bonus, shouldn't be appealing. Except his irritation made her want to rise to the unspoken challenge. To try to turn that spark into something else. Turn that irritation into something more...

"Are you eating my Pop-Tarts?"

The voice cut through the music and she jumped, flinging the toaster pastry into the air. She ripped her headphones out of her ears and turned around to see Joshua, his arms crossed over his broad chest, his eyebrows flat on his forehead, his expression unreadable.

"You said whatever was in your house was mine to use," she squeaked. "And a warning would've been good. You just about made me jump out of my skin. Which was maybe your plan all along. If you wanted to make me into a skin suit."

"That's ridiculous. I would not fit into your skin."

She swallowed hard, her throat dry. "Well, it's a figure of speech, isn't it?"

"Is it?" he asked.

"Yes. Everybody knows what that means. It means that I think you might be a serial killer."

"You don't really think I'm a serial killer, or you wouldn't be here."

"I am pretty desperate." She lifted her hand and licked off a remnant of jam. "I mean, obviously."

"There are no Pop-Tarts left," he said, his tone filled with annoyance.

"You said I could have whatever I wanted. I wanted Pop-Tarts."

"You ate all of them."

"Why do you even have Pop-Tarts?" She stood up, crossing her arms, mimicking his stance. "You don't look like a man who eats Pop-Tarts."

"I like them. I like to eat them after I work outside."

"You work outside?"

"Yes," he said. "I have horses."

Suddenly, all of her annoyance fell away. Like it had been melted by magic. *Equine* magic. "You have horses?" She tried to keep the awe out of her voice, but it was nearly impossible.

"Yes," he said.

"Can I… Can I see them?"

"If you want to."

She had checked the range on the baby monitor, so depending on how far away from the house the horses were, she could go while Riley was napping.

"Could we see the house from the barn? Or wherever you keep them?"

"Yeah," he said, "it's just right across the driveway."

"Can I see them *now*?"

"I don't know. You ate my Pop-Tarts. Actually, more egregious than eating my Pop-Tarts, you threw the last half of one on the ground."

"Sorry about your Pop-Tarts. But I'm sure that a man who can have an entire nursery outfitted in less than twenty-four hours can certainly acquire Pop-Tarts at a moment's notice."

"Or I could just go to the store."

She had a hard time picturing a man like Joshua Grayson walking through the grocery store. In fact, the image almost made her laugh. He was way too commanding to do something as mundane as pick up a head of lettuce and try to figure out how fresh it was. Far too…masculine to go around squeezing avocados.

"What?" he asked, his eyebrows drawing together.

"I just can't imagine you going to the grocery store. That's all."

"Well, I do. Because I like food. Food like Pop-Tarts."

"My mom would never buy those for me," she said. "They were too expensive."

He huffed out a laugh. "My mom would never buy them for me."

"This is why being an adult is cool, even when it sucks."

"Pop-Tarts whenever you want?"

She nodded. "Yep."

"That seems like a low bar."

She lifted a shoulder. "Maybe it is, but it's a tasty one."

He nodded. "Fair enough. Now, why don't we go look at the horses."

Joshua didn't know what to expect by taking Danielle outside to see the horses. He had been irritated that she had eaten his preferred afternoon snack, and then, perversely, even more irritated that she had questioned the fact that it was his preferred afternoon snack. Irritated that he was put in the position of explaining to someone what he did with his time and what he put into his body.

He didn't like explaining himself.

But then she saw the horses. And all his irritation faded as he took in the look on her face. She was filled with…wonder. Absolute wonder over this thing he took for granted.

The fact that he owned horses at all, that he had felt compelled to acquire some once he had moved into this place, was a source of consternation. He had hated doing farm chores when he was a kid. Hadn't been able to get away from home and to the city fast enough. But in recent years, those feelings had started to change. And he'd found himself seeking out roots. Seeking out home.

For better or worse, this was home. Not just the misty Oregon coast, not just the town of Copper Ridge. But a ranch. Horses. A morning spent riding until the sun rose over the mountains, washing everything in a pale gold.

Yeah, that was home.

He could tell this ranch he loved was something beyond a temporary home for Danielle, who was looking at the horses and the barn like they were magical things.

She wasn't wearing her beanie today. Her dark brown hair hung limply around her face. She was pale, her chin pointed, her nose slightly pointed, as well. She was elfin, and he wasn't tempted to call her beautiful, but there was something captivating about her. Something fascinating. Watching her with the large animals was somehow just as entertaining as watching football and he couldn't quite figure out why.

"You didn't grow up around horses?"

"No," she said, taking a timid step toward the paddock. "I grew up in Portland."

He nodded. "Right."

"Always in apartments," she said. Then she frowned. "I think one time we had a house. I can't really remember it. We moved a lot. But sometimes when we lived with my mom's boyfriends, we had nicer places. It had its perks."

"What did?"

"My mom being a codependent hussy," she said, her voice toneless so it was impossible to say whether or not she was teasing.

"Right." He had grown up in one house. His family had never moved. His parents were still in that same farmhouse, the one his family had owned for a couple of generations. He had moved away to go to college and then to start the business, but that was different. He had always known he could come back here. He'd always had roots.

"Will you go back to Portland when you're finished here?" he asked.

"I don't know," she said, blinking rapidly. "I've never really had a choice before. Of where I wanted to live."

It struck him then that she was awfully young. And that he didn't know quite *how* young. "You're twenty-two?"

"Yes," she said, sounding almost defensive. "So I haven't really had a chance to think about what all I want to do and, like, be. When I grow up and stuff."

"Right," he said.

He'd been aimless for a while, but before he'd graduated high school, he'd decided he couldn't deal with a life of ranching in Copper Ridge. He had decided to get out of town. He had wanted more. He had wanted bigger. He'd gone to school for marketing because he was good at selling ideas. Products. He wasn't necessarily the one who created them, or the one who dreamed them up, but he was the one who made sure a consumer would see them and realize that product was what their life had been missing up until that point.

He was the one who took the straw and made it into gold.

He had always enjoyed his job, but it would have been especially satisfying if he'd been able to start his career by building a business with his brother and sister. To be able to market Faith's extraordinary talent to the world, as he did now. But he wasn't sure that he'd started out with a passion for what he did so much as a passion for wealth and success, and that had meant leaving behind his sister and brother too, at first. But his career had certainly grown into a passion. And he'd learned that he was the practical piece. The part that everybody needed.

A lot of people had ideas, but less than half of them had the follow-through to complete what they started. And less than half of *those* people knew how to get to the consumer. That was where he came in.

He'd had his first corporate internship at the age of twenty. He couldn't imagine being aimless at twenty-two.

But then, Danielle had a baby and he couldn't imagine having a baby at that age either.

A hollow pang struck him in the chest.

He didn't like thinking of babies at all.

"You're judging me," she said, taking a step back from the paddock.

"No, I'm not. Also, you can get closer. You can pet them."

Her head whipped around to look at the horses, then back to him, her eyes round and almost comically hopeful. "I can?"

"Of course you can. They don't bite. Well, they *might* bite, just don't stick your fingers in their mouths."

"I don't know," she said, stuffing her hands in her pockets. Except he could tell she really wanted to. She was just afraid.

"Danielle," he said, earning himself a shocked look when he used her name. "Pet the horses."

She tugged her hand out of her pocket again, then took a tentative step forward, reaching out, then drawing her hand back just as quickly.

He couldn't stand it. Between her not knowing what she wanted to be when she grew up and watching her struggle with touching a horse, he just couldn't deal with it. He stepped forward, wrapped his fingers around her wrist and drew her closer to the paddock. "It's fine," he said.

A moment after he said the words, his body registered what he had done. More than that, it registered the fact that she was very warm. That her skin was smooth.

And that she was way, way too thin.

A strange combination of feelings tightened his whole body. Compassion tightened his heart; lust tightened his groin.

He gritted his teeth. "Come on," he said.

He noticed the color rise in her face, and he wondered if she was angry, or if she was feeling the same flash of awareness rocking through him. He supposed it didn't matter either way. "Come on," he said, drawing her hand closer to the opening of the paddock. "There you go, hold your hand flat like that."

She complied, and he released his hold on her, taking a step back. He did his best to ignore the fact that he could still feel the impression of her skin against his palm.

One of his horses—a gray mare named Blue—walked up to the bars and pressed her nose against Danielle's outstretched hand. Danielle made a sharp, shocked sound, drew her hand back, then giggled. "Her whiskers are soft."

"Yeah," he said, a smile tugging at his lips. "And she is about as gentle as they come, so you don't have to be afraid of her."

"I'm not afraid of anything," Danielle said, sticking her hand back in, letting the horse sniff her.

He didn't believe that she wasn't afraid of anything. She was definitely tough. But she was brittle. Like one of those people who might withstand a beating, but if something ever hit a fragile spot, she would shatter entirely.

"Would you like to go riding sometime?" he asked.

She drew her hand back again, her expression… Well, he couldn't quite read it. There was a softness to it, but also an edge of fear and suspicion.

"I don't know. Why?"

"You seem to like the horses."

"I do. But I don't know how to ride."

"I can teach you."

"I don't know. I have to watch Riley." She began to withdraw, both from him and from the paddock.

"I'm going to hire somebody to help watch Riley," he said, making that decision right as the words exited his mouth.

There was that look again. Suspicion. "Why?"

"In case I need you for something that isn't baby friendly. Which will probably happen. We have over a month ahead of us with you living with me, and one never knows what kinds of situations we might run into. I wasn't expecting you to come with a baby, and while I agree that it will definitely help make the case that you're not suitable for me, I also think we'll need to be able to go out without him."

She looked very hesitant about that idea. And he could understand why. She clung to that baby like he was a life preserver. Like if she let go of him, she might sink and be in over her head completely.

"And I would get to ride the horses?" she asked, her eyes narrowed, full of suspicion still.

"I said so."

"Sure. But that doesn't mean a lot to me, Mr. Grayson," she said. "I don't accept people at their word. I like legal documents."

"Well, I'm not going to draw up a legal document about giving you horse-riding lessons. So you're going to have to trust me."

"You want me to trust the sketchy rich dude who put an ad in the paper looking for a fake wife?"

"He's the devil you made the deal with, Ms. Kelly. I would say it's in your best interest to trust him."

"We shake on it at least."

She stuck her hand out, and he could see she was

completely sincere. So he stuck his out in kind, wrapping his fingers around hers, marveling at her delicate bone structure. Feeling guilty now about getting angry over her eating his Pop-Tarts. The woman needed him to hire a gourmet chef too. Needed him to make sure she was getting three meals a day. He wondered how long it had been since she'd eaten regularly. She certainly didn't have the look of a woman who had recently given birth. There was no extra weight on her to speak of. He wondered how she had survived something so taxing as labor and delivery. But those were questions he was not going to ask. They weren't his business.

And he shouldn't even be curious about them.

"All right," she said. "You can hire somebody. And I'll learn to ride horses."

"You're a tough negotiator," he said, releasing his hold on her hand.

"Maybe I should go into business."

He tried to imagine this fragile, spiky creature in a boardroom, and it nearly made him laugh. "If you want to," he said, instead of laughing. Because he had a feeling she might attack him if he made fun of her. And another feeling that if Danielle attacked, she would likely go straight for the eyes. Or the balls.

He was attached to both of those things, and he liked them attached to him.

"I should go back to the house. Riley might wake up soon. Plus, I'm not entirely sure if I trust the new baby monitor. I mean, it's probably fine. But I'm going to have to get used to it before I really depend on it."

"I understand," he said, even though he didn't.

He turned and walked with her back toward the

house. He kept his eyes on her small, determined frame. On the way, she stuffed her hands in her pockets and hunched her shoulders forward. As though she were trying to look intimidating. Trying to keep from looking at her surroundings in case her surroundings looked back.

And then he reminded himself that none of this mattered. She was just a means to an end, even if she was a slightly more multifaceted means than he had thought she might be.

It didn't matter how many facets she had. Danielle Kelly needed to fulfill only one objective. She had to be introduced to his parents and be found completely wanting.

He looked back at her, at her determined walk and her posture that seemed to radiate with *I'll cut you*.

Yeah. He had a feeling she would fulfill that objective just fine.

Four

Danielle was still feeling wobbly after her interaction with Joshua down at the barn. She had touched a horse. And she had touched *him*. She hadn't counted on doing either of those things today. And he had told her they were going to have dinner together tonight and he was going to give her a crash course on the Grayson family. She wasn't entirely sure she felt ready for that either.

She had gone through all her clothes, looking for something suitable for having dinner with a billionaire. She didn't have anything. Obviously.

She snorted, feeling like an idiot for thinking she could find something relatively appropriate in that bag of hers. A bag he thought had scabies.

She turned her snort into a growl.

Then, rebelliously, she pulled out the same pair of faded pants she had been wearing yesterday.

He had probably never dealt with a woman who wore the same thing twice. Let alone the same thing two days in a row. Perversely, she kind of enjoyed that. Hey, she was here to be unsuitable. Might as well start now.

She looked in the mirror, grabbed one stringy end of her hair and blew out a disgusted breath. She shouldn't care how her hair looked.

But he was just so good-looking. It made her feel like a small, brown mouse standing next to him. It wasn't fair, really. That he had the resources to buy himself nice clothes and that he just naturally looked great.

She sighed, picking Riley up from his crib and sticking him in the little carrier she would put him in for dinner. He was awake and looking around, so she wanted to be in his vicinity, rather than leaving him upstairs alone. He wasn't a fussy baby. Really, he hardly ever cried.

But considering how often his mother had left him alone in those early days of his life, before Danielle had realized she couldn't count on her mother to take good care of him, she was reluctant to leave him by himself unless he was sleeping.

Then she paused, going back over to her bag to get the little red, dog-eared dictionary inside. She bent down, still holding on to Riley, and retrieved it. Then she quickly looked up scabies.

"I knew it," she said derisively, throwing the dictionary back into her bag.

She walked down the stairs and into the dining room, setting Riley in his seat on the chair next to hers. Joshua was already sitting at the table, looking as though he had been waiting for them. Which, she had a feeling, he was doing just to be annoying and superior.

"My bag can't have scabies," she said by way of greeting.

"Oh really?"

"Yes. I looked it up. Scabies are mites that burrow into your skin. Not into a duffel bag."

"They have to come from somewhere."

"Well, they're not coming from my bag. They're more likely to come from your horses, or something."

"You like my horses," he said, his tone dry. "Anyway, we're about to have dinner. So maybe we shouldn't be discussing skin mites?"

"You're the one who brought up scabies. The first time."

"I had pretty much dropped the subject."

"Easy enough for you to do, since it wasn't your hygiene being maligned."

"Sure." He stood up from his position at the table. "I'm just going to go get dinner, since you're here. I had it warming."

"Did you cook?"

He left the room without answering and returned a moment later holding two plates full of hot food. Her stomach growled intensely. She didn't even care what was on the plates. As far as she was concerned, it was gourmet. It was warm and obviously not from a can or a frozen pizza box. Plus, she was sitting at a real dining table and not on a patio set that had been shoved into her tiny living room.

The meal looked surprisingly healthy, considering she had discovered his affinity for Pop-Tarts earlier.

And it was accompanied by a particularly nice-looking rice. "What is this?"

"Chicken and risotto," he said.

"What's risotto?"

"Creamy rice," he said. "At least, that's the simple explanation."

Thankfully, he wasn't looking at her like she was an alien for not knowing about risotto. But then she remembered he had spoken of having simple roots. So maybe he was used to dealing with people who didn't have as sophisticated a palate as he had.

She wrinkled her nose, then picked up her fork and took a tentative bite. It was good. So good. And before she knew it, she had cleared out her portion. Her cheeks heated when she realized he had barely taken two bites.

"There's plenty more in the kitchen," he said. Then he took her plate from in front of her and went back into the kitchen. She was stunned, and all she could do was sit there and wait until he returned a moment later with the entire pot of risotto, another portion already on her plate.

"Eat as much as you want," he said, setting everything in front of her.

Well, she wasn't going to argue with that suggestion. She polished off the chicken, then went back for thirds of the risotto. Eventually, she got around to eating the salad.

"I thought we were going to talk about my responsibilities for being your fiancée and stuff," she said after she realized he had been sitting there staring at her for the past ten minutes.

"I thought you should have a chance to eat a meal first."

"Well," she said, taking another bite, "that's unexpectedly kind of you."

"You seem…hungry."

That was the most loaded statement of the century. She was so hungry. For so many things. Food was kind of the least of it. "It's just been a really crazy few months."

"How old is the baby? Riley. How old is Riley?"

For the first time, because of that correction, she became aware of the fact that he seemed reluctant to call Riley by name. Actually, Joshua seemed pretty reluctant to deal with Riley in general.

Riley was unperturbed. Sitting in that reclined seat, his muddy blue eyes staring up at the ceiling. He lifted his fist, putting it in his mouth and gumming it idly.

That was one good thing she could say about their whole situation. Riley was so young that he was largely unperturbed by all of it. He had gone along more or less unaffected by their mother's mistakes. At least, Danielle hoped so. She really did.

"He's almost four months old," she said. She felt a soft smile touch her lips. Yes, taking care of her half brother was hard. None of it was easy. But he had given her a new kind of purpose. Had given her a kind of the drive she'd been missing before.

Before Riley, she had been somewhat content to just enjoy living life on her own terms. To enjoy not cleaning up her mother's messes. Instead, working at the grocery store, going out with friends after work for coffee or burritos at the twenty-four-hour Mexican restaurant.

Her life had been simple, and it had been carefree. Something she hadn't been afforded all the years she'd lived with her mother, dealing with her mother's various heartbreaks, schemes to try to better their circumstances and intense emotional lows.

So many years when Danielle should have been a child but instead was expected to be the parent. If her mother passed out in the bathroom after having too much to drink, it was up to Danielle to take care of her. To put a pillow underneath her mother's head, then make herself a piece of toast for dinner and get her homework done.

In contrast, taking care of only herself had seemed simple. And in truth, she had resented Riley at first, resented the idea that she would have to take care of another person again. But taking care of a baby was different. He wasn't a victim of his own bad choices. No, he was a victim of circumstances. He hadn't had a chance to make a single choice for himself yet.

To Danielle, Riley was the child she'd once been.

Except she hadn't had anyone to step in and take care of her when her mother failed. But Riley did. That realization had filled Danielle with passion. Drive.

And along with that dedication came a fierce, unexpected love like she had never felt before toward another human being. She would do anything for him. Give anything for him.

"And you've been alone with him all this time?"

She didn't know why she was so reluctant to let Joshua know that Riley wasn't her son. She supposed it was partly because, for all intents and purposes, he was her son. She intended to adopt him officially as soon as she had the means to do so. As soon as everything in her life was in order enough that Child Services would respond to her favorably.

The other part was that as long as people thought Riley was hers, they would be less likely to suggest she make a different decision about his welfare. Joshua Grayson had a coldness to him. He seemed to have a family who loved and supported him, but instead of finding it endearing, he got angry about it. He was using her to get back at his dad for doing something that, in her opinion, seemed mostly innocuous. And yes, she was benefiting from his pettiness, so she couldn't exactly judge.

Still, she had a feeling that if he knew Riley wasn't her son, he would suggest she do the "responsible" thing and allow him to be raised by a two-parent family, or whatever. She just didn't even want to have that discussion with him. Or with anybody. She had too many things against her already.

She didn't want to fight about this too.

"Mostly," she said carefully, treading the line between the truth and a lie. "Since he was about three weeks old. And I thought… I thought I could do it. I'd been self-sufficient for a long time. But then I realized there are a lot of logistical problems when you can't just leave your apartment whenever you want. It's harder to get to work. And I couldn't afford childcare. There wasn't any space at the places that had subsidized rates. So I was trading childcare with a neighbor, but sometimes our schedules conflicted. Anyway, it was just difficult. You can imagine why responding to your ad seemed like the best possible solution."

"I already told you, I'm not judging you for taking me up on an offer I made."

"I guess I'm just explaining that under other circumstances I probably wouldn't have sought you out. But things have been hard. I lost my job because I wasn't flexible enough and I had missed too many shifts because babysitting for Riley fell through."

"Well," he said, a strange expression crossing his face, "your problems should be minimized soon. You should be independently wealthy enough to at least afford childcare."

Not only that, she would actually be able to make decisions about her life. About what she wanted. When Joshua had asked her earlier today about whether or not she would go back to Portland, it had been the first time she had truly realized she could make decisions about where she wanted to live, rather than just parking herself somewhere because she happened to be there already.

It would be the first time in her life she could make proactive decisions rather than just reacting to her situation.

"Right. So I guess we should talk about your family," she said, determined to move the conversation back in the right direction. She didn't need to talk about herself. They didn't need to get to know each other. She just needed to do this thing, to trick his family, lie…whatever he needed her to do. So she and Riley could start their new life.

"I already told you my younger sister is an architectural genius. My older brother Isaiah is the financial brain. And I do the public relations and marketing. We have another brother named Devlin, and he runs a small ranching operation in town. He's married, no kids. Then there are my parents."

"The reason we find ourselves in this situation," she said, folding her hands and leaning forward. Then she cast a glance at the pot of risotto and decided to grab the spoon and serve herself another helping while they were talking.

"Yes. Well, not my mother so much. Sure, she wrings her hands and looks at me sadly and says she wishes I would get married. My father is the one who…actively meddles."

"That surprises me. I mean, given what I know about fathers. Which is entirely based on TV. I don't have one."

He lifted a brow.

"Well," she continued, "sure, I guess I do. But I never met him. I mean, I don't even know his name."

She realized that her history was shockingly close to the story she had given about Riley. Which was a true one. It just wasn't about Danielle. It was about her mother. And the fact that her mother repeated the same cycle over and over again. The fact that she never seemed to change. And never would.

"That must've been hard," he said. "I'm sorry."

"Don't apologize. I bet he was an ass. I mean, circumstances would lead you to believe that he must be, right?"

"Yeah, it's probably a pretty safe assumption."

"Well, anyway, this isn't about my lack of a paternal figure. This is about the overbearing presence of yours."

He laughed. "My mother is old-fashioned—so is my father. My brother Devlin is a little bit too, but he's also something of a rebel. He has tattoos and things. He's a likely ally for you, especially since he got married a few months ago and is feeling soft about love and all of that. My brother Isaiah isn't going to like you. My sister, Faith, will try. Basically, if you cuss, chew with your mouth open, put your elbows on the table and in general act like a feral cat, my family will likely find you unsuitable. Also, if you could maybe repeatedly bring up the fact that you're really looking forward to spending my money, and that you had another man's baby four months ago, that would be great."

She squinted. "I think the fact that I have a four-month-old baby in tow will be reminder enough."

The idea of going into his family's farmhouse and behaving like a nightmare didn't sit as well with her as it had when the plan had been fully abstract. But now he had given names to the family members. Now she had been here for a while. And now it was all starting to feel a little bit real.

"It won't hurt. Though, he's pretty quiet. It might help if he screamed."

She laughed. "Oh, I don't know about that. I have a feeling your mom and sister might just want to hold him. That will be the real problem. Not having everyone hate me. That'll be easy enough. It'll be keeping everyone from loving him."

That comment struck her square in the chest, made her realize just what they were playing at here. She was going to be lying to these people. And yes, the idea was to alienate them, but they were going to think she might be their daughter-in-law, sister-in-law…that Riley would be their grandson or nephew.

But it would be a lie.

That's the point, you moron. And who cares? They're strangers. Riley is your life. He's your responsib lity. And you'll never see these people again.

"We won't let them hold the baby," he said, his expression hard, as if he'd suddenly realized she wasn't completely wrong about his mother and sister and it bothered him.

She wished she could understand why he felt so strongly about putting a stop to his father playing matchmaker. As someone whose parents were ambivalent about her existence, his disregard for his family's well wishes was hard to comprehend.

"Okay," she said. "Fine by me. And you just want me to…be my charming self?"

"Obviously we'll have to come up with a story about our relationship. We don't have to make up how we met. We can say we met through the ad."

"The ad your father placed, not the ad you placed."

"Naturally."

She looked at Joshua then, at the broad expanse of table between them. Two people who looked less like a couple probably didn't exist on the face of the planet. Honestly, two strangers standing across the street from each other probably looked more like a happily engaged unit than they did.

She frowned. "This is very unconvincing."

"What is? Be specific."

She rolled her eyes at his impatience. "Us."

She stood up and walked toward him, sitting down in the chair right next to him. She looked at him for a moment, at the sharp curve of his jaw, the enticing shape of his lips. He was an attractive man. That was an understatement. He was also so uptight she was pretty sure he had a stick up his ass.

"Look, you want your family to think you've lost your mind, to think you have hooked up with a totally unsuitable woman, right?"

"That is the game."

"Then you have to look like you've lost your mind over me. Unfortunately, Joshua, you look very much in your right mind. In fact, a man of sounder mind may not exist. You are…responsible. You literally look like The Man."

"Which man?"

"Like, The Man. Like, fight the power. *You're* the power. Nobody's going to believe you're with me. At least, not if you don't seem a little bit…looser."

A slight smile tipped up those lips she had been thinking about only a moment before. His blue eyes warmed, and she felt an answering warmth spread low in her belly. "So what you're saying is we need to look like we have more of a connection?"

Her throat went dry. "It's just a suggestion."

He leaned forward, his gaze intent on hers. "An essential one, I think." Then he reached up and she jerked backward, nearly toppling off the side of her chair. "It looks like I'm not the only one who's wound a bit tight."

"I'm not," she said, taking a deep breath, trying to get her jittery body to calm itself down.

She wasn't used to men. She wasn't used to men touching her. Yes, intermittently she and her mother had lived with some of her mother's boyfriends, but none of them had ever been inappropriate with her. And she had never been close enough to even give any of them hugs.

And she really, really wasn't used to men who were so beautiful it was almost physically painful to look directly at them.

"You're right. We have to do a better job of looking like a couple. And that would include you not scampering under the furniture when I get close to you."

She sat up straight and folded her hands in her lap. "I did not scamper," she muttered.

"You were perilously close to a scamper."

"Was not," she grumbled, and then her breath caught in her throat as his warm palm made contact with her cheek.

He slid his thumb down the curve of her face to that dent just beneath her lips, his eyes never leaving hers. She felt…stunned and warm. No, hot. So very hot. Like there was a furnace inside that had been turned up the moment his hand touched her bare skin.

She supposed she was meant to be flirtatious. To play the part of the moneygrubbing tart with loose morals he needed her to be, that his family would expect her to be. But right now, she was shocked into immobility.

She took a deep breath, fighting for composure. But his thumb migrated from the somewhat reasonable point just below her mouth to her lip and her composure dissolved completely. His touch felt… shockingly intimate and filthy somehow. Not in a bad way, just in a way she'd never experienced before.

For some reason she would never be able to articulate—not even to herself—she darted her tongue out and touched the tip to his thumb. She tasted salt, skin and a promise that arrowed downward to the most private part of her body, leaving her feeling breathless. Leaving her feeling new somehow.

As if a wholly unexpected and previously unknown part of herself had been uncovered, awoken. She wanted to do exactly what he had accused her of doing earlier. She wanted to turn away. Wanted to scurry beneath the furniture or off into the night. Somewhere safe. Somewhere less confrontational.

But he was still looking at her. And those blue eyes were like chains, lashing her to the seat, holding her in place. And his thumb, pressed against her lip, felt heavy. Much too heavy for her to push against. For her to fight.

And when it came right down to it, she didn't even want to.

Something expanded in her chest, spreading low, opening up a yawning chasm in her stomach. Deepening her need, her want. Her desire for things she hadn't known she could desire until now.

Until he had made a promise with his touch that she hadn't known she wanted fulfilled.

She was just about to come back to herself, to pull away. And then he closed the distance between them.

His lips were warm and firm. The kiss was nothing like she had imagined it might be. She had always thought a kiss must reach inside and steal your brain. Transform you. She had always imagined a kiss to be powerful, considering the way her mother acted.

When her mother was under the influence of love—at least, that was what her mother had called it; Danielle had always known it was lust—she acted like someone entirely apart from herself.

Yes, Danielle had always known a kiss could be powerful. But what she hadn't counted on was that she might feel wholly like *herself* when a man fused his lips to hers. That she would be so perfectly aware of where she was, of what she was doing.

Of the pressure of his lips against hers, the warmth of his hand as he cradled her face, the hard, tightening knot of desire in her stomach that told her how insufficient the kiss was.

The desire that told her just how much more she wanted. Just how much more there could be.

He was kissing her well, this near stranger, and she never wanted it to end.

Instinctively, she angled her head slightly, parting her lips, allowing him to slide his tongue against hers. It was unexpectedly slick, unexpectedly arousing. Unexpectedly everything she wanted.

That was the other thing that surprised her. Because not only had she imagined a woman might lose herself entirely when a man kissed her, she had also imagined she would be immune. Because she knew better. She knew the cost. But she was sitting here, allowing him to kiss her and kiss her and kiss her. She was Danielle Kelly, and she was submitting herself to this sensual assault with almost shocking abandon.

Her hands were still folded in her lap, almost primly, but her mouth was parted wide, gratefully receiving every stroke of his tongue, slow and languorous against her own. Sexy. Deliciously affecting.

He moved his hands then, sliding them around the

back of her neck, down between her shoulder blades, along the line of her spine until his hands spanned her waist. She arched, wishing she could press her body against his. Wishing she could do something to close the distance between them. Because he was still sitting in his chair and she in hers.

He pulled away, and she followed him, leaning into him with an almost humiliating desperation, wanting to taste him again. To be kissed again. By Joshua Grayson, the man she was committing an insane kind of fraud with. The man who had hired her to play the part of his pretend fiancée.

"That will do," he said, lifting his hand and squeezing her chin gently, those blue eyes glinting with a sharpness that cut straight to her soul. "Yes, Ms. Kelly, that will do quite nicely."

Then he released his hold on her completely, settling back in his seat, his attention returning to his dinner plate.

A slash of heat bled across Danielle's cheekbones. He hadn't felt anything at all. He had been proving a point. Just practicing the ruse they would be performing for his family tomorrow night. The kiss hadn't changed anything for him at all. Hadn't been more than the simple meeting of mouths.

It had been her first kiss. It had been everything.

And right then she got her first taste of just how badly a man could make a woman feel. Of how—when wounded—feminine pride could be a treacherous and testy thing.

She rose from her seat and rounded to stand behind his. Then, without fully pausing to think about what she might be doing, she placed her hands on his shoulders, leaned forward and slid her hands beneath the collar of his shirt and down his chest.

Her palms made contact with his hot skin, with hard muscle, and she had to bite her lip to keep from groaning out loud. She had to plant her feet firmly on the wood floor to keep herself from running away, from jerking her hands back like a child burned on a hot oven.

She'd never touched a man like this before. It was shocking just how arousing she found it, this little form of revenge, this little rebellion against his blasé response to the earthquake he had caused in her body.

She leaned her head forward, nearly pressing her lips against his ear. Then her teeth scraped his earlobe.

"Yes," she whispered. "I think it's quite convincing."

She straightened again, slowly running her fingernails over his skin as she did. She didn't know where this confidence had come from. Where the know-how and seemingly deep, feminine instinct had come from that allowed her to toy with him. But there it was.

She was officially playing the part of a saucy minx. Considering that was what he had hired her for, her flirtation was a good thing. But her heart thundered harder than a drum as she walked back to Riley, picked up his carrier and flipped her hair as she turned to face Joshua.

"I think I'm going to bed. I had best prepare myself to meet your family."

"You'll be wearing something different tomorrow," he said, his tone firm.

"Why?" She looked down at her ragged sweatshirt and skinny jeans. "That doesn't make any sense. You wanted me to look unsuitable. I might as well go in this."

"No, you brought up a very good point. You have to look unsuitable, but this situation also has to be believable. Plus, I think a gold digger would demand a new wardrobe, don't you?" One corner of his lips quirked upward, and she had a feeling he was punishing her for her little display a moment ago.

If only she could work out quite where the trap was.

"I don't know," she said, her voice stiff.

"But, Ms. Kelly, you told me yourself that you *are* a gold digger. That's why you're here, after all. For my gold."

"I suppose so," she said, keeping her words deliberately hard. "But I want actual gold, not clothes. So this is another thing that's going to be on you."

Those blue eyes glinted, and right then she got an idea of just how dangerous he was to her. "Consider it done."

And if there was one thing she had learned so far about Joshua Grayson, it was that if he said something would be done, it would be.

Five

Joshua wasn't going to try to turn Danielle into a sophisticate overnight. He was also avoiding thinking about the way it had felt to kiss her soft lips. Was avoiding remembering the way her hands had felt sliding down his chest.

He needed to make sure the two of them looked like a couple, that much was true. But he wouldn't allow himself to be distracted by her. There were a million reasons not to touch Danielle Kelly—unless they were playing a couple. Yes, there would have to be some touching, but he was not going to take advantage of her.

First of all, she was at his financial mercy. Second of all, she was the kind of woman who came with entanglements. And he didn't want any entanglements.

He wasn't the type to have trouble with self-control. If it wasn't a good time to seek out a physical relationship, he didn't. It wasn't a good time now, which meant he would defer any kind of sexual gratification until the end of his association with Danielle.

That should be fine.

He should be able to consider any number of women who he had on-again, off-again associations with, choose one and get in touch with her after Danielle left. His mind and body should be set on that.

Sadly, all he could think of was last night's kiss and the shocking heat that had come with it.

And then Danielle came down the stairs wearing the simple black dress he'd had delivered for her.

His thoughts about not transforming her into a sophisticated woman overnight held true. Her long, straight brown hair still hung limp down to her waist, and she had no makeup on to speak of except pale pink gloss on her lips.

But the simple cut of the dress suited her slender figure and displayed small, perky breasts that had been hidden beneath her baggy, threadbare sweaters.

She was holding on to the handle of the baby's car seat with both hands, lugging it down the stairs. For one moment, he was afraid she might topple over. He moved forward quickly, grabbing the handle and taking the seat from her.

When he looked down at the sleeping child, a strange tightness invaded his chest. "It wouldn't be good for you or for Riley if you fell and broke your neck trying to carry something that's too heavy for you," he said, his tone harder than he'd intended it to be.

Danielle scowled. "Well, offer assistance earlier next time. I had to get down the stairs somehow. Anyway, I've been navigating stairs like this with the baby since he was born. I lived in an apartment. On the third floor."

"I imagine he's heavier now than he used to be."

"An expert on child development?" She arched one dark brow as she posed the question.

He gritted his teeth. "Hardly."

She stepped away from the stairs, and the two of them walked toward the door. Just because he wanted to make it clear that he was in charge of the evening, he placed his hand low on her back, right at the dip where her spine curved, right above what the dress revealed to be a magnificent ass.

He had touched her there to get to her, but he had not anticipated the touch getting to him.

He ushered her out quickly, then handed the car seat to her, allowing her to snap it into the base—the one he'd had installed in his car when all of the nursery accoutrements had been delivered—then sat waiting for her to get in.

As they started to pull out of the driveway, she wrapped her arms around herself, rubbing her hands over her bare skin. "Do you think you could turn the heater on?"

He frowned. "Why didn't you bring a jacket?"

"I don't have one? All I have are my sweaters. And I don't think either of them would go with the dress. Would kind of ruin the effect."

He put the brakes on, slipped out of his own jacket and handed it to her. She just looked at him like he was offering her a live gopher. "Take it," he said.

She frowned but reached out, taking the jacket and

slipping it on. "Thank you," she said, her voice sounding hollow.

They drove to his parents' house in silence, the only sounds coming from the baby sitting in the back seat. A sobering reminder of the evening that was about to unfold. He was going to present a surprise fiancée and a surprise baby to his parents, and suddenly, he didn't look at this plan in quite the same way as he had before.

He was throwing Danielle into the deep end. Throwing Riley into the deep end.

Joshua gritted his teeth, tightening his hold on the steering wheel. Finally, the interminable drive through town was over. He turned left off a winding road and onto a dirt drive that led back to the familiar, humble farmhouse his parents still called home.

That some part of his heart still called home too.

He looked over at Danielle, who had gone pale. "It's fine," he said.

Danielle looked down at the ring on her finger, then back up at him. "I guess it's showtime."

Danielle felt warm all over, no longer in need of Joshua's jacket, and conflicted down to the brand-new shoes Joshua had ordered for her.

But it wasn't the dress, or the shoes, that had her feeling warm. It was the jacket. Well, obviously a jacket was supposed to make her warm, but this was different. Joshua had realized she was cold. And it had mattered to him.

He had given her his own jacket so she could keep warm.

It was too big, the sleeves went well past the edges

of her fingertips, and it smelled like him. From the moment she had slipped it on, she had been fighting the urge to bury her nose in the fabric and lose herself in the sharp, masculine smell that reminded her of his skin. Skin she had tasted last night.

Standing on the front step of this modest farmhouse that she could hardly believe Joshua had ever lived in, wearing his coat, with him holding Riley's car seat, it was too easy to believe this actually was some kind of "meet the parents" date.

In effect, she supposed it was. She was even wearing his jacket. His jacket that was still warm from his body and smelled—

Danielle was still ruminating about the scent of Joshua's jacket when the door opened. A blonde woman with graying hair and blue eyes that looked remarkably like her son's gave them a warm smile.

"Joshua," she said, glancing sideways at Danielle and clearly doing her best not to look completely shocked, "I didn't expect you so early. And I didn't know you were bringing a guest." Her eyes fell to the carrier in Joshua's hand. "Two guests."

"I thought it would be a good surprise."

"What would be?"

A man who could only be Joshua's father came to the door behind the woman. He was tall, with dark hair and eyes. He looked nice too. They both did. There was a warmth to them, a kindness, that didn't seem to be present in their son.

But then Danielle felt the warmth of the jacket again, and she had to revise that thought. Joshua might not exude kindness, but it was definitely there, buried. And for the life of her, she couldn't figure out why he hid it.

She was prickly and difficult, but at least she had an excuse. Her family was the worst. As far as she could tell, his family was guilty of caring too much. And she just couldn't feel that sorry for a rich dude whose parents loved him and were involved in his life more than he wanted them to be.

"Who is this?" Joshua's father asked.

"Danielle, this is my mom and dad, Todd and Nancy Grayson. Mom, Dad, this is Danielle Kelly," Joshua said smoothly. "And I have you to thank for meeting her, Dad."

His father's eyebrows shot upward. "Do you?"

"Yes," Joshua said. "She responded to your ad. Mom, Dad, Danielle is my fiancée."

They were ushered into the house quickly after that announcement, and there were a lot of exclamations. The house was already full. A young woman sat in the corner holding hands with a large, tattooed man who was built like a brick house and was clearly related to Joshua somehow. There was another man, as tall as Joshua, with slightly darker hair and the same blue eyes but who didn't carry himself quite as stiffly. His build was somewhere in between Joshua and the tattooed man, muscular but not a beast.

"My brother Devlin," Joshua said, indicating the tattooed man before putting his arm around Danielle's waist as they moved deeper into the room, "and his wife, Mia. And this is my brother Isaiah. I'm surprised his capable assistant, Poppy, isn't somewhere nearby."

"Isaiah, did you want a beer or whiskey?" A petite woman appeared from the kitchen area, her curly, dark hair swept back into a bun, a few stray pieces bouncing around her pretty face. She was impeccable. From that elegant updo down to the soles of her tiny, high-heeled feet. She was wearing a high-waisted skirt that flared out at the hips and fell down past her knees, along with a plain, fitted top.

"Is that his...girlfriend?" Danielle asked.

Poppy laughed. "Absolutely not," she said, her tone clipped. "I'm his assistant."

Danielle thought it strange that an assistant would be at a family gathering but didn't say anything.

"She's more than an assistant," Nancy Grayson said. "She's part of the family. She's been with them since they started the business."

Danielle had not been filled in on the details of his family's relationships because she only needed to know how to alienate them, not how to endear herself to them.

The front door opened again and this time it was a younger blonde woman whose eyes also matched Joshua's who walked in. "Sorry I'm late," she said, "I got caught up working on a project."

This had to be his sister, Faith. The architect he talked about with such pride and fondness. A woman who was Danielle's age and yet so much more successful they might be completely different species.

"This is Joshua's fiancée," Todd Grayson said. "He's engaged."

"Shut the front door," Faith said. "Are you really?"

"Yes," Joshua said, the lie rolling easily off his tongue.

Danielle bit back a comment about his PR skills. She

was supposed to be hard to deal with, but they weren't supposed to call attention to the fact this was a ruse.

"That's great?" Faith took a step forward and hugged her brother, then leaned in to grab hold of Danielle, as well.

"Is nobody going to ask about the baby?" Isaiah asked.

"Obviously *you* are," Devlin said.

"Well, it's kind of the eight-hundred-pound gorilla in the room. Or the ten-pound infant."

"It's my baby," Danielle said, feeling color mount in her cheeks.

She noticed a slight shift in Joshua's father's expression. Which was the general idea. To make him suspicious of her. To make him think he had gone and caught his son a gold digger.

"Well, that's..." She could see Joshua's mother searching for words. "It's definitely unexpected." She looked apologetically at Danielle the moment the words left her mouth. "It's just that Joshua hasn't shown much interest in marriage or family."

Danielle had a feeling that was an understatement. If Joshua was willing to go to such lengths to get his father out of his business, then he must be about as anti-marriage as you could get.

"Well," Joshua said, "Danielle and I met because of Dad."

His mother's blue gaze sharpened. "How?"

His father looked guilty. "Well, I thought he could use a little help," he said finally.

"What kind of help?"

"It's not good for a man to be alone, especially not our boys," he said insistently.

"Some of us like to be alone," Isaiah pointed out.

"You wouldn't feel that way if you didn't have a woman who cooked for you and ran your errands," his father responded, looking pointedly at Poppy.

"She's an employee," Isaiah said.

Poppy looked more irritated and distressed by Isaiah's comment than she did by the Grayson family patriarch's statement. But she didn't say anything.

"You were right," Joshua said. "I just needed to find the right woman. You placed that ad, listing all of my assets, and the right woman responded."

This was so ridiculous. Danielle felt her face heating. The assets Joshua's father had listed were his bank account, and there was no way in the world that wasn't exactly what everyone in his family was thinking.

She knew this was her chance to confirm her gold-digging motives. But right then, Riley started to cry.

"Oh," she said, feeling flustered. "Just let me... I need to..."

She fumbled around with the new diaper bag, digging around for a bottle, and then went over to the car seat, taking the baby out of it.

"Let me help," Joshua's mother said.

She was being so kind. Danielle felt terrible.

But before Danielle could protest, the other woman was taking Riley from her arms. Riley wiggled and fussed, but then she efficiently plucked the bottle from Danielle's hand and stuck it right in his mouth. He quieted immediately.

"What a good baby," she said. "Does he usually go to strangers?"

Danielle honestly didn't know. "Other than a neighbor whose known him since he was born, I'm the only one who takes care of him," she said.

"Don't you have any family?"

Danielle shook her head, feeling every inch the curiosity she undoubtedly was. Every single eye in the room was trained on her, and she knew they were all waiting for her to make a mistake. She was *supposed* to make a mistake, dammit. That was what Joshua was paying her to do.

"I don't have any family," she said decisively. "It's just been me and Riley from the beginning."

"It must be nice to have some help now," Faith said, not unkindly, but definitely probing.

"It is," Danielle said. "I mean, it's really hard taking care of a baby by yourself. And I didn't make enough money to…well, anything. So meeting Joshua has been great. Because he's so…helpful."

A timer went off in the other room and Joshua's mother blinked. "Oh, I have to get dinner." She turned to her son. "Since you're so helpful, Joshua." And before Danielle could protest, before Joshua could protest, Nancy dumped Riley right into his arms.

He looked like he'd been handed a bomb. And frankly, Danielle felt a little bit like a bomb might detonate at any moment. It had not escaped her notice that Joshua had never touched Riley. Yes, he had carried his car seat, but he had never voluntarily touched the baby. Which, now that she thought about it, must have been purposeful. But then, not everybody liked babies. She had never been particularly drawn to them before Riley. Maybe Joshua felt the same way.

She could tell by his awkward posture, and the way

Riley's small frame was engulfed by Joshua's large, muscular one, that any contact with babies was not something he was used to.

She imagined Joshua's reaction would go a long way in proving how unsuitable she was. Maybe not in the way he had hoped, but it definitely made his point.

He took a seat on the couch, still holding on to Riley, still clearly committed to the farce.

"So you met through an ad," Isaiah said, his voice full of disbelief. "An ad that Dad put in the paper."

Everyone's head swiveled, and they looked at Todd. "I did what any concerned father would do for his son."

Devlin snorted. "Thank God I found a wife on my own."

"You found a wife by pilfering from my friendship pool," Faith said, her tone disapproving. "Isaiah and Joshua have too much class to go picking out women that young."

"Actually," Danielle said, deciding this was the perfect opportunity to highlight another of the many ways in which she was unsuitable, "I'm only twenty-two."

Joshua's father looked at him, his gaze sharp. "Really?"

"Really," Danielle said.

"That's unexpected," Todd said to his son.

"That's what's so great about how we met," Joshua said. "Had I looked for a life partner on my own, I probably would have chosen somebody with a completely different set of circumstances. Had you asked me only a few short weeks ago, I would have said I didn't want children. And now look at me."

Everybody *was* looking at him, and it was clear he was extremely uncomfortable. Danielle wasn't entirely sure he was making the point he hoped to make, but he did make a pretty amusing picture. "I also would have chosen somebody closer to my age. But the great thing about Danielle is that she is so mature. I think it's because she's a mother. And yes, it happened for her in non-ideal circumstances, but her ability to rise above her situation and solve her problems—namely by responding to the ad—is one of the many things I find attractive about her."

She wanted to kick him in the shin. He was being an asshole, and he was making her sound like a total flake... But that was the whole idea. And, honestly, given the information Joshua had about her life...he undoubtedly thought she *was* a flake. It was stupid, and it wasn't fair. One of the many things she had learned about people since becoming the sole care-giver for Riley was that even though everyone had sex, a woman was an immediate pariah the minute she bore the evidence of that sex.

All that mattered to the hypocrites was that Danielle appeared to be a scarlet woman, therefore she was one.

Never mind that in reality she was a virgin.

Which was not a word she needed to be thinking while sitting in the Grayson family living room.

Her cheeks felt hot, like they were being stung by bees.

"Fate is a funny thing," Danielle said, edging closer to Joshua. She took Riley out of his arms, and from the way Joshua surrendered the baby, she could tell he was more than ready to hand him over.

The rest of the evening passed in a blur of awkward moments and stilted conversation. It was clear to her that his family was wonderful and warm, but that they were also seriously questioning Joshua's decision making. Todd Grayson looked as if he was going to be physically assaulted by his wife.

Basically, everything was going according to Joshua's plan.

But Danielle couldn't feel happy about it. She couldn't feel triumphant. It just felt awful.

Finally, it was time to go, and Danielle was ready to scurry out the door and keep on scurrying away from the entire Grayson family—Joshua included.

She was gathering her things, and Joshua was talking to one of his brothers, when Faith approached.

"We haven't gotten a chance to talk yet," she said.

"I guess not," Danielle said, feeling instantly wary. She had a feeling that being approached by Joshua's younger sister like this wouldn't end well.

"I'm sure he's told you all about me," Faith said, and Danielle had a feeling that statement was a test.

"Of course he has." She sounded defensive, even though there was no reason for her to feel defensive, except that she kind of did anyway.

"Great. So here's the thing. I don't know exactly what's going on here, but my brother is not a 'marriage and babies' kind of guy. My brother dates a seemingly endless stream of models, all of whom are about half a foot taller than you without their ridiculous high heels on. Also, he likes blondes."

Danielle felt her face heating again as the other woman appraised her and found her lacking. "Right. Well. Maybe I'm a really great conversationalist. Although, it could be the fact that I don't have a gag reflex."

She watched the other woman's cheeks turn bright pink and felt somewhat satisfied. Unsophisticated, virginal Danielle had made the clearly much more sophisticated Faith Grayson blush.

"Right. Well, if you're leading him around by his… *you know*…so you can get into his wallet, I'm not going to allow that. There's a reason he's avoided commitment all this time. And I'm not going to let you hurt him. He's been hurt enough," she said.

Danielle could only wonder what that meant, because Joshua seemed bulletproof.

"I'm not going to break up with him," Danielle said. "Why would I do that? I'd rather stay in his house than in a homeless shelter."

She wanted to punch her own face. And she was warring with the fact that Faith had rightly guessed that she was using Joshua for his money—though not in the way his sister assumed. And Danielle needed Faith to think the worst. But it also hurt to have her assume something so negative based on Danielle's circumstances. Based on her appearance.

People had been looking at Danielle and judging her as low-class white trash for so long—not exactly incorrectly—that it was a sore spot.

"We're a close family," Faith said. "And we look out for each other. Just remember that."

"Well, your brother loves me."

"If that's true," Faith said, "then I hope you're very happy together. I actually do hope it's true. But the problem is, I'm not sure I believe it."

"Why?" Danielle was bristling, and there was no

reason on earth why she should be. She shouldn't be upset about this. She shouldn't be taking it personally. But she was.

Faith Grayson had taken one look at Danielle and judged her. Pegged her for exactly the kind of person she was, really—a low-class nobody who needed the kind of money and security a man like Joshua could provide. Danielle had burned her pride to the ground to take part in this charade. Poking at the embers of that pride was stupid. But she felt compelled to do it anyway.

"Is it because I'm some kind of skank he would never normally sully himself with?"

"Mostly, it's because I know my brother. And I know he never intended to be in any kind of serious relationship again."

Again.

That word rattled around inside of Danielle. It implied he had been in a serious relationship before. He hadn't mentioned that. He'd just said he didn't want his father meddling. Didn't want marriage. He hadn't said it was because he'd tried before.

She blinked.

Faith took that momentary hesitation and ran with it. "So you don't know that much about him. You don't actually know anything about him, do you? You just know he's rich."

"And he's hot," Danielle said.

She wasn't going to back down. Not now. But she would have a few very grumpy words with Joshua once they left.

He hadn't prepared her for this. She looked like an idiot. As she gathered her things, she realized looking like an idiot was his objective. She could look bad in a great many ways, after all. The fact that they might be an unsuitable couple because she didn't know anything about him would be one way to accomplish that.

When she and Joshua finally stepped outside, heading back to the car amid a thunderous farewell from the family, Danielle felt like she could breathe for the first time in at least two hours. She hadn't realized it, but being inside that house—all warm and cozy and filled with the kind of love she had only ever seen in movies—had made her throat and lungs and chest, and even her fingers, feel tight.

They got into the car, and Danielle folded her arms tightly, leaning her head against the cold passenger-side window, her breath fanning out across the glass, leaving mist behind. She didn't bother fighting the urge to trace a heart in it.

"Feeling that in character?" Joshua asked, his tone dry, as he put the car in Reverse and began to pull out of the driveway.

She stuck her tongue out and scribbled over the heart. "Not particularly. I don't understand. Now that I've met them, I understand even less. Your sister grilled me the minute she got a chance to talk to me alone. Your father is worried about the situation. Your mother is trying to be supportive in spite of the fact that we are clearly the worst couple of all time. And you're doing this why, Joshua? I don't understand."

She hadn't meant to call him out in quite that way. After all, what did she care about his motivations? He was paying her. The fact that he was a rich, eccentric idiot kind of worked in her favor. But tonight had felt wrong. And while she was more into survival than into the nuances of right and wrong, the ruse was getting to her.

"I explained to you already," he said, his tone so hard it elicited a small, plaintive cry from Riley in the back.

"Don't wake up the baby," she snapped.

"We really are a convincing couple," he responded.

"Not to your sister. Who told me we didn't make any sense together because you had never shown any interest in falling in love *again*."

It was dark in the car, so she felt rather than saw the tension creep up his spine. It was in the way he shifted in his seat, how his fists rolled forward as he twisted his hands on the steering wheel.

"Well," he said, "that's the thing. They all know. Because family like mine doesn't leave well enough alone. They want to know about all your injuries, all your scars, and then they obsess over the idea that they might be able to heal them. And they don't listen when you tell them healing is not necessary."

"Right," she said, blowing out an exasperated breath. "Here's the thing. I'm just a dumb bimbo you picked up through a newspaper ad who needed your money. So I don't understand all this coded nonsense. Just tell me what's going on. Especially if I'm going to spend more nights trying to alienate your family— who are basically a childhood sitcom fantasy of what a family should be."

"I've done it before, Danielle. Love. It's not worth it. Not considering how badly it hurts when it ends. But even more, it's not worth it when you consider how badly you can hurt the other person."

His words fell flat in the car, and she didn't know how to respond to them. "I don't…"

"Details aren't important. You've been hurt before, haven't you?"

He turned the car off the main road and headed up the long drive to his house. She took a deep breath. "Yes."

"By Riley's father?"

She shifted uncomfortably. "Not exactly."

"You didn't love him?"

"No," she said. "I didn't love him. But my mother kind of did a number on me. I do understand that love hurts. I also understand that a supportive family is not necessarily guaranteed."

"Yeah," Joshua said, "supportive family is great." He put the car in Park and killed the engine before getting out and stalking toward the house.

Danielle frowned, then unbuckled quickly, getting out of the car and pushing the sleeves of Joshua's jacket back so she could get Riley's car seat out of the base. Then she headed up the stairs and into the house after him.

"And yet you are trying to hurt yours. So excuse me if I'm not making all the connections."

"I'm not trying to hurt my family," he said, turning around, pushing his hand through his blond hair. His blue eyes glittered, his jaw suddenly looking sharper, his cheekbones more hollow. "What I want is for them to leave well enough alone. My father doesn't understand. He thinks all I need is to find somebody to love again and I'm going to be fixed. But there is no fixing this. There's no fixing me. I don't want it. And yeah, maybe this scheme is over the top, but don't you think putting an ad in the paper looking for a wife for your son is over the top too? I'm not giving him back anything he didn't dish out."

"Maybe you could talk to him."

"You think I haven't talked to him? You think this was my first resort? You're wrong about that. I tried reasonable discourse, but you can't reason with an unreasonable man."

"Yeah," Danielle said, picking at the edge of her thumbnail. "He seemed like a real monster. What with the clear devotion to your mother, the fact that he raised all of you, that he supported you well enough that you could live in that house all your life and then go off to become more successful than he was."

She set the car seat down on the couch and unbuckled it, lifting Riley into her arms and heading toward the stairs.

"We didn't have anything when I was growing up," he said, his tone flat and strange.

Danielle swallowed hard, lifting her hand to cradle Riley's soft head. "I'm sorry. But unless you were homeless or were left alone while one of your parents went to work all day—and I mean *alone*, not with siblings—then we might have different definitions of nothing."

"Fine," he said. "We weren't that poor. But we didn't have anything extra, and there was definitely nothing to do around here but get into trouble when you didn't have money."

She blinked. "What kind of trouble?"

"The usual kind. Go out to the woods, get messed up, have sex."

"Last I checked, condoms and drugs cost money."

She held on to Riley a little bit tighter. "Pretty sure you could have bought a movie ticket."

He lifted his shoulder. "Look, we pooled our money. We did what we did. Didn't worry about the future, didn't worry about anything."

"What changed?" Because obviously something had. He hadn't stayed here. He hadn't stayed aimless.

"One day I looked up and realized this was all I would ever have unless I changed something. Let me tell you, that's pretty sobering. A future of farming, barely making it, barely scraping by? That's what my dad had. And I hated it. I drank in the woods every night with my friends to avoid that reality. I didn't want to have my dad's life. So I made some changes. Not really soon enough to improve my grades or get myself a full scholarship, but I ended up moving to Seattle and getting myself an entry-level job with a PR firm."

"You just moved? You didn't know anybody?"

"No. I didn't know anyone. But I met people. And, it turned out, I was good at meeting people. Which was interesting because you don't meet very many new people in a small town that you've lived in your entire life. But in Seattle, no one knew me. No one knew who my father was, and no one had expectations for me. I was judged entirely on my own merit, and I could completely rewrite who I was. Not just some small-town deadbeat, but a young, bright kid who had a future in front of him."

The way he told that story, the very idea of it, was tantalizing to Danielle. The idea of starting over. Having a clean slate. Of course, with a baby in tow, a change like that would be much more difficult. But her association with Joshua would allow her to make it happen.

It was…shocking to realize he'd had to start over once. Incredibly encouraging, even though she was feeling annoyed with him at the moment.

She leaned forward and absently pressed a kiss to Riley's head. "That must've been incredible. And scary."

"The only scary thing was the idea of going back to where I came from without changing anything. So I didn't allow that to happen. I worked harder than everybody else. I set goals and I met them. And then I met Shannon."

Something ugly twisted inside of Danielle's stomach the moment he said the other woman's name. For the life of her she couldn't figure out why. She felt… curious. But in a desperate way. Like she needed to know everything about this other person. This person who had once shared Joshua's life. This person who had undoubtedly made him the man standing in front of her. If she didn't know about this woman, then she would never understand him.

"What, then? Who was Shannon?" Her desperation was evident in her words, and she didn't bother hiding it.

"She was my girlfriend. For four years, while I was getting established in Seattle. We lived together. I was going to ask her to marry me."

He looked away from her then, something in his blue eyes turning distant. "Then she found out she was pregnant, and I figured I could skip the elaborate proposal and move straight to the wedding."

She knew him well enough to know this story

wasn't headed toward a happy ending. He didn't have a wife. He didn't have a child. In fact, she was willing to bet he'd never had a child. Based on the way he interacted with Riley. Or rather, the very practiced way he avoided interacting with Riley.

"That didn't happen," she said, because she didn't know what else to say, and part of her wanted to spare him having to tell the rest of the story. But, also, part of her needed to know.

"She wanted to plan the wedding. She wanted to wait until after the baby was born. You know, wedding dress sizes and stuff like that. So I agreed. She miscarried late, Danielle. Almost five months. It was…the most physically harrowing thing I've ever watched anyone go through. But the recovery was worse. And I didn't know what to do. So I went back to work. We had a nice apartment, we had a view of the city, and if I worked, she didn't have to. I could support her, I could buy her things. I could do my best to make her happy, keep her focused on the wedding."

He had moved so quickly through the devastating, painful revelation of his lost baby that she barely had time to process it. But she also realized he had to tell the story this way. There was no point lingering on the details. It was simple fact. He had been with a woman he loved very much. He had intended to marry her, had been expecting a child with her. And they had lost the baby.

She held on a little bit more tightly to Riley.

"She kept getting worse. Emotionally. She moved into a different bedroom, then she didn't get out of bed. She had a lot of pain. At first, I didn't question it, because it seemed reasonable that she'd need pain medication after what she went through. But then she kept taking it. And I wondered if that was okay. We had a fight about it. She said it wasn't right for me to question her pain—physical or otherwise—when all I did was work. And you know... I thought she was probably right. So I let it go. For a year, I let it go. And then I found out the situation with the prescription drugs was worse than I realized. But when I confronted Shannon, she just got angry."

It was so strange for Danielle to imagine what he was telling her. This whole other life he'd had. In a city where he had lived with a woman and loved her. Where he had dreamed of having a family. Of having a child. Where he had buried himself in work to avoid dealing with the pain of loss, while the woman he loved lost herself in a different way.

The tale seemed so far removed from the man he was now. From this place, from that hard set to his jaw, that sharp glitter in his eye, the way he held his shoulders straight. She couldn't imagine this man feeling at a loss. Feeling helpless.

"She got involved with another man, someone I worked with. Maybe it started before she left me, but I'm not entirely sure. All I know is she wasn't sleeping with me at the time, so even if she was with him before she moved out, it hardly felt like cheating. And anyway, the affair wasn't really the important part. That guy was into recreational drug use. It's how he functioned. And he made it all available to her."

"That's...that's awful, Joshua. I know how bad that stuff can be. I've seen it."

He shook his head. "Do you have any idea what it's like? To have somebody come into your life who's beautiful, happy, and to watch her leave your life as something else entirely. Broken, an addict. I ruined her."

Danielle took a step back, feeling as though she had been struck by the impact of his words. "No, you didn't. It was drugs. It was…"

"I wasn't there for her. I didn't know how to be. I didn't like hard things, Danielle. I never did. I didn't want to stay in Copper Ridge and work the land—I didn't want to deal with a lifetime of scraping by, because it was too hard."

"Right. You're so lazy that you moved to Seattle and started from scratch and worked your way to the highest ranks of the company? I don't buy that."

"There's reward in that kind of work, though. And you don't have to deal with your life when it gets bad. You just go work more. And you can tell yourself it's fine because you're making more money. Because you're making your life easier, life for the other person easier, even while you let them sit on the couch slowly dying, waiting for you to help them. I convinced myself that what I was doing was important. It was the worst kind of narcissism, Danielle, and I'm not going to excuse it."

"But that was… It was a unique circumstance. And you're different. And…it's not like every future relationship…"

"And here's the problem. You don't know me. You don't even like me and yet you're trying to fix this. You're trying to convince me I should give relationships another try. It's your first instinct, and you don't even actually care. My father can't stop any more than you could stop yourself just now. So I did this." He gestured between the two of them. "I did this because he escalated it all the way to putting an ad in the paper. Because he won't listen to me. Because he knows my ex is a junkie somewhere living on the damned street, and that I feel responsible for that, and still he wants me to live his life. This life here, where he's never made a single mistake or let anyone down."

Danielle had no idea what to say to that. She imagined that his dad had made mistakes. But what did she know? She only knew about absentee fathers and mothers who treated their children like afterthoughts.

Her arms were starting to ache. Her chest ached too. All of her ached.

"I'm going to take Riley up to bed," she said, turning and heading up the stairs.

She didn't look back, but she could hear the heavy footfalls behind her, and she knew he was following her. Even if she didn't quite understand why.

She walked into her bedroom, and she left the door open. She crossed the space and set Riley down in the crib. He shifted for a moment, stretching his arms up above his head and kicking his feet out. But he didn't wake up. She was sweaty from having his warm little body pressed against her chest, but she was grateful for that feeling now. Thinking about Joshua and his loss made her feel especially grateful.

Joshua was standing in the doorway, looking at her. "Did you still want to argue with me?"

She shook her head. "I never wanted to argue with you."

She went to walk past him, but his big body blocked her path. She took a step toward him, and he refused to move, his blue eyes looking straight into hers.

"You seemed like you wanted to argue," he responded.

"No," she said, reaching up to press her hand against him, to push him out of the way. "I just wanted an explanation."

The moment her hand made contact with his shoulder, something raced through her. Something electric. Thrilling. Something that reached back to that feeling, that tightening low in her stomach when he'd first mentioned Shannon.

The two feelings were connected.

Jealousy. That was what she felt. Attraction. That was what this was.

She looked up, his chin in her line of sight. She saw a dusting of golden whiskers, and they looked prickly. His chin looked strong. The two things in combination—the strength and the prickliness—made her want to reach out and touch him, to test both of those hypotheses and see if either was true.

Touching him was craziness. She knew it was. So she curled her fingers into a fist and lowered her hand back down to her side.

"Tell me," he said, his voice rough. "After going through what you did, being pregnant. Being abandoned... You don't want to jump right back into relationships, do you?"

He didn't know the situation. And he didn't know it because she had purposefully kept it from him. Still, because of the circumstances surrounding Riley's birth, because of the way her mother had always conducted relationships with men, because of the way they had always ended, Danielle wanted to avoid romantic entanglements.

So she could find an honest answer in there somewhere.

"I don't want to jump into anything," she said, keeping her voice even. "But there's a difference between being cautious and saying never."

"Is there?"

He had dipped his head slightly, and he seemed to loom over her, to fill her vision, to fill her senses. When she breathed in, the air was scented with him. When she felt warm, the warmth was from his body.

Her lips suddenly felt dry, and she licked them. Then became more aware of them than she'd ever been in her entire life. They felt…obvious. Needy.

She was afraid she knew exactly what they were needy for.

His mouth. His kiss.

The taste of him. The feel of him.

She wondered if he was thinking of their kiss too. Of course, for him, a kiss was probably a commonplace event.

For her, it had been singular.

"You can't honestly say you want to spend the rest of your life alone?"

"I'm only alone when I want to be," he said, his voice husky. "There's a big difference between wanting to share your life with somebody and wanting to share your bed sometimes." He tilted his head to the side. "Tell me. Have you shared your bed with anyone since you were with him?"

She shook her head, words, explanations, getting stuck in her throat. But before she knew it, she couldn't speak anyway, because he had closed the distance between them and claimed her mouth with his.

Six

He was hell bound, that much was certain. After everything that had happened tonight with his family, after Shannon, his fate had been set in stone. But if it hadn't been, then this kiss would have sealed that fate, padlocked it and flung it right down into the fire.

Danielle was young, she was vulnerable and contractually she was at his mercy to a certain degree. Kissing her, wanting to do more with her, was taking being an asshole to extremes.

Right now, he didn't care.

If this was hell, he was happy to hang out for a while. If only he could keep kissing her, if only he could keep tasting her.

She held still against his body for a moment before angling her head, wrapping her arms around his neck, sliding her fingers through his hair and cupping the back of his head as if she was intent on holding him against her mouth.

As if she was concerned he might break the kiss. As if he was capable of that.

Sanity and reasonable decision making had exited the building the moment he had closed the distance between them. It wasn't coming back anytime soon. Not as long as she continued to make those sweet, kittenish noises. Not as long as she continued to stroke her tongue against his—tentatively at first and then with much more boldness.

He gripped the edge of the doorjamb, backing her against the frame, pressing his body against hers. He was hard, and he knew she would feel just how much he wanted her.

He slipped his hands around her waist, then down her ass to the hem of her dress. He shoved it upward, completely void of any sort of finesse. Void of anything beyond the need and desperation screaming inside of him to be inside her. To be buried so deep he wouldn't remember anything.

Not why he knew her. Why she was here. Not what had happened at his parents' house tonight. Not the horrific, unending sadness that had happened in his beautiful high-rise apartment overlooking the city he'd thought of as his. The penthouse that should have kept him above the struggle and insulated him from hardship.

Yeah, he didn't want to think about any of it.

He didn't want to think of anything but the way Danielle tasted. How soft her skin was to the touch.

Why the hell some skinny, bedraggled urchin had

suddenly managed to light a fire inside of him was beyond him.

He didn't really care about the rationale right now. No. He just wanted to be burned.

He moved his hands around, then dipped one between her legs, rubbing his thumb against the silken fabric of her panties. She gasped, arching against him, wrenching her mouth away from his and letting her head fall back against the door frame.

That was an invitation to go further. He shifted his stance, drawing his hand upward and then down beneath the waistband of her underwear. He made contact with slick, damp skin that spoke of her desire for him. He had to clench his teeth to keep from embarrassing himself then and there.

He couldn't remember the last time a woman had affected him like this, if ever. When a simple touch, the promise of release, had pushed him so close to the edge.

When so little had felt like so much.

He stroked her, centering his attention on her clit. Her eyes flew open wide as if he had discovered something completely new. As if she was discovering something completely new. And that did things to him. Things it shouldn't do. Mattered in ways it shouldn't.

Because this shouldn't matter and neither should she.

He pressed his thumb against her chin, leaned forward and captured her open mouth with his.

"I have to have you," he said, the words rough, unpracticed, definitely not the way he usually propositioned a woman.

His words seemed to shock her. Like she had made contact with a naked wire. She went stiff in his arms, and then she pulled away, her eyes wide. "What are we doing?"

She was being utterly sincere, the words unsteady, her expression one of complete surprise and even… fear.

"I'm pretty sure we were about to make love," he said, using a more gentle terminology than he normally would have because of that strange vulnerability lurking in her eyes.

She shook her head, wiggling out of his hold and moving away from the door, backing toward the crib. "We can't do that. We can't." She pressed her hand against her cheek, and she looked so much like a stereotypical distressed female from some 1950s comic that he would have laughed if she hadn't successfully made him feel like he would be the villain in that piece. "It would be… It would be wrong."

"Why exactly?"

"Because. You're paying me to be here. You're paying me to play the part of your fiancée, and if things get physical between us, then I don't understand exactly what separates me from a prostitute."

"I'm not paying you for sex," he said. "I'm paying you to pretend to be my fiancée. I want you. And that's entirely separate from what we're doing here."

She shook her head, her eyes glistening. "Not to me. I already feel horrible. Like the worst person ever, after what I did to your family. After the way we tricked them tonight. After the way we will continue to trick them. I can't add sex to this situation. I have to walk away from this, Joshua. I have to walk away and not feel like I lost myself. I can't face the idea that I might finally sort out the money, where I'm going to live, how I'll survive…and lose the only thing I've always had. Myself. I just can't."

He had never begged a woman in his life, but he realized right then that he was on the verge of begging her to agree that it would feel good enough for whatever consequences to be damned. But as he looked behind her at the crib—the crib with the woman's baby in it, for heaven's sake—he realized the argument wasn't going to work with her.

She had been badly used, and though she had never really given him details, the evidence was obvious. She was alone. She had been abandoned at her most vulnerable. For her, the deepest consequences of sex were not hypothetical.

Though, they weren't for him either. And he was a stickler for safe sex, so there was that. Still, he couldn't blame her for not trusting him. And he should want nothing more than to find a woman who was less complicated. One who didn't have all the baggage that Danielle carried.

Still, he wanted to beg.

But he didn't.

"Sex isn't that big of a deal for me," he said. "If you're not into it, that's fine."

She nodded, the gesture jerky. "Good. That's probably another reason we shouldn't."

"I'm going to start interviewing nannies tomorrow," he said, abruptly changing the subject, because if he didn't, he would haul her back into his arms and finish what he had started.

"Okay," she said, looking shell-shocked.

"You'll have a little bit more freedom then. And we can go out riding."

She blinked. "Why? I just turned you down. Why do you want to do anything for me?"

"I already told you. None of this is a trade for sex. You turning me down doesn't change my intentions."

She frowned. "I don't understand." She looked down, picking at her thumbnail. "Everything has a price. There's no reason for you to do something for me when you're not looking for something in return."

"Not everything in life is a transaction, Danielle."

"I suppose it's not when you care about somebody." She tilted her head to the side. "But nobody's ever really cared about me."

If he hadn't already felt like an ass, then her words would have done it. Because his family did care about him. His life had been filled with people doing things for him just because they wanted to give him something. They'd had no expectation of receiving anything in return.

But after Shannon, something had changed inside of him. He wanted to hold everybody at arm's length. Explaining himself felt impossible.

He hadn't wanted to give to anyone, connect with anyone, in a long time. But for some reason, he wanted to connect with Danielle. Wanted to give to that fragile, sweet girl.

It wasn't altruistic. Not really. She had so little that it was easy to step in and do something life altering. She didn't understand the smallest gesture of kindness, which meant the smallest gesture was enough.

"Tomorrow the interview process starts. I assume you want input?"

"Do I want input over who is going to be watching my baby? Yeah. That would be good."

She reached up, absently touching her lips, then lowered her hand quickly, wiggling her fingers slightly. "Good night," she said, the words coming out in a rush.

"Good night," he said, his voice hard. He turned, closing the door resolutely behind him, because if he didn't, he couldn't be responsible for what he might do.

He was going to leave her alone. He was going to do something nice for her. As if that would do something for his tarnished soul.

Well, maybe it wouldn't. But maybe it would do something for her. And for some reason, that mattered.

Maybe that meant he wasn't too far gone after all.

Danielle had never interviewed anyone who was going to work for her. She had interviewed for several jobs herself, but she had never been on the reverse side. It was strange and infused her with an inordinate sense of power.

Which was nice, considering she rarely felt powerful.

Certainly not the other night when Joshua had kissed her. Then she had felt weak as a kitten. Ready to lie down and give him whatever he wanted.

Except she hadn't. She had said no. She was proud of herself for that, even while she mourned the loss of whatever pleasure she might have found with him.

It wasn't about pleasure. It was about pride.

Pride and self-preservation. What she had said to

him had been true. If she walked away from this situation completely broken, unable to extricate herself from him, from his life, because she had allowed herself to get tangled up in ways she hadn't anticipated, then she would never forgive herself. If she had finally made her life easier in all the ways she'd always dreamed of, only to snare herself in a trap she knew would end in pain…

She would judge herself harshly for that.

Whatever she wanted to tell herself about Joshua—he was a tool, he didn't deserve the wonderful family he had—she was starting to feel things for him. Things she really couldn't afford to feel.

That story about his girlfriend had hit her hard and deep. Hit her in a place she normally kept well protected.

Dammit.

She took a deep breath and looked over at the new nanny, Janine, who had just started today, and who was going to watch Riley while Joshua and Danielle went for a ride.

She was nervous. Unsteady about leaving Riley for the first time in a while. Necessity had meant she'd had to leave him when she was working at the grocery store. Still, this felt different. Because it wasn't necessary. It made her feel guilty. Because she was leaving him to do something for herself.

She shook her head. Her reaction was ridiculous. But she supposed it was preferable to how her mother had operated. Which was to never think about her children at all. Her neglect of Danielle hadn't come close to her disinterest in her youngest child. Danielle supposed that by the time Riley was born, her mother had been fully burned-out. Had exhausted whatever maternal instinct she'd possessed.

Danielle shook her head. Then took a deep breath and turned to face Janine. "He should nap most of the time we're gone. And even if he wakes up, he's usually really happy."

Janine smiled. "He's just a baby. I've watched a lot of babies. Not that he isn't special," she said, as though she were trying to cover up some faux pas. "I just mean, I'm confident that I can handle him."

Danielle took a deep breath and nodded. Then Joshua came into the room and the breath she had just drawn into her lungs rushed out.

He was wearing a dark blue button-down shirt and jeans, paired with a white cowboy hat that made him look like the hero in an old Western movie.

Do not get that stupid. He might be a hero, but he's not your hero.

No. Girls like her didn't get heroes. They had to be their own heroes. And that was fine. Honestly, it was.

If only she could tell her heart that. Her stupid heart, which was beating out of control.

It was far too easy to remember what it had been like to kiss him. To remember what it had felt like when his stubble-covered cheek scraped against hers. How sexy it had felt. How intoxicating it had been to touch a man like that. To experience the differences between men and women for the first time.

It was dangerous, was what it was. She had opened a door she had never intended to open, and now it was hard to close.

She shook her hands out, then balled them into

fists, trying to banish the jitters that were racing through her veins.

"Are you ready?" he asked.

His eyes met hers and all she could think was how incredible it was that his eyes matched his shirt. They were a deep, perfect shade of navy.

There was something wrong with her. She had never been this stupid around a man before.

"Yes," she said, the answer coming out more as a squeak than an actual word. "I'm ready."

The corner of his mouth lifted into a lopsided grin. "You don't have to be nervous. I'll be gentle with you."

She nearly choked. "Good to know. But I'm more worried about the horse being gentle with me."

"She will be. Promise. I've never taught a girl how to ride before, but I'm pretty confident I can teach you."

His words ricocheted around inside of her, reaching the level of double entendre. Which wasn't fair. That wasn't how he'd meant it.

Or maybe it was.

He hadn't been shy about letting her know exactly what he wanted from her that night. He had put his hand between her legs. Touched her where no other man ever had. He'd made her see stars, tracked sparks over her skin.

It was understandable for her to be affected by the experience. But like he'd said, sex didn't really matter to him. It wasn't a big deal. So why he would be thinking of it now was beyond her. He had probably forgotten already. Probably that kiss had become an indistinct blur in his mind, mixed with all his other sexual encounters.

There were no other encounters for her. So there

he was in her mind, and in front of her, far too sharp and far too clear.

"I'm ready," she said, the words rushed. "Totally ready."

"Great," he said. "Let's go."

Taking Danielle out riding was submitting himself to a particular kind of torture, that was for sure. But he was kind of into punishing himself...so he figured it fit his MO.

He hadn't stopped thinking about her since they had kissed—and more—in her bedroom the other night. He had done his best to throw himself into work, to avoid her, but still, he kept waking up with sweat slicked over his skin, his cock hard and dreams of...her lips, her tongue, her scent...lingering in his thoughts.

Normally, the outdoors cleared his mind. Riding his horse along the length of the property was his therapy. Maneuvering her over the rolling hills, along the ridge line of the mountain, the evergreen trees rising behind them in a stately backdrop that left him feeling small within the greater context of the world. Which was something a man like him found refreshing some days.

But not today.

Today, he was obsessing. He was watching Danielle's ass as she rode her horse in front of him, the motion of the horse's gait making him think of what it would look like if the woman was riding him instead of his mare.

He couldn't understand this. Couldn't understand this obsession with her.

She wasn't the kind of sophisticated woman he

tended to favor. In a lot of ways, she reminded him of the kind of girl he used to go for here in town, back when he had been a good-for-nothing teenager spending his free time drinking and getting laid out in the woods.

Back then he had liked hometown girls who wanted the same things he did. A few hours to escape, a little bit of fun.

The problem was, he already knew Danielle didn't want that. She didn't find casual hookups fun. And he didn't have anything to offer beyond a casual hookup.

The other problem was that the feelings he had for her were not casual. If they were, then he wouldn't be obsessing. But he was.

In the couple of weeks since she had come to live with him, she had started to fill out a bit. He could get a sense of her figure, of how she would look if she were thriving rather than simply surviving. She was naturally thin, but there was something elegant about her curves.

But even more appealing than the baser things, like the perky curve of her high breasts and the subtle slope of her hips, was the stubborn set of her jaw. The straight, brittle weight of her shoulders spoke of both strength and fragility.

While there was something unbreakable about her, he worried that if a man ever were to find her weakness, she would do more than just break. She would shatter.

He shook his head. And then he forced himself to look away from her, forced himself to look at the scenery. At the mountain spread out before them, and the ocean gray and fierce behind it.

"Am I doing okay?"

Danielle's question made it impossible to ignore her, and he found himself looking at her ass again. "You haven't fallen off yet," he said, perhaps a bit unkindly.

She snorted, then looked over her shoulder, a challenging light glittering in her brown eyes. "Yet? I'm not going to fall off, Joshua Grayson. It would take a hell of a lot to unseat me."

"Says the woman who was shaking when I helped her mount up earlier."

She surprised him by releasing her hold on the reins with one hand and waving it in the air. "Well, I'm getting the hang of it."

"You're a regular cowgirl," he said.

Suddenly, he wanted that to be true. It was the strangest thing. He wanted her to have this outlet, this freedom. Something more than a small apartment. Something more than struggle.

You're giving her that. That's what this entire bargain is for. Like she said, she's a gold digger, and you're giving her your gold.

Yes, but he wanted to give her more than that.

Just like he had told her the other day, what he wanted to give her wasn't about an exchange. He wanted her to have something for herself. Something for Riley.

Maybe it was a misguided attempt to atone for what he hadn't managed to give Shannon. What he hadn't ever been able to give the child he lost.

He swallowed hard, taking in a deep breath of the sharp pine and salt air, trying to ease the pressure in his chest.

She looked at him again, this time a dazzling smile on her lips. It took all that pressure in his chest and punched a hole right through it. He felt his lungs expand, all of him begin to expand.

He clenched his teeth, grinding them together so hard he was pretty sure his jaw was going to break. "Are you about ready to head back?"

"No. But I'm not sure I'm ever going to be ready to head back. This was... Thank you." She didn't look at him this time. But he had a feeling it was because she was a lot less comfortable with sincere connection than she was with sarcasm.

Well, that made two of them.

"You're welcome," he said, fixing his gaze on the line of trees beside them.

He maneuvered his horse around in front of hers so he could lead the way back down to the barn. They rode on in silence, but he could feel her staring holes into his back.

"Are you looking at my butt, Danielle?"

He heard a sputtering noise behind him. "No."

They rode up to the front of the barn and he dismounted, then walked over to her horse. "Liar. Do you need help?"

She frowned, her brows lowering. "Not from you. You called me a liar."

"Because you were looking at my ass and we both know it." He raised his hand up, extending it to her. "Now let me help you so you don't fall on your pretty face."

"Bah," she said, reaching out to him, her fingers brushing against his, sending an electrical current arcing between them. He chose to ignore it. Because there was no way in the whole damn world that the brush of a woman's fingertips against his should get him hot and bothered.

He grabbed hold of her and helped get her down from the horse, drawing her against him when her feet connected with the ground. And then it was over.

Pretending that this wasn't a long prelude to him kissing her again. Pretending that the last few days hadn't been foreplay. Pretending that every time either of them had thought about the kiss hadn't been easing them closer and closer to the inevitable.

She wanted him, he knew that. It was clear in the way she responded to him. She might have reservations about acting on it, and he had his own. But need was bigger than any of that right now, building between them, impossible to ignore.

He was a breath away from claiming her mouth with his when she shocked him by curving her fingers around his neck and stretching up on her toes.

Her kiss was soft, tentative. A question where his kiss would have been a command. But that made it all the sweeter. The fact that she had come to him. The fact that even though she was still conflicted about all of it, she couldn't resist any longer.

He cupped her cheek, calling on all his restraint— what little there was—to allow her to lead this, to allow her to guide the exploration. There was something so unpracticed about that pretty mouth of hers, something untutored about the way her lips skimmed over his. About the almost sweet, soft way her tongue tested his.

What he wanted to do was take it deep. Take it hard. What he wanted to do was grab hold of her hips and press her back against the barn. Push her jeans down her thighs and get his hand back between her gorgeous legs so he could feel all that soft, slick flesh.

What he wanted was to press his cock against her entrance and slide in slowly, savoring the feel of her desire as it washed over him.

But he didn't.

And it was the damned hardest thing he had ever done. To wait. To let her lead. To let her believe she had the control here. Whatever she needed to do so she wouldn't get scared again. If he had to be patient, if he had to take it slow, he could. He would.

If it meant having her.

He had to have her. Had to exorcise the intense demon that had taken residence inside of him, that demanded he take her. Demanded he make her his own.

His horse snickered behind them, shifting her bulk, drawing Danielle's focus back to the present and away from him. Dammit all.

"Let me get them put away," he said.

He was going to do it quickly. And then he was going to get right back to tasting her. He half expected her to run to the house as he removed the tack from the animals and got them brushed down, but she didn't. Instead, she just stood there watching him, her eyes large, her expression one of absolute indecision.

Because she knew.

She knew that if she stayed down here, he wasn't going to leave it at a kiss. He wasn't going to leave it at all.

But he went about his tasks, slowing his movements, forcing himself not to rush. Forcing himself to draw it out. For her torture as well as his. He wanted her to need it, the way that he did.

And yes, he could see she wanted to run. He could also tell she wanted him, she wanted this. She was unbearably curious, even if she was also afraid.

And he was counting on that curiosity to win out.

Finally, she cleared her throat, shifting impatiently. "Are you going to take all day to do that?"

"You have to take good care of your horses, Danielle. I know a city girl like you doesn't understand how that works."

She squinted, then took a step forward, pulling his hat off his head and depositing it on her own. "Bullshit. You're playing with me."

He couldn't hold back the smile. "Not yet. But I plan to."

After that, he hurried a bit. He put the horses back in their paddock, then took hold of Danielle's hand, leading her deeper into the barn, to a ladder that went up to the loft.

"Can I show you something?"

She bit her lip, hesitating. "Why do I have a feeling that it isn't the loft you're going to show me?"

"I'm going to show you the loft. It's just not all I'm going to show you."

She took a step back, worrying her lip with her teeth. He reached out, cupping the back of her head and bringing his mouth down on hers, kissing her the way he had wanted to when she initiated the kiss outside. He didn't have patience anymore. And he wasn't going to let her lead. Not now.

He cupped her face, stroking her cheeks with his thumbs. "This has nothing to do with our agreement.

It has nothing to do with the contract. Nothing to do with the ad or my father or anything other than the fact that I want you. Do you understand?"

She nodded slowly. "Yes," she said, the word coming out a whisper.

Adrenaline shot through him, a strange kind of triumph that came with a kick to the gut right behind it. He wanted her. He knew he didn't deserve her. But he wasn't going to stop himself from having her in spite of that.

Then he took her hand and led her up the ladder.

Seven

Danielle's heart was pounding in her ears. It was all she could hear. The sound of her own heart beating as she climbed the rungs that led up to the loft.

It was different than she had imagined. It was clean. There was a haystack in one corner, but beyond that the floor was immaculate, every item stored and organized with precision. Which, knowing Joshua like she now did, wasn't too much of a surprise.

That made her smile, just a little. She did know him. In some ways, she felt like she knew him better than she knew anyone.

She wasn't sure what that said about her other relationships. For a while, she'd had friends, but they'd disappeared when she'd become consumed with caring for her pregnant mother and working as much as possible at the grocery store. And then no one had come back when Danielle ended up with full care of Riley.

In some ways, she didn't blame them. Life was hard enough without dealing with a friend who was juggling all of that. But just because she understood didn't mean she wasn't lonely.

She looked at Joshua, their eyes connecting. He had shared his past with her. But she was keeping something big from him. Even while she was prepared to give him her body, she was holding back secrets.

She took a breath, opening her mouth to speak, but something in his blue gaze stopped the words before they could form. Something sharp, predatory. Something that made her feel like she was the center of the world, or at least the center of his world.

It was intoxicating. She'd never experienced it before.

She wanted more, all of it. Wherever it would lead.

And that was scary. Scarier than agreeing to do something she had never done before. Because she finally understood. Understood why her mother had traded her sanity, and her self-worth, for that moment when a man looked at you like you were his everything.

Danielle had spent so long being nothing to anyone. Nothing but a burden. Now, feeling like the solution rather than the problem was powerful, heady. She knew she couldn't turn back now no matter what.

Even if sanity tried to prevail, she would shove it aside. Because she needed this. Needed this balm for all the wounds that ran so deep inside of her.

Joshua walked across the immaculate space and opened up a cabinet. There were blankets inside, thick, woolen ones with geometric designs on them. He pulled out two and spread one on the ground.

She bit her lip, fighting a rising tide of hysteria, fighting a giggle that was climbing its way up her throat.

"I know this isn't exactly a fancy hotel suite."

She forced a smile. "It works for me."

He set the other blanket down on the end of the first one, still folded, then he reached out and took her hand, drawing her to him. He curved his fingers around her wrist, lifting her arm up, then shifted his hold, lacing his fingers through hers and dipping his head, pressing his lips to her own.

Her heart was still pounding that same, steady beat, and she was certain he must be able to hear it. Must be aware of just how he was affecting her.

There were all sorts of things she should tell him. About Riley's mother. About this being her first time.

But she didn't have the words.

She had her heartbeat. The way her limbs trembled. She could let him see that her eyes were filling with tears, and no matter how fiercely she blinked, they never quite went away.

She was good at manipulating conversation. At giving answers that walked the line between fact and fiction.

Her body could only tell the truth.

She hoped he could see it. That he understood. Later, they would talk. Later, there would be honesty between them. Because he would have questions. God knew. But for now, she would let the way her finger-tips trailed down his back—uncertain and tentative—

the way she peppered kisses along his jaw—clumsy and broken—say everything she couldn't.

"It doesn't need to be fancy," she said, her voice sounding thick even to her own ears.

"Maybe it should be," he said, his voice rough. "But if I was going to take you back to my bedroom, I expect I would have to wait until tonight. And I don't want to wait."

She shook her head. "It doesn't have to be fancy. It just has to be now. And it has to be you."

He drew his head back, inhaling sharply. And then he cupped her cheek and consumed her. His kiss was heat and fire, sparking against the dry, neglected things inside her and raging out of control.

She slid her hands up his arms, hanging on to his strong shoulders, using his steadiness to hold her fast even as her legs turned weak.

He lifted her up against him, then swept his arm beneath her legs, cradling her against his chest like she was a child. Then he set her down gently on the blanket, continuing to kiss her as he did so.

She was overwhelmed. Overwhelmed by the intensity of his gaze, by his focus. Overwhelmed by his closeness, his scent.

He was everywhere. His hands on her body, his face filling her vision.

She had spent the past few months caring for her half brother, pouring everything she had onto one little person she loved more than anything in the entire world. But in doing so, she had left herself empty. She had been giving continually, opening a vein and bleeding whenever necessary, and taking nothing in to refill herself.

But this… This was more than she had ever had. More than she'd ever thought she could have. Being the focus of a man's attention. Of his need.

This was a different kind of need than that of a child. Because it wasn't entirely selfish. Joshua's need gave her something in return; it compelled him to be close. Compelled him to kiss her, to skim his hands over her body, teasing and tormenting her with the promise of a pleasure she had never experienced.

Before she could think her actions through, she was pushing her fingertips beneath the hem of his shirt, his hard, flat stomach hot to the touch. And then it didn't matter what she had done before or what she hadn't done. Didn't matter that she was a virgin and this was an entirely new experience.

Need replaced everything except being skin to skin with him. Having nothing between them.

Suddenly, the years of feeling isolated, alone, cold and separate were simply too much. She needed his body over hers, his body inside hers. Whatever happened after that, whatever happened in the end, right now she couldn't care.

Because her desire outweighed the consequences. A wild, desperate thing starving to be fed. With his touch. With his possession.

She pushed his shirt up, and he helped her shrug it over his head. Her throat dried, her mouth opening slightly as she looked at him. His shoulders were broad, his chest well-defined and muscular, pale hair spreading over those glorious muscles, down his ridged abdomen, disappearing in a thin trail beneath the waistband of his low-slung jeans.

She had never seen a man who looked like him

before, not in person. And she had never been this close to a man ever. She pressed her palm against his chest, relishing his heat and his hardness beneath her touch. His heart raging out of control, matching the beat of her own.

She parted her thighs and he settled between them. She could feel the hard ridge of his arousal pressing against that place where she was wet and needy for him. She was shocked at how hard he was, even through layers of clothing.

And she lost herself in his kiss, in the way he rocked his hips against hers. This moment, this experience was like everything she had missed growing up. Misspent teenage years when she should have been making out with boys in barns and hoping she didn't get caught. In reality, her mother wouldn't have cared.

This was a reclamation. More than that, it was something completely new. Something she had never even known she could want.

Joshua was something she had never known she could want.

It shouldn't make sense, the two of them. This brilliant businessman in his thirties who owned a ranch and seemed to shun most emotional connections. And her. Poor. In her twenties. Desperately clinging to any connection she could forge because each one was so rare and special.

But somehow they seemed to make sense. Kissing each other. Touching each other. For some reason, he was the only man that made sense.

Maybe it was because he had taught her to ride a horse. Maybe it was because he was giving her and

Riley a ticket out of poverty. Maybe it was because he was handsome. She had a feeling this connection transcended all those things.

As his tongue traced a trail down her neck to the collar of her T-shirt, she was okay with not knowing. She didn't need to give this connection a name. She didn't even want to.

Her breath caught as he pushed her shirt up and over her head, then quickly dispensed with her bra using a skill not even she possessed. Her nipples tightened, and she was painfully aware of them and of the fact that she was a little lackluster in size.

If Joshua noticed, he didn't seem to mind.

Instead, he dipped his head, sucking one tightened bud between his lips. The move was so sudden, so shocking and so damned unexpected that she couldn't stop herself from arching into him, a cry on her lips.

He looked up, the smile on his face so damned cocky she should probably have been irritated. But she wasn't. She just allowed herself to get lost. In his heat. In the fire that flared between them. In the way he used his lips, his teeth and his tongue to draw a map of pleasure over her skin. All the way down to the waistband of her pants. He licked her. Just above the snap on her jeans. Another sensation so deliciously shocking she couldn't hold back the sound of pleasure on her lips.

She pressed her fist against her mouth, trying to keep herself from getting too vocal. From embarrassing herself. From revealing just how inexperienced she was. The noises she was making definitely announced the fact that these sensations were revelatory to her. And that made her feel a touch too vulnerable.

She was so used to holding people at a distance. So used to benign neglect and general apathy creating a shield around her feelings. Her secrets.

But there was no distance here.

And certainly none as he undid the button of her jeans and drew the zipper down slowly. As he pushed the rough denim down her legs, taking her panties with them.

If she had felt vulnerable a moment before, that was nothing compared to now. She felt so fragile. So exposed. And then he reached up, pressing his hand against her leg at the inside of her knee, spreading her wide so he could look his fill.

She wanted to snap her legs together. Wanted to cover up. But she was immobilized. Completely captive to whatever might happen next. She was so desperate to find out, and at the same time desperate to escape it.

Rough fingertips drifted down the tender skin on her inner thigh, brushing perilously close to her damp, needy flesh. And then he was there. His touch in no way gentle or tentative as he pressed his hand against her, the heel of his palm putting firm pressure on her clit before he pressed his fingers down and spread her wide.

He made his intentions clear as he lowered his head, tasting her deeply. She lifted her hips, a sharp sound on her lips, one she didn't even bother to hold back. He shifted his hold, gripping her hips, holding her just wide enough for his broad shoulders to fit right there, his sensual assault merciless.

Tension knotted her stomach like a fist, tighter and tighter with each pass of his tongue. Then he pressed his thumb against her clit at the same time as he flicked his tongue against that sensitive bundle of nerves. She grabbed hold of him, her fingernails digging into his back.

He drew his thumb down her crease, teasing the entrance of her body. She rocked her hips with the motion, desperate for something. Feeling suddenly empty and achy and needy in ways she never had before.

He rotated his hand, pressing his middle finger deep inside of her, and she gasped at the foreign invasion. But any discomfort passed quickly as her body grew wetter beneath the ministrations of his tongue. By the time he added a second finger, it slipped in easily.

He quickened his pace, and it felt like there was an earthquake starting inside her. A low, slow pull at her core that spread outward, her limbs trembling as the pressure at her center continued to mount.

His thumb joined with his tongue as he continued to pump his fingers inside her, and it was that added pressure that finally broke her. She was shaken. Rattled completely. The magnitude of measurable aftershocks rocking her long after the primary force had passed.

He moved into a sitting position, undoing his belt and the button on his jeans. Then he stood for a moment, drawing the zipper down slowly and pushing the denim down his muscular thighs.

She had never seen a naked man in person before, and the stark, thick evidence of his arousal standing out from his body was a clear reminder that they weren't finished, no matter how wrung out and replete she felt.

Except, even though she felt satisfied, limp from the intensity of her release, she did want more. Because there was more to have. Because she wanted to be close to him. Because she wanted to give him even an ounce of the satisfaction that she had just experienced.

He knelt back down, pulling his jeans closer and taking his wallet out of his back pocket. He produced a condom packet and she gave thanks for his presence of mind. She knew better than to have unprotected sex with someone. For myriad reasons. But still, she wondered if she would have remembered if he had not.

Thank God one of them was thinking. She was too overwhelmed. Too swamped by the release that had overtaken her, and by the enormity of what was about to happen. When he positioned himself at the entrance of her body and pressed the thick head of his cock against her, she gasped in shock.

It *hurt*. Dear God it hurt. His fingers hadn't prepared her for the rest of him.

He noticed her hesitation and slowed his movements, pressing inside her inch by excruciating inch. She held on to his shoulders, closing her eyes and burying her face in his neck as he jerked his hips forward, fully seating himself inside her.

She did her best to breathe through it. But she was in a daze. Joshua was inside her, and she wasn't a virgin anymore. It felt… Well, it didn't feel like losing anything. It felt like gaining something. Gaining a whole lot.

The pain began to recede and she looked up, at his face, at the extreme concentration there, at the set of his jaw, the veins in his neck standing out.

"Are you okay?" he asked, his voice strangled.

She nodded wordlessly, then flexed her hips experimentally.

He groaned, lowering his head, pressing his forehead against hers, before kissing her. Then he began to move.

Soon, that same sweet tension began to build again in her stomach, need replacing the bone-deep satisfaction that she had only just experienced. She didn't know how it was possible to be back in that needy place only moments after feeling fulfilled.

But she was. And then she was lost in the rhythm, lost in the feeling of his thick length stroking in and out of her, all of the pain gone now, only pleasure remaining. It was so foreign, so singular and unlike anything she had ever experienced. And she loved it. Reveled in it.

But even more than her own pleasure, she reveled in watching his unraveling.

Because he had pulled her apart in a million astounding ways, and she didn't know if she could ever be reassembled. So it was only fair that he lost himself too. Only fair that she be his undoing in some way.

Sweat beaded on his brow, trickled down his back. She reveled in the feel of it beneath her fingertips. In the obvious evidence of what this did to him.

His breathing became more labored, his muscles shaking as each thrust became less gentle. As he began to pound into her. And just as he needed to go harder, go faster, so did she.

Her own pleasure wound around his, inextricably linked.

On a harsh growl he buried his face in her neck,

his arms shaking as he thrust into her one last time, slamming into her clit, breaking a wave of pleasure over her body as he found his own release.

He tried to pull away, but she wrapped her arms around him, holding him close. Because the sooner he separated from her body, the sooner they would have to talk. And she wasn't exactly sure she wanted to talk.

But when he lifted his head, his blue eyes glinting in the dim light, she could tell that whether or not she wanted to talk, they were going to.

He rolled away from her, pushing into a sitting position. "Are you going to explain all of this to me? Or are you going to make me guess?"

"What?" She sounded overly innocent, her eyes wider than necessary.

"Danielle, I'm going to ask you a question, and I need you to answer me honestly. Were you a virgin?"

Joshua's blood was still running hot through his veins, arousal still burning beneath the surface of his skin. And he knew the question he had just asked her was probably insane. He could explain her discomfort as pain because she hadn't taken a man to her bed since she'd given birth.

But that wasn't it. It wasn't.

The more credence he gave to his virgin theory, the more everything about her started to make sense. The way she responded to his kiss, the way she acted when he touched her.

Her reaction had been about more than simple attraction, more than pleasure. There had been wonder there. A sense of discovery.

But that meant Riley wasn't her son. And it meant she had been fucking lying to him.

"Well, Joshua, given that this is not a New Testament kind of situation…"

He reached out, grabbing hold of her wrist and tugging her upward, drawing her toward him. "Don't lie to me."

"Why would you think that?" she asked, her words small. Admission enough as far as he was concerned.

"A lot of reasons. But I have had sex with a virgin before. More accurately, Sadie Miller and I took each other's virginity in the woods some eighteen years ago. You don't forget that. And, I grant you, there could be other reasons for the fact that it hurt you, for the fact that you were tight." A flush spread over her skin, her cheeks turning beet red. "But I don't think any of those reasons are the truth. So what's going on? Who is Riley's mother?"

A tear slid down her cheek, her expression mutinous and angry. "I am," she said, her voice trembling. "At least, I might as well be. I should be."

"You didn't give birth to Riley."

She sniffed loudly, another tear sliding down her cheek. "No. I didn't."

"Are you running from somebody? Is there something I need to know?"

"It's not like that. I'm not hiding. I didn't steal him. I have legal custody of Riley. But my situation was problematic. At least, as far as Child Services was concerned. I lost my job because of the babysitting situation and I needed money."

She suddenly looked so incredibly young, so vulnerable… And he felt like the biggest prick on planet Earth.

She had lied to him. She had most definitely led him to believe she was in an entirely different circumstance than she was, and still, he was mostly angry at himself.

Because the picture she was painting was even more desperate than the one he had been led to believe. Because she had been a virgin and he had just roughly dispensed with that.

She had been desperate. Utterly desperate. And had taken this post with him because she hadn't seen another option. Whatever he'd thought of her before, he was forced to revise it, and there was no way that revision didn't include recasting himself as the villain.

"Whose baby is he?"

She swallowed hard, drawing her knees up to her chest, covering her nudity. "Riley is my half brother. My mother showed up at my place about a year ago pregnant and desperate. She needed someone to help her out. When she came to me, she sounded pretty determined to take care of him. She even named him. She told me she would do better for him than she had for me, because she was done with men now and all of that. But she broke her promises. She had the baby, she met somebody else. I didn't know it at first. I didn't realize she was leaving Riley in the apartment alone sometimes while I was at work."

She took a deep, shuddering breath, then continued. "I didn't mess around when I found out. I didn't wait for her to decide to abandon him. I called Child Services. And I got temporary guardianship. My mother left. But then things started to fall apart with the work, and I didn't know how I was going to pay for the apartment... Then I saw your ad."

He swore. "You should have told me."

"Maybe. But I needed the money, Joshua. And I didn't want to do anything to jeopardize your offer. I could tell you were uncomfortable that I brought a baby with me, and now I know why. But, regardless, at the time, I didn't want to do anything that might compromise our arrangement."

He felt like the ass he undoubtedly was. The worst part was, it shone a light on all the bullshit he'd put her through. Regardless of Riley's parentage, she'd been desperate and he'd taken advantage of that. Less so when he'd been keeping his hands to himself. At least then it had been feasible to pretend it was an even exchange.

But now?

Now he'd slept with her and it was impossible to keep pretending.

And frankly, he didn't want to.

He'd been wrestling with this feeling from the moment they'd gone out riding today, or maybe since they'd left his parents' house last week.

But today...when he'd looked at her, seen her smile...noticed the way she'd gained weight after being in a place where she felt secure...

He'd wanted to give her more of that.

He'd wanted to do more good than harm. Had wanted to fix something instead of break it.

It was too late for Shannon. But he could help Danielle. He could make sure she always felt safe. That she and Riley were always protected.

The realization would have made him want to laugh if it didn't all feel too damned grim. Somehow his father's ad had brought him to this place when he'd been determined to teach the old man a lesson.

But Joshua hadn't counted on Danielle.

Hadn't counted on how she would make him feel. That she'd wake something inside him he'd thought had been asleep for good.

It wasn't just chemistry. Wasn't just sex. It was the desire to make her happy. To give her things.

To fix what was broken.

He knew the solution wouldn't come from him personally, but his money could sure as hell fix her problems. And they did have chemistry. The kind that wasn't common. It sure as hell went beyond anything he'd ever experienced before.

"The truth doesn't change anything," she said, lowering her face into her arms, her words muffled. "It doesn't."

He reached out, taking her chin between his thumb and forefinger, tilting her face back up. "It does. Even if it shouldn't. Though, maybe it's not Riley that changes it. Maybe it's just the two of us."

She shook her head. "It doesn't have to change anything."

"Danielle... I can't..."

She lurched forward, grabbing his arm, her eyes wide, her expression wild. "Joshua, please. I need this money. I can't go back to where we were. I'm being held to a harsher standard than his biological mother would be and I can't lose him."

He grabbed her chin again, steadying her face, looking into those glistening brown eyes. "Danielle,

I would never let you lose him. I want to protect you. Both of you."

She tilted her head to the side, her expression growing suspicious. "You...do?"

"I've been thinking. I was thinking this earlier when we were riding, but now, knowing your whole story... I want you and Riley to stay with me."

She blinked. "What?"

"Danielle, I want you to marry me."

Eight

Danielle couldn't process any of this.

She had expected him to be angry. Had expected him to get mad because she'd lied to him.

She hadn't expected a marriage proposal.

At least, she was pretty sure that was what had just happened. "You want to…marry me? For real marry me?"

"Yes," he said, his tone hard, decisive. "You don't feel good about fooling my family—neither do I. You need money and security and, hell, I have both. We have chemistry. I want… I don't want to send you back into the world alone. You don't even know where you're going."

He wasn't wrong. And dammit his offer was tempting. They were both naked, and he was so beautiful, and she wanted to kiss him again. Touch him again.

But more than that, she wanted him to hold her in his arms again.

She wanted to be close to him. Bonded to him.

She wanted—so desperately—to not be alone.

But there had to be a catch.

There was always a catch. He could say whatever he wanted about how all of this wasn't a transaction, how he had taken her riding just to take her riding. But then they'd had sex. And he'd had a condom in his wallet.

So he'd been prepared.

That made her stomach sour.

"Did you plan this?" she asked. "The horse-riding seduction?"

"No, I didn't plan it. I carry a condom because I like to be prepared to have sex. You never know. You can get mad at me for that if you want, but then, we did need one, so it seems a little hypocritical."

"Are you tricking me?" she asked, feeling desperate and panicky. "Is this a trick? Because I don't understand how it benefits you to marry me. To keep Riley and me here. You don't even like Riley, Joshua. You can't stand to be in the same room with him."

"I broke Shannon," he said, his voice hard. "I ruined her. I did that. But I won't break you. I want to fix this."

"You can't slap duct tape and a wedding band on me and call it done," she said, her voice trembling. "I'm not a leaky faucet."

"I didn't say you were. But you need something I have and I… Danielle, I need you." His voice was rough, intense. "I'm not offering you love, but I can be faithful. I was ready to be a husband years ago, that part doesn't faze me. I can take care of you. I can keep you safe. And if I send you out into the world with nothing more than money and something happens to you or Riley, I won't forgive myself. So stay with me. Marry me."

It was crazy. He was crazy.

And she was crazy for sitting there fully considering everything he was offering.

But she was imagining a life here. For her, for Riley. On Joshua's ranch, in his beautiful house.

And she knew—she absolutely knew—that what she had felt physically with him, what had just happened, was a huge reason why they were having this conversation at all.

More than the pleasure, the closeness drew her in. Actually, that was the most dangerous part of his offer. The idea that she could go through life with somebody by her side. To raise Riley with this strong man backing her up.

Something clenched tight in her chest, working its way down to her stomach. Riley. He could have a father figure. She didn't know exactly what function Joshua would play in his life. Joshua had trouble with the baby right now. But she knew Joshua was a good man, and that he would never freeze Riley out intentionally. Not when he was offering them a life together.

"What about Riley?" she asked, her throat dry. She swallowed hard. She had to know what he was thinking.

"What about him?"

"This offer extends to him too. And I mean...not

just protection and support. But would you… Would you teach him things? Would your father be a grandfather to him? Would your brothers be uncles and your sister be an aunt? I understand that having a child around might be hard for you, after you lost your chance at being a father. And I understand you want to fix me, my situation. And it's tempting, Joshua, it's very tempting. But I need to know if that support, if all of that, extends to Riley."

Joshua's face looked as though it had been cast in stone. "I'm not sure if I would be a good father, Danielle. I was going to be a father, and so I was going to figure it out—how to do that, how to be that. I suppose I can apply that same intent here. I can't guarantee that I'll be the best, but I'll try. And you're right. I have my family to back me up. And he has you."

That was it.

That was the reason she couldn't say no. Because if she walked away from Joshua now, Riley would have her. Only her. She loved him, but she was just one person. If she stayed here with Joshua, Riley would have grandparents. Aunts and uncles. Family. People who knew how to be a family. She was doing the very best she could, but her idea of family was somewhere between cold neglectful nightmare and a TV sitcom.

The Grayson family knew—Joshua knew—what it meant to be a family. If she said yes, she could give that to Riley.

She swallowed again, trying to alleviate the scratchy feeling in her throat.

"I guess… I guess I can't really say no to that."

She straightened, still naked, and not even a little bit embarrassed. There were bigger things going on here than the fact that he could see her breasts. "Okay, Joshua. I'll marry you."

Nine

The biggest problem with this sudden change in plan was the fact that Joshua had deliberately set out to make his family dislike Danielle. And now he was marrying her for real.

Of course, the flaw in his original plan was that Danielle *hadn't* been roundly hated by his family. They'd distrusted the whole situation, certainly, but his family was simply too fair, too nice to hate her.

Still, guilt clutched at him, and he knew he was going to have to do something to fix this. Which was why he found himself down at the Gray Bear Construction office rather than working from home. Because he knew Faith and Isaiah would be in, and he needed to have a talk with his siblings.

The office was a newly constructed building fashioned to look like a log cabin. It was down at the edge of town, by where Rona's diner used to be, a former greasy spoon that had been transformed into a series of smaller, hipper shops that were more in line with the interests of Copper Ridge's tourists.

It was a great office space with a prime view of the ocean, but still, Joshua typically preferred to work in the privacy of his own home, secluded in the mountains.

Isaiah did too, which was why it was notable that his brother was in the office today, but he'd had a meeting of some kind, so he'd put on a decent shirt and a pair of nice jeans and gotten his ass out of his hermitage.

Faith, being the bright, sharp creature she was, always came into the office, always dressed in some variation of her personal uniform. Black pants and a black top—a sweater today because of the chilly weather.

"What are you doing here?" Faith asked, her expression scrutinizing.

"I came here to talk to you," he said.

"I'll make coffee." Joshua turned and saw Poppy standing there. Strange, he hadn't noticed. But then, Poppy usually stayed in the background. He couldn't remember running the business without her, but like useful office supplies, you really only noticed them when they didn't work. And Poppy always worked.

"Thanks, Poppy," Faith said.

Isaiah folded his arms over his chest and leaned back in his chair. "What's up?"

"I'm getting married in two weeks."

Faith made a scoffing sound. "To that child you're dating?"

"She's your age," he said. "And yes. Just like I said I was."

"Which begs the question," Isaiah said. "Why are you telling us again?"

"Because. The first time I was lying. Dad put that ad in the paper trying to find a wife for me, and I selected Danielle in order to teach him a lesson. The joke's on me it turns out." Damn was it ever.

"Good God, Joshua. You're such an ass," Faith said, leaning against the wall, her arms folded, mirroring Isaiah's stance. "I knew something was up, but of all the things I suspected, you tricking our mother and father was not one of them."

"What did you suspect?"

"That you were thinking with your... Well. And now I'm back to that conclusion. Because why are you marrying her?"

"I care about her. And believe me when I say she's had it rough."

"You've slept with her?" This question came from Isaiah, and there was absolutely no tact in it. But then, Isaiah himself possessed absolutely no tact. Which was why he handled money and not people.

"Yes," Joshua said.

"She must be good. But I'm not sure that's going to convince either of us you're thinking with your big brain." His brother stood up, not unfolding his arms.

"Well, you're an asshole," Joshua returned. "The sex has nothing to do with it. I can get sex whenever I want."

Faith made a hissing sound. He tossed his younger sister a glance. "You can stop hissing and settle down," he said to her. "You were the one who brought sex into it, I'm just clarifying. You know what I went through with Shannon, what I put Shannon through. If I send Danielle and her baby back out into the world and something happens to them, I'll never forgive myself."

"Well, Joshua, that kind of implies you aren't already living in a perpetual state of self-flagellation," Faith said.

"Do you want to see if it can get worse?"

She shook her head. "No, but marrying some random woman you found through an ad seems like an extreme way to go about searching for atonement. Can't you do some Hail Marys or something?"

"If it were that simple, I would have done it a long time ago." He took a deep breath. "I'm not going to tell Mom and Dad the whole story. But I'm telling you because I need you to be nice about Danielle. However it looked when I brought her by to introduce her to the family… I threw her under the bus, and now I want to drag her back out from under it."

Isaiah shook his head. "You're a contrary son of a bitch."

"Well, usually that's your function. I figured it was my turn."

The door to the office opened and in walked their business partner, Jonathan Bear, who ran the construction side of the firm. He looked around the room, clearly confused by the fact that they were all in residence. "Is there a meeting I didn't know about?"

"Joshua is getting married," Faith said, looking sullen.

"Congratulations," Jonathan said, smiling, which was unusual for the other man, who was typically pretty taciturn. "I can highly recommend it."

Jonathan had married the pastor's daughter, Hayley Thompson, in a small ceremony recently.

In the past, Jonathan had walked around like he had his own personal storm cloud overhead, and since meeting Hayley, he had most definitely changed. Maybe there was something to that whole marriage thing. Maybe Joshua's idea of atonement wasn't as outrageous as it might have initially seemed.

"There," Joshua said. "Jonathan recommends it. So you two can stop looking at me suspiciously."

Jonathan shrugged and walked through the main area and into the back, toward his office, leaving Joshua alone with his siblings.

Faith tucked her hair behind her ear. "Honestly, whatever you need, whatever you want, I'll help. But I don't want you to get hurt."

"And I appreciate that," he said. "But the thing is, you can only get hurt if there's love involved. I don't love her."

Faith looked wounded by that. "Then what's the point? I'm not trying to argue. I just don't understand."

"Love is not the be-all and end-all, Faith. Sometimes just committing to taking care of somebody else is enough. I loved Shannon, but I still didn't do the right thing for her. I'm older now. And I know what's important. I'm going to keep Danielle safe. I'm going to keep Riley safe. What's more important than that?" He shook his head. "I'm sure Shannon would have rather had that than any expression of love."

"Fine," she said. "I support you. I'm in."

"So you aren't going to be a persnickety brat?"

A small smile quirked her lips upward. "I didn't

say that. I said I would support you. But as a younger sister, I feel the need to remind you that being a persnickety brat is sometimes part of my support."

He shot Isaiah a baleful look. "I suppose you're still going to be an asshole?"

"Obviously."

Joshua smiled then. Because that was the best he was going to get from his siblings. But it was a step toward making sure Danielle felt like she had a place in the family, rather than feeling like an outsider.

And if he wanted that with an intensity that wasn't strictly normal or healthy, he would ignore that. He had never pretended to be normal or healthy. He wasn't going to start now.

Danielle was getting fluttery waiting for Joshua to come home. The anticipation was a strange feeling. It had been a long time since she'd looked forward to someone coming home. She remembered being young, when it was hard to be alone. But she hadn't exactly wished for her mother to come home, because she knew that when her mother arrived, she would be drunk. And Danielle would be tasked with managing her in some way.

That was the story of her life. Not being alone meant taking care of somebody. Being alone meant isolation, but at least she had time to herself.

But Joshua wasn't like that. Being with him didn't mean she had to manage him.

She thought of their time together in the barn, and the memory made her shiver. She had gone to bed in her own room last night, and he hadn't made any move toward her since his proposal. She had a feeling his hesitation had something to do with her inexperience.

But she was ready for him again. Ready for more.

She shook her hands out, feeling jittery. And a little scared.

It was so easy to want him. To dream about him coming home, how she would embrace him, kiss him. And maybe even learn to cook, so she could make him dinner. Learn to do something other than warm up Pop-Tarts.

Although, he liked Pop-Tarts, and so did she.

Maybe they should have Pop-Tarts at their wedding. That was the kind of thing couples did. Incorporate the cute foundations of their relationships into their wedding ceremonies.

She made a small sound that was halfway between a whimper and a growl. She was getting loopy about him. About a guy. Which she had promised herself she would never do. But it was hard *not* to get loopy. He had offered her support, a family for Riley, a house to live in. He had become her lover, and then he had asked to become her husband.

And in those few short moments, her entire vision for the rest of her life had changed. It had become something so much warmer, so much more secure than she had ever imagined it could be. She just wasn't strong enough to reject that vision.

Honestly, she didn't know a woman who would be strong enough. Joshua was hot. And he was nice. Well, sometimes he was kind of a jerk, but mostly, at his core, he was nice and he had wonderful taste in breakfast food.

That seemed like as good a foundation for a marriage as any.

She heard the front door open and shut, and as it slammed, her heart lurched against her breastbone.

Joshua walked in looking so intensely handsome in a light blue button-up shirt, the sleeves pushed up his arms, that she wanted to swoon for the first time in her entire life.

"Do you think they can make a wedding cake out of Pop-Tarts?" She didn't know why that was the first thing that came out of her mouth. Probably, it would have been better if she had said something about how she couldn't wait to tear his clothes off.

But no. She had led with toaster pastry.

"I don't know. But we're getting married in two weeks, so if you can stack Pop-Tarts and call them a cake, I suppose it might save time and money."

"I could probably do that. I promise that's not all I thought about today, but for some reason it's what came out of my mouth."

"How about I keep your mouth busy for a while," he said, his blue gaze getting sharp. He crossed the space between them, wrapping his arm around her waist and drawing her against him. And then he kissed her.

It was so deep, so warm, and she felt so…sheltered. Enveloped completely in his arms, in his strength. Who cared if she was lost in a fantasy right now? It would be the first time. She had never had the luxury of dreaming about men like him, or passion this intense.

It seemed right, only fair, that she have the fantasy. If only for a while. To have a moment where she actually dreamed about a wedding with cake. Where she fantasized about a man walking in the door and kissing her like this, wanting her like this.

"Is Janine here?" he asked, breaking the kiss just long enough to pose the question.

"No," she said, barely managing to answer before he slammed his lips back down on hers.

Then she found herself being lifted and carried from the entryway into the living room, deposited on the couch. And somehow, as he set her down, he managed to raise her shirt up over her head.

She stared at him, dazed, while he divested himself of his own shirt. "You're very good at this," she said. "I assume you've had a lot of practice?"

He lifted an eyebrow, his hands going to his belt buckle. "Is this a conversation you want to have?"

She felt…bemused rather than jealous. "I don't know. I'm just curious."

"I got into a lot of trouble when I was a teenager. I think I mentioned the incident with my virginity in the woods."

She nodded. "You did. And since I lost my virginity in a barn, I suppose I have to reserve judgment."

"Probably. Then I moved to Seattle. And I was even worse, because suddenly I was surrounded by women I hadn't known my whole life."

Danielle nodded gravely. "I can see how that would be an issue."

He smiled. Then finished undoing his belt, button and zipper before shoving his pants down to the floor. He stood in front of her naked, aroused and beautiful.

"Then I got myself into a long-term relationship,

and it turns out I'm good at that. Well, at the being faithful part."

"That's a relief."

"In terms of promiscuity, though, my behavior has been somewhat appalling for the past five years. I have picked up a particular set of skills."

She wrinkled her nose. "I suppose that's something."

"You asked."

She straightened. "And I wanted to know."

He reached behind her back, undoing her bra, pulling it off and throwing it somewhere behind him. "Well, now you do." He pressed his hands against the back of the couch, bracketing her in. "You still want to marry me?"

"I had a very tempting proposal from the UPS man today. He asked me to sign for a package. So I guess you could say it's getting kind of serious."

"I don't think the UPS man makes you feel like this." He captured her mouth with his, and she found herself being pressed into the cushions, sliding to the side, until he'd maneuvered her so they were both lying flat on the couch.

He wrapped his fingers around her wrists, lifting them up over her head as he bent to kiss her neck, her collarbone, to draw one nipple inside his mouth.

She bucked against him, and he shifted, pushing his hand beneath her jeans, under the fabric of her panties, discovering just how wet and ready she was for him.

She rolled her hips upward, moving in time with the rhythm of his strokes, lights beginning to flash behind her eyelids, orgasm barreling down on her at an embarrassingly quick rate.

Danielle sucked in a deep breath, trying her best to hold her climax at bay. Because how embarrassing would it be to come from a kiss? A brief bit of attention to her breast and a quick stroke between the legs?

But then she opened her eyes and met his gaze. His lips curved into a wicked smile as he turned his wrist, sliding one finger deep inside her as he flicked his thumb over her clit.

All she could do then was hold on tight and ride out the explosion. He never looked away from her, and as much as she wanted to, she couldn't look away from him.

It felt too intense, too raw and much too intimate.

But she was trapped in it, drowning in it, and there was nothing she could do to stop it. She just had to surrender.

While she was still recovering from her orgasm, Joshua made quick work of her jeans, flinging them in the same direction her bra had gone.

Then, still looking right at her, he stroked her, over the thin fabric of her panties, the tease against her overly sensitized skin almost too much to handle.

Then he traced the edge of the fabric at the crease of her thigh, dipping one finger beneath her underwear, touching slick flesh.

He hooked his finger around the fabric, pulling her panties off and casting them aside. And here she was, just as she'd been the first time, completely open and vulnerable to him. At his mercy.

It wasn't as though she didn't want that. There was something wonderful about it. Something incredible about the way he lavished attention on her, about being his sole focus.

But she wanted more. She wanted to be… She wanted to be equal to him in some way.

He was practiced. And he had skill. He'd had a lot of lovers. Realistically, she imagined he didn't even know exactly how many.

She didn't have skill. She hadn't been tutored in the art of love by anyone. But she *wanted*.

If desire could equal skill, then she could rival any woman he'd ever been with. Because the depth of her need, the depth of her passion, reached places inside her she hadn't known existed.

She pressed her hands down on the couch cushions, launching herself into a sitting position. His eyes widened, and she reveled in the fact that she had surprised him. She reached out, resting one palm against his chest, luxuriating in the feel of all that heat, that muscle, that masculine hair that tickled her sensitive skin.

"Danielle," he said, his tone filled with warning.

She didn't care about his warnings.

She was going to marry this man. He was going to be her husband. That thought filled her with such a strange sense of elation.

He had all the power. He had the money. He had the beautiful house. What he was giving her…it bordered on charity. If she was ever going to feel like she belonged—like this place was really hers—they needed to be equals in some regard.

She had to give him something too.

And if it started here, then it started here.

She leaned in, cautiously tasting his neck, tracing a line down to his nipple. He jerked beneath her touch, his reaction satisfying her in a way that went well beyond the physical.

He was beautiful, and she reveled in the chance to explore him. To run her fingertips over each well-defined muscle. Over his abs and the hard cut inward just below his hip bone.

But she didn't stop there. No, she wasn't even remotely finished with him.

He had made her shake. He had made her tremble. He had made her lose her mind.

And she was going to return the favor.

She took a deep breath and kissed his stomach. Just one easy thing before she moved on to what she wanted, even though it scared her.

She lifted her head, meeting his gaze as she wrapped her fingers around his cock and squeezed. His eyes glittered like ice on fire, and he said nothing. He just sat there, his jaw held tight, his expression one of absolute concentration.

Then she looked away from his face, bringing her attention to that most masculine part of him. She was hungry for him. There was no other word for it.

She was starving for a taste.

And that hunger overtook everything else.

She flicked her tongue out and tasted him, his skin salty and hot. But the true eroticism was in his response. His head fell back, his breath hissing sharply through his teeth. And he reached out, pressing his hand to her back, spreading his fingers wide at the center of her shoulder blades.

Maybe she didn't have skill. Maybe she didn't know what she was doing. But he liked it. And that made her feel powerful. It made her feel needed.

She slid her hand down his shaft, gripping the base before taking him more deeply into her mouth. His groan sounded torn from him, wild and untamed, and she loved it.

Because Joshua was all about control. Had been from the moment she'd first met him.

That was what all this was, after all. From the ad in the paper to his marriage proposal—all of it was him trying to bend the situation to his will. To bend those around him to his will, to make them see he was right, that his way was the best way.

But right now he was losing control. He was at her mercy. Shaking. Because of her.

And even though she was the one pleasuring him, she felt an immense sense of satisfaction flood her as she continued to taste him. As she continued to make him tremble.

He needed her. He wanted her. After a lifetime of feeling like nobody wanted her at all, this was the most brilliant and beautiful thing she could ever imagine.

She'd heard her friends talk about giving guys blow jobs before. They laughed about it. Or said it was gross. Or said it was a great way to control their boyfriends.

They hadn't said what an incredible thing it was to make a big, strong alpha male sweat and shake. They hadn't said it could make you feel so desired, so beloved. Or that giving someone else pleasure was even better—in some ways—than being on the receiving end of the attention.

She swallowed more of him, and his hand jerked up to her hair, tugging her head back. "Careful," he said, his tone hard and thin.

"Why?"

"You keep doing that and I'm going to come," he said, not bothering to sugarcoat it.

"So what? When you did it for me, that's what I did."

"Yes. But you're a woman. And you can have as many orgasms as I can give you without time off in between. I don't want it to end like this."

She was about to protest, but then he pulled her forward, kissing her hard and deep, stealing not just her ability to speak, but her ability to think of words.

He left her for a moment, retrieving his wallet and the protection in it, making quick work of putting the condom on before he laid her back down on the couch.

"Wait," she said, the word husky, rough. "I want... Can I be on top?"

He drew back, arching one brow. "Since you asked so nicely."

He gripped her hips, reversing their position, bringing her to sit astride him. He was hard beneath her, and she shifted back and forth experimentally, rubbing her slick folds over him before positioning him at the entrance of her body.

She bit her lip, lowering herself onto him, taking it slow, relishing that moment of him filling her so utterly and completely.

"I don't know what I'm doing," she whispered when he was buried fully inside of her.

He reached up, brushing his fingertips over her cheek before lowering his hand to grip both her hips tightly, lift her, then impale her on his hard length again.

"Just do what feels good," he ground out, the words strained.

She rocked her hips, then lifted herself slightly before taking him inside again. She repeated the motion. Again and again. Finding the speed and rhythm that made him gasp and made her moan. Finding just the right angle, just the right pressure, to please them both.

Pleasure began to ripple through her, the now somewhat familiar pressure of impending orgasm building inside her. She rolled her hips, making contact right where she needed it. He grabbed her chin, drawing her head down to kiss her. Deep, wet.

And that was it. She was done.

Pleasure burst behind her eyes, her internal muscles gripping him tight as her orgasm rocked her.

She found herself being rolled onto her back and Joshua began to pound into her, chasing his own release with a raw ferocity that made her whole body feel like it was on fire with passion.

He was undone. Completely. Because of her.

He growled, reaching beneath her to cup her ass, drawing her hard against him, forcing her to meet his every thrust. And that was when he proved himself right. She really could come as many times as he could make her.

She lost it then, shaking and shivering as her second orgasm overtook her already sensitized body.

He lowered his head, his teeth scraping against her collarbone as he froze against her, finding his own release.

He lay against her for a moment, his face buried in her neck, and she sifted her fingers through his hair, a small smile touching her lips as ripples of lingering pleasure continued to fan out through her body.

He looked at her, then brushed his lips gently over hers. She found herself being lifted up, cradled against his chest as he carried her from the couch to the stairs.

"Time for bed," he said, the words husky and rough.

She reached up and touched his face. "Okay."

He carried her to his room, laid her down on the expansive mattress, the blanket decadent and soft beneath her bare skin.

This would be their room. A room they would share.

For some reason, that thought made tears sting her eyes. She had spent so long being alone that the idea of so much closeness was almost overwhelming. But no matter what, she wanted it.

Wanted it so badly it was like a physical hunger.

Joshua joined her on the bed and she was overwhelmed by the urge to simply fold herself into his embrace. To enjoy the closeness.

But then he was naked. And so was she. So the desire for closeness fought with her desire to play with him a little more.

He pressed his hand against her lower back, then slid it down to her butt, squeezing tight. And he smiled.

Something intense and sharp filled her chest. It was almost painful.

Happiness, she realized. She was happy.

She knew in that moment that she never really had been happy before. At least, not without an equally weighty worry to balance it. To warn her that on the other side of the happiness could easily lie tragedy.

But she wasn't thinking of tragedy now. She couldn't.

Joshua filled her vision, and he filled her brain, and for now—just for now—everything in her world felt right.

For a while, she wanted that to be the whole story.

So she blocked out every other thought, every single what-if, and she kissed him again.

When Joshua woke up, the bedroom was dark. There was a woman wrapped around him. And he wasn't entirely sure what had pulled him out of his deep slumber.

Danielle was sleeping peacefully. Her dark hair was wrapped around her face like a spiderweb, and he reached down to push it back. She flinched, pursing her lips and shifting against him, tightening her arms around his waist.

She was exhausted. Probably because he was an animal who had taken her three, maybe four times before they'd finally both fallen asleep.

He looked at her, and the hunger was immediate. Visceral. And he wondered if he was fooling himself pretending, even for a moment, that any of this was for her.

That he had any kind of higher purpose.

He wondered if he had any purpose at all beyond trying to satisfy himself with her.

And then he realized what had woken him up.

He heard a high, keening cry that barely filtered through the open bedroom door. Riley.

He looked down at Danielle, who was still fast asleep, and who would no doubt be upset that they had forgotten to bring the baby monitor into the room.

Joshua had barely been able to remember his own name, much less a baby monitor.

He extricated himself from her hold, scrubbing his hand over his face. Then he walked over to his closet, grabbing a pair of jeans and pulling them on with nothing underneath.

He had no idea what in the hell to do with the baby. But Danielle was exhausted, because of him, and he didn't want to wake her up.

The cries got louder as he made his way down the hall, and he walked into the room to see flailing movement coming from the crib. The baby was very unhappy, whatever the reason.

Joshua walked across the room and stood above the crib, looking down. If he was going to marry Danielle, then that meant Riley was his responsibility too.

Riley would be his son.

Something prickled at the back of his throat, making it tight. So much had happened after Shannon lost the baby that he didn't tend to think too much about what might have been. But it was impossible not to think about it right now.

His son would have been five.

He swallowed hard, trying to combat the rising tide of emotion in his chest. That emotion was why he avoided contact with Riley. Joshua wasn't so out of touch with his feelings that he didn't know that.

But his son wasn't here. He'd never had the chance to be born.

Riley was here.

And Joshua could be there for him.

He reached down, placing his hand on the baby's chest. His little body started, but he stopped crying.

Joshua didn't know the first thing about babies. He'd never had to learn. He'd never had the chance to hold his son. Never gone through a sleepless night because of crying.

He reached down, picking up the small boy from his crib, holding the baby close to his chest and supporting Riley's downy head.

There weren't very many situations in life that caused Joshua to doubt himself. Mostly because he took great care to ensure he was only ever in situations where he had the utmost control.

But holding this tiny creature in his arms made him feel at a loss. Made him feel like his strength might be a liability rather than an asset. Because at the moment, he felt like this little boy could be far too easily broken. Like he might crush the baby somehow.

Either with his hands or with his inadequacy.

Though, he supposed that was the good thing about babies. Right now, Riley didn't seem to need him to be perfect. He just needed Joshua to be there. Being there he could handle.

He made his way to the rocking chair in the corner and sat down, pressing Riley to his chest as he rocked back and forth.

"You might be hungry," Joshua said, keeping his voice soft. "I didn't ask."

Riley turned his head back and forth, leaving a small trail of drool behind on Joshua's skin. He had a feeling if his brother could see him now, he would mock him mercilessly. But then, he couldn't imagine Isaiah with a baby at all. Devlin, yes. But only since he had married Mia. She had changed Devlin completely. Made him more relaxed. Made him a better man.

Joshua thought of Danielle, sleeping soundly back in his room. Of just how insatiable he'd been for her earlier. Of how utterly trapped she was, and more or less at his mercy.

He had to wonder if there was any way she could make him a better man, all things considered.

Though, he supposed he'd kind of started to become a better man already. Since he had taken her on. And Riley.

He had to be the man who could take care of them, if he was so intent on fixing things.

Maybe they can fix you too.

Even though there was no one in the room but the baby, Joshua shook his head. That wasn't a fair thing to put on either of them.

"Joshua?"

He looked up and saw Danielle standing in the doorway. She was wearing one of his T-shirts, the hem falling to the top of her thighs. He couldn't see her expression in the darkened room.

"Over here."

"Are you holding Riley?" She moved deeper into the room and stopped in front of him, the moonlight streaming through the window shadowing one side of her face. With her long, dark hair hanging loose around her shoulders, and that silver light casting her in a glow, she looked ethereal. He wondered how he had ever thought she was pitiful. How he had ever imagined she wasn't beautiful.

"He was crying," he responded.

"I can take him."

He shook his head, for some reason reluctant to give him up. "That's okay."

A smile curved her lips. "Okay. I can make him a bottle."

He nodded, moving his hand up and down on the baby's back. "Okay."

Danielle rummaged around for a moment and then went across the room to the changing station, where he assumed she kept the bottle-making supplies. Warmers and filtered water and all of that. He didn't know much about it, only that he had arranged to have it all delivered to the house to make things easier for her.

She returned a moment later, bottle in hand. She tilted it upside down and tested it on the inside of her wrist. "It's all good. Do you want to give it to him?"

He nodded slowly and reached up. "Sure."

He shifted his hold on Riley, repositioning him in the crook of his arm so he could offer him the bottle.

"Do you have a lot of experience with babies?"

"None," he said.

"You could have fooled me. Although, I didn't really have any experience with babies until Riley was born. I didn't figure I would ever have experience with them."

"No?"

She shook her head. "No. I was never going to get married, Joshua. I knew all about men, you see. My mother got pregnant with me when she was fourteen. Needless to say, things didn't get off to the best start. I never knew my father. My upbringing was…unstable. My mother just wasn't ready to have a baby, and honestly, I don't know how she could have been. She didn't have a good home life, and she was so young. I think she wanted to keep me, wanted to do the right thing—it was just hard. She was always looking for something else. Looking for love."

"Not in the right places, I assume."

She bit her lip. "No. To say the least. She had a lot of boyfriends, and we lived with some of them. Sometimes that was better. Sometimes they were more established than us and had better homes. The older I got, the less like a mom my mom seemed. I started to really understand how young she was. When she would get her heart broken, I comforted her more like a friend than like a daughter. When she would go out and get drunk, I would put her to bed like I was the parent." Danielle took a deep breath. "I just didn't want that for myself. I didn't want to depend on anybody, or have anyone depend on me. I didn't want to pin my hopes on someone else. And I never saw a relationship that looked like anything else when I was growing up."

"But here you are," he said, his chest feeling tight. "And you're marrying me."

"I don't know if you can possibly understand what this is like," she said, laughing, a kind of shaky nervous sound. "Having this idea of what your life will be and just…changing that. I was so certain about what I would have, and what I wouldn't have. I would never get married. I would never have children. I would never have…a beautiful house or a yard." Her words got thick, her throat sounding tight. "Then there was Riley. And then there was your ad. And then there was you. And suddenly everything I want is different, everything I expect is different. I actually hope for things. It's kind of a miracle."

He wanted to tell her that he wasn't a miracle. That whatever she expected from him, he was sure to disappoint her in some way. But what she was describing was too close to his own truth.

He had written off having a wife. He had written off having children. That was the whole part of being human he'd decided wasn't for him. And yet here he was, feeding a baby at three in the morning staring at a woman who had just come from his bed. A woman who was wearing his ring.

The way Joshua needed it, the way he wanted to cling to his new reality, to make sure that it was real and that it would last, shocked him with its ferocity.

A moment later, he heard a strange sucking sound and realized the bottle was empty.

"Am I supposed to burp him?"

Danielle laughed. "Yes. But I'll do that."

"I'm not helpless."

"He's probably going to spit up on your hot and sexy chest. Better to have him do it on your T-shirt." She reached out. "I got this."

She took Riley from him and he sat back and admired the expert way she handled the little boy. She rocked him over her shoulder, patting his back lightly until he made a sound that most definitely suggested he had spit up on the T-shirt she was wearing.

Joshua had found her to be such a strange creature when he had first seen her. Brittle and pointed. Fragile.

But she was made of iron. He could see that now.

No one had been there to raise her, not really.

And then she had stepped in to make sure that her half brother was taken care of. Had upended every plan she'd made for her life and decided to become a mother at twenty-two.

"What?" she asked, and he realized he had been sitting there staring at her.

"You're an amazing woman, Danielle Kelly. And if no one's ever told you that, it's about time someone did."

She was so bright, so beautiful, so fearless.

All this time she had been a burning flame no one had taken the time to look at. But she had come to him, answered his ad and started a wildfire in his life.

It didn't seem fair, the way the world saw each of them. He was a celebrated businessman, and she... Well, hadn't he chosen her because he knew his family would simply see her as a poor, unwed mother?

She was worth ten of him.

She blinked rapidly and wasn't quite able to stop a tear from tracking down her cheek. "Why...why do you think that?"

"Not very many people would have done what you did. Taking your brother. Not after everything your mother already put you through. Not after spending your whole life taking care of the one person who should have been taking care of you. And then you came here and answered my ad."

"Some people might argue that the last part was taking the easy way out."

"Right. Except that I could have been a serial killer."

"Or made me dress like a teddy bear," she said,

keeping her tone completely serious. "I actually feel like that last one is more likely."

"Do you?"

"There are more furries than there are serial killers, thank God."

"I guess, lucky for you, I'm neither one." He wasn't sure he was the great hope she seemed to think he was. But right now, he wanted to be.

"Very lucky for me," she said. "Oh... Joshua, imagine if someone were both."

"I'd rather not."

She went to the changing table and quickly set about getting Riley a new diaper before placing him back in the crib. Then she straightened and hesitated. "I guess I could... I can just stay in here. Or..."

"Get the baby monitor," he said. "You're coming back to my bed."

She smiled, and she did just that.

The next day there were wedding dresses in Danielle's room. Not just a couple of wedding dresses. At least ten, all in her size.

She turned in a circle, looking at all of the garment bags with heavy white satin, beads and chiffon showing through.

Joshua walked into the room behind her, his arms folded over his chest. She raised her eyebrows, gesturing wildly at the dresses. "What is this?"

"We are getting married in less than two weeks. You need a dress."

"A fancy dress to eat my Pop-Tart cake in," she said, moving to a joke because if she didn't she might cry. Because the man had ordered wedding dresses and brought them into the house.

And because if she were normal, she might have friends to share this occasion with her. Or her mother. Instead, she was standing in her bedroom, where her baby was napping, and her fiancé was the only potential spectator.

"You aren't supposed to see the dresses, though," she said.

"I promise you I cannot make any sense out of them based on how they look stuffed into those bags. I called the bridal store in town and described your figure and had her send dresses accordingly."

Her eyes flew wide, her mouth dropping open. "You described my figure?"

"To give her an idea of what would suit you."

"I'm going to need a play-by-play of this description. How did you describe my figure, Joshua? This is very important."

"Elfin," he said, surprising her because he didn't seem to be joking. And that was a downright fanciful description coming from him.

"Elfin?"

A smile tipped his lips upward. "Yes. You're like an elf. Or a nymph."

"Nympho, maybe. And I blame you for that."

He reached out then, hooking his arm around her waist and drawing her toward him. "Danielle, I am serious."

She swallowed hard. "Okay," she said, because she didn't really know what else to say.

"You're beautiful."

Hearing him say that made her throat feel all dry

and scratchy, made her eyes feel like they were burning. "You don't have to do that," she said.

"You think I'm lying? Why would I lie about that? Also, men can't fake this." He grabbed her hand and pressed it up against the front of his jeans, against the hardness there.

"You're asking me to believe your penis? Because penises are notoriously indiscriminate."

"You have a point. Plus, mine is pretty damn famously indiscriminate. By my own admission. But the one good thing about that is you can trust I know the difference between generalized lust and when a woman has reached down inside of me and grabbed hold of something I didn't even know was there. I told you, I like it easy. I told you… I don't deal with difficult situations or difficult people. That was my past failing. A huge failing, and I don't know if I'm ever going to forgive myself for it. But what we have here makes me feel like maybe I can make up for it."

There were a lot of nice words in there. A lot of beautiful sentiments tangled up in something that made her feel, well, kind of gross.

But he was looking at her with all that intensity, and there were wedding dresses hung up all around her, his ring glittering on her finger. And she just didn't want to examine the bad feelings. She was so tired of bad feelings.

Joshua—all of this—was like a fantasy. She wanted to live in the fantasy for as long as she could.

Was that wrong? After everything she had been through, she couldn't believe that it was.

"Well, get your penis out of here. The rest of you too. I'm going to try on dresses."

"I don't get to watch?"

"I grant you nothing about our relationship has been typical so far, but I would like to surprise you with my dress choice."

"That's fair. Why don't you let me take Riley for a while?"

"Janine is going to be here soon."

He shrugged. "I'll take him until then." He strode across the room and picked Riley up, and Riley flashed a small, gummy smile that might have been nothing more than a facial twitch but still made Danielle's heart do something fluttery and funny.

Joshua's confidence with Riley was increasing, and he made a massive effort to be proactive when it came to taking care of the baby.

Watching Joshua stand there with Riley banished any lingering gross feelings about being considered difficult, and when Joshua left the room and Danielle turned to face the array of gowns, she pushed every last one of her doubts to the side.

Maybe Joshua wasn't perfect. Maybe there were some issues. But all of this, with him, was a damn sight better than anything she'd had before.

And a girl like her couldn't afford to be too picky.

She took a deep breath and unzipped the first dress.

Ten

The day of the wedding was drawing closer and Danielle was drawing closer to a potential nervous breakdown. She was happy, in a way. When Joshua kissed her, when he took her to bed, when he spent the whole night holding her in his strong arms, everything felt great.

It was the in-between hours. The quiet moments she spent with herself, rocking Riley in that gray time before dawn. That was when she pulled those bad feelings out and began to examine them.

She had two days until the wedding, and her dress had been professionally altered to fit her—a glorious, heavy satin gown with a deep V in the back and buttons that ran down the full skirt—and if for no other reason than that, she couldn't back out.

The thought of backing out sent a burst of pain blooming through her chest. Unfurling, spreading, expanding. No. She didn't want to leave Joshua. No matter the strange, imbalanced feelings between them, she wanted to be with him. She felt almost desperate to be with him.

She looked over at him now, sitting in the driver's seat of what was still the nicest car she had ever touched, much less ridden in, as they pulled up to the front of his parents' house.

Sometimes looking at him hurt. And sometimes looking away from him hurt. Sometimes everything hurt. The need to be near him, the need for distance.

Maybe she really had lost her mind.

It took her a moment to realize she was still sitting motionless in the passenger seat, and Joshua had already put the car in Park and retrieved Riley from the back seat. He didn't bother to bring the car seat inside this time. Instead, he wrapped the baby in a blanket and cradled him in his arms.

Oh, that hurt her in a whole different way.

Joshua was sexy. All the time. There was no question about that. But the way he was with Riley... Well, she was surprised that any woman who walked by him when he was holding Riley didn't fall immediately at his feet.

She nearly did. Every damned time.

She followed him to the front door, looking down to focus on the way the gravel crunched beneath her boots—new boots courtesy of Joshua that didn't have holes in them, and didn't need three pairs of socks to keep her toes from turning into icicles—because otherwise she was going to get swallowed up by the nerves that were riding through her.

His mother had insisted on making a prewedding dinner for them, and this was Danielle's second chance to make a first impression. Now it was real and she felt an immense amount of pressure to be better than she was, rather than simply sliding into the lowest expectation people like his family had of someone like her, as she'd done before.

She looked over at him when she realized he was staring at her. "You're going to be fine," he said.

Then he bent down and kissed her. She closed her eyes, her breath rushing from her lungs as she gave herself over to his kiss.

That, of course, was when the front door opened. "You're here!"

Nancy Grayson actually looked happy to see them both, and even happier that she had caught them making out on the front porch.

Danielle tucked a stray lock of hair behind her ear. "Thank you for doing this," she said, jarred by the change in her role, but desperate to do a good job.

"Of course," the older woman said. "Now, let me hold my grandbaby."

Those words made Danielle pause, made her freeze up. Made her want to cry. Actually, she *was* crying. Tears were rolling down her cheeks without even giving her a chance to hold them back.

Joshua's mother frowned. "What's wrong, honey?"

Danielle swallowed hard. "I didn't ever expect that he would have grandparents. That he would have a family." She took a deep breath. "I mean like this. It means a lot to me."

Nancy took Riley from Joshua's arms. But then she reached out and put her hand on Danielle's shoulder. "He's not the only one who has a family. You do too."

Throughout the evening Danielle was stunned by the warm acceptance of Joshua's entire family. By the way his sister-in-law, Mia, made an effort to get to know her, and by the complete absence of antagonism coming from his younger sister, Faith.

But what really surprised her was when Joshua's father came and sat next to her on the couch during dessert. Joshua was engaged in conversation with his brothers across the room while Mia, Faith and Joshua's mother were busy playing with Riley.

"I knew you would be good for him," Mr. Grayson said.

Danielle looked up at the older man. "A wife, you mean," she said, her voice soft. She didn't know why she had challenged his assertion, why she'd done anything but blandly agree. Except she knew she wasn't the woman he would have chosen for his son, and she didn't want him to pretend otherwise.

He shook his head. "I'm not talking about the ad. I know what he did. I know that he placed another ad looking for somebody he could use to get back at me. But the minute I met you, I knew you were exactly what he needed. Somebody unexpected. Somebody who would push him out of his comfort zone. It's real now, isn't it?"

It's real now.

Those words echoed inside of her. What did real mean? They were really getting married, but was their relationship real?

He didn't love her. He wanted to fix her. And somehow, through fixing her, he believed he would fix himself.

Maybe that wasn't any less real than what most people had. Maybe it was just more honest.

"Yes," she said, her voice a whisper. "It's real."

"I know that my meddling upset him. I'm not stupid. And I know he felt like I wasn't listening to him. But he has been so lost in all that pain, and I knew… I knew he just needed to love somebody again. He thought everything I did, everything I said was because I don't understand a life that goes beyond what we have here." He gestured around the living room— small, cozy, essentially a stereotype of the happy, rural family. "But that's not it. Doesn't matter what a life looks like, a man needs love. And *that* man needs love more than most. He always was stubborn, difficult. Never could get him to talk about much of anything. He needs someone he can talk to. Someone who can see the good in him so he can start to see it too."

"Love," Danielle said softly, the word a revelation she had been trying to avoid.

That was why it hurt. When she looked at him. When she was with him. When she looked away from him. When he was gone.

That was the intense, building pressure inside her that felt almost too large for her body to contain.

It was every beautiful, hopeful feeling she'd had since meeting him.

She loved him.

And he didn't love her. That absence was the cause of the dark disquiet she'd felt sometimes. He wanted to use her as a substitute for his girlfriend, the one he thought he had failed.

"Every man needs love," Todd said. "Successful businessmen and humble farmers. Trust me. It's the thing that makes life run. The thing that keeps you going when crops don't grow and the weather doesn't cooperate. The thing that pulls you up from the dark pit when you can't find the light. I'm glad he found his light."

But he hadn't.

She had found hers.

For him, she was a Band-Aid he was trying to put over a wound that would end up being fatal if he didn't do something to treat it. If he didn't do something more than simply cover it up.

She took a deep breath. "I don't…"

"Are you ready to go home?"

Danielle looked up and saw Joshua standing in front of her. And those words…

Him asking if she wanted to go home, meaning to his house, with him, like that house belonged to her. Like he belonged to her…

Well, his question allowed her to erase all the doubts that had just washed through her. Allowed her to put herself back in the fantasy she'd been living in since she'd agreed to his proposal.

"Sure," she said, pushing herself up from the couch.

She watched as he said goodbye to his family, as he collected Riley and slung the diaper bag over his shoulder. Yes. She loved him.

She was an absolute and total lost cause for him. In love. Something she had thought she could never be.

The only problem was, she was in love alone.

It was his wedding day.

Thankfully, only his family would be in attendance. A small wedding in Copper Ridge's Baptist church, which was already decorated for Christmas and so saved everyone time and hassle.

Which was a good thing, since he had already harassed local baker Alison Donnelly to the point where she was ready to assault him with a spatula over his demands related to a Pop-Tart cake.

It was the one thing Danielle had said she wanted, and even if she had been joking, he wanted to make it happen for her.

He liked doing things for her. Whether it was teaching her how to ride horses, pleasuring her in the bedroom or fixing her nice meals, she always expressed a deep and sweet gratitude that transcended anything he had ever experienced before.

Her appreciation affected him. He couldn't pretend it didn't.

She affected him.

He walked into the empty church, looking up at the steeply pitched roof and the thick, curved beams of wood that ran the length of it, currently decked with actual boughs of holly.

Everything looked like it was set up and ready, all there was to do now was wait for the ceremony to start.

Suddenly, the doors that led to the fellowship hall opened wide and in burst Danielle. If he had thought she looked ethereal before, it was nothing compared to how she looked at this moment. Her dark hair was swept back in a loose bun, sprigs of baby's breath woven into it, some tendrils hanging around her face.

And the dress...

The bodice was fitted, showing off her slim figure, and the skirt billowed out around her, shimmering with each and every step. She was holding a bouquet of dark red roses, her lips painted a deep crimson to match.

"I didn't think I was supposed to see you until the wedding?" It was a stupid thing to say, but it was about the only thing he could think of.

"Yes. I know. I was here getting ready, and I was going to hide until everything started. Stay in the dressing room." She shook her head. "I need to talk to you, though. And I was already wearing this dress, and all of the layers of underwear that you have to wear underneath it to make it do this." She kicked her foot out, causing the skirt to flare.

"To make it do what?"

"You need a crinoline. Otherwise your skirt is like a wilted tulip. That's something I learned when the wedding store lady came this morning to help me get ready. But that's not what I wanted to talk to you about."

He wasn't sure if her clarification was a relief or not. He wasn't an expert on the subject of crinolines, but it seemed like an innocuous subject. Anything else that had drawn her out of hiding before the ceremony probably wasn't.

"Then talk."

She took a deep breath, wringing her hands around the stem of her bouquet. "Okay. I will talk. I'm going to. In just a second."

He shook his head. "Danielle Kelly, you stormed into my house with a baby and pretty much refused to leave until I agreed to give you what you wanted—don't act like you're afraid of me now."

"That was different. I wasn't afraid of losing you

then." She looked up at him, her dark eyes liquid. "I'm afraid right now."

"You?" He couldn't imagine this brave, wonderfully strong woman being afraid of anything.

"I've never had anything that I wanted to keep. Or I guess, I never did before Riley. Once I had him, the thought of losing him was one of the things that scared me. It was the first time I'd ever felt anything like it. And now…it's the same with you. Do you know what you have in common with Riley?"

"The occasional tantrum?" His chest was tight. He knew that was the wrong thing to say, knew it was wrong to make light of the situation when she was so obviously serious and trembling.

"Fair enough," she said. Then she took a deep breath. "I love you. That's what you have in common with Riley. That's why I'm afraid of losing you. Because you matter. Because you more than matter. You're…everything."

Her words were like a sucker punch straight to the gut. "Danielle…"

He was such an ass. Of course she thought she was in love with him. He was her first lover, the first man to ever give her an orgasm. He had offered her a place to live and he was promising a certain amount of financial security, the kind she'd never had before.

Of course such a vulnerable, lonely woman would confuse those feelings of gratitude with love.

She frowned. "Don't use that tone with me. I know you're about to act like you're the older and wiser of the two of us. You're about to explain why I don't understand what I'm talking about. Remember when you told me about your penis?"

He looked over his shoulder, then back at Danielle. "Okay, I'm not usually a prude, but we are in a church."

She let out an exasperated sound. "Sorry. But the thing is, remember when you told me that because you had been indiscriminate you knew the difference between common, garden-variety sex—"

"Danielle, Pastor John is around here somewhere."

She straightened her arms at her sides, the flowers in her hand trembling with her unsuppressed irritation. "Who cares? This is our life. Anyway, what little I've read in the Bible was pretty honest about people. Everything I'm talking about—it's all part of being a person. I'm not embarrassed about any of it." She tilted her chin up, looking defiant. "My point is, I don't need you telling me what you think I feel. I have spent so much time alone, so much time without love, that I've had a lot of time to think about what it might feel like. About what it might mean."

He lowered his voice and took a step toward her. "Danielle, feeling cared for isn't the same as love. Pleasure isn't the same as love."

"I know that!" Her words echoed in the empty sanctuary. "Trust me. If I thought being taken care of was the same thing as love, I probably would have repeated my mother's pattern for my entire life. But I didn't. I waited. I waited until I found a man who was worth being an idiot over. Here I am in a wedding dress yelling at the man I'm supposed to marry in an hour, wanting him to understand that I love him. You can't be much more of an idiot than that, Joshua."

"It's okay if you love me," he said, even though it made his stomach feel tight. Even though it wasn't okay at all. "But I don't know what you expect me to do with that."

She stamped her foot, the sound ricocheting around them. "Love me back, dammit."

He felt like someone had grabbed hold of his heart and squeezed it hard. "Danielle, I can't do that. I can't. And honestly, it's better if you don't feel that way about me. I think we can have a partnership. I'm good with those. I'm good with making agreements, shaking hands, holding up my end of the deal. But feelings, all that stuff in between… I would tell you to call Shannon and ask her about that, but I don't think she has a phone right now, because I'm pretty sure she's homeless."

"You can't take the blame for that. You can't take the blame for her mistakes. I mean, I guess you can, you've been doing a great job of it for the past five years. And I get that. You lost a child. And then you lost your fiancée, the woman you loved. And you're holding on to that pain to try to insulate yourself from more."

He shook his head. "That's not it. It would be damned irresponsible of me not to pay attention to what I did to her. To what being with me can do to a woman." He cleared his throat. "She needed something that I couldn't give. I did love her—you're right. But it wasn't enough."

"You're wrong about that too," she said. "You loved her enough. But sometimes, Joshua, you can love somebody and love somebody, but unless they do something with that love it goes fallow. You can sow the seeds all you want, but if they don't water them, if they don't nurture them, you can't fix it for them."

"I didn't do enough," he said, tightening his jaw, hardening his heart.

"Maybe you were difficult. Maybe you did some wrong things. But at some point, she needed to reach out and tell you that. But she didn't. She shut down. Love can be everything, but it can't all be coming from one direction. The other person has to accept it. You can't love someone into being whole. They have to love themselves enough to want to be whole. And they have to love you enough to lay down their pain, to lay down their selfishness, and change—even when it's hard."

"I can't say she was selfish," he said, his voice rough. "I can't say she did anything wrong."

"What about my mother? God knows she had it hard, Joshua. I can't imagine having a baby at four-teen. It's hard enough having one at twenty-two. She has a lot of excuses. And they're valid. She went through hell, but the fact of the matter is she's choosing to go through it at this point. She has spent her whole life searching for the kind of love that either one of her children would have given her for nothing. I couldn't have loved her more. Riley is a baby, completely and totally dependent on whoever might take care of him. Could we have loved her more? Could we have made her stay?"

"That's different."

She stamped her foot again. "It is fucking not!"

He didn't bother to yell at her about them being in a church again. "I understand that all of this is new to you," he said, fighting to keep his voice steady. "And honestly? It feels good, selfishly good, to know you see all this in me. It's tempting to lie to you, Danielle.

But I can't do that. What I offered you is the beginning and end of what I have. Either you accept our partnership or you walk away."

She wouldn't.

She needed him too much. That was the part that made him a monster.

He knew he had all the power here, and he knew she would ultimately see things his way. She would have to.

And then what? Would she wither away living with him? Wanting something that he refused to give her?

The situation looked too familiar.

He tightened his jaw, steeling himself for her response.

What he didn't expect was to find a bouquet of flowers tossed at him. He caught them, and her petite shoulders lifted up, then lowered as she let out a shuddering breath. "I guess you're the next one to get married, then. Congratulations. You caught the flowers."

"Of course I damn well am," he said, tightening his fist around the roses, ignoring the thorn that bit into his palm. "Our wedding is in an hour."

Her eyes filled with tears, and she shook her head. Then she turned and ran out of the room, pausing only to kick her shoes off and leave them lying on the floor like she was Cinderella.

And he just stood there, holding on to the flowers, a trickle of blood from the thorn dripping down his wrist as he watched the first ray of light, the first bit of hope he'd had in years, disappear from his life.

Of course, her exit didn't stop him from standing at the altar and waiting. Didn't stop him from acting like the wedding would continue without a hitch.

He knew she hadn't gone far, mostly because Janine was still at the church with Riley, and while Danielle's actions were painful and mystifying at the moment, he knew her well enough to know she wasn't going to leave without Riley.

But the music began to play and no bride materialized.

There he was, a giant dick in a suit, waiting for a woman who wasn't going to come.

His family looked at each other, trading expressions filled with a mix of pity and anger. But it was his father who spoke up. "What in hell did you do, boy?"

A damned good question.

Unfortunately, he knew the answer to it.

"Why are you blaming him?" Faith asked, his younger sister defending him to the bitter end, even when he didn't deserve it.

"Because that girl loves him," his father said, his tone full of confidence, "and she wouldn't have left him standing there if he hadn't done something."

Pastor John raised his hands, the gesture clearly meant to placate. "If there are any doubts about a marriage, it's definitely best to stop and consider those doubts, as it is a union meant for life."

"And she was certain," Joshua's father said. "Which means he messed it up."

"When two people love each other…" The rest of Pastor John's words were swallowed up by Joshua's family, but those first six hit Joshua and pierced him right in the chest.

When two people love each other.

Two people. Loving each other.

Love going both ways. Giving and taking.

And he understood then. He really understood.

Why she couldn't submit to living in a relationship that she thought might be one-sided. Because she had already endured it once. Because she'd already lived it with her mother.

Danielle was willing to walk away from everything he'd offered her. From the house, from the money, from the security. Even from his family. Because for some reason his love meant that much to her.

That realization nearly brought him to his knees.

He had thought his love insufficient. Had thought it destructive. And as she had stood there, pleading with him to love her back, he had thought his love unimportant.

But to her, it was everything.

How dare he question her feelings for him? Love, to Danielle, was more than a ranch and good sex. And she had proved it, because she was clearly willing to sacrifice the ranch and the sex to have him return her love.

"It was my fault," he said, his voice sounding like a stranger's as it echoed through the room. "She said she loved me. And I told her I couldn't love her back."

"Well," Faith said, "not even I can defend you now, dumbass."

His mother looked stricken, his father angry. His brothers seemed completely unsurprised.

"You do love her, though," his father said, his tone steady. "So why did you tell her you didn't?"

Of course, Joshua realized right then something else she'd been right about. He was afraid.

Afraid of wanting this life he really had always dreamed of but had written off because he messed up his first attempt so badly. Afraid because the first time had been so painful, had gone so horribly wrong.

"Because I'm a coward," he said. "But I'm not going to be one anymore."

He walked down off the stage and to the front pew, picking up the bouquet. "I'm going to go find her," he said. "I know she's not far, since Riley is here."

Suddenly, he knew exactly where she was.

"Do you have any other weddings today, Pastor?"

Pastor John shook his head. "No. This is the only thing I have on my schedule today. Not many people get married on a Thursday."

"Hopefully, if I don't mess this up, we'll need you."

Eleven

It was cold. And Danielle's bare feet were starting to ache. But there had been no way in hell she could run in those high heels. She would have broken her neck.

Of course, if she had broken her neck, she might have fully severed her spinal cord and then not been able to feel anything. A broken heart sadly didn't work that way. She felt everything. Pain, deep and unending. Pain that spread from her chest out to the tips of her fingers and toes.

She wiggled her toes. In fairness, they might just be frostbitten.

She knew she was being pathetic. Lying down on that Pendleton blanket in the loft. The place where Joshua had first made love to her. Hiding.

Facing everyone—facing Joshua again—was inevitable. She was going to have to get Riley. Pack up her things.

Figure out life without Joshua's money. Go back to working a cash register at a grocery store somewhere. Wrestling with childcare problems.

She expected terror to clutch her at the thought. Expected to feel deep sadness about her impending poverty. But those feelings didn't come.

She really didn't care about any of that.

Well, she probably would care once she was neck deep in it again, but right now all she cared about was that she wouldn't have Joshua.

If he had no money, if he was struggling just like her, she would have wanted to struggle right along with him.

But money or no money, struggle or no struggle, she needed him to love her. Otherwise…

She closed her eyes and took in a breath of sharp, cold air.

She had been bound and determined to ignore all of the little warnings she'd felt in her soul when she'd thought about their relationship. But in the end, she couldn't.

She knew far too well what it was like to pour love out and never get it back. And for a while it had been easy to pretend. That his support, and the sex, was the same as getting something back.

But they were temporary.

The kinds of things that would fade over the years.

If none of his choices were rooted in love, if none of it was founded in love, then what they had couldn't last.

She was saving herself hideous heartbreak down the road by stabbing herself in the chest now.

She snorted. Right now, she kind of wondered what the point was.

Pride?

"Screw pride," she croaked.

She heard the barn door open, heard footsteps down below, and she curled up into a ball, the crinoline under her dress scratching her legs. She buried her face in her arm, like a child. As if whoever had just walked into the barn wouldn't be able to see her as long as she couldn't see him.

Then she heard footsteps on the ladder rungs, the sound of calloused hands sliding over the metal. She knew who it was. Oh well. She had already embarrassed herself in front of him earlier. It was not like him seeing her sprawled in a tragic heap in a barn was any worse than her stamping her foot like a dramatic silent-film heroine.

"I thought I might find you here."

She didn't look up when she heard his voice. Instead, she curled into a tighter, even more resolute ball.

She felt him getting closer, which was ridiculous. She knew she couldn't actually feel the heat radiating from his body.

"I got you that Pop-Tart cake," he said. "I mean, I had Alison from Pie in the Sky make one. And I have to tell you, it looks disgusting. I mean, she did a great job, but I can't imagine that it's edible."

She uncurled as a sudden spout of rage flooded through her and she pushed herself into a sitting position. "Fuck your Pop-Tart cake, Joshua."

"I thought we both liked Pop-Tarts."

"Yes. But I don't like lies. And your Pop-Tarts would taste like lies."

"Actually," he said slowly, "I think the Pop-Tart

cake is closer to the truth than anything I said to you back in the church. You said a lot of things that were true. I'm a coward, Danielle. And guilt is a hell of a lot easier than grief."

"What the hell does that mean?" She drew her arm underneath her nose, wiping snot and tears away, tempted to ask him where his elfin princess was now. "Don't tease me. Don't talk in riddles. I'm ready to walk away from you if I need to, but I don't want to do it. So please, don't tempt me to hurt myself like that if you aren't..."

"I love you," he said, his voice rough. "And my saying so now isn't because I was afraid you were a gold digger and you proved you weren't by walking away. I realize what I'm about to say could be confused for that, but don't be confused. Because loving you has nothing to do with that. If you need my money... I've never blamed you for going after it. I've never blamed you for wanting to make your and Riley's lives easier. But the fact that you *were* willing to walk away from everything over three words... How can I pretend they aren't important? How can I pretend that I don't need your love when you demonstrated that you need my love more than financial security. More than sex. How can I doubt you and the strength of your feelings? How can I excuse my unwillingness to open myself up to you? My unwillingness to make myself bleed for you?"

He reached out, taking hold of her hands, down on his knees with her.

"You're going to get your suit dirty," she said inanely.

"Your dress is filthy," he returned.

She looked down at the dirt and smudges on the beautiful white satin. "Crap."

He took hold of her chin, tilting her face up to look at him. "I don't care. It doesn't matter. Because I would marry you in blue jeans, or I would marry you in this barn. I would sure as hell marry you in that dirty wedding dress. I… You are right about everything.

"It was easy to martyr myself over Shannon's pain. To blame myself so I didn't have to try again. So I didn't have to hurt again. Old pain is easier. The pain from that time in my life isn't gone, but it's dull. It throbs sometimes. It aches. When I look at Riley, he reminds me of my son, who never took a breath, and it hurts down deep. But I know that if I were to lose either of you now… That would be fresh pain. A fresh hell. And I have some idea of what that hell would be like because of what I've been through before.

"But it would be worse now. And… I was protecting myself from it. But now, I don't care about the pain, the fear. I want it all. I want you.

"I love you. Whatever might happen, whatever might come our way in the future… I love you. And I am going to do the hard fucking yards for you, Danielle."

His expression was so fierce, his words so raw and real, all she could do was stare at him, listening as he said all the things she had never imagined she would hear.

"I was young and stupid the last time I tried love. Selfish. I made mistakes. I can't take credit for everything that went wrong. Some of it was fate. Some of it was her choices. But when things get hard this time, you have my word I won't pull away. I'm not going to let you shut me out. If you close the door on me, I'm going to kick it down. Because what we have is special. It's real. It's hope. And I will fight with everything I have to hold on to it."

She lurched forward, wrapping her arms around his neck, making them both fall backward. "I'll never shut you out." She squeezed her eyes closed, tears tracking down her cheeks. "Finding you has been the best thing that's ever happened to me. I don't feel alone, Joshua. Can you possibly understand what that means to me?"

He nodded gravely, kissing her lips. "I do understand," he said. "Because I've been alone in my own swamp for a long damned time. And you're the first person who made me feel like it was worth it to wade out."

"I love you," she said.

"I love you too. Do you still want to marry me?"

"Hell yeah."

"Good." He maneuvered them both so they were upright, taking her hand and leading her to the ladder. They climbed down, and she hopped from foot to foot on the cold cement floor. "Come on," he said, grabbing her hand and leading her through the open double doors.

She stopped when she saw that his whole family, Janine and Riley, and Pastor John were standing out there in the gravel.

Joshua's mother was holding the bouquet of roses, and she reached out, handing it back to Danielle. Then Joshua went to Janine and took Riley from her arms, holding the baby in the crook of his own. Then Joshua went back to Danielle, taking both of her hands with his free one.

"I look bedraggled," she said.

"You look perfect to me."

She smiled, gazing at everyone, at her new family. At this new life she was going to have.

And then she looked back at the man she loved with all her heart. "Well," she said, "okay, then. Marry me, cowboy."

Epilogue

December 5, 2017
FOUND A WIFE—

Local rancher Todd Grayson and his wife, Nancy, are pleased to announce the marriage of their son, a wealthy former bachelor, Joshua Grayson (no longer irritated with his father) to Danielle Kelly, formerly of Portland, now of Copper Ridge and the daughter of their hearts. Mr. Grayson knew his son would need a partner who was strong, determined and able to handle an extremely stubborn cuss, which she does beautifully. But best of all, she loves him with her whole heart, which is all his meddling parents ever wanted for him.

* * * * *

CHRISTMAS
SEDUCTION

JESSICA LEMMON

For all my friends at the lake – you are the
embodiment of a true community, and
I'm so blessed to know you.

One

Outside the Brass Pony, a five-star restaurant where he'd nursed more than one whiskey at the bar, Tate Duncan stood beneath the canopy and watched the rain come down in sheets.

He'd picked a hell of a night to walk.

But, that's the way the streets here were designed in Spright Wellness Community. With plenty of sidewalks and paths cutting through the woods, making a walk more convenient than a winding car ride to your destination. This was a wellness community, after all.

Tate and a dedicated team of contractors had developed the health and wellness community five years ago. Its location? Spright Island, an enviable utopia thirty-minutes by ferry from Seattle, Washington, and Tate's twenty-fifth birthday gift from his adoptive parents. The island had been, and remained, a nature preserve and was the perfect spot to build a sustainable, peaceful, modern neighborhood that would attract curious city dwellers.

He'd imagined into existence the luxury wellness enclave, which had become a refuge of sorts for those who desired a strong sense of community, and wanted to be surrounded by lush greenery rather than concrete. As a re-

sult, Spright Wellness Community teemed with residents
who glowed with wealth and stank of wellness. There was
a big demand to live small and, even though it wasn't all
that small, SWC had that feel about it.

"Umbrella, Mr. Duncan?" The manager of the Brass
Pony, Jared Tomalin, leaned out the door and offered a
black umbrella by it's U-shaped handle. His smile faded
much as it had earlier when he'd attempted to make small
talk and learned that "Mr. Duncan" wasn't in the mood for
small talk tonight.

There had been a time, and it wasn't that long ago, that
Tate would have turned, given Jared a smile and accepted
the offer, saying, "Thank you. I'll bring it back by tomorrow." Now, he gave the manager a withering glare and
stalked off into the abysmal weather. A twenty-minute
jaunt—soggy, chilling and wet—was a good metaphor for
the downward spiral his life had taken recently.

Everything in Tate's world had been on an upward track,
steady and stable until...

Until.

He popped his collar and tucked his hands into the pockets of his leather jacket. Chin down, eyes on the gathering
puddles under his feet, he began to walk.

Surrounding neighborhoods were marked by a variety
of shops; markets with fresh produce and organic goods,
restaurants like the Pony with reputations that drew diners
from the coast, plus plenty of service-based businesses like
salons, art stores and yoga studios. With its high-end wellness fare, SWC was part luxury living, part hippie commune, but to Tate, simply home.

A rare flash of headlights caught his attention and he
lifted his head. Summer's Market stood on the opposite
side of the street, the wooden shelves and brightly-colored
stacks of produce visible from the windows. The safety
lights spotlighted wheels of cheese and boxed crackers ar-

ranged near a selection of wine. It was hard to believe he'd once had nothing better to do than pop into Summer's for a wine-tasting and cheese-pairing and have a chat with his neighbors.

Back when I knew who I was.

Tate had never thought of identity as a wily thing, but lately his own had been wriggling, slippery in his grip. He'd known once, with certainty, who he was: the son of William and Marion Duncan, from California. Life, apparently, had other plans for him. Plans that had sent him careening, grappling to understand how he'd *become* the son of William and Marion Duncan, right around the same time the woman who was supposed to marry him had walked away.

I can't do this, Tate, Claire had told him, her delicate features screwed into an expression of regret. Then she'd given back the engagement ring. That was two weeks ago. Since then, he'd become a ripe bastard.

The rhythm of his breath paced the time along with his steps. Rainwater beat drumlike on his head and soaked into his Italian leather shoes.

On his side of the street, he came upon a building that held an array of businesses, including an acupuncture office, a family doctor and a yoga studio. The yoga studio was the only one lit inside, by a pair of pink hued salt lamps glowing warmly on top of a desk. He peered through the window, wishing he'd have accepted the damn umbrella. Wishing he could absorb the warmth emitting from the place. It was orderly, homey, with its scarred wooden floors and stacks of cubbies for storing shoes and cell phones during class.

He'd been inside once before, to greet the new owner who'd leased the space. Yoga by Hayden was run by Hayden Green, a new resident who'd been in SWC a little over a year now. He saw her around town sometimes. She was the equivalent of looking at the sun. Bright, glowing, joyful. She had a skip in her step and a smile on her face most days. He wondered if yoga was her secret to being happy, if maybe he should try it—make that his new therapy. God knew he wasn't heading back to Dr. Schroder any time soon.

The first-world problems he used to bring to his therapist were laughable considering the *actual* drama surrounding him now. He could imagine that conversation, his doc's eyebrows climbing her forehead into her coifed dark hair.

Yeah, so I found out I was kidnapped when I was three, adopted out for a large sum of money and my real parents live in London. No, my adoptive parents didn't know I was kidnapped. Yes, London. Oh, and I have a brother. We're twins.

Eerie. That's what this was. Like a scary story told around a campfire, there was a large chunk of him that wanted to believe it was false. That the repressed memory of big hands cuffing him under the arms and dragging him away from his and his twin brother's birthday party had been a nightmare he could awaken from. That George and Jane Singleton were no more related to him than the Queen of England.

Though he was from the UK, so God help him, he *could be* related to the Queen of England.

Ice-cold raindrops soaked through his hair to his scalp, and he shuddered. His mind had been bobbing in the atmosphere like a lost balloon for going on two months now. He wasn't sure he'd ever get back to normal at this rate. Wasn't sure if he knew what normal *was* any longer.

This entire situation was surreal. And after living an organized, regimented, successful life, a shock he hadn't been prepared to deal with.

What were the odds of two estranged London-born twin brothers bumping into each other in a Seattle coffee shop nearly thirty years later?

Astronomical.

He let out a fractured laugh. "You're not well enough to be in a wellness community."

Overhead, he admired a streetlamp like the others lining the sidewalks, remembering how a formerly sane version of himself had commissioned a welder to design them. They resembled tree branches, complete with curling leaves along the top, the lights encased in a bell-shaped flower. Tate mused that they had a fairy-tale quality. Like that smoking caterpillar or the Cheshire cat from *Alice in Wonderland* could appear perched on one at any moment.

"You're losing it, Duncan."

But his smile was short-lived when he abruptly remembered that he wasn't a Duncan. Not really.

He was a Singleton.

Whatever the hell that meant.

The sharp whistle of the teakettle pulled Hayden Green's attention from her book. She made the short trek to her kitchen, flipped the gas burner off and reached for her waiting teacup.

Through the driving rain, she could barely make out the shape of the market across the street and yet her senses prickled. Stepping closer to her upstairs window, she squinted at the street below and found her senses were, as usual, spot-on.

In the deluge lurked a figure. Right outside her yoga studio. It was a man, most definitely, his dark leather jacket unable to hide the breadth of his shoulders.

She pressed her forehead against the pane to get a better look, confident he couldn't see her since the kitchen light was off. He tilted his head back; the street light overhead illuminating him as the rain splashed his upturned face and closed eyelids.

Hayden recognized her unexpected visitor instantly. "Tate Duncan, what are you doing?"

Tate's reputation had reached almost mythical proportions on Spright Island. He owned the island, so everyone knew him or knew *of him*, anyway. Hayden was somewhere in between. She knew of him—of his legendary pushbacks on the laws that stated their community had to have standard streetlamps and ugly yellow concrete curbs. Tate had fought for, and won, the right to design streetlamps that were art sculptures and to install curbs of sparkling quartz. He'd personally overseen every detail because to him, the details mattered.

Hayden had been romanced by SWC. It was a relaxing, serene place to live—a retreat from bustling city life. She had been born in Seattle into a busy, distracting, dysfunctional household, and had longed her entire adult life to be somewhere less busy and distracting.

When she'd learned about Spright Island's wellness community a year and a half ago, she'd come to visit. Days later, she'd taken out as big a business loan as the bank would give her and leased the space for her yoga studio. She'd quit her job at the YMCA, finagled her way out of her Seattle apartment's lease and moved here with minimal belongings.

It'd been her fresh start.

Shortly after, Tate had stopped by her studio to personally welcome her to the neighborhood and invite her to a wine tasting happening that weekend at Summer's Market. It was a kindness she hadn't expected, and without it, she might never have met and grown to know her neighbors.

She rarely saw a suit and tie step foot into a yoga studio, so Tate's presence had garnered every ounce of her attention. One of his signature quick, potent smiles later, she'd promptly lost any train of thought she'd had. As it turned out, the legendary Tate Duncan was also stupidly attractive, and when he smiled, that attractiveness doubled.

She'd grown used to his presence around town, if not his mind-numbing male beauty. She and Tate had bumped into each other several times in town, from the market to the restaurant to her favorite café. He'd always offered a smile and asked her how the studio was doing. Come to think of it, it'd been a while since she'd spoken to him. She'd seen him in recent weeks—*or was that a month ago?*—when she'd left the post office. He'd had his cell phone to his ear and was talking to someone, a deep frown marring his perfect brow.

He'd scanned the road and she'd waved when his eyes reached her, but he didn't react at all, only kept talking on the phone. It was strange behavior for Tate, but she'd written it off.

But now, watching him stand in the rain and willingly get soaked, she wondered if his behavior that day had been strange after all. She glanced over at her teakettle, considering. It wouldn't hurt to invite him in for a cup…

Once he'd gone out of his way to make her feel welcome. The least she could do was offer him a friendly ear to bend. Just in case he needed one.

She bypassed her front door for the door next to her coat closet. It led to a private staircase and down to her yoga studio. She shared the building with a few other businesses, but her apartment was in a hallway all its own. The attached studio and private entryway were her favorite aspects of the unique building.

Downstairs, she flipped on the studio's overhead lights and Tate blinked over at her, recognition dawning. He lifted a hand in a semblance of a wave, like he was embarrassed to be caught outside her place of business.

The stirring of her senses reinforced her instincts to come down here. Tate needed someone to talk to even more than he needed a warm space to dry off.

She unlocked the door and held it open for him, tipping her head to invite him in. "Wet night for a walk."

He ran a hand through his soaking hair and offered a chagrined twist of his lips, a far cry from the genuine smile he'd given her almost every other time she'd seen him.

He wore dark pants and shoes, his leather coat zipped to his chin. Her day had been packed with errands, so she still wore her jeans and soft, cream-colored sweater from earlier. If she'd greeted him wearing her usual—leggings and slouchy sweatshirt, minus the bra—he wouldn't have been the only one of them embarrassed.

"My teakettle whistled and then I spotted you down here. You look like you could use a warm drink."

"Do I?" He palmed his neck and glanced behind him. Maybe she'd misread this situation after all.

"Unless you're waiting for someone?"

She'd seen him in town with a waifish blonde woman a handful of times. *Claire*, Hayden had gleaned. Tate's girl-friend and very recently, fiancée. The other woman seemed proper and rigid, and Hayden's first thought was that she was an odd match for the always bright and cheery Tate… though he wasn't bright or cheery at the moment.

"No. I was at the Pony," he said of the restaurant up the hill from here. "The rain caught me."

"I'd offer to drive you home, but I don't have a car." One of the luxuries she'd given up to afford to move to Spright Island, but the sacrifice had been worth it. *Peace* had been worth it.

Every shop or store in the community could be reached on foot if she planned ahead, and she had a few friends in the area or could call a car service if she needed to venture farther.

"But I do have tea." She opened the door wider.

"Of course. Thank you." He stepped into the studio, his shoes squishing on her welcome mat. "Sorry about this."

"No worries." She locked the door behind him and grabbed a towel from a nearby cabinet. "Clean, fluffy towel? They're for my hot yoga classes."

He accepted with a nod and sopped the water from his hair.

"Tea's in my apartment." She gestured to the open doorway leading upstairs. "Don't worry about wet shoes. I'm not that formal."

Tate followed her upstairs and inside her *blessedly spotless* apartment. She'd cleaned yesterday. She was fairly tidy, but some weeks got the best of her and she didn't get around to vacuuming or changing her sheets.

By the time he was in the center of her living room and she was shutting the door to the staircase behind her, she was questioning her invitation.

A man in her apartment shrank it down until it felt like she lived in a cereal box—and this man in particular infused the immediate space with a sizzling attraction she'd felt since he first shook her hand.

Hayden Green, he'd said. *You have the perfect last name for this community.*

Now, he pegged her with a look that could only be described as vulnerable, as if something was really, *really* off. She wanted nothing more than to cross the room and scoop him into her arms. But she couldn't do that. He had a fiancée. And she wasn't looking for a romantic relationship.

No matter how hot he was.

"Tea," she reminded herself and then stepped around him to walk to the kitchen.

Two

Tate slipped out of his leather jacket and hung it on an honest-to-goodness coatrack in between the door and the television. His shirt beneath was dry, thank goodness, and his pants were in the process of drying, but he kicked off his shoes rather than track puddles through Hayden's apartment.

Since he'd personally approved the design of every structure in SWC, he knew this building. He'd expected her place to be both modern and cozy, but she'd added her own sense of unique style. Much like Hayden herself, her apartment was laid-back with a Zen feel. From the live potted plants near the window to the black-and-white woven rug on the floor. A camel-brown sofa stood next to a coffee table, its surface cluttered with books. Oversize deep gold throw pillows were stacked on the floor for sitting, a journal and a pen resting on top of one of them.

"I like what you've done with the place." He was still drying his hair with the towel when he leaned forward to study the photos on the mantel above a gas fireplace. He'd expected family photos, maybe one of a boyfriend, or a niece or nephew. Instead the frames held quotes. One of them was the silhouette of a woman in a yoga pose with wording underneath that read, *I bend so I don't break*, and the other a plain black background with white lettering: *If you stumble, make it part of the dance.*

"Do you have a tea preference?" she called from the kitchen.

"Not really."

He didn't drink tea, though he supposed he should, since he'd recently learned he was *from fucking London*.

"I have green, peppermint and chai. Green has caffeine, so let's not go there." She peeked at him before tucking the packet back into the drawer like she'd intuited a pending breakdown.

Great. Nothing like an emasculating bout of anxiety to finish up his day.

"Peppermint would be good if you were nauseous or ate too much, and chai will warm you up." She narrowed her eyes, assessing him anew. "Chai."

"Chai's fine. Thanks again."

She set about making his tea and he watched her, the fluid way she moved as she hummed to herself in the small kitchen. Stepping into Hayden's apartment was a lot like stepping into a therapist's office, only not as stuffy. As if being in her space tempted him to open up. Whether it was the rich, earthy colors or the offer of a soothing, hot drink he didn't know. Maybe both.

He was surprised she'd invited him in, considering she'd found him standing in a downpour staring blankly at the window.

Probably he should get around to addressing that.

She set the mugs on the coffee table, and he moved to the sofa, debating whether or not to sit.

"You're dry enough," she said, reading his mind. She swiped the towel and disappeared into the bedroom before coming back out. Her walk was as confident as they came, with an elegance reminding him of Claire.

Claire. Her last words to him two weeks ago kept him awake at night, along with the other melee of crap bouncing around in his head.

I can't handle this right now, Tate. I have a job. A life. Let's have a cooling-off period. I'm sure you'd like some time alone.

He felt alone, more alone than ever now that the holidays were coming up. His adoptive parents were fretting, though he tried to reassure them. Nothing would reassure his mother, he knew. Guilt was a carnivorous beast.

Hayden lit a candle on a nearby shelf, and he took back his earlier comparison to Claire. Hayden was completely different. From her dark hair to her curvy dancer's body.

Pointing to the quote on the mantel, he said, "I bet you've never stumbled a day in your life."

With a smile, she sat next to him and lifted her mug. "I've stumbled many times. Do you know how hard it is to do a headstand in yoga?"

"How is the studio doing? I was considering trying a class." A clumsy segue, but that might explain why he'd been lingering outside like a grade A creeper. "I've been... stressed. I thought yoga might be a good de-stressor."

"Yoga's a *great* de-stressor," she said conversationally, as if him coming to this conclusion while standing in a downpour was normal. "I teach scheduled group classes as well as private sessions."

"One on one?" He'd bet her schedule was packed. Being in her presence for a few minutes had already made him feel more relaxed.

"Yep. A lot of people around here prefer one-on-one help with their practice. Others just like being alone with no help at all, which is why I open the space for members once a week."

"That's a lot of options." She must work around the clock.

"There are a lot of people here, or haven't you noticed, Mr. Spright Island?" She winked, thick dark lashes closing over one chocolate-brown iris. Had she always been this beautiful?

"I noticed." He returned her smile. There were just shy of nine hundred houses in SWC. That made for plenty of residents milling around town and, more often than he was previously aware, apparently in Hayden's yoga studio.

"I don't believe you want to talk about yoga." Her gaze was a bare lightbulb on a string over his head, as if there was no way to hide what had been rattling around in his brain tonight. She lifted dark, inquisitive eyebrows. "You look like you have something interesting to talk about."

The pull toward her was real and raw—the realest sensation he'd felt in a while. It grounded him, grabbed him by the balls and demanded his full attention.

"I didn't plan on talking about it..." he admitted, but she must have heard the ellipsis at the end of that sentence.

She tilted her head, sage interest in whatever he might say next. Wavy dark brown hair surrounded a cherubic heart-shaped face, her deep brown eyes at once tender and inviting. *Inviting.* There was that word again. Unbidden, his gaze roamed over her tanned skin, her V-necked collar and delicate collarbone. How had he not noticed before? She was *alarmingly* beautiful.

"I'm sorry." Her palm landed on his forearm. "I'm prying. You don't have to say anything."

She moved to pull her hand away but he captured her fingers in his, studying her shiny, clear nails and admiring the olive shade of her skin and the way her hand offset his own pinker hue.

"There are aspects of my life I was certain of a month and a half ago," he said, idly stroking her hand with his thumb. "I was certain that my parents' names were William and Marion Duncan." He offered a sad smile as Hayden's eyebrows dipped in confusion. "I suppose they technically still are my parents, but they're also not. I'm adopted."

Her plush mouth pulled into a soft frown, but she didn't interrupt.

"I recently learned that the agency—" *or more accurately, the kidnappers* "—lied about my birth parents. Turns out they're alive and living in London. And I have a brother." He paused before clarifying, "A twin brother."

Hayden's lashes fluttered. "Wow."

"Fraternal, but he's a good-looking bastard."

She squeezed his fingers. There for him in spite of owing him nothing. That should've been Claire's job.

"I was certain that I was the owner/operator of Spright Island's premier, thriving wellness community," he stated in his radio-commercial voice. "That, thank God, hasn't changed. SWC is a sanctuary of sorts. There is a different vibe here that you can't find inland."

"I know exactly what you mean. I stepped foot in my studio downstairs that first time, and it had this positive energy about it. Does that sound unbelievable?"

No more unbelievable than being kidnapped in another country and having no memory of it.

"It doesn't sound unbelievable." He took pride in what he'd built. He'd poured himself, body and soul, into what he created, so it wasn't surprising some of that had leaked into the energy of this place.

"I was also certain I was going to be married to Claire Waterson."

At the mention of a fiancée, Hayden tugged her hand from his and wrapped her fingers around her mug. He didn't think it was because she was thirsty.

"When I found out about my family tree, she bailed on me," he told her. "I didn't expect that."

He raked his hands through his damp hair, unable to stop the flow of words now that he'd undammed them. "You invited me in for tea thinking I had something on my mind. Bet you didn't expect a full-blown identity crisis."

Her eyebrows dipped in sympathy.

"I just need… I need…" Dropping his head in his hands, he trailed off, muttering to the floor, "Christ, I have no idea what I need."

He felt the couch shift and dip, and then Hayden's hand was on his back, moving in comforting circles.

"I've had my share of family drama, trust me. But nothing like what you're going through. It's okay for you to feel unsure. Lost."

He faced her. This close, he could smell her soft lavender perfume and see the gold flecks in her dark eyes. He hadn't planned on coming here, or on sitting on her couch and spilling his heart out. He and Hayden were *friendly*, not friends. But her comforting touch on his back, the way her words seemed to soothe the recently broken part of him…

Maybe what he needed was *her*.

He leaned forward, his eyes focused on her mouth and the satisfaction kissing her would bring.

"Tate." She jerked away, sobering him instantly.

"Sorry. I'm sorry." What the hell was he thinking? That Hayden invited him in to make out on her couch? That sharing his sob story would somehow turn her on? As if any woman wanted to be with a man who was in pieces.

He stood to leave. She stood with him.

"Listen, Tate—"

"I shouldn't have come here." He pulled his coat on and shoved his feet in his shoes, grateful for the leather slip-ons. At least there wouldn't be an awkward interlude while he tied his laces. "Thank you for listening. I'm really very sorry."

"Wait." She arrived at the coatrack as he was stuffing his arms into his still-wet leather coat.

"I'm going to go." He turned to apologize again, but was damn near knocked off his feet when Hayden pushed to her toes, cuffed the back of his neck and pulled his mouth down to hers.

Three

Hayden had fantasized of kissing Tate ever since she first laid eyes on him. She knew he wasn't meant to be hers in real life, but in her fantasies, well, there were no rules.

Of all the imagined kisses they'd shared, none compared to the actual kiss she was experiencing now.

The moment their lips touched, he grabbed on to her like a lifeline, eagerly plunging his tongue into her mouth. His skin was chilly from the rain, but his body radiated heat. She was downright toasty in his arms…and getting hotter by the second.

She tasted dark liquor—bourbon or whiskey—on his tongue, but there was a tinge of something else. Sadness, if she wasn't mistaken. Sadness over learning he had a brother after all these years—a twin brother. Wow, that was wild…

A pair of strong hands gripped her waist. Tate tugged her close, and when her breasts flattened against his chest all other thoughts flew from her head. The water clinging to his coat soaked through her sweater, causing her nipples to bead to tight peaks inside her bra.

Still, she kissed him.

She wasn't done with this real-life fantasy. A brief thought of Claire Waterson crashed into her mind, and she shoved it out. They were broken up—he'd said so himself. Hayden had nothing to feel guilty about.

Besides, he needed her. Whenever she'd been lost or sad, she'd taken solace in her friends. That was what she offered to him now.

A safe space.

She pulled her lips from Tate's to catch her breath, her mind buzzing and her limbs vibrating. His chest and shoulders rose and fell, the hectic rhythm set by the brief make-out session. An unsure smile tilted his mouth, and she returned it with one of her own.

"Better?" she asked.

His low laugh soaked into her like rum on spongecake. He pulled his hand over his mouth and then back through his hair, and her knees nearly gave way. It'd be so easy to lean in and taste him again, to offer her body as a place for him to lay his worries…

"I didn't mean to take advantage of your hospitality. Honest." His blue eyes shimmered in the candlelight.

"You didn't. I always serve tea with French kisses. It's a package deal."

"The best deal in town," he murmured. He stroked her jaw tenderly, those tempting lips offering the sincerest "thank you" she'd ever heard.

"Call a car," she said, before she asked him to stay. "It's pouring out there."

"Actually—" he opened the door that led down to her studio "—I could use a cool, brisk walk after that kiss."

She smiled, pleased. It wasn't every day she could curl a hot guy's toes. She considered this rare feat a victory.

"I'll lock the studio door behind me. There are some real weirdos out there…"

She grinned, knowing he was referring to himself.

Before he pulled the door shut, he stuck his head through

the crack. "You don't really kiss everyone you offer tea, do you?"

"Wouldn't you like to know." She was tempted to put another brief peck on his mouth, but he disappeared through the gap before she could. A fraction of a second later, she was looking at the wood panel instead of his handsome face and wondering if she'd hallucinated the entire thing.

"Hayden, Hayden," she chastised gently as she engaged the lock and drew the chain. She turned and eyed the mugs of tea, Tate's untouched and hers barely drunk. His lips hadn't so much as grazed the edge of that mug.

But they were all over yours.

That spontaneous kiss had rocked her world.

She dashed to the window and peered out into the rain, hoping for one more glance at her nighttime visitor. A dark figure passed under a streetlamp, his shoulders under his ears, his hair wet all over again. Before he disappeared from sight, he turned to face her building and walked a few steps backward. She couldn't see his face from that far away, but she liked to believe he was smiling.

She touched her lips.

So was she.

Three wet days later, the rain had downgraded from downpour to light drizzle. Even walking across the street to Summer's Market yesterday for ingredients for blueberry muffins had left Hayden wet and cold. She'd returned home soaked to the bone, her hair smelling of rainwater.

Which, of course, reminded her of *The Kiss* from the other day. She hadn't seen Tate since. Not that she'd expected him to stop by, but… Well, was *hope* the wrong word to use?

Over and over, she'd remembered the feel of Tate's firm lips, his capable hands gripping her hips, the vulnerability in his smile. The ways his eyes shined with curiosity afterward.

Knowing she'd erased some of his sadness made her feel special. She was beginning to think she actually *missed him*. Odd, considering the concept of missing him was foreign until that kiss.

The chilly bite of the wind cut through her puffy, light-weight coat, and she tucked her chin behind the zipped collar as she crossed the street to the café.

Nothing better for walking off sexual frustration than a brisk November stroll.

She had an advanced yoga class in an hour and was tired just thinking about it. A hot cup of coffee would put some much-needed pep in her step.

She wasn't the only resident of SWC taking advantage of the drier weather. Cold drizzles they were willing to brave. Drenching downpours, not so much. As a result, there was a buzz in the air, an audible din of chatter amongst the couples or single professionals lounging in the outdoor patio. It was closed off for the winter, the temporary walls and tall gas heaters making the space warm enough for the over-flow of customers.

Inside, Hayden rubbed her hands together, delighted to find that the person in line ahead of her was finished ordering. The only thing better than a Sprightly Bean coffee at the start of a day was not waiting in line to get one. She ordered a large caramel latte and stepped to the side to wait. Not thirty seconds into her studying the glass case of doughnuts and other sinful baked goods, the low voice from her dreams spoke over her shoulder.

"I've seen regret before, and it looks a lot like the expression on your face, Ms. Green."

Her smile crested her mouth before she turned. She thought she was prepared to come face-to-face with Tate until she did. His dark wool coat was draped over a charcoal-gray suit, his hair neatly styled against his head and slightly damp, she guessed from a recent shower. And wasn't that a pleasant image? Him naked, water flowing over lean muscle, corded forearms, long, strong legs...

"Am I broadcasting regret?" she asked, her voice a flirty lilt.

He pointed at the bakery case. "Was it the éclair or the lemon–poppy seed muffin that caused it?"

"Hmm." She pretended to consider. "I could be regretting my impulsive behavior three days ago."

His eyebrows rose like she'd stunned him. She wasn't much of a wallflower, which he should know after she'd grabbed him up and kissed him.

He opened his mouth to reply when a thin blonde woman glided around the corner, tugging a glove onto her hand. *Claire.*

"I'm ready to go," she announced without preamble. Or manners. Or delicacy.

As if her frosty entrance had chilled them both, Hayden's smile vanished and Tate retreated.

He nodded at Claire Waterson, his frown appearing both on his mouth and forehead. "Hayden, this is Claire. Claire, this is Hayden Green. She owns the yoga studio down the road."

"Charmed." Claire nodded curtly as she tugged on her other glove. No offer of a handshake, but Hayden didn't want to shake the other woman's hand, anyway.

"See you around," Tate told Hayden.

She watched them leave, her forehead scrunching when Tate touched Claire's back on the walk out to a car. He hadn't walked to the café today. Hayden would bet *Priss in Boots* hadn't allowed it.

"Grande caramel latte." The cheery barista handed over Hayden's coffee, and she managed a genial smile before walking out the front door, her steps heavy. Tate, in the driver's seat, pulled away from the curb on the opposite side of the street. He didn't wave, but did manage a compressed half smile.

While Hayden didn't have any claim on him, she'd admit she felt like an idiot for believing him. He'd sounded so sincere when he said his relationship with Claire was over. Or had he implied it was over? Either way, if she'd had any idea Tate and Claire would be sharing morning coffee a few days later, Hayden never would have kissed him. From the looks of it, he and Claire were very much *together*.

Ew.

She started her march home, an unhealthy dose of anger seeping into her bloodstream. The first sip of her coffee burned her tongue, and the wind blew directly into her face, cold and bitter.

A series of beeps sounded from her pocket and Hayden's back stiffened. That was her mother's ringtone. It never failed to cause a cocktail of panic, fear and resentment to boil over. She ignored the second ring and then the third and, a minute later, the chime of her voice mail.

When Hayden left Seattle, it had felt like more of an escape. Her mother had been—and was still—stressed to the max, refusing to draw boundary lines around the one woman causing problems in their lives: Hayden's alcoholic grandmother. Grandma Winnie favored drama and bottom-shelf vodka in equal measures, and Hayden's mother, Patti, had turned codependency into an art form. Hayden's dad, Glenn, was content to let the matriarchs rule the roost, as if he'd eschewed himself from the chaos in the only way he knew how: silence.

After years of trying to balance family drama with her own desperate need for stability, Hayden left Seattle and her family behind for the oasis of Spright Island.

By the time she was changing for her class, her coffee was cool and her mind was numb. She paused in the living room of her apartment, put her hands over her heart and took three deep breaths.

There was no sense in being angry at Grandma Winnie for being an alcoholic. It wasn't her fault she had a disease. Similarly, she let go of worrying over her mother's codependence and her father's blind eye.

"Everyone is doing the best they can," she said aloud.

But as she trotted down the stairs to the studio and unlocked the door for a few waiting guests, she found that there was one person in her life she didn't feel as magnanimous toward.

The man who'd kissed her soundly, scrambled her senses and then showed up in town with the very woman he claimed had left him behind.

"Hi, Hayden," greeted Jan, the first of her students through the door.

Hayden returned Jan's smile and shoved aside her tumultuous thoughts. She owed it to her class to be present and bring good energy, not bad.

Family drama—and Tate drama—would be waiting for her when the class was over, whether she wanted it or not.

Four

The bell over her studio entrance jangled as Hayden's evening class filed out of the building. She was behind the desk, jotting down a note for Marla, who'd been coming for individual classes but decided tonight she wanted to join the group. Since Marla hadn't brought her credit card, Hayden had promised to email her in the morning.

Hayden stuck a reminder Post-it note onto the cover of her hardbound planner and looked up, expecting to see the last of her students leave. Instead, someone was coming *in*.

A certain someone who hadn't left her mind no matter how hard she tried to stop thinking about him.

Dressed in black athletic pants and a long-sleeved black T-shirt, Tate shrugged out of the same leather jacket he'd worn the night they kissed. It'd been five days since that kiss. Two days since the coffee shop.

She still wasn't happy with him, but it was impossible not to admire his exquisite hotness.

"Hey," she blurted, unsure what else to say.

"Hey." He looked over his shoulder. "I know I missed class, but I was hoping to schedule a one-on-one."

Her mind went to the last "one-on-one" session they'd

had. She hadn't forgotten that kiss. She probably never would. It was burned onto her frontal lobe.

"Individual sessions have to be scheduled ahead of time," she said as tartly as she could manage. The vision of him with Claire was too fresh in her mind for her to be cordial.

"Are you sure?" He tilted his head as he stepped closer to her.

"If you're here because you feel you owe me an explanation or you need to air your regrets—"

"No. Nothing like that."

She lifted her eyebrows, asking a silent *well?*

"I haven't been in control of my life lately. Everything's moving at warp speed, and I'm caught in the undertow. You ever feel like you've lost control? Once upon a time you had it in your hands, and now..." He looked down at his own fists gripping his coat as his mouth pulled down at the corners.

She knew exactly what that was like, but in reverse order. Her world had been moving at warp speed since birth, and only moving to SWC had stopped its trajectory.

She sympathized with Tate, though she was tempted to cut her losses and show him the door.

"And taking a yoga class with me would help you feel in control?" she asked anyway.

"Ah, well. Not exactly." Palm on his neck, he studied the floor and then peeked up at her with a look of chagrin so magnetic, her heart skipped a beat. "I'm really good at turning you on. At least I think I would be. Are you still doling out kisses with every cup of tea?"

She gripped the edge of the front desk, digesting what he'd just said. He *was* good at turning her on. She knew that, but what was she supposed to do with it? Especially when Tate stood in front of her looking coy and cunning and yet vulnerable and was offering… Wait… Was this *a booty call*?

"Sorry. That offer expired." Not that she was above kissing him, but… "I'm not going to be your girl on the side, Tate. What would Claire say?"

"That's over. It's *been* over. What you saw at the coffee shop was her finalizing things. You know, like you do after someone dies."

He paced to the salt lamp on her desk and stared at it for a beat. "She dropped off a box of my stuff at my house and then asked if we could grab a coffee and talk. I told her she could talk to me there, but she said she preferred neutral territory."

"Oh." It was a breakup. Hayden had misread that entire exchange. Still… "And you didn't feel the need to explain yourself after I saw you at the café? You thought you'd instead come here and…" She waved a hand uselessly, unable to finish her thought, since she wasn't 100 percent sure why he was here.

"I thought we could start with a yoga session." He dipped his chin. "If you have any openings for, say, now."

She tried to tell him no, but found she couldn't. Tate Duncan didn't have to work hard to charm her on any given day, and today he was actually trying.

"How about…" She flipped open her planner and traced her finger down the page. "Tomorrow. Noon."

"Deal."

"I'll need your credit card. I require a nonrefundable down payment for the first appointment."

"Smart."

She hummed. She wasn't so sure this was smart, but was too curious to turn him away.

The morning of his yoga appointment, Tate set out for Hayden's studio. The day was dry if chilly, but he welcomed the burning cold in his lungs as he cut through a path in the woods.

He'd been out for a quick trip to Summer's Market when he'd witnessed Hayden's evening class letting out. He hadn't planned on walking across the street and inside, but when he found himself in front of her, he had to have a reason for being there.

Besides the obvious.

Hayden had consumed damn near every one of his waking thoughts, which was a relief compared to his usual pastime: turning over his parentage, the truth about where he came from, or the disastrous outcome since.

He'd blamed the kiss on whiskey and a need for connection. The liquor buzz was long gone, but the imprint of her kiss remained like a brand. It was reckless to leap into the flames after he'd just escaped a fire—Claire should've rendered him numb. But Hayden…she was different.

Not only had she been there for him when he'd been adrift on his own, but she replaced his tumultuous thoughts with something a hell of a lot better.

Sex.

He wanted her. He wanted her in his arms and in his bed. He wanted her moaning beneath him, her nails scratching down his back.

It was as if he'd devolved to his most carnal desires when she was around, and for a change, he was all for it. He was tired of feeling unmoored, helpless. Sad. With her he felt strong, capable. She'd come apart in his arms during that kiss. She may have put him through his paces last night, but he respected her for it.

Hell, he knew he'd stepped in it with Hayden the moment he left that café with Claire. But he'd owed Claire that meeting. They'd dated for three years and had been recently engaged, though he now wondered if that was more of a technicality. She'd never lived with him—never wanted to. She didn't treasure Spright Island or his community the way he did.

The way Hayden does. That kiss with Hayden was about far more than their lips meeting and an attraction they weren't aware of blooming. For Tate, it was about discovering that he'd been sleepwalking through his life.

Tate had never been ill-equipped for a task set before him. He'd accepted the gift of Spright Island from his father without qualms and had set about building an entire town and community even when he'd never worked on his own before. He'd learned by doing. Each time adversity had come up, he'd defeated it.

When he'd found out that Reid was his brother, Tate felt like a superhero who'd stumbled across his fatal weakness. He didn't have a single weapon in his arsenal to handle the situation set before him.

His previously drama-free life had begun to look more like a Netflix feature with him in the center as the hapless protagonist.

Until the kiss with Hayden.

That night had changed him, changed his outlook. And after a numb month of disbelief, feeling something—feeling anything other than stark shock—was as welcome as… well, as the kiss itself.

Yoga by Hayden came into sight and he crossed the street with a neat jog. A smile inched across his face, but flagged when he noticed the Closed sign on the door. He tugged the handle.

Locked.

He checked the clock on his phone. 12:04 p.m. He was late. Maybe she drew a hard line when it came to promptness.

Then he looked up and there she was, her curves barely contained in colorful leggings and a long-sleeved green shirt. She flipped the lock and opened the door, reminding him of the night he'd been standing outside this very studio in the rain.

Reminding him that she'd climbed to her toes to lay the mother of all kisses on him and had changed his life for the better.

"Sorry. Typically, I'm more punctual than this," she said.

God, he wanted to kiss her. The timing was wrong, though. She hadn't yet met his eyes save for a brief flicker that bounced away the second she caught him staring.

She was hard not to stare at, all that silken dark hair and the grace in her every movement...

"I thought maybe you'd changed your mind." He hung his coat on a hook and perused a small display of yoga mats, blocks and water bottles. "I'll have to buy a mat. I don't have one."

"Help yourself." Hayden's gaze glanced off him again, and then almost relieved, she said, "Oh, good, she's here."

A fortysomething blonde woman ran toward the building, her yoga mat under her arm.

"Sherry had a last-minute need for an appointment, so I piggybacked onto your session. With the holiday week being so busy, I couldn't fit her in any other time." Hayden blew out the news in a nonstop stream. "I hope you don't mind."

Of course he minded. He'd scheduled a one-on-one with Hayden, and now he had to share his time with Sherry Baker, SWC's premiere real estate agent.

"Oh, hi, Tate." Sherry patted him on the shoulder before hanging her coat and scarf on the hook next to his. "I didn't know you practiced yoga."

He slid his eyes to Hayden, who bit her lip and locked the door. She'd double booked herself on purpose. *For some reason.*

"You know me," he told Sherry. "I'm always trying to support more local businesses."

"Get this one." Sherry handed him a black yoga mat. "It's manly and the same brand as mine."

"Done." He turned to Hayden with a million questions he couldn't ask. "Mind if I pay you after?"

Her mouth hovered open for a beat as Sherry unrolled her yoga mat. With an audience, Hayden didn't have much of a choice other than being polite.

"Sure."

"Great." He took his spot on the studio floor. He'd won that round. He planned on sticking around after Sherry left. He wanted answers.

Five

For Hayden, doing yoga was like breathing. She slipped into each pose easily, pausing to instruct Sherry and Tate through the movements.

Sherry was in her midforties with two teenagers. Her son had recently moved to a college campus and her younger daughter was thirteen and embroiled in a teenage spat with her two best friends, Callie and Samantha. Hayden knew this because Sherry hadn't stopped talking since class had started.

Sherry also mentioned her twenty unwanted pounds and a caffeine habit that bordered on addiction, and said she hoped doing one healthy thing like yoga would lead to other healthy things like cutting down on coffee and overtime at work.

Tate remained resolutely silent, though she'd caught a small smile on his mouth more than once as he'd eased from one pose into the other.

During downward dog pose Hayden moved to assist Sherry with her alignment. "Push your five fingertips into the mat rather than the palm of your hand," she instructed. "We don't want compressed wrists."

Hayden turned to Tate next, willing herself to remember she was a teacher and a professional. There was never anything sexual involved in helping a student.

Until now.

One look at Tate's ass, his legs and arms strong and straight, and a wave of attraction walloped her in the stomach. As fate would have it, she was also going to have to touch his hips to move him into more of a V form than a U.

Dammit.

One hand on his back, the other on his hips, she instructed him to lower his heels to the floor as much as he was able. He breathed out with the effort, that breath reverberating along her arm and hand, and she became even more aware of him than before.

Who knew that was possible?

Those sorts of thoughts were exactly what Sherry's presence was supposed to *quell.*

She led them from downward dog to cobra, encouraging Sherry to use her knees if she needed to. When Hayden turned to tell Tate the same thing, he lowered into the pushup-like pose with what appeared to be very little effort. A closer look at his biceps and she realized they shook subtly as he took his time, holding himself in plank pose a moment before dropping his waist and pushing up with his arms.

She stared, unabashedly, which he must've noticed a moment later, when he sent her a cocky smirk.

Show-off.

She returned to her mat and walked them through one more sun salutation, ending in mountain pose: standing, hands in prayer pose at the chest.

"Namaste," Hayden said. "That concludes our lesson for the day."

"Woo! That was intense, girlfriend!" Sherry waved her hands in front of her pink face. "I'm sure Tate would've preferred a less chatty partner, though."

Sherry winked at him, and Hayden smothered a laugh. Sherry was happily married and treated Tate like she would a friend or any other familiar resident of SWC.

You know, the same way you *should be treating him.*

"I have to return to the office," Sherry announced. "Can I call to schedule a follow-up after the holiday?"

"Whenever you like." Hayden walked Sherry to the door, chatting to stall while waiting for Tate to leave. Instead, Tate was at the front desk, his rolled mat on the surface.

Crap. She forgot he needed to pay.

Sherry left and Hayden made her way to the front desk, her heart hammering.

"If you admit that you booked Sherry because you couldn't trust yourself to be alone with me, I'll forgive you for it," he told her.

"Ha!" She left it at that because any response other than "Yep, that's correct!" would have been a lie.

She *didn't* trust herself alone with him. His kiss the other night had been too welcome, his presence too distracting. She had enough drama in her life without creating some of her own.

Last night after he left she'd thought more about the chaos in Tate's life. Not one parental pair but two. And a surprise twin brother. Hayden had come to Spright Island specifically to avoid drama not become embroiled in it. That, and the fact she didn't trust herself to be alone with him, was why she'd scheduled Sherry for the same timeslot.

Tate wasn't unlike that second serving of ice cream she knew she shouldn't have. It seemed that no amount of will-power could keep her from one more taste.

"Thirty-two dollars."

He handed her his credit card.

"It's a really good mat," she explained needlessly as she charged his card. Anything to fill the dead air between them.

"I wasn't arguing."

"No, I guess you wouldn't." She imagined thirty-two dollars to Tate Duncan must be what thirty-two *cents* felt like to her.

"What's going on, Hayden? Do you find me particularly hard to get along with?"

"I— Sorry. That was rude." She handed his card back and flipped the screen around for him to sign it. When he was finished, she tucked her iPad into the drawer and, with no other task before her, was forced to meet his eyes.

He stood there like he had nowhere else to be.

"I didn't schedule Sherry *only* because I didn't want to be alone with you. It worked well since you're both beginners."

He nodded slowly.

"Plus, what did you expect after you barged in here—"

"I barged?"

"—and demanded—"

"Demanded?"

She huffed out a breath. If was going to continue calling her bluff, she really should stop lying about her true intentions. But there was a nugget of truth she could cling to.

"My schedule has been nuts this week. Everyone's trying to get in before Thanksgiving."

"Ah. And you fit me in." He grinned. "Because you couldn't tell me no."

She made a pathetic choking sound. How arrogant was this guy, anyway? And how did he keep guessing right?

"Because I have to make a living. I don't have billions stashed away..." She almost added "like some people" but she was already protesting too much.

"Right," he agreed, but something in his expression told her he'd gleaned what she hadn't said. "Well, thank you. For the mat."

He went to grab his coat, slipping it over his arms and holding the rolled mat between his knees.

Feeling a dab of guilt, she moved toward him and vomited out a generic nicety. "Thank you for booking your session. I hope you'll consider a membership."

His hand resting on the door handle, he turned as she stopped advancing, putting her mere inches from his handsome face. "I was thinking about another kind of one-on-one session. Are you available for dinner?"

She hadn't been prepared for that. Words eluded her. She knew that agreeing to go out with him was a bad idea, but when faced with his glittering blue eyes she couldn't quite remember why.

"Just so you know—" that blue gaze dipped to her mouth "—if you were ready, I'd kiss the hell out of you right now. Just to make sure I didn't imagine how good you tasted before."

She gaped at him, but he didn't advance to kiss her. Instead he turned around and stepped outside.

Before she could shut the door, he pushed it open a crack. "Think about dinner. I'll ask again."

She locked up behind him, watching him through the glass. He had a sure, strong gait, a disgustingly handsome mug, and looked as good in a suit as he did in sweatpants.

There were a multitude of reactions fighting for first place. She wanted to open the door and yell for him to come back. She wanted to run upstairs and shut the blinds. She wanted to jog across the street and grab him by the ears and kiss the hell out of *him*.

Especially that last one.

While she warred with those options, frozen in stunned bliss at the possibilities, Tate grew farther and farther away until he was a shadowy blur disappearing into a path into the woods.

"Damn him." But she didn't mean it. She was looking forward to next time—when she would leave *him* slack-jawed and without a response.

Six

Chaz's Pub in Seattle was a far cry from the Brass Pony, with its scuffed floors and beaten tables. Tate walked in for the first time, took in the colorful red and green decorations, and decided he liked the place. Any establishment that decorated for Christmas before Thanksgiving had his undying respect.

His brother Reid had invited him out to celebrate "the biggest drinking day of the year," tacking on, "You're British and it's your duty to get pissed."

As overwhelming as it was to learn he had a brother and a set of parents he'd never met, Tate had to smile. Could've been the yoga. He'd been more relaxed since the session with Hayden, though the buzz afterwards could likely be blamed more on sexual tension than downward dog.

The sexual tension part wasn't entirely her fault. Tate and Claire hadn't slept together since he'd found out about his family, and shortly after that she'd ended their engagement. In other words, it'd been a while.

Plus, Hayden was sexy as hell, had a way of revving him up and calming him down simultaneously. When she hadn't been touching him to move his body into proper form, he'd noticed her sliding from position to position. It'd been like watching an erotic dance.

She was a unique experience, that was for damn sure.

"Tate, hey!"

A petite brunette bounced over to him, pulling him from his thoughts. Reid's fiancée, Drew Fleming was as sweet as she was adorable and at the same time up to absolutely no good. He'd met her before—Reid had brought her when they'd gone out for drinks or dinners.

She looped her left arm in Tate's, and he glanced down at the sizable diamond ring on her hand. Reid had proposed around the time Tate's engagement had ended, as if Reid was an alien who had taken over Tate's life. Wasn't Tate supposed to be the one with the stable family life and fiancée?

"The boys are over there. I'll walk with you. But then I'm returning to the dance floor with the girls. Andy and Sabrina," she reminded him.

"Fiancées of Gage and Flynn."

"You remembered!"

He had. Gage and Flynn were Reid's best friends and coworkers. He'd met the whole gang in passing at one time or another.

Drew guided Tate to a high, round table with several stools surrounding it. Full glasses of Guinness were in front of each of the guys, suggesting they hadn't been here long.

"There he is." Reid wore the wide smile Tate envied. Not that Tate didn't want his brother to be happy, but he'd like to stockpile some of that for himself. Wanted to feel with certainty that tomorrow would come, and things would return to normal again.

"Found a stray," Drew released Tate and laid a kiss on Reid's cheek. He didn't let her get away, snagging her waist and dipping her low while kissing her thoroughly. Next to them, Flynn grinned, but Gage was less enthralled by the PDA.

"Still getting used to that," Gage grumbled as Tate took his seat. Gage was Drew's older brother, and Reid and Drew had kept their relationship from Gage until long after things had gotten serious between them.

"Hang in there, buddy." Flynn slapped Gage's back and let out a baritone chuckle. "Tate, man, how are you?"

Tate nodded, having no other word than a generic "fine."

"You need a beer," Flynn announced, waving down a waitress and to order one.

"Off with you, then." Reid swatted his fiancée's butt and she giggled, radiantly aglow. Once she'd scampered off, Reid's smile stuck to his face like glue. "She's pregnant."

Flynn nearly spit out his beer.

Gage turned an interesting shade of pale green.

"Congratulations," Tate said, figuring that was a safe response given the size of Reid's grin.

"Are pigs flying?" Flynn asked, his eyebrows meeting over the bridge of his nose. "Did hell freeze over? Am I having a stroke?" He turned to Gage and asked, "Do you smell burned toast?"

Gage shook his head, but his color returned. "Maybe we're all suffering from strokes. Reid Singleton: engaged and soon-to-be dad. What gives?"

"Drew. She's… Drew." Reid grinned bigger.

"I know how amazing she is. She's *my* sister." Then, as if it dawned on him at that moment, Gage smiled, too. "I'm going to be an uncle."

"Me, too. Technically." Flynn shrugged.

"And you," Reid dipped his chin at Tate. "Legitimately."

Right. Tate hadn't thought about that. Reid wasn't only a friend he was getting to know. He was a blood relative. The waitress delivered a Guinness, and Tate drank down the top third without coming up for air.

A pair of high-pitched squeals lifted on the air, and the guys turned toward the dance floor, where a brunette with glasses and a tall redhead were hugging Drew simultaneously.

"She told 'em. I knew she couldn't hold out." Reid said that with a smile as well, and if Tate had to guess, he'd say his brother's joy wasn't going anywhere soon.

"Sláinte." Flynn held his glass aloft, and the four of them banged the beers together. "So what have you been up to with the wellness commune, Duncan?"

He'd only met Flynn twice, but had determined that joking was Flynn's style. Tate liked Reid's friends and their fiancées. They were good people.

"Planning on a big Thanksgiving dinner Friday for the residents," Tate answered. "Serving Kool-Aid at the end for the really dedicated."

The guys laughed at the cult reference. Tate took it as a win. He knew the way Spright Wellness Community had been perceived it the past, but the place had gained a reputation for luxury living, thanks to Tate. Visitors flocked to the island and filled their community to capacity to eat, shop or simply spend time in nature.

"What about you guys?" Tate asked.

"Family dinner." Reid slid a glance at Gage. "With that wanker."

"I tried to disinvite him, but Mom said it'd ruin the holiday," Gage returned, poker-faced.

"We're going to California to Sab's parents. Her brother, Luke, is flying in from Chicago to join us."

"He's in Chi-town now?" Reid asked. "Sabrina never told me that."

"Yeah. His new gym franchise took off and he moved there to open another one. Rumor has it he's bringing a girl. Another one bites the dust." Flynn hadn't kept it a secret that his family was no longer. He'd mentioned inheriting Monarch Consulting after his father had died. That had brought mention of his late mother followed by a taste-less joke about how his brother was "banging my ex-wife." Flynn didn't seem as bitter about it as he was matter-of-fact, which Tate respected. Here he was trying to handle one curveball, and Flynn had been swinging at them his entire adult life.

"What about you?" Reid asked. "Other than Friday. Any plans?"

"Uh, no. Not really. Couldn't make the trip to Cali to see the parents."

Reid nodded slowly, like there was a thought he didn't want to say aloud in front of the guys. Like maybe he'd fig-ured out that Tate couldn't handle a family holiday with his adoptive parents after finding out they'd basically bought him off the black market. They hadn't known the truth, though, and that was the only reason he was still speaking to them. "The Brass Pony is serving an eight-course din-ner. I thought about going."

"You're welcome to join us," Gage said, even as Tate held up a hand to tell him he didn't have to do that. "I'm not asking because you're a charity case. I'm asking be-cause you're Reid's brother. Plus my parents cook enough to feed the county."

As kind as the invite was, a holiday spent with a fam-ily he didn't know and as the only single guy at the table sounded like Tate's worst nightmare. Rather than say that, he covered with, "Actually, I have a friend who lives in town. I asked her to join me."

Technically he hadn't asked Hayden out for that specific night but the dinner invitation could have been for when-ever, wherever.

"You *dog*. Dating again already?" Reid smirked.

"Claire and I weren't..." Tate took in the three girls who belonged with the men at the table as he tried to decide how to finish that sentence. For lack of a better term, he landed on, "Like you and your girls."

"Enviably gorgeous?" Reid said.

"In love," Tate said, bringing the table's laughter to a halt.

"Damn." Flynn finished his beer and gestured for another round for the table. Tate took another hearty gulp to catch up, but he still wasn't close. "Duncan called us out."

"He does that," Reid said.

"I like him," Gage decided. "Even if he doesn't want to hang out with my loony family on turkey day."

The guys continued bantering, and Tate, for a change, found himself relaxing into the conversation, the beer and the round of appetizers they ended up ordering. He didn't feel like the odd man out with the girls back at the table, tittering about Drew's pregnancy and making sure she had first dibs on every appetizer plate, but it did make him think of Hayden and how well she would've fit in here.

It was time to extend that dinner invitation again. And this time, earn a yes.

Seven

Hayden, sitting at a table in Succulence, a trendy, gourmet vegetarian restaurant in SWC, waved her friends over. Arlene gave an exuberant wave and pulled Emily in alongside her.

Hayden had met Arlene and Em last year, and they'd become fast friends. In SWC, residents were more interested in what they had in common rather than what set them apart. It made for deep discussions early on and, had cemented the three of them.

Well, originally there had been four. But Bailey had been AWOL since having a baby. Joyously married, she'd always been in a category of her own. Hayden recalled many, many nights when she and Arlene and Em would complain about their recent bad date or #singlelife and Bailey didn't have anything to contribute. Hayden missed her, but was confident Bailey would fold back into the fray. They were too close for their friendship to end over a few lifestyle differences. Besides, one of the three of them was bound to be married or at least happily coupled off eventually…right?

"Girls' night is on!" Arlene, boisterous and bold, had so much confidence it was infectious. She was also hilarious.

More often than not she had Hayden clutching her side in laughter while tears streamed down her face.

"So good to see you!" Emily gave Hayden a tight squeeze. "I feel like I've been gone a year." Emily had recently gone on an excursion to Spain for the lifestyle blog she wrote.

"It felt that way for all of us," Hayden agreed.

"Except we remembered you and you forgot all about us." Arlene threw her purse onto the chair. "First round on me. What's your pleasure? And before you ask, we're doing a shot followed by a cocktail. That's the minimum."

"Uh…" Hayden wasn't exactly a shot kind of girl. Not anymore.

"It ain't like any of us drove here." Arlene's blond hair was big with a lot of volume, like the rest of her. "And it *is* the biggest drinking holiday of the year."

"Because everyone dreads going home to family," Emily supplied. "Peppermint schnapps followed by a cosmo."

"I like your style." Arlene raised her brows at Hayden.

"Well…"

"Tequila," Arlene decided.

"What? No!" Hayden laughed.

"Yes. You can follow it with a light beer."

"I'll have a white Russian." Hayden lifted an eyebrow.

"Vodka shot on the side, then." Arlene didn't wait for an argument, only zoomed over to the bar to place their orders.

"Will you hold my hair?" Emily asked with a bright smile. She was ridiculously adorable with her dark hair in a sassy pixie cut. She folded her arms on the tabletop— white frosted glass balanced on a single silver pedestal. Succulence's mod design resembled a health spa, with its white and silver and neon-green accents. They were also pricey, but Hayden gladly overpaid for the fantastic food and cocktails.

A waiter came by. "Ladies."

"Hi, Josh." Em smiled up at him, as smitten as she was the first time they'd come in here. Hayden took pride in the fact that she'd arrived early enough to request his table.

"Eating or drinking tonight?" Josh was probably five years younger than all of them, but damned if Emily cared. She leaned heavily on a palm.

"Drinking, but snacks later. We'll probably camp here a while, but I promise to leave you a pile of money for a tip."

"Your beauty is enough of a tip for me." His cunning smile scrunched his dark eyes up at the corners. Paired with his tanned complexion and dark hair, Hayden had to agree he was pretty darn cute.

"You are full of it," Arlene told him as she returned to the table, tray in hand.

"Give me that." Josh swiped the tray and pointed at a seat. Arlene obediently sat and let Josh serve their drinks. "I know the peppermint schnapps is Em's."

Emily batted her lashes.

"Arlene has to be the tequila. And Hayden—" he sniffed her clear shot "—vodka. Nice choice. Enjoy, ladies." Then he was off, but not before winking at Emily.

"Oh, will you two screw each other already?" Arlene drank down a healthy swallow of her margarita .

"Shh! These walls have ears. And eyes. And cell phones with cameras." Emily jerked her gaze around the room.

Emily was right. SWC was high-end, luxurious and nature- and wellness-focused, but it was also a dressed-up small town. Everyone knew everyone and therefore knew everyone's *business*.

"We should've gone to the city where we could gossip properly," Arlene said. "Shots, ladies."

"If we were in the city, then I couldn't request Josh as

a server and watch Emily light up like a Christmas tree," Hayden said.

"I do not!" Emily turned a stunning shade of red as she lifted her shot glass.

"Did you think it was coincidence that we're always at his table?" Arlene asked with a raspy chuckle.

"You should ask him out," Hayden said.

"No way. He's just patronizing me."

"He'd like to be doing more than that." Arlene slanted a glance at Hayden.

"Why don't *you* ask someone out?" Em shot back, her shot wobbling at the edge of the glass. "How long's it been since you dated Derek?"

"Not long enough." Arlene held her shot aloft and shouted, "Cheers to years of beers and pap smears!"

Emily turned bright pink, Hayden groaned and hid behind a hand, and Arlene let out a bawdy laugh. That broad. God. Hayden loved her, though. They chucked back their shots, only Em coughing and waving the air like she'd swallowed gasoline.

"What about you, Hayd?" Em croaked.

"What about me what?"

"When are you going to ask someone out?"

"Why would I ask someone out?" Hayden purposely widened her eyes to look more innocent and then tacked on, "When I can kiss…" She looked around the restaurant teeming with their neighbors. Everyone here knew or had at least heard of Tate Duncan, so she couldn't very well blurt out his name. "*Someone* any time I'd like," she finished with an arch of one eyebrow.

"Shut. Up." Emily leaned in. "Who?"

"Someone we know." Arlene assessed Hayden. "But who?"

Unable to resist, Hayden mouthed his name. "Tate."

"Duncan?" Arlene bleated.

"Shh!" Hayden hissed.

"See? It's not fun when she does it to *you*." Em stuck her tongue out at Arlene, who returned the sentiment.

"He was standing outside my studio in the rain one night, and he looked so lost. I invited him up for tea and then…"

"You had sex with him?" Arlene cried.

"Keep it down, and no, I didn't!"

"Why not?" Emily asked with a small pout.

"For the same reason you won't ask out Josh," Hayden answered. "I was too terrified to consider it."

Which was the truth, if not for different reasons than Em. Hayden had fought hard to be fiercely independent, to escape the chaos that bubbled over in her family on a daily basis. Tate wasn't exactly a complete set. Some of his parts were scattered across the damn globe.

"I heard he and the blonde split up," Arlene said.

"Where did you hear that?"

"Naomi. She was at the café and overheard them talking."

Damn. This place really was a gossip mill. Hayden didn't dare mention Tate's learning of his birth parents and a twin brother.

"So, I'd be rebound girl," Hayden said, and it wasn't an entirely bad setup. Seeing how mired her mother was with her father certainly hadn't made it look appealing.

"Sounds like a superhero," Em said. "Rebound Girl! Able to leap tall, handsome billionaires in a single bound."

"I don't think he's a *billionaire*," Hayden said through her laughter.

"Have you seen this place?" Arlene gestured beyond the restaurant to the rows of houses on one side and the retail establishments on the other. "He built it, Hayd. From scratch."

"I have nothing against wealthy men," Emily said. "Except I'm attracted to the ones who aren't." She sent another longing glance to Josh, who was jotting down another group's order.

"He doesn't count, since he owns Succulence. He could be a billionaire restaurant owner. You never know," Hayden supplied.

Em pursed her lips in consideration.

"Well, I wouldn't kick Tate Duncan out of bed for any reason. *Especially* if it was because he was loaded." Arlene waggled her eyebrows, Emily agreed and Hayden found herself easing into the conversation as her mind wandered along the path of what-if and arrived at Tate's bed.

And Tate's couch. And Tate's shower…

"You're thinking about sex!" Arlene said. "Josh! We need another round!"

"No, we don't." But Hayden's smile was too big to be denied. She *was* thinking about sex. Tate was too fun not to kiss, not to do a host of other things to, especially since his last words to her were about kissing the hell out of her when she was ready. "I don't know if I'm ready."

Then again…

Just because Hayden wanted to have an affair with a gorgeous rich guy didn't mean she had to give up her autonomy. Tate didn't *have* to be ice cream. He could be a perfectly reasonable kale salad, which she enjoyed immensely and never suffered cravings for afterwards.

Aw, who was she kidding? Tate could never be kale salad. He was too tempting. Too hot. Too distracting!

But she should give herself more credit. She was independent. She'd moved away from her family and started over with her new family: her friends at SWC. She was a successful business owner, to boot.

Plus she really, *really* wanted to say yes to Tate the next time he asked. For dinner, for a kiss, for anything…

"On second thought, I *could be* ready." Hayden stirred the cream into her dark drink.

"Attagirl." Arlene pinned Emily with a meaningful look. "Now are you going to ask out Josh, or do I have to do it for you?"

Eight

Laughing, the three ladies stumbled out of Succulence and onto the sidewalk.

Arlene curled her arm around Emily and let out a shout of triumph. "You freaking did it!"

Emily giggled, proud of herself. She should be. After round two of drinks, she'd looked up at Josh and purred, "We should go on a date sometime. My friends agree we'd look good together."

To Hayden's complete delight, Josh's lids had lowered sexily and he'd replied, "What took you so long to ask?"

"Don't get too excited." Emily belted her coat against the wind. "It's only the beginning. And beginnings are fragile."

"You mean the other F-word," Arlene said. "Fun."

"They are fun," Emily agreed.

"Well, I had a fantastic time. Goodnight, loves." Hayden kissed Emily's cheek and pulled Arlene into a hug. "Be safe!"

They'd eaten enough appetizers to soak up the alcohol and had switched to water after the drinks. Two hours of fun and laughter later, Hayden's heart was full and happy. Her walk home might not be warm, but it would be welcome. Moving her body always made her feel better.

Back home in Seattle, Hayden used to hang out with the wrong crowd. She used to drink not for recreation, but with the goal of being completely drunk. She used to wake up with hangovers and headaches and, one time, no memory of how she'd gotten home. Nothing was more sobering than realizing she was repeating a pattern that her grandmother had started. Worried that she might end up exactly like Grandma Winnie, a belligerent, controlling, bitter alcoholic, Hayden decided that maybe drinking shouldn't be her main focus in life.

Enter exercise. She'd started with running early in the morning, which kept her from staying up too late. Running didn't require special equipment or training, and she found she had a proclivity for it. She set goals to be better each week and before she knew it, she was running every day.

Bitten by the fitness bug, she left her sedentary office job, where her derriere was widening by the day, to work at a local gym. She took advantage of her employee discount to purchase yoga classes.

It was love at first warrior pose.

Yoga gave her something running didn't. *Peace.*

Rather than her heart rate ratcheting up and her feet pounding the pavement—it was hell on her knees, anyway—she spent each hour-long yoga class in an almost meditative state. Working quietly and silently on moving her body and stretching stubborn muscles.

Yoga had been the first domino to fall in her quest for self-care. She wanted to be good to herself rather than continue the abuse she'd started in her twenties. Yoga led her to Spright Island. Yoga awakened her to the unhealthy relationship she had with her family. Yoga made her want to be better *for herself.*

At her studio, she rounded the corner to enter the side door that led up to her apartment. She should hang lights this year. Every year she balked at hanging outdoor holiday lights, seeing it as a hassle and dreading taking them down after the season was over. But maybe it was time to stretch another muscle and step beyond her comfort zone. Besides, it would be worth it to see them and smile, knowing she cared enough to adorn her little porch with Christmas cheer.

Doorknob in hand, she didn't make it inside before friendly honk sounded. A white Mercedes with tinted windows pulled to her side of the street, the car belonging to the man who wouldn't leave her mind.

Tate stepped out and rounded the car, his hands in the pockets of his leather jacket. His long legs were encased in denim, ending in leather slip-ons. Even several yards away he was tempting and potent.

Totally more like ice cream than kale salad.

"I'm not stalking you, I swear." He grinned, and damned if she couldn't help returning it. "I was thinking of you tonight."

She'd been thinking of him, too, but couldn't quite bring herself to admit it.

"Can I buy you a drink? A meal?"

"I was just out with friends. I'm fed, and I've had all the drinks I'm having for one night." Tonight had been a little over-the-top for her. She rarely indulged, for obvious reasons.

Tate fell silent and Hayden wondered she was playing too hard to get. Before she could worry she'd thwarted his efforts entirely, he asked, "Can I show you my place?"

Her teeth stabbed her lip, her smile struggling to stay restrained. Emily had mentioned beginnings and how fragile they were while Arlene had argued that they were fun. Given Hayden's thundering pulse and warmth pooling in her belly, she'd have to agree with Arlene.

"Okay."

He closed the distance between them and held out a hand. Hayden slipped her palm into his. With each step, she was reassured she'd made the right decision. She'd had an amazing night already. Capping it off with a visit to Tate's house that would lead to whatever they pleased was the ultimate way to end it.

"You keep getting hotter." He shook his head as if awed.

"Yeah, well, so do you."

They stood in the street and grinned at each other like idiots for a beat, and then he helped her into the car.

When he pulled away from the curb her belly tightened in anticipation. It had been a long while since she'd felt wanted. A few years since she'd attempted to have a relationship. Her last boyfriend, Alan, had been good for her at the time. He was stable, nice and had a great job. But the more time she spent with him the less like herself she'd felt. He enjoyed staying in so she found herself staying in more. He didn't like seafood and she realized at one point that she hadn't cooked her favorite shrimp pasta in months. She'd lost herself in him, and again those old patterns she'd seen in her family became apparent. After Alan, she decided to make sure she never lost herself again.

Which made her briefly question how hard she'd fought Tate's advances. She'd resisted him in the name of maintaining her independence. Now that they were in his Mercedes gliding along the tree-lined streets, she had to question her reasoning. What could be more pro-self than indulging in the attraction pounding between them?

"I was thinking about you tonight, too," she said. She was done resisting.

His face was lit by the blue dashboard lights of his car, his grin one for the books.

He cut through Summer's Drift, one of her favorite neighborhoods in SWC. The theme was water, the palette white and sand and pale blues. Residents took the theme to heart and decorated accordingly. There were coils of rope resting on porches and miniature lighthouses standing in yards. One house even had upstairs windows that resembled ship's portals.

"Where'd you have dinner?" Tate asked.

"Succulence."

"Best sweet potato gnocchi in town."

"Not afraid of veggie fare?"

"Would a guy who built this community fear vegetables?" he joked.

"Fair point. What about you?"

"I was out with my brother. A bar called Chaz's Pub in Seattle."

"Chaz. One of the lesser-known Irishmen. How was it?"

"Good. Really good." He didn't say more but he didn't have to. She could tell by his tone and the quiet way he finished their trip that he'd had a "really good" evening. She was glad to hear he was getting along well with his newfound brother.

He turned down a long drive hooded by trees and marked by a private sign. Hayden was excited to see Tate's house. She'd always been curious what kind of house the builder of Spright Wellness Community had built for himself.

The trees ended and the house came into view. The structure was boxy but interesting thanks to the slanted roof that lent a modern, artistic quality to the home. It was big, but not as big as she was expecting. Arlene's billionaire reference had Hayden expecting an over-the-top fifty-room mansion.

"It's beautiful," she commented as he pulled into a driveway.

In the light glowing from the porch and the car's headlights she could make out the details. A sturdy stone wall climbed to the top of the house, while the rest of it was dark metal beams and wood. At the highest point of the roof, one entire side was almost nothing but windows, intersected with a set of stairs that led to an outdoor patio.

"Wait till you see the inside." He unbuckled her belt for her and they climbed out of the car.

"Living room through here." He gestured as they walked into the foyer, pausing to shrug out of his leather coat. "Kitchen's to your right. Can I take your coat?"

"Sure." Big hands moved to her shoulders. Flanked by his heat from behind, it took everything in her not to lean into his warmth.

He slipped the garment from her shoulders, leaning close to her ear to mutter, "Better?"

A tight breath was all she could manage.

She walked through the living room and admired the décor. Metal and wood and stone converged in a modern, artistic, comfortable way. Everywhere she looked, there was nature. From the petrified wood on a stand on the bookshelf to the woven rug beneath the black leather sofa and chairs.

"Mind if I powder my nose?" she asked when Tate walked into the room with her.

He pointed to the slatted-step staircase framed with an iron railing. "Top of the stairs. Take a right. Can I get you anything to drink?"

"Sparkling water? Or still, if that's too fussy."

"Lucky you. We specialize in fussy here."

In the bathroom mirror she fluffed her hair and gave herself a once-over. She looked good tonight. Thank goodness she'd worn her favorite low-heeled boots. They made her ass look amazing.

Tate had turned on music. She heard the croony voice of Michael Bublé drifting through the downstairs. Curious to see the rest of the house, she peeked down the hallway on one side and then the other. Admittedly she was being nosy, but she couldn't help it. She'd always been epically curious about how the other half lived.

At best guess Tate had spared no expense when it came to decorating and furnishing his house.

There were four bedrooms upstairs alone, and still more house to explore downstairs. One of the rooms was being used as an office, the tidy space both masculine and attractive. The enormous L-shaped desk was deep brown in color, the desk chair the same pale beige as the reading chair in the corner. A laptop was centered on the desk's surface, a square pen holder holding three pens next to it. Bookshelves lined the wall stuffed with an array of architectural books and business titles.

She bypassed a guest room, and another being used for storage. A box marked "Claire" sat on the floor, and she peeked inside. A white sweater and pair of oversize headphones were all she'd evidently left behind.

The last bedroom at the end of the hall held a model of a neighborhood in the center of a large folding table. The model had several buildings, including apartments and what looked like a retail area, as well as a a green slab with tiny benches and a swing set.

"You found my secret project," said a voice behind her.

"Oh!" Startled, she straightened quickly and bumped the table. She turned just as quickly to steady the model, grateful she didn't knock it off and turn the impressive work of art into a pile of matchsticks.

"Sorry. I'm sorry." She backed away from the table. "I was… Um. I like how you decorate. Your house is amazing."

"Relax, Hayden. I don't think you were casing my house in search of the good silver." He handed her a champagne flute. "Your sparkling water. I added a wedge of lime. I do well with fussy."

She hummed, keeping her thoughts about Claire to herself.

"Is it really secret?" she asked of the model.

"No, but very few people know about it. This neighborhood is going to sit behind Summer's Drift. We're building around the trees. The architecture is Swedish. Row houses, a few restaurants." He pointed out the various elements.

"And a park."

"And a park." He assessed her, eyes narrowed.

"What?"

"It's just—"

"What is it?" She straightened her sweater and reached for her hair, fidgeting.

"You look ready now, Hayden Green."

Oh.

Oh.

"To have the hell kissed out of me?" she guessed.

He set her glass aside, his gaze zooming in on her mouth. "I'm guessing that's going to require a lot of kissing."

She rested her arms on his shoulders. "Are you up for the task?"

"Hell, *yes*," he said, his voice gravel. And then he smothered her laughter with a rough kiss.

Nine

Kissing Hayden was like being kissed for the first time.

He moved his lips over hers, a unique thrill jolting him as she gripped the back of his head and dove in for more. Her tongue came out to play, nudging his top lip before her teeth nipped his bottom lip.

No, screw that. Kissing Hayden was like being kissed *by Hayden* for the first time. If he'd been kissed like this for his first kiss, he would've had no idea what to do next.

Thank God he knew now.

Opening to accept her tongue, he deepened the kiss, wrapping his arms around her lower back and pressing her soft body against his. She was fit, muscular and curvy, but there was give where there should be. In her breasts flattening against his chest, and her belly, which made for a perfect place to nudge the hint of his erection.

Kissing Claire was never like this.

He shouldn't compare, but he couldn't keep from doing it. Couldn't keep from noticing that Hayden's strength and softness were two attributes that his ex had never had. Claire was controlled, buttoned-up. Tate had mirrored those attributes, which made for some uninspired sex.

He couldn't think of a scenario where *Hayden* and *un-inspired* would go together in a sentence.

"I promised myself," she whispered, tugging his hair, "the next chance I had—" she stole a quick kiss "—I'd do this."

"Kiss me?" he asked before she lit him up with another tongue lashing.

She pulled her lips away and regarded him with disbelief. "Have sex with you."

"You want to have sex with me?" he growled.

She rolled her eyes. "Oh, like you don't want to have sex with me?"

Her confidence was his favorite part about her. The second was her body. He gripped her hips and squeezed, loving the contrasting strength and give there, as well. "I do. I really, *really* do."

Something serious shadowed her eyes. The tugging she'd done earlier to his hair changing to gentle strokes. She tipped her chin and took him in, her dark eyes both earnest and vulnerable.

Leaning in slowly, he gave her the chance to change her mind, to back away and thank him for the invite and insist he drive her home. He would. He didn't want to, but he would.

She instead closed the gap between them, her lips barely brushing his as she gave him room to initiate.

Hell. Yes.

He wouldn't miss the chance to sleep with her tonight. Not when she tasted and felt this good—and he sensed she needed the physical connection as badly as he did.

Threading her hair through his fingers, he took charge of her mouth. He bent his knees to lower them to the floor and she followed, easing down with him in one fluid, graceful movement. He took a mental snapshot of her on his carpeted floor, her hair spread around her like a dark halo. She was gorgeous and, for now, *his*.

He braced his weight on his arms and hovered over her, studying her unique beauty. Until her lips spread into an uncertain smirk. "You're staring again."

"Can't help it."

"Why? Is there a problem?"

"Holding out longer than ten minutes, maybe."

"Well, forget it then." She winked, saucy, which only made him harder.

"I was admiring you. And wondering how I missed that you were this exquisite until the night you found me loitering outside your studio in the driving rain."

She stroked his hair gently. "I was admiring you that night, too."

"I was kidding about the ten minutes. Let's make this last." He covered her mouth with his own, and she returned his efforts. While her fingernails tickled his scalp, he skimmed his hand along her sweater, lifting it until he encountered a slice of soft skin. A low groan reverberated from his chest, and he reminded himself that he'd promised to make this last. As badly as he wanted her naked, he was going to take his time. He had one shot at convincing her to sleep with him more than once. After that first kiss she'd so boldly initiated, he knew *once* would not be enough.

He had to impress her.

He rucked her shirt up and exposed her taut abdomen— delicately defined, he could make out the muscles above her belly button. There was softness to the bit below, and he again admired the juxtaposition. Beauty wasn't found in the expected, but in the surprises; the imperfect.

He moved down her body to kiss her stomach and then back up to her bra. Gold and black and lace held breasts that were large and round. He was definitely going to need a moment with each of them. He helped her sit up and divested her of her sweater. Hayden shivered.

"Cold?" he asked.

"Excited," she answered. He loved her honesty.

"Flattery, Ms. Green, will get you absolutely *everywhere*."

"Sucker," she whispered.

Smacking a brief kiss onto the center of her cunning mouth, he found the hook of her bra, failed at releasing it and tried again.

"Out of practice?" She reached behind her to unhook it herself.

"Yeah. I guess I am." It'd been a while since he'd undressed Claire. He realized with stark discomfort that they'd usually undressed themselves before sex. What a waste. This was the best part.

Bra loosened, Hayden slipped it from her arms, watching his reaction as she exposed her breasts to the cooler air in the room.

Dusky rose, her nipples pebbled. He took one into his mouth and sucked gently. She reacted like he'd plugged her into an electric socket, zapping to life with an encouraging gasp as she raked her hands into his hair again.

He swirled the tender bud and then dragged his tongue over the other nipple and started on that one. She squirmed beneath him, lifting her hips to bump his. He was hard and well past ready but unwilling to rush—or so he had to keep reminding himself.

After she'd thoroughly wrecked his hair, he abandoned her breasts to undo her belt and unbutton her jeans. Halfway through unzipping, she reached for his sweater and yanked.

"Take this off."

It wasn't hard to take orders from a rosy-cheeked, topless woman on her back. Not even a little.

He whipped off the shirt and she ran her fingertips over

his pectorals and stomach, and then along the line of hair that vanished into his jeans. She bypassed the belt and zipper and molded her hand around the stiff denim hiding his cock. If he thought he was hard before, that was nothing compared to the inches of steel created by her tenderly stroking hand.

Moving her wrist, he reprimanded her with a headshake and yanked her pants from her legs. He had her short boots to contend with, so that took a second or two of struggle.

Her black and gold panties made it worth the work.

"Tell me you always wear lingerie."

"I always wear lingerie."

"Even under your yoga pants?"

"I don't wear anything under my yoga pants."

Great. He could never take a class from her again without embarrassing himself.

"Your face." She chuckled, returning her hands to his abs. "Where have you been hiding this body? I guess I wasn't looking hard enough."

"Neither of us were." He kissed her palm and pulled the sides of her panties down her thighs as he laid kisses on her belly and thighs. Once he'd stripped them from her, he lifted one of her legs and rested it on his shoulder, enjoying the way she propped herself up to watch. She opened wider to accommodate him, not the least bit shy about accepting what she wanted.

And he wasn't the least bit shy about giving it to her.

It'd been so long since a man's mouth had been between her legs she was almost too excited to concentrate. *Almost*.

Tate worked his magic until she was forced to close her eyes, lie back and give herself over to his ministrations. He paid careful attention to what she liked, doubling his efforts whenever she let out a whimper of approval.

Which she did *a lot*.

The man had skills. She had the stray thought that she'd never dump a guy who could make her come as easily as Tate Duncan. That alone would be worth the price of admission.

A gentle series of orgasms hit her like rolling waves. Arching her back, she parted her thighs. He gripped her hips and tugged her toward his mouth, continuing his delicious assault until she was moaning again. There was another orgasm waiting on the cusp. She could feel it. She reached up to tug her own nipples, and that was exactly the move that took her over. Like one of those earlier waves, she came on a cry, undulating as pleasure rocked her body and erased her mind.

Her breath sawed from her lungs, leaving her body warm and buzzing. A shadow darkened her vision behind her eyelids.

"Open your eyes, beautiful girl," Tate murmured before kissing the corner of her mouth.

She was confronted with a tender ocean-blue stare.

"Hi," he said.

"Hi." She laughed at the absurdity of the greeting, at the sheer delight of it. She'd never had this much fun having sex, and technically they hadn't had sex yet.

"Condoms are in the bathroom across the hall," he told her. "Which means I have to leave the cradle of your incredible thighs, find one and come back."

"Okay." She nodded quickly to let him know she wasn't suffering an ounce of doubt where making love to him was concerned. She was all for it.

"Okay." He stood and stepped over her, adjusting the hard ridge pushing the fly of his jeans to capacity, and then walked into the hallway.

Hayden slapped her hands over her face and smiled into her palms. She was really doing this. And it was *really* freaking incredible.

Tate returned in record time and, holding the condom wrapper between his teeth, wrestled free from his belt and jeans. She simply lay there and watched as he stripped for her, admiring the strong planes of his muscular body and the strength he exuded.

When he tugged off black boxer briefs, she felt her mouth go very dry. It was…well, it was gorgeous, was what it was. Long and thick and inviting, all brought to stark attention as he rolled the protection over his length.

"Keep looking at me like that, and we'll be done sooner than you'd like," he warned, lowering over her willing body.

"I don't believe you." She hooked her heels over his ass and tugged him forward, his heated skin warming hers. The hardness between his legs met her plush, wet folds and she gasped.

"You're far too capable, Tate Duncan—" she paused as he notched her entrance "—to finish before you're good and ready."

A feral, cocky glint lit his eyes as he seated himself deep inside her. Her mind blanked of thought as moved, slipping along the wetness he'd created with his talented mouth.

Hayden stopped teasing him and gave in to the pleasure he doled out blow by exquisite blow.

Ten

"Mmm." Hayden hummed, pure satisfaction.

Tate smiled over at the dark-haired beauty on the floor next to him, proud of those three letters making up one truncated sound. He'd worked hard.

"We're good at that," he stated.

"We are." Her throat bobbed with a husky, sexy laugh She turned her head to face him, and he was struck momentarily speechless by the unwavering eye contact. "I had complete faith in you."

Goose bumps prickled her arms and she shivered. He rolled to the side and rubbed her biceps with his hand in an attempt to warm her.

"How about some hot cocoa or tea?"

"I'd never turn down cocoa. Do you have marshmallows?"

"What am I, a barbarian? I have *homemade* marshmallows from Blossom Bakery."

"I love those." Her expression was a lot like her last O face, which made him grin.

He offered a hand and helped her sit up.

"Wow. I'm zapped." She put a hand to her hair. "I must be a mess."

"You are a mess. A complete and utter, distracting, hot mess."

"That…was a compliment, I assume?" She narrowed one eye.

"Yes." He kissed her succinctly. "What time are you going to Thanksgiving dinner tomorrow?" He knew some families ate earlier in the day—hell, his own mother set the table at 11:00 a.m.

"I'm—" She shook her head in a rare show of discomfort. "I'm not going anywhere for Thanksgiving. My family…we're sort of distant." The arms she'd wrapped around herself tightened.

"If you don't have anywhere to be in the morning then you should stay the night here."

"You want me to stay?"

"I do. Yes. And then I want to do what we just did three or four more times."

"Four!" she said on a laugh. "Four times before tomorrow morning?"

"Preferably."

He'd hardly know himself right now if he were an outside observer. He was beyond what should be comfortable with Hayden this soon.

After he'd learned of his actual birth parents and twin brother, Tate had vowed to deal with it like he had any other moment of adversity. Just plow through with certainty and confidence that it would work out in the end. He'd underestimated the emotional toll of finding out his entire existence was a lie.

His relationship with his adoptive parents had become strained—a totally new dynamic for them—and then Claire had ended the engagement. Tate began thinking that closeness wasn't something he was meant to have on a long-term basis.

He was having trouble categorizing Hayden, though. He

liked being close to her. He liked her honesty and wit. He just plain liked her. Way more than he should.

Tate had played safe his entire life. Had laid out each step after the last in a predictable, cautious way. What good had playing it safe done him? He'd lost everything unexpectedly.

A part of him argued that he should be smart about this thing with Hayden—that he shouldn't get in too deep—and in response he raised a middle finger. He was trying a new tack. He was embracing danger and unpredictability for a change.

He needed to shake off the caution from his past. Needed to feel *alive*. And since no one made him feel more alive than Hayden Green, he needed *her*.

They both dressed, pausing to send satisfied smiles over at each other in between zipping and buckling. She tugged on her boots and pulled a hair tie from her pocket. In two seconds, and barely trying, she'd fashioned a ponytail.

"Impressive." Everything about her.

He took her hand and walked with her downstairs. Five minutes later he served her at his kitchen table, setting a mug piled high with sticky, square marshmallows in front of her.

She cradled the mug before navigating a sip of the cocoa around the melting marshmallows. "Mmm."

"When you made that sound earlier, I liked it then, too."

"Yes, well, you earned it."

Confidence straightened his shoulders at the comment and again when she looked around the room. He admired it with her—the stylish gas fireplace, the wide open windows with nothing but dark woods beyond. His carefully chosen furnishings, earthy in both materials and color.

"I'd love to have this much space." She tilted her head back to admire the overhead lighting. "Not that I don't love living above my studio. But this…" She let out a wistful sigh. "This is beautiful."

"Does that mean you're staying?"

"I didn't bring any clothes." She pressed a finger to his lips when he opened his mouth to argue. "You're going to say I don't need them."

"Damn straight." Movement outside caught his attention and he pulled her finger from his lips. "Look."

A deer poked its head from the trees, cocking its ears to listen. Hayden let out a soft gasp of surprise.

"This is why I tucked my house into the woods. So? You staying?"

"You think a deer is enough to get me to agree?"

"I was hoping that and the promise of sex four more times before morning might seal the deal."

She chuckled, but didn't answer him.

"Tell me about your twin brother." She lifted her mug.

"Not the smoothest segue."

"Go big or go home. Except I'm not going home. Not yet, anyway."

"Tease." It was easy to be with her, even when she asked questions about his newfound family.

"It has to be mind-boggling to have a twin. To have that connection with someone. Do you see aspects of yourself when you look at him?"

He had to think about how to answer that. Not because he was choosing his words, but because he hadn't really thought of Reid and himself in that way. What was it like to look at Reid, whom Tate had *shared a womb with*, for God's sake?

"We both gesture with our hands when we talk. Not wildly or anything, but subtly. We do this—" he pressed his index finger and thumb together like he was popping a balloon with a pin "—when we want to make a point. I

never paid attention to that until Reid did it. And then I noticed I did it, too. That I've always done it."

"So you make the same gestures even though you
haven't been around each other for decades."

"Apparently. It's surreal. I always thought I was an only
child and then I meet this stranger and a few dinners later
it's like I've known him my whole life."

"I guess in a way, you have." Hayden rested her hand
on Tate's thigh.

"He invited me to London for Christmas." Tate took a
deep breath. He wasn't sure how he felt about that invitation. "Where my parents live."

"That's exciting," she said, but there was caution in her
tone.

"I didn't give him an answer yet, but Reid and Drew—
his pregnant fiancée—are going."

"You're going to be an uncle." Her face brightened.
"Lucky. I'm an only child. No hope of being an aunt unless I'm made honorary aunt by one of my friends."

And to think he used to be an only child, too. "It's…
overwhelming to have this all happening at once."

"I'm sure it is. I bet your adoptive parents are having a
hard time letting you navigate the holidays now that they
have to share you."

"You have no idea." He rubbed his temple, a headache
forming behind his fingers. His mother had cried when he'd
told her he wouldn't be home for Thanksgiving or Christmas, and his father had demanded he consider someone
other than himself. Tate hadn't argued, simply explaining
that he was doing what he had to do. A breath later his father was apologizing and his mother had stopped crying.
Tate still felt the sting from their reactions, though. He'd
had an almost consuming need to give in to what they
wanted. In the end he'd stood his ground.

"I'm sorry. Just tell me to shut up. I didn't mean to encroach on your—"

"I was kidnapped," he interrupted, and Hayden's jaw went slack. She didn't know the whole truth, and he needed her to see the full picture. If only to understand why he was making the decisions he was making "At age three. I was taken from my and my brother's birthday party in London, and our parents never found me again. My adoptive parents assumed the agency they were adopting me from was legitimate until that agency extorted money from them. They suspected something was off, but they wanted a child so badly."

His budding headache took root and throbbed like a truth bomb ready to detonate.

"The Duncans were told my birth parents were dead— they were given falsified death certificates filled out with fake names. Eventually, my real birth parents believed I was dead. They buried an empty casket five years after my disappearance."

"Oh, Tate." Sympathy flooded Hayden's dark eyes.

He continued, monotone. Might as well share it all. "My adoptive parents paid the so-called agency's exorbitant fees without asking too many questions. My mother said she never would've imagined I was kidnapped. She had an inkling that the agency was unscrupulous, but if money was the only thing standing in the way of bringing me home…"

He shook his head. It wasn't their fault. Not really. But he couldn't help blaming them for not acting on their instincts. Had Marion explored that inkling he might've been raised in London rather than California. He might've been returned to his rightful home, to his actual birth parents who were no more than strangers to him now.

And you wouldn't have been raised by the Duncans. Which meant never knowing the family he loved dearly.

Never setting foot on Spright Island to build a community that he treasured. Never meeting the people who lived here—Hayden included.

He wasn't sure which thought was more chill-inducing.

Spooked, the deer became suddenly alert, before turning and darting off into the trees, his white tail a visible exclamation point in the dark. Had his parents been equally afraid of digging for the truth?

"Then a month ago I was in a coffee shop in Seattle, and this guy in front of me in line starts babbling about how I was his twin brother."

Hayden's hand formed a fist and she seemed to keep herself in check. Like she wanted to touch him but didn't know if she should. "You must've been…"

"Terrified," Tate finished for her. "I called my mom after, expecting her to laugh it off. She didn't. And the next night when I had dinner with Claire, I drank a stupid amount of wine and told her everything I just told you, and…"

"She left you."

"Not that night, but eventually. Yes." He gave Hayden a sad smile. "Now's your chance."

But she didn't heed his warning, stand up and put on her coat. She gripped the back of his neck and kissed him soft and long. Achingly gentle. He returned her kiss, tasting on her lips the newfound courage she'd uncovered.

She made him feel strong, confident. All the ways he used to be that had gone missing recently. He felt as if he'd been tossed overboard into a churning sea of uncertainty and was only now clawing his way onto dry land.

"Most complicated one-night stand ever," she said, rubbing her thumb along his bottom lip.

"Is that enough for you?" God knew it was all he had to give. He couldn't rely on the future any longer. Certainty was a myth.

She tilted her head and watched him. "I'm not opposed to two nights."

He smiled. "How about we take it one night at a time?" He was already mentally undressing her, wanting more of the earlier taste she gave him.

She unbuttoned a button on his shirt and then the one under it. "One night at a time."

He covered her lips with a kiss, the sweetness from the marshmallow on her tongue. One night at a time was as unchartered as territory came for him. Completely opposite of how he'd operated before.

He had no idea where they would end up. One night at a time broke every rule he had, every guideline he'd followed previously. Which was exactly what he needed.

Different. New. Exciting.

In a word: *Hayden*.

Eleven

One night turned into two and two into three and three into more. Hayden and Tate had been saying yes to almost three weeks' worth of nights so far.

It was December and Christmas was in full swing at SWC. Colorful lights and garland were wrapped around lampposts, retail shop doors boasted gold-and-green wreaths and holiday music was piped through speakers inside.

Hayden had decorated her small, but pretty, tree in her apartment with red and gold decorations, and the larger one in her studio with silver and blue. She even went through the trouble of hanging outdoor lights for the first time.

As loath as she was to admit it, life really *was* better when she wasn't alone during the holidays.

She'd spent a lot of time at Tate's house, in front of the fireplace and in his bed. So much time that she hadn't been at her own apartment much, save for running upstairs to change or showering after her classes. With her schedule trimmed back for the holidays, though, she had a decent amount of free time.

She'd finished up her last class of the year ten minutes ago and was just updating her planner and checking her email when the bell over the door dinged to alert her someone was coming in.

Since she knew exactly who that someone was, she didn't bother calling out that she was closed.

Tate looked like the billionaire Arlene had accused him of being, his expensive trousers in deep charcoal gray, his shoes black and shiny. The part of him that deviated was the ever-present dark leather jacket that hung over his muscular, round shoulders.

"Now that's a nice scarf," she commented about the red scarf looped around his neck. She'd purchased it for him, for no reason except she'd seen it and thought of him.

His sexy grin was missing as he stalked toward her in the empty studio, however, causing her nerves to prickle, and not pleasantly.

And since that prickle came with fear that things had changed and she didn't know why or how, she didn't like it at all.

Breathe. He's allowed to have a bad day.

Plus, he was here. That's what mattered.

"What's up?" she asked, forcing a bright tone.

He seemed to snap out of it at the question. "Nothing. The scarf—" he lifted one side of it "—was a gift from an incredibly beautiful woman."

He was joking, that was a good sign. "Should I be jealous?"

He kissed her hello, a long and lingering press of his lips that assuaged her fears some. Maybe she'd overreacted. It wasn't like she was accustomed to being happy and in a relationship. Getting used to both simultaneously would take some doing.

Hayden reminded herself not to put too much pressure on the outcome. Years ago she'd decided that being on her own was A-okay. She didn't need a family or a marriage, or even a boyfriend, to feel whole. Even so, she couldn't deny that she was happy with Tate. She was going to enjoy it, no matter how finite.

And she was *so* into Tate Duncan. More than any guy she'd ever met. It'd only been three weeks, and already he was more than a friend—way more than a sex buddy. He was just plain *more*, and she'd left it at that in her head. Labeling what they had was dangerous. Like naming it would lead to its inevitable end sooner rather than later.

"How did the meeting go?" she asked.

Tate had stopped by a planning meeting for the New Year's Eve gala, which consisted of a lush black-tie party with cocktails and dancing.

"Well. Ran into Nick there. He invited us to the Purple Rose for lunch."

Nick was, hands down, Hayden's favorite chef. He made some of freshest, most delicious meals, all using simple ingredients.

"Us?" Without her permission, her heart lifted at the reference that Tate had mentioned her to Nick.

"We're hardly under the radar, Ms. Green." But Tate's smile told her that he didn't mind they were SWC-official. "Are you available?"

"I am," she said with a smile of her own.

An hour later they were enjoying roasted vegetable–white bean salad, a quinoa bowl and a plate of crispy Brussels sprouts drenched in a sweet Thai dressing.

"As I suspected," Hayden said as she spooned another healthy portion of Brussels sprouts onto her plate. "Nick sold his soul to the devil in exchange for the recipe for this sauce."

Plus it wasn't on the menu yet. She could get used to this sort of special treatment. She hadn't been in the market for a boyfriend, if that's what Tate was, but having one that held the golden key to the city was the way to go.

Tate placed his fork on his table, swiping his mouth with a napkin. His gaze was unfocused, his demeanor shifting abruptly. She was reminded of the mood he'd been in when he stepped into her studio.

"I have something to ask you." His eyebrows compressed.

Even as her heart ka-thumped a worried staccato, Hayden said, "Okay."

"It's a big ask."

"Okay."

"Reid called me this morning, asking again if I'd consider going to London for Christmas." His Adam's apple jumped when he swallowed, and he reached for his water glass. "I've decided to go."

"That's great." She meant it. Meeting his birth parents was a huge leap for him.

"I want you to go with me."

Hayden sagged in her seat, shocked down to her toes. Everything about the way he'd been behaving would have her assuming he'd dump her not...take her to London?

She couldn't say yes to *going to London* with him. Even though she'd wanted to visit England for as long as she could remember.

Meeting his family was *huge*. And at Christmas? That was monumental.

He continued to watch her, waiting for acknowledgment, or maybe for her to shout an exuberant *yes!* Since she didn't know what to say, she sort of repeated his words. "Go with you? To London?"

"Yes. There's more."

More than inviting her to London for Christmas to meet his birth parents? She slicked damp palms on her jeans. She wasn't sure she wanted to know, but for the sake of her sanity, she *had* to know, or else the possibilities would stack themselves to the heavens before falling onto her and crushing her to death.

Calm down. It's not like he's going to propose.

But then he said, "The Singletons are under the assumption that I'm engaged. Because I *was* engaged. Reid knows Claire and I ended, but I asked him not to tell George and Jane that my engagement was off."

Oh, God. *Was* he going to propose?

"Why not tell them?" she croaked, her mind and heart racing like they were vying for first place.

"I'm not sure." His frown deepened. "I was concerned they'd think I wasn't doing well, I guess? That they would assume their son's life was unraveling because of the news. I guess I didn't want them to worry."

He was one of the kindest men she'd ever met. Even amidst the turmoil in his own life, he was looking out for those who loved him. Even those he had no memory of knowing.

"If you don't have a passport, I can pay to have it expedited for you."

"I have a passport," she said. "What is it, exactly, that you need from me?"

He nodded, his expression an unsure mix of dread and concern. "If they assume you're my fiancée—if they even remember I have one—all you have to do is not argue. You don't have to pretend your name is Claire, or anything."

"Good. I wouldn't." She quirked her lips and Tate's mouth shifted into a smile.

"I don't want to keep you from your plans, but it'd be a huge favor for me. Your travel and incidentals would be covered."

She started to say he didn't have to do that but with her light work schedule and shopping for the holidays she hadn't exactly stashed away a few thou for a trip to another country.

"I've always wanted to go to London."

She might be sweating the fact that Tate, who was basically a really meaningful fling, was sort of proposing to her and asking her to go to a foreign country, but she couldn't not be there for him when he needed her. Going to celebrate Christmas with a bunch of strangers might be weird for her, but she imagined for him, it'd be downright uncomfortable.

Plus, visiting London would be a dream come true. The alternative would be going home to Seattle to endure her grandmother's drunkenness, her mother's scrambling after her like a servant and her father's apathy.

Tate was still watching her carefully, as if he was deciding whether or not to sweeten the pot by offering something more. He didn't have to. She wanted to be with him, and this was a unique situation.

"I'll do it."

"Yeah?" He grinned, the agony from earlier sweeping away with that smile.

Tate deserved a win, and, dammit so did she. If pretending to be his fiancée would give them both a sense of triumph, why the hell not?

But a small voice in her head whispered, *so many reasons*.

Twelve

Reid and Drew had flown to London two days ago. There was a reason Tate didn't sync his flight with his twin's: he wanted to keep his stay in the UK as brief as possible. With the excuse of work—partially true—he'd instead booked his and Hayden's international flight to arrive at 11:15 a.m. December 23. That gave them the day to hide away to rest, and then they could emerge for cocktail hour and dinner before ducking away again to sleep. Then all he'd have to endure was Christmas Eve and Christmas Day before flying home the next morning. Which, thanks to an eight-hour time difference, would land them in Seattle just two hours after they left England.

He'd booked first-class business tickets on the flight out, not because he was planning on working but because they were the best seats the airline had to offer. Hayden was doing him a solid by joining him—he wanted to make sure she felt special.

When Hayden sat in her seat next to a bulky armrest-slash-desk, her eyebrows were so high on her forehead it was almost comical. "Tate."

She took in the cabin around her, which consisted of thirty business-class "pods," each with its own private, wraparound seat dividers. There was a divider that could separate his and Hayden's seats as well, but he'd lowered it the second they found their seats.

"Sorry, this was the nicest seat the airline had."

"Smart-ass." Subtly, she shook her head, her smile tolerant. "I usually sit in the middle of coach with my knees smashed into the seat in front of me."

She stretched her legs out, unable to touch the pod in front of her with her toes. Then her smile faded. "It's too much."

"Let's revisit that claim five hours into a nine-and-a-half-hour flight." He lifted an eyebrow. "You'll be thanking me for copious legroom and a chair that reclines."

"And my own TV." She gestured at the screen in front of her. "And tray table, and—" She lifted a black bag labeled Amenity Kit and held it up to show him.

"Sleep mask, lavender spray and a Casper-brand pillow and fleece blanket."

She laughed, an effervescent sound, and the tightness in his chest eased. There would be a lot of people and overwhelming circumstances to deal with shortly after they landed at Heathrow, but for right now, he had it easy. With Hayden.

She'd made this trip better already and it hadn't started yet. Plus, watching her wide eyes gobble up the luxury that had become pedestrian to him was a good reminder of how far he'd come. The dose of confidence and self-assuredness would go a long way when he was a stranger in a strange land... Except it wasn't a strange land. It was his *hometown*.

Would that ever sink in?

Hayden was oohing and ahhing over the lavender spray and mentioned again how fluffy the pillow was, and he had to grin.

"You're easy to spoil, Ms. Green."

Her cheeks pinked. "I'm acting like a total country mouse, aren't I?"

"A little, but I'm enjoying it." He'd never done without. Trips he'd taken with his family had always been in first class or via private flight. Seeing this experience through fresh eyes was damned refreshing. Just like the rest of her.

"I can't help it. It's new to me." She narrowed her eyes in faux suspicion. "Are you making sure I'm not going to back out at the last second? Have you heard all sorts of horrifying secrets about your family? Am I in for the ride of my life?"

"The opposite. Reid gushes over them. And Drew hasn't met them but she says she's spent a lot of time on the phone with Reid's, um, our mother, Jane." He paused while that soaked in. "Anyway, Drew loves her already, and she hasn't met her."

"That's good news." Hayden's encouragement was careful, but Tate had a feeling they'd survive this awkward holiday regardless of what he had to face. At least he wouldn't be facing it alone.

He appreciated the hell out of her for being here.

It wasn't something he'd successfully put into words, but he hoped the first-class flight, the trip to London and every last way he planned on worshipping her in the bedroom would say what he couldn't: That there was no one he'd rather navigate this patch of his life with other than Hayden.

One day at a time.

Seven hours into the flight Hayden was feeling the fatigue of traveling tenfold. The longest flight she'd been on had been a five-hour flight to Toronto for a yoga conference last year. She could thank that trip for her having a passport.

She'd already been to the bathroom and had moved around to stretch her legs. Even the roomy pod, complete with seat and desk, couldn't cure her craving for movement. She struck a few poses as best she could from her chair, regardless of who watched. Though, she doubted anyone was paying attention to her or her seated warrior pose. There were only thirty seats in this section of the plane, and she assumed everyone desired privacy first and foremost. It was by far the best way to travel.

She would've liked to give Tate at least *some* money for her travel expenses, no matter how trivial. Yes, they were dating, but this went beyond their agreement to take things as they came. But each time she brought it up, he shook his head denoting the end of the discussion. An hour into their flight she'd tried again and his, "It's a gift, Hayden, stop asking," told her she had surpassed insistence and tiptoed into ungratefulness.

She couldn't help it. Financial arguments had been commonplace in her family's home especially since her grandmother drank away every dollar she wrapped her fist around, leaving her wellbeing to Hayden's parents.

Hayden hadn't grown up with a healthy view of much of anything as a kid. As an adult she'd studied her backside off trying to learn how to save and invest for her future. Since the bulk of care and concern from her mother was lavished on her father and grandmother, Hayden had been on her own.

She'd learned to care for herself, knowing no one else would take care of her. It was the harder path, but at least reliable. It was also the main reason she'd chose to stay unmarried. Trusting herself was easy. Trusting others, not so much.

Tate, reclined in his seat, arms folded over his chest, was asleep. She watched his chest lift and fall and considered how much she'd trusted him already, without realizing she was doing it.

Anyone would assume he was peacefully snoozing except for the furrow in his brow. He was worried about meeting them—his parents. She couldn't imagine how she'd feel if she'd found out she had a whole other family who lived in London.

Relieved, probably, she thought with a bittersweet smile.

Thirteen

When Hayden first laid eyes on Tate's brother, Reid, she thought, *My God, there really are two of them.*

They weren't identical twins, but there was no denying the set of their mouths and—Tate was right—they both made the same gestures when they talked.

In the back seat of Reid's rental car, she sat next to his fiancée Drew while the guys carried on a conversation up front.

"They're both so attractive it's stupefying," Drew stated. "Don't you think?"

The question was asked at a near whisper, even though the guys were chattering loud enough that they likely hadn't overheard.

"It doesn't take much to stupefy me after that flight," Hayden joked. The truth, had she been forced to admit it, was that 100 percent of the attraction coming from her was aimed directly at Tate.

"No kidding." Drew snorted, and like the rest of her, it was darling. "We arrived three days ago, and my body is just now accepting that I'm supposed to be awake."

"So by the time I'm used to the time change, I'll be on my way back home."

"You're seriously leaving on Boxing Day? Criminal!" Drew clutched her nonexistent pearls. "It is sad that you're not staying longer, though."

Hayden felt similarly. She liked Drew, even having only known her for a few minutes. The other woman was both scrappy and easygoing. Hayden didn't know much about how Drew and Reid got together, except that she was the little sister of one of Reid's best friends. Hayden would bet there was a story there. She'd have to extract details from Drew over dinner.

"Hey! I heard you're engaged!" Drew exclaimed.

"Uh…"

"*Pretending* to be engaged, love," Reid corrected his fiancée, throwing a wink at her in the rearview mirror. "I told you that."

"I *know*. Mind your own business up there, Gorgeous Inc. That's his new nickname." Drew pursed her lips. "I guess though, if Reid is the CEO of Gorgeous Inc., Tate has to be, at the very least, COO." She glanced first at Reid's profile, then Tate's. "Stupefying."

Hayden giggled, but it led to a yawn. She was feeling every hour of their lengthy travel.

"Do you want coffee?" Drew offered, clearly discerning what that yawn was about. "It's easier to find tea here, but there are a few really good shops that serve both. We stopped by one when we finished Christmas shopping yesterday."

"Mum is serving tea when we arrive." Reid said as he drove past pubs and shops downtown. "Can't rob her of that."

Tate rubbed his palms down his dark jeans, and Hayden thought she saw his shoulders stiffen. No doubt the mention of his "mum" had set him on edge.

Reid, consummate entertainer, launched into his tour

guide voice and pointed out a few buildings beyond the car's window.

Drew leaned closer to Hayden, keeping her voice low. "I can't imagine how difficult this must be for Tate."

"Yes."

"And you." Sincerity swam in the other brunette's dark gaze. "If you need anyone to talk to while you're here... about family stuff or girl stuff...or *engagement* stuff."

Hayden laughed. "You're not going to give up on that, are you?"

"Nope." Drew grinned, seemingly pleased with herself, and pleased in general. She palmed her still-flat, pregnant belly. "I'm just saying, you can't predict where you'll end up with these Singleton boys. Right, Gorgeous, Inc.?"

The look Reid sent through the rearview was a smolder if Hayden had ever seen one. And when Tate peeked over his shoulder at her, that look held a certain smolder for her as well.

Those Singleton boys, indeed.

Tate took in the rows of houses they drove past, most tightly packed in next to each other. Having not been here past the age of three, he had no recollection of the area. Nothing looked familiar and the foreignness only made him long for his parents' home in California. His chest grew tight. He'd never been a homesick kid, but he felt that way now.

The cocktail of excitement and nerves over meeting the man and woman who'd created him had been shaken, stirred and then thrown into a blender for good measure. He'd had a million silent discussions with himself on the flight over about expectations, reasoning that this meeting didn't have to be anything more than cordial. But it was hard not to have expectations when Reid went on and on about their parents. He meant well, but it'd almost been too much to absorb for Tate.

"They're getting on well," Reid said. "We'll have to keep an eye on that, brother, in case they decide to team up on us."

Reid pulled into a long asphalt driveway flanked by short, decorative stone pillars. "Here we are."

The Singleton house was in Berkshire, about half an hour from the airport, and sat on three acres of land which backed up to the very wooded area Tate had been dragged to when he was a toddler.

He repressed a shudder.

"Mum's bloody gorgeous, by the way." Reid smirked, proud. "She was a fashion model in her twenties, not that she looks a day past thirty-seven." He threw the car into Park and faced Tate. "Mate. Welcome home." Then Reid lightened the heavy sentiment with, "I've already warned Mum not to smother you. You're welcome."

Tate had to hand it to his brother—Reid hadn't acted as if this was strange for a while now. Ironically, that made this entirely strange situation easier to accept.

As the four of them climbed from the car and approached the house, the dark wood front door with iron handles swung open.

He'd seen photos of Jane and George, but nothing could have prepared him for seeing his birth parents in the flesh for the first time in decades.

"Silver fox, am I right?" Drew murmured under her breath to Hayden. "His mom's hot, too."

Hayden replied, but Tate couldn't hear anything save the blood rushing past his eardrums. His poised mother was stationed at the threshold, dressed in white slacks and a cowl-necked gray sweater. She held on to Tate's father, who wore a casual suit and looked much younger than his stately name implied. Jane's hair was stylishly gray, but

George's maintained most of its dark brown with only a feathering of gray at the temples.

Tate took in every detail of the pair as he walked on stiff legs. Reid mentioned the traffic going easy before gently gripping his—*their*—mother's shoulders and guiding her inside. Before Tate stepped over the threshold, he felt Hayden's hand in his.

"Piece of cake," she whispered, looking beautiful but jet-lagged. Tate might be in unfamiliar territory but she'd become familiar. He would be here, facing this moment alone, if it wasn't for her.

He squeezed her fingers with his, unable to tell her what it meant to him that she was here, but hoping she knew anyway. Her tired wink suggested she might.

He'd make sure she had time to rest during the next few days. He pulled her to walk beside him and stole a kiss before following everyone inside. Reid led his mother into the entryway and then stood next to Drew.

George offered Tate a palm, the first to break the invisible wall between them. Looking into his father's face was like seeing someone you thought you might know but couldn't remember from where. Tate gripped George's hand.

"Good handshake, son. I'm your father, George Singleton. This is your mother, Jane." He cupped his wife's shoulder as she began to cry. Pretty at first, her high cheekbones and full lips barely shifting from their neutral positions, but a moment later, tears fell and that perfect bone structure seemed to dissolve.

Her outstretched arms shook when she reached for Tate. "Please, may I?" Her voice was broken, and Tate wasn't far behind, nodding his acceptance as tears blurred his vision.

He held his mother, expecting awkwardness, but it never came. Odd as it was to feel a connection with her, he did. The same way he'd felt it with Reid since the first moment he saw him in that coffee shop. As if a connection deep in his soul had been forged eons ago.

"Oh, my Wesley," she murmured repeatedly as she held on to him. "My sweet Wesley." She must have felt his arms go rigid, because she abruptly pulled away and corrected herself. "Tate. Tate is your name."

"They're both my names." He'd come to accept that recently. Easier now that the woman who'd carried him in her womb was standing in the circle of his arms.

Jane embraced him again, holding on for a long moment. A few other sniffs sounded in the room—from the direction of Drew and Hayden if Tate wasn't mistaken.

Jane let go of Tate, nodding with finality, her tears no longer falling. "One thing's for certain," she said as she studied his face. "You're much better looking than your brother."

"Hey!" Reid protested. The rest of them laughed and the tension that had built receded some.

It was *really* good to laugh.

"All right, then. Tea." Jane clapped her hands and led them farther into the house. Rich, caramel brown floors matched the doorframes and windowsills, and the walls were painted a soft white. The color palette was mostly burgundies and pine greens, and everywhere Tate looked was a reminder of nature. *Like my house*, he thought as he admired a piece of petrified wood in a slightly misshapen hand-thrown clay bowl.

"I made it. It's rubbish," Jane said of the bowl, bypassing it to walk to a cart in the corner of the room.

"So's what's in it," George agreed, his tone teasing. "A stick that's turned into a rock."

"Tate has petrified wood in his house," Hayden said, meeting his eyes and then Jane's. "You two have that in common." She stroked his arm with a hand as they lowered onto a jewel-toned settee, but then rose a moment later to help his mother serve.

"…lucky to have such a caring fiancée," Tate heard his mother say.

Hayden shot a quick glance to Tate, her expression no doubt matching his own. She recovered smoothly, flashing his mother a grin and offering a generic, polite response. "Thank you, Jane. I'm happy to help."

"I hear you own a nature preserve," George said, drawing Tate's attention from his fake fiancée.

Hayden handed Tate a cup of tea and sat with him and he renewed the promise he'd made to himself on the trip over. He was definitely making time to show Hayden his appreciation later.

Fourteen

"Your parents are sort of incredible." Hayden unpacked her suitcase, stashing her clothes in the dresser in the guest bedroom.

On that count, Tate had to agree. The weirdest part about meeting them was that they no longer felt like strangers. They'd discussed Spright Island, Jane and George both eager to hear of Tate's success with the community. Jane abashedly admitted that she'd "Googled it" and was "quite impressed."

He'd always been proud of the work he'd done there. The wellness community was his passion, but also his legacy. He'd never thought much about having a family of his own, always focusing instead on work. Claire had been equally focused on her career and stated she'd never wanted to have children. After having met the members of his actual family tree, though, Tate had briefly entertained the idea of having a family of his own. He supposed that was inevitable considering the circumstances.

Hayden hid her suitcase in the closet, yawning as she shut the bedroom door. He wondered if she wanted children. She'd never mentioned it before, but given the hints that her family was rife with conflict, maybe she didn't.

It wasn't the kind of discussion two people having a day-to-day affair would have, but he couldn't stop the vision of a little boy with dark hair and his blue eyes. Or twins.

"Jesus." He pulled a hand down his face to staunch the thoughts.

"I know. I'm tired, too." Hayden yawned again and he was glad she'd assumed he was tired rather than considering her potentially bearing his children. Maybe he could blame fatigue on his thoughts. They certainly weren't par for course.

Is any of this?

"Why don't you stay up here and rest." The guest room was hidden away at the back of the upstairs hallway, and he knew his parents wouldn't mind Hayden not showing for cocktail hour. Besides, it'd been George that had had invited Tate and Reid for brandy. Pregnant Drew had begged off to bed and his mother told Tate she'd happily join Hayden for a nip, but only if Hayden wasn't too tired. "Jane meant what she said when she told you to do what you like."

Hayden tilted her head and studied him, a spark of interest in her eyes despite the fatigue. "Do you think you'll ever be comfortable calling her Mom? Or Mum, as Reid calls her?"

Tate sucked in a breath. He guessed it wasn't that alarming to be thinking of having a family. He was surrounded by family and piecing the relationships together as best he could.

"Maybe someday," he said, but oddly that felt like a betrayal to his adoptive mother.

"You're handling this really well." Hayden palmed his cheek.

Placing his hands on her hips, Tate pulled her closer, and she draped her forearms over his shoulders. She fit there, in his embrace. Claire hadn't fit in his arms like she was meant to be there—a detail he'd always overlooked. And now that he'd met George and Jane and Reid Singleton, he wondered if in hindsight he'd find that he never fit with his family in California, either.

"Deep thoughts?"

"How do you know where you belong? Is it with the people who are familiar, or the people who are related?"

"That's a whopper, Tate Duncan," She paused to consider. "I used to feel comfortable in chaos, but now I crave a stable environment. In your very unique case, I don't think you'll have to choose. You have room in your life for your adoptive parents and your birth parents, for Reid and Drew, and for your new niece or nephew when he or she is born."

And you.

Pretending to be engaged to Hayden, pretending they had a future with "forever" implied, it wasn't hard to picture her there during his brother's wedding, the birth of a niece or nephew, or even a vacation to California to meet his adoptive parents.

That, too, felt dangerous, but this was also a safe place to consider the possibility of what life would be like if he and Hayden were truly engaged.

How it'd be expected to linger in their shared bedroom…

"How tired are you?" Tate lowered his mouth to her neck.

"Mmm," she purred.

He took to her lips for a brief kiss that didn't stay that way. Sliding his tongue along hers was the foolproof cure for jet lag. He backed her toward the bed.

"Tate," she whispered, and he was sure "we can't" would follow.

"Don't tell me to stop." He needed her. Needed to ground himself in the only reality that made sense right now. If there was one component that wasn't pretend, it was their explosive chemistry.

She raised and lowered one eyebrow, suddenly alert. "I was going to say brandy with George and Reid can wait."

"Hell, yes, it can."

She'd dressed for dinner in a long-sleeved black shirt made from material that held the slightest shimmer. He slipped a hand beneath it and along her smooth skin.

She tipped her head back, her dark hair falling over her shoulders while his hands explored her full breasts over the smooth cups of her bra.

Her moan of approval spurred him on. And like that first time he was with her, he didn't want to rush. Brandy with his family be damned.

He made short work of stripping her of her shirt and bra. Cupping her breasts, he thumbed her nipples and then kissed the tips of each. Her hands explored his hair, wrecking it. He took that as encouragement and continued circling one nipple with his tongue.

He unbuttoned her dark pants, slipping his hand past the waistband of her panties to tease her smooth folds. Spreading that wetness over her clit, he guided his fingers back and forth, until Hayden's hands clutched his shoulders and her moans elevated to bleats of pleasure.

Yanking his head from her chest, she kissed him with ferocity, none of her earlier fatigue present. He tenderly stroked her into her first orgasm. Watching her mouth round in pleasure and her beautiful face contort wouldn't be a sight he'd soon forget.

She shuddered in his arms, and he supported her weight, bracing her waist and kissing a trail from her jaw to her ear.

"You're so fucking gorgeous when you do that," he rasped. "This time, do it again, but with me inside you."

"Sounds good to me." She smiled. A challenge.

He lifted her into his arms and tossed her onto the bed. She bounced, stifling her laugh with a hand over her lips while he tugged off her heeled shoes and pants.

She daintily scooted back, folding her long legs to one side and looking up at him sexily. She was like every wet dream he'd ever had, only better—because she was here. She was real. And he was *really* going to enjoy coaxing forth her next orgasm.

Tate took off his shirt, and Hayden's dark eyes flared. That she looked at him the way he looked at her—like she couldn't believe how damn lucky she was to have him naked—hardened his erection and sharpened his desire.

He finished undressing and climbed over her, tickling her lips with a series of gentle kisses before trailing his mouth down her neck to her breasts. He made a pit stop at each one—he'd never be able to resist the lure of her perfect nipples—and then made himself comfortable between her thighs.

Ruined.

Tate had ruined her for anyone else. Which was alarming, since she didn't spend much time considering a man permanently being around for sex, or dating, or…anything, really.

But, she wasn't above having fun.

Which was what this is, she reminded herself sternly.

George and Jane, and even Reid and Drew who knew the engagement was for show, had treated Hayden like family tonight. There was a part of her that had basked in that attention. At the idea of being a part of a family that genuinely seemed to want for each other, not from each other.

But Tate wasn't a permanent fixture. This was a fairy tale. One where she'd been whisked to London by a wealthy prince—one who *really* knew how to use his freaking tongue.

The sound of the condom wrapper being torn open jolted her out of her post-orgasmic bliss.

"Wait!"

Tate looked almost alarmed at her outburst, which was sort of funny.

"Let's hold off on this part." She took the condom from his hand. "There's something I wanted to do first."

Shoving him onto his back, she pressed a kiss to first one pectoral and then the other and positioned herself over him. As she kissed her way down his torso, Tate grew reverently silent. She knew he'd figured out her intentions the moment he scooped her hair into his hands and watched her work.

And oh, did she *work*.

She held his shaft at the base, flicking him a sultry glance while licking the tip of his cock. His mouth dropped open, the tendons in his neck standing out in stark relief.

He smelled of soap from their earlier—and sadly, separate—showers, and the musky smell that was his and his alone.

She alternated with teasing licks and loving kisses and then swallowed him whole, tickling his balls while the air sawed out of his lungs in uneven gasps.

Moments before she would have swallowed his release, he tugged her hair, still wrapped in his fists. "Hayden."

When she didn't stop right away, his voice grew gruff, more demanding, *"Hayden."*

She let him go with a soft pop, licking her lips. "Fine. I'll stop, but only bec—"

Without warning, he flipped her to her back and was over her in an instant. She yelped in surprise then slapped a hand over her mouth. The house was large, but not *that* large. No need to broadcast that she was upstairs shagging the Singletons' newfound son.

"Condom," she reminded him as he nudged her entrance with his very hard member.

"Right. Of course." He blinked once, then twice like he was trying to bring his brain back online. He rolled on the condom in record time and, before her next breath, entered her in one long, slow slide. Buried to the root, he paused to blow out a careful, measured breath.

"You okay, COO of Gorgeous Inc.?" She feathered his hair from his forehead, and he offered a narrow-eyed glare. "COO? Founder? Which do you prefer?"

"I prefer—" he slid out and then in again "—for you to call me by my name. Repeatedly. And with growing enthusiasm," he added as he continued moving.

"Tate." He seemed to gain strength as she repeated his name over and over. As if he'd needed, more than anything, that reminder of who he was. As if hearing his name had anchored him.

"Come for me, Hayden." He lifted her calf, and she stretched her leg to rest it easily on his shoulder. The angle made it easier for him to hit her G-spot, which he had a knack for finding.

"There," she said with a gasp. Damn, he was good.

"One more for me. Then I'll let you sleep for a few hours."

He grinned, and she returned it. Her smile fell when she felt the telltale building of a showstopper of an orgasm.

"Tate." She continued worshipping as she gripped the blankets with kneading fists. Her nipples pebbled in the cool bedroom air even as sweat beaded his forehead from his workout.

The fourth stroke was the charm.

She dissolved, the release hitting her so hard she squeezed her eyes shut to absorb the impact. He wasn't far behind her, growling his release. He came to a jerky stop moments before collapsing on top of her.

His weight pressed her into the mattress, a thin sheen of sweat sticking his chest to hers. "By far my favorite work out is having sex with you."

"Agreed." She swept a hand through his hair and kissed his temple.

He left to deal with the condom, but by the time he returned, her eyes refused to stay open. She was vaguely aware of the sound of him pulling on his clothes, barely awake when he feathered a kiss on her cheek.

The last words she remembered was his whispered promise of, "Rest up. You'll need your strength for later."

Fifteen

"He had no idea who you were?" Hayden leaned closer to Drew at the tightly packed bar.

When they'd first stepped into the Churchill, she'd been agape with wonder. The outside of the building was draped with Christmas trees. "Eighty of them and eighteen thousand fairy lights," Reid had shared. From that point on, the place had fascinated her.

Hanging from the ceiling were numerous beaten-copper pots, pans and lights, and at one point she spotted a guitar case and even an accordion. As its name suggested, the Churchill was dripping with memorabilia, in memory of the man after which it was named. The walls were wooden and dotted with framed photos and paintings, the tables and chairs well worn from plenty of use.

"There's no better place to be than Church on Christmas Eve," Reid had told Tate, looping a brotherly arm around his neck as he'd dragged him inside.

Hayden was ridiculously happy for Tate. He had a fun, boisterous, lovable family. She could see clearly that his mother had wanted to accompany him out tonight only to be close to him awhile longer. And who could blame her? The woman had gone decades believing her other son was *deceased*. In the end George had wrangled Jane in, encouraging her to "let the lads and lasses have their fun."

Drew circled the straws in her club soda with lime before confirming Hayden's question. "Reid had no clue it was me."

"Then what?" Hayden was on the edge of her seat hearing how Drew and Reid had bumped into each other at a work conference. She stirred her own club soda with lime, content with the mocktail and Drew's company. She listened intently as Drew told her about the huge crush she'd had on Reid when she was sixteen years old and how running into him again was her very narrow window to properly seduce him.

"So I'm lying in his hotel room bed fast asleep and he does this—" Drew snapped her fingers in Hayden's face "—and literally *scolds* me for not telling him who I was!"

Hayden laughed. It'd be a story for the grandkids, without a doubt... An edited version, but still.

Drew was beaming, glowing. Even though half her story was shouted so as to be heard over a rowdy group of *lads* chugging down their ciders and ales.

The patrons of Churchill had worn their Christmas finery. For most of the ladies, sparkly dresses—one lass wore an elf costume—and the guys, including Reid and Tate, wore funny hats. Reid, a court jester hat and he'd talked Tate into the one shaped like a giant pint of ale.

"He's doing well, Tate," Drew pulled her eyes away from their guys to say. "I've been trying not to watch him with George and Jane, but it's so beautiful to see them together. And when Reid joins the mix..." Her eyelashes fluttered. "Sorry. Hormones."

"You don't have to explain. I've felt that same sort of emotion being around them. Tate's doing amazingly well."

"I remember the first time I had that look in my eye. It's unique to a woman falling in love."

Hayden tried not to overreact, but she was relatively certain her shocked expression rivaled the one she'd worn when she stepped into Church for the first time tonight. Except instead of awe over garland and pinecones, flickering candles in lanterns and sleigh bells strewn hither and yon, her shock was due to her inability to agree with her new friend.

"It's not love."

"Oh." Drew was uncharacteristically chagrined. "Sorry. I didn't mean to assume…"

Hayden waved a hand to cut off Drew's needless apology. "I can see how you'd draw that conclusion. We have a great time together. He asked me to come here and support him, and I couldn't turn down a friend."

Though *friend* seemed a lame word for what they had been doing together in bed every time they were alone. It sounded lame saying it out loud, too, but if Drew noticed, she was too polite to point it out.

"I'm glad he has you. No matter how you define it. And there's no need to define anything, is there? It's Christmas!" Drew lifted her glass, and Hayden tapped her own against it.

On the other side of the bar, the guys sat close to the fireplace, glasses of bourbon or some kind of brown liquid in hand. Reid tossed his head back and laughed, his throat bobbing, and Tate swiped his eyes as he laughed along with him. Hayden was hit with the oddest sense of pleasure at seeing Tate happy. And not the way she might mildly appreciate someone enjoying themselves. More like she was *invested* in him. Her assuredness about not being in love with him didn't stop her from having feelings that were, while not love, definitely love-*like*.

If there was a real fiancé in Hayden's life, Tate would be the ideal candidate.

* * *

Tate sat by the fireplace while Reid fetched refills at the bar. On the way he stopped and placed a hand on Hayden's shoulder and smiled down at her. When she replied with an eye roll, Reid winked.

They'd accepted her, his family. His parents, his brother and Drew. The same way they'd accepted him into their lives. There were rough patches, of course. Awkward moments where the air was stale and no one spoke. But ultimately someone thought of something to say, and it was always in order to help Tate feel at home.

His mother had been asking about wedding plans almost nonstop. "Let me know the date as soon as you're certain," she'd said. "I'll book a flight."

I'll book a flight had been Jane Singleton's mantra since Tate arrived. She was anxious to come to the States, and when Tate agreed at lunch that he'd enjoy showing her around Spright Island, she'd promptly pressed her lips together to quell more tears.

Her crying over him made him uncomfortable, but he understood. He felt as if he'd been robbed, and yet at the same time he wouldn't trade his childhood or his adoptive parents for anything in the world.

Hayden turned her head to look over at him and he waved. She smiled, demurely at first, but then her teeth stabbed her lower lip to keep away a full grin.

My fiancée, he thought when he returned her smile. What had he been thinking asking her to play the role? She was great at it, though. So great that it wasn't hard to imagine her in that role for real. But the timing was so off it wasn't even funny. He was scrambling to keep his life sewn together at the seams and Hayden… He kept referring back to their conversation the first night they were together. One night at a time had been the promise—a reprieve for them both.

Pretending was fine. Short-term. *Fun*. But reality came with an entirely new set of rules.

"Cheers." Reid returned and handed Tate one of the drinks. "Hayden is gorgeous and funny and you're not likely to do better." Reid's cheeks puffed as he held the liquor in them for a beat before swallowing and wincing. "Holy hellfire." He coughed.

Tate opted for a sip rather than a gulp.

"I never saw myself married or a dad, but it's about to happen for me. I'm one of those happy idiots I used to feel sorry for." Reid was more careful taking his next drink. "And before you accuse me of trying to induct you into the married people hall of fame, just know that I have no agenda other than your happiness."

Rare was the moment Reid was sincere, but he appeared so as he held his glass aloft. Even wearing the jester hat.

"I appreciate you looking out for me." Tate sat back into the stuffed chair. "What Hayden and I have now, it's working. It's easy. Simple."

Tate nodded, liking the sound of both of those words. Easy and simple wasn't something his life had been lately.

"Simple has its merits," Reid said, but it sounded like a line. Something to say to fill the air rather than the truth, which reflected in blue eyes that matched Tate's own.

Outside the Singleton home, Tate stood in the backyard, a brisk wind stinging his reddened cheeks. He'd gone to bed around 1:00 a.m., after several glasses of the burning liquid Reid kept bringing him. He'd come back here, passed out and then woke at 3:30 a.m., his heart racing like it was trying to escape his chest.

After three big glasses of water—one of them with an aspirin chaser—Tate wandered outside. The in-ground pool was draped with a black tarp, closed this time of year. He had vague thoughts of swimming in it, of losing a toy and of his mother diving in after it wearing all her clothes.

He didn't know how much of the memory was memory or how much was his mind desperately trying to connect the dots of his checkered past. Bits of information were missing and colored in with other bits from an entirely different life. He'd yet to piece himself together.

"Wesl—Tate," came his mother's voice from behind him. "Darling, what are you doing?" She bundled a thick parka around her. "It's freezing out here, you'll catch your—"

"Death?" he finished for her. "Too late."

She gave him a light shove in the arm. "Comedian like your brother. Bloody hell! It really is freezing out here."

"We can go in."

"No, no it's fine." She assessed him, something sad in her eyes before she said, "Your adoptive parents contacted us."

He felt the blood rush from his cheeks. He'd had no idea.

"Don't be angry. We contacted them first, hoping if we reached out, they'd reply. I begged Marion—ah, your mother—not to say anything to you. By the look on your face, I assume she complied."

"She didn't tell me." He felt his worlds colliding, fearing that collision and at the same time anxiously anticipating it. He couldn't be two people the rest of his life. At some point he'd have to accept that he was Tate *and* Wesley. Son of Marion and William *and* son of George and Jane.

"I wanted to…understand, I suppose," Jane said. "They're lovely. And as much as I wanted to rage at the couple who kept my son from me all those years, I realize it's not their fault they loved you so fiercely. At least that's what my therapist says I'm supposed to feel." Her mouth quirked. "But I love you, Wes—Tate. And that means I will prioritize your happiness above my own."

A surge of emotion pushed against his rib cage. After

a month of damming it up, only allowing it to release at a trickle, he was due for a tsunami.

His chin shook as another memory crawled out of the recesses of his mind. Jane jumping into the pool after his favorite stuffed toy. He hadn't imagined it. It wasn't made up. The memory was from his toddler-height point of view. And when Jane handed it back sopping wet, he'd cried more and George had helped Jane to her feet, his rumbling laughter encompassing them.

It was *real*, his life here in London. No longer a fuzzy impression he was trying to bring into focus.

"Call me Wesley, Mum," he wrapped an arm around his mother. "That's the name you gave me."

This time when she cried, he held on and cried with her. For the many years they'd lost, and the many years, God willing, they had left.

Sixteen

Dinner was set on the Singleton table, the candles lit, tablecloth spread, and the poinsettia table markers next to embroidered cloth napkins. The Christmas tree was bedazzled with lights in the corner, though Jane mentioned to Hayden they didn't often buy a tree.

"It's a special occasion," Jane had said with a warm smile.

George and Jane sat at either end of the mahogany table while Drew and Reid took their seats side by side. Hayden settled in next to Tate, surprised that spending the holiday away from home, and in a strikingly different environment, hadn't made her feel out of place. She suspected the Singletons had something to do with that—all of them.

Her family holidays were hectic and loud, and not in the charming way. Usually her mother was arguing with her grandmother, who was pouring her third cocktail before dinner. Mom's cooking was good, though—Hayden wouldn't begrudge her that. But one look at the Singleton spread hinted that Jane knew her way around the kitchen, as well.

A whole turkey was the centerpiece, carved in neat slices and glistening with butter, its skin a crisp golden brown.

Sides of diced potatoes and onions, stuffing—though it looked more like hush puppies to Hayden—and vegetables like cabbage, parsnips and a dish of green peas filled in the gaps.

"Right, then. Let's get started." George unfurled his napkin and held out his hands on either side of him. After a beat, Drew and Hayden gathered that they should each take hold of the patriarch's hands for prayer. Hayden held Tate's hand and he in turn held his mother's, who gripped Reid's fingers as he reached for Drew's.

The prayer was brief and proper, and by the time the word *Amen* was uttered, there wasn't a dry eye in the house. Could've had something to do with George giving thanks for "Wesley" being home. "For the first time in nearly three decades," Tate's father had said, "both my sons are under this roof again."

"Gravy," Jane announced, dousing her plate of food with the stuff before passing it on. Hayden politely took the dish from Tate after he'd put some on his potatoes before handing it to George without partaking.

"No sense in watching your waistline, love," George teased with a wink. "All of the veg on this table have been cooked in duck fat." He offered the dish back as though passing on the gravy wasn't an option. She put a dollop on her potatoes. When in Rome, and all that.

Dinner was delicious, if heavy, and once the meal was finished, no one moved to scurry from the table. Typically, at her house, her mother had the food in the fridge the very moment the last plate was cleared. Here, though, Jane made no move to rush around putting food away. Instead she tossed her napkin onto the table saying, "Crackers! I nearly forgot the crackers!"

"Crackers?" Tate asked, and Hayden shared his mild alarm. After stuffing themselves with a rich, two-helpingsof-everything Christmas dinner, who could possibly have room for crackers.

"Oh! I've been wanting to do this!" Drew applauded from her seat.

Jane came out from under the tree with gift-wrapped oblong paper packages tied with ribbons on both ends. They looked like giant, festively wrapped Tootsie Rolls.

"Tradition," Reid explained to the three Americans. He took the gift his mother passed out and explained. "I hold one end, Drew holds the other." A delighted Drew gripped one end of the wrapping. "And then we pull."

A small cracking sound came and the paper tore. Out fell a bauble and a few bits of folded paper. "Looks like I've won a ring." Reid, pleased with his trinket, stuffed it onto his pinky, the purple stone set in plastic not exactly his style. He then unfolded a gold crepe-like paper crown, which he proudly perched on his head. "There, now. I'm ready for my joke."

He reached for the square of paper on the table and read, "What do Santa's little helpers learn at school?" When no one answered, he shared, "The elf-abet."

Jane, George and Reid chuckled. Drew raised an eyebrow. "These are supposed to be bad jokes, right?"

"Oh, the worst." Reid kissed her. "Now yours. Come on then." Drew's cracker held a tiny stapler that couldn't have been longer than her thumb. George's contained a bag of marbles, Jane's a puzzle game with a ball and a maze. Their included jokes were as lame as Reid's.

Tate's Christmas cracker held a small stuffed bear. One he stared at for an inordinately long time. His eyes tracked to his mother's, who blinked away tears as she shook her head.

"What a silly coincidence." She waved a hand but Hayden knew that symbol of a special moment between mother and son was anything but silly.

"Your turn," Tate told Hayden as she took the end of her cracker and he took the other. After the pop, a gaudy ring fell from her cracker. "Look at that. A matching set."

"Not quite. Mine's bigger than Reid's." Hayden eyed Tate's brother, trying to keep things light.

"Maybe you should see if it fits." Drew's winked, pure, adorable *evil*. Not at all interested in keeping the focus off Hayden's ring.

Hayden cast Tate an unsure look but he didn't waver. He took the ring from her hand and slid it onto her ring finger, admiring it in the candlelight.

The tacky plastic trinket shimmered, silver glitter swimming within the blue stone. It was gumball-machine quality, and completely ridiculous, but there was something symbolic about Tate slipping it onto her hand in front of his family that caused a lump to rise in her throat.

"The perfect placeholder while yours is being sized, then," Jane said, repeating the false story Hayden had given about why she wasn't wearing a ring.

"Right."

"My boys. Married and happy. It's all I ever wanted." Jane folded her hands at her chest and Hayden hoped it escaped notice that she and Tate were silent on the matter.

The only real part of their relationship was that she and Tate liked each other a whole hell of a lot.

"Your crown," Tate slipped the thin paper ring over Hayden's hair and, following tradition, she reached for her joke.

"Why does Santa have three gardens?" She waited a beat and then wrinkled her nose. "So he can 'ho ho ho.'" She groaned but everyone at the table erupted in laughter.

"Worst one yet." Tate leaned forward to kiss her. It occurred to her that he'd been careful about being affectionate with her in front of his family, and she him. Now he lingered over her lips, placing a second kiss there before murmuring, "Merry Christmas, Hayden."

"Jane wants us to delay our flight," Tate said as he packed away another sweater into his suitcase. They'd stayed downstairs after dinner, drinking and laughing and enjoying his their family's traditional Christmas pudding.

That brought discussion of more of his newfound family, which had led to photo albums. Turned out he had a lot of cousins, aunts, uncles and one living grandfather in the area.

"When you return, we'll have a visit," Jane had told him, hinting that she'd been careful not to overwhelm him this trip.

"It's Boxing Day tomorrow, which is a national holiday here," he continued telling Hayden, who sat on the bed. Things had gone well so far, but staying longer seemed to be pushing his luck. "They go to a restaurant and out shopping, and then there's a duck race with rubber duckies for charity in the afternoon." He raised his eyebrows. "I had no idea."

He'd booked their flights to be in and out quickly, figuring he'd be ready to retreat to the sanctity of Spright Island as soon as possible. But he wasn't as ready as he'd originally thought. He was enjoying his parents, Reid and Drew, and Hayden.

She still wore the ring he'd put on her finger at dinner. When Drew had suggested she try it on, Tate hadn't hesitated. Part of living dangerously included not overthinking moments like that one. But he couldn't deny the part of him that wanted it to be real—as real as the family who, before this trip, had been no more than a story. Would bringing Hayden deeper into his life be the same as it'd been with the Singletons? At first a vague notion, and then 3D reality come to life... Did he *want* to be in deeper?

Discomfort bubbled in his gut, and the thought of "don't push your luck" occurred again. There was fun and then there was stupid, and he'd been walking that razor's edge.

"You should take that off before it turns your finger green."

Hayden gave her finger one lingering look before agreeing, "I guess you're right." She tugged the ring from her hand and set it on the night table next to the bed.

See? She doesn't want to go deeper either.

"With everything going on, I hadn't so much as thought about putting a real ring on your finger for show. I should've known everyone would expect it." Not that he'd have even considered giving her the one Claire had worn. That thing was a bad omen. He hadn't gotten around to selling it yet, but he would. Another act in the one-man play he was calling *Moving On*.

"You've had a lot on your mind." Hayden came to him and traced the lines bracketing his mouth. "This will become easier, Tate. You'll see. You'll get used to having extra family, and then you'll find a way to include them all into your big, amazing life."

"You always know what to say." Always knew how to put everything into instant perspective. His lips hovered dangerously close to hers. "Thank you for coming. I couldn't have done this without you."

He meant it. Considering the depth of the emotional pitfalls he'd experienced recently, he'd tackled them with relative ease. Hayden had his back, and he didn't take that lightly.

Hayden tilted her face, her lips brushing his. "I'm glad I could help." One eyebrow lifted impishly. "You owe me, Duncan."

He gave her bottom lip a gentle nip. "Will you take payment in sexual favors?"

"My favorite kind of currency."

He kissed her, his lips sliding over hers as he settled against her in bed. He lost himself in her plush mouth, the friction from her writhing hips into his crotch giving him a damn good idea.

Her soft moans urged him on, and Tate had them out of their clothes a short while later. He was suddenly very grateful he'd stopped in the rain outside her studio that night.

Grateful for her in any capacity, even a temporary one. Maybe they were only meant to be together through this particularly difficult part of his life. Maybe once the storms cleared and the sun shined, they'd be ready to move on.

Somehow, though, he doubted it.

He took his time kissing every inch of her he exposed. Every soft, muscular, firm yet giving bit of her, until her breaths were short and fast.

She stroked his jaw with cool fingertips as she murmured her praise. And he took his time, memorizing the details of her beneath him just in case their time together ended before he was ready.

Seventeen

"Are you sure you don't want to come along?" Tate asked his mother.

"You kids go on without us. I've had my fun."

After making love to Hayden last night, she'd convinced Tate to stay another day. She argued that she didn't have classes until after the new year, anyway, then added, "You're enjoying yourself. It'd be good for you." When he hesitated, she resorted to teasing him. "What's wrong? Can't afford to change our flight times?"

That had earned her a tickle fight that turned into slow, openmouthed kisses. When he tried to pull her under him again, she'd shoved him in the direction of his laptop. He'd reluctantly left the warm bed and made the necessary changes to their tickets.

"Listen to your mother," George warned now, beer glass raised. They'd spent the Boxing Day in downtown London for the most part, shopping and visiting a variety of booths in what was normally a concrete jungle. From there they'd gone to a pub for a beer and snacks, when Jane mentioned "you'd better see yourselves to Hyde Park before it's too late."

"Yeah, listen to your mother," Reid echoed George.

"Look at her. A woman her age probably needs to rest her weary bones."

Jane Singleton was nowhere near "weary." Her blue eyes were bright and sparkling, her smile soft and easy. No longer did she have that haunted look in her eyes like she'd seen a ghost—though Tate reasoned that he *was* a ghost in a way.

"She needs tea," Reid continued, not heeding the warning glare from Jane. "And a nap."

"Careful, son, or you'll be wearing that drink," George warned with a chuckle. "The truth of the matter is we want the house to ourselves." He wrapped his arms around his wife and kissed her neck while Jane laughed and gave his arm a halfhearted swat.

Tate smiled at the display, grateful they'd had each other while he was missing. Grateful that what had happened to him hadn't torn apart their marriage.

"What do you think?" Tate asked Hayden, but he could've guessed her thoughts given the size of her grin.

"I'd be remiss to leave London without seeing a light garden in Hyde Park." She turned to Jane. "And I'd never rob you of an evening with your very handsome husband."

"Hear, hear," Drew said with enthusiasm, holding her club soda in the air.

"But take photos!" Jane requested. "Of the light garden, the observation wheel, roller coasters and, oh! Ice skating!"

"Do you ice skate, *darling*?" Hayden asked, her syrupy tone teasing.

"You've seen me move," Tate murmured into her ear before kissing her warm cheek. "What do you think?"

Reid, ever the encourager of public displays of affection, put his fingers between his lips and whistled.

London had been culture shock for Hayden since she arrived, so she was pleasantly surprised to find the winter wonderland event in Hyde Park was similar to what she'd come to expect of carnivals and fairs back home.

Well, aside from the aged, regal architecture she'd seen driving in, which had been preserved from another era entirely.

The park itself was overdone in the best way imaginable. Gaudy, blinking bulbs decorated every stall and stand, including on the huge lit entrance sign announcing "Winter Wonderland."

Entry was free, but there were opportunities to buy everything from food to shirts and jewelry to artwork. Bars dotted the park as well as venues for live shows, a funhouse, and a Ferris wheel—which must've been what Jane meant by "observation" wheel. The ice skating rink was *enormous*, children and adults alike moving across the slick surface with various stages of skill. Some gliding, others flailing.

Hayden would probably manage something between a glide and a flail if they ventured that direction.

Tate waggled their hands. They were connected by interlocked fingers and she'd gone without gloves given the mild weather. It was chilly, but not cold and while fog threatened, it hadn't brought rain.

"Since I can't have beer, I insist upon sugar," Drew announced, pointing at a stall with candy bins filled with lollipops, candy necklaces and gummy everything.

"Done. Should we meet up at the light garden?" Reid asked.

"Yeah, one hour. We're going to try to skate," Tate called to his brother. Reid nodded his acknowledgment.

Tate, bracketing Hayden's hips with his hands, pulled her ass against his crotch. "Let's see what you're made of, gorgeous."

Snow machines blew flaked ice into the air as they laced up, Hayden unsure what she was getting herself into.

"I'm sure it's like riding a bike," she'd famously said before falling onto her backside. They made their way clumsily around the rink once, and by round two, while they hadn't exactly glided, they had swept across the ice in a way that was at least semicompetent.

Skates off, boots on, she and Tate made their way to the closest booth that sold beverages and sat on a nearby bench with their drinks.

"Thank God for my core strength," she said with a laugh over her paper cup of wassail.

"I enjoyed watching you wobbling across the ice."

She nudged him, careful not to spill his drink into his lap. "You actually did better than me. I'm impressed." She poked him in the belly, and his abdomen clenched into a wall of muscle beneath her finger. Which reminded her of what he looked like without any clothes, and that in turn reminded her of what they did together best. "It's kind of a turn-on."

"Ice skating turns you on?" Tate lifted a dubious eyebrow.

"Pretty sure you doing anything turn me on." She said it with an almost disappointed lilt. This fantasy of being fake engaged, the fairy tale of Christmas in London, was about to come to an end. She'd been tempering her reactions, trying to monitor the way she responded to him, but she wasn't always able to keep her true feelings from surfacing.

She issued a reminder that it was smart not to grow accustomed to flying business class to London at Christmas, or having a Hallmark-style scene on ice skates…

Hayden had become independent out of necessity. Since the moment she'd invited Tate into her apartment—into her *life*—he'd been chipping away at the wall she safely hid behind. She felt a pull toward him that was simply undeniable.

"I could say the same to you, Ms. Green." She was rewarded with a kiss that reminded her of the wassail. Sweet, clovey, cinnamony…*temporary.*

"You freak me out a little," she admitted. "I'm not used to…so much lavish treatment."

"Excuse me? Lavish? We hopped on a plane. We're at a park."

"You flew us to London in our own private pods! We're at *Hyde Park.* You own an entire community, meanwhile I'm leasing my studio and my apartment."

"And my treating you to what you deserve is making you uncomfortable?"

"I…" But her pending argument died on her tongue. She was stuck on the "deserve" part. Tate had no problem filling the silence.

"You do deserve it, Hayden. The good life. It's not reserved to people who were lucky enough to be born into it. Or adopted into it," he added softly.

"My grandmother's an alcoholic," she blurted out, as if the secret of her own parentage refused to be stuffed down any longer. "And my mother is a master of guilt. Both at absorbing it and doling it out."

Tate's eyebrows knitted, but he stayed quiet. She hadn't opened up to him about just how wide the gap was between his life and hers, and it seemed wrong not to share at this point. She knew his secrets.

"When I moved out on my own for the first time, they didn't let a day go by without reminding me that I was betraying them in the worst way possible. And when I moved to the refuge of Spright Island, they were jealous. Enormously jealous." She rolled her eyes as she replayed her mother's words about Hayden being *too good for them.* "I saved and saved and saved. And I work hard. I earned the right to live there. I made that decision on my own. It didn't come without a price, though. I'm not sure I have what I deserve."

She smiled sadly as she remembered another conversation with her mom, this one before she left for London. Patti Green hadn't been supportive of her daughter choosing to "flit around the globe" over spending time with family.

"Sometimes the healthiest choice for you isn't the popular one," Tate said. "I love my adoptive parents but when I found out about the Singletons visiting them became hard. I drew boundary lines around them even though I knew it would hurt my mother's feelings."

She heaved a sigh. "Adulting is hard."

"The worst," he agreed, but his smile was light, and she felt the weight lift from her shoulders having admitted some family conflict of her own.

"After the new year, life will return to normal," she reminded both of them. "But getting lost in this—" she gestured to the gazebo with a decorated tree in the center and the many, many ropes of lights strung in every direction "—is worth it."

"Good."

"Thank you, Tate. I really appreciate you—this. You've been generous."

"Stop making this sound like goodbye." A little lean forward would be all it took to kiss him. A tiny nudge all it would take for him to mean so, so much more to her.

But it was Christmastime, and Tate smelled like wassail and leather, so Hayden lost herself in the heat of his mouth, and postponed worrying about the consequences for a little while longer.

Eighteen

Recovering from jet lag took a lot longer than Hayden anticipated.

The flight back from London was unremarkable and a lot less comfortable than the flight there. Despite Tate's insistence they change airlines to book first class or charter a private jet to go home, Hayden refused. She'd assured him that any seat was fine. He'd finally let her convince him and they'd ended up crammed in a middle aisle in a tight seat for the incredibly long flight home.

She'd needed the reminder that life wasn't all champagne and caviar. Halfway through the flight, however, as she was trying to stretch in the pitiful space between her seat and the one in front of her she realized she was being ridiculous. Why was it so hard for her to indulge?

As part of her new year's resolutions next year, she was just going to enjoy her damn self. Tate had been a good sport, sending her a weary "I told you so" glance, but never bothering with the sentiment. She'd ended up apologizing once they were back in SWC, but he'd only kissed her forehead and sent her up to her apartment before returning home himself.

Now that she'd been home for a few days and was well

rested, she was having what might be the most productive day of her life. She'd finished her laundry, planned her meals for the week, *and* finalized her class schedule for January as well as posting it on her website.

A knock at her door came earlier than she expected. Tate had made dinner plans for them to eat at the Brass Pony. She was wearing one of two new dresses she'd purchased since she'd returned home. One in black for the New Year's Eve party, which was much fancier than the red one she wore now.

"You weren't supposed to be here until six," she said as she pulled open the door. He was dressed handsomely in a suit sans tie, the collar open on a crisp white shirt. But his face was drawn, his mouth downturned.

"Wow. Rough day?"

"You could say that." He handed her a tall white cup from EterniTea. "They haven't opened yet, but I know a guy. Thought you might like to try the green tea latte."

"Thanks."

He leaned in and kissed her, lingering over her lips as he pulled in a breath. "Ready to go?"

"Are you sure you *want* to go?"

"Of course." He made a half-assed attempt at a smile but it didn't reach his eyes.

"Do you want to talk about it?" The second she asked her phone beeped—her mother's ringtone, which was as dooming as Darth Vader's theme song.

She staunchly ignored it, sipping her tea instead. "This is delicious."

"Don't you want to get that?" He frowned.

"No." Hayden had tried to call her mother to let her know she'd returned from London. She hadn't heard back and had counted herself lucky. "It's my mom."

"We have time."

"Trust me. Answering that call isn't about *time*. My family's...not like yours."

"British?" he teased.

"Normal."

"No family is normal. Answer it. If you do and find it's more drama with no real point, then mention we are headed to dinner and hang up. It's just that easy."

"And if it's an actual emergency?"

"Then we'll deal with it."

We.

She realized upon hearing that word that she'd never had support when it came to her family. It'd always been more of an "us versus them" situation.

"I'm sure your day was rough enough without dealing with—" the phone beeped again "—whatever this is."

Tate remained resolutely silent, even when the chime of her voice mail sounded.

"Fine," she told him, lifting her cell phone and turning on the speaker. "Here we go."

The recording started with a frantic "Oh, Hayden" that chilled her blood. Hayden's mother spoke between nervous breaths.

"Your grandmother is in the ER." Her mother's recorded voice shook. "This is worse than usual, Hayden. Much worse." Patti went on dispensing one horrific detail after the last, which made Hayden worry all the more. Patti ended the call with the name of the hospital.

Hayden crossed the living room to grab her keys and purse but was confronted by Tate, who plucked the keys from her hand.

"I'll drive."

Her head was already shaking. "I can't ask you to do that."

"You didn't ask. I told you we'd deal with it. Let's deal with it."

After years of independence and relying on herself, Tate, even after hearing that voice mail, was willing to go with her. It was hard to accept.

"Yes, but…"

"You met my family."

As if that was the same? But then she thought about how he'd been brave enough to ask for her help. Was she brave enough to accept his?

"Hayden." He held her hand. That was all it took to convince her. She let him lead her to the door and the uncertainty that waited for them at Seattle Memorial Hospital.

A hard, bitter line was the best description of Hayden's mouth as she navigated the hospital's hallways. She was a woman on a mission, and reminded Tate more of a woman who was walking into a courtroom to hear a verdict than someone visiting her sick grandmother.

He'd dealt with his own bullshit today in the form of Casey Huxley. Tate had spent an hour arguing with the jackass head contractor who was spearheading the new neighborhood in SWC—that "secret" project model Hayden had stumbled upon in Tate's upstairs bedroom.

Casey had been amenable to the design until recently. Now they were arguing over bulldozing more trees to expand. It wasn't happening. Tate wouldn't compromise nature simply because Casey was too lazy to find a workaround.

At the nurse's desk, they learned that Hayden's grandmother had been downgraded from ICU to a room of her own, which only firmed the bitter line of Hayden's lips, causing them to vanish altogether.

He didn't have a lot of experience with true dysfunction and had zero experience with alcoholism, but he knew stressful situations which was clearly what she was involved in here.

"When's the last time you took a deep breath?" he asked, catching her wrist before she could march in the direction of her grandmother's room.

Hayden glared up at him, unwilling to let go and let God.

"Wouldn't it be better to walk into that room calm and collected?" he tried again. Advice he could've taken from himself earlier when he'd been in a screaming match with Casey in the trailer at the worksite. Tate would have some backpedaling to do if he hoped to quell the gossip train. Destroying land was a hot button for him. He refused to compromise his integrity, or his island's.

She didn't look happy about it, but Hayden took one breath, then another. "You don't have to go in with me. My family is… They're…" She shook her head, giving up.

"Family," he answered. "Not serial killers. Family. Messy, complicated, unpredictable."

"The student becomes the teacher." Her smile was faint.

"I'm a fast learner."

In the hospital room, there was an empty bed by the door and a frail, pale woman in a bed by the window. He guessed the woman at her side holding her hand to be Hayden's mother. She had the same dark brown hair, but shot through with gray. She carried more weight than Hayden and her face was lined.

A man in jeans and a long-sleeved sweater approached from the corridor, limping like he had a bum knee. He didn't seem very old, but his beer belly and the dark circles beneath his eyes aged him.

"Hayd. You made it." His voice was bright, almost cheery. Odd considering the situation.

"Hi, Dad." Hayden's smile was cautious as she held herself in check. No warm family greetings here.

"Went to grab a coffee. Guess we'll be here awhile." He sipped from his cup before turning to Tate. "Hello."

"Dad, this is Tate Duncan. He drove me here. Tate, my father, Glenn."

"Nice to see you, Tate. Can I grab either of you a cup of coffee?"

"No, thank you," Hayden told him.

Tate tried not to take her "he drove me here" comment personally, as if he was a chauffer and not the man who'd taken her to London over the holidays.

"Okey-doke. Well, I'll let you go in and visit, then. I'll wander around." In place of goodbye, he said, "Tate," and then turned and walked away from them.

"He's mellow." It might've been the strangest interaction Tate had ever had with a parent, and that was saying something.

"It's a coping mechanism," she said.

"Hayden? Oh, Hayden!" Her mother, having just noticed them at the threshold, frantically waved her deeper into the room. Hayden's grandmother lifted her head, her eyelids narrowing. Tate could've sworn the temperature of the room went down a few degrees.

"Hi, Mom." Hayden gave her mother a side hug and then dipped her chin to acknowledge her grandmother. "Grandma Winnie. How are you feeling?"

"Welllll, if it isn't the princess from the high tower," came Winnie's barbed reply, her voice dripping with sarcasm. "So nice of you to deign to come visit us common folk." She turned stony eyes on Tate and barked, "Who the hell are you?"

Nineteen

Here we go.

Hayden shot Tate an apologetic smile, feeling instantly guilty that she hadn't warned him. Anyone she'd dated as an adult had no reason to meet *the fam*, and the guys she dated when she was living at home weren't exactly the kinds of guys to bring home to mom.

"Mother, your heart," Patti warned Winnie.

"Don't worry about my heart," Winnie snapped. "Worry about smuggling in a cocktail. It's long past five o'clock. Keeping an old woman from one of her only pleasures in life is criminal."

What's her other pleasure in life? Bossing around my mother? Hayden wisely kept the snide thought to herself.

"Well?" Winnie speared Tate with a glare. "Introduce yourself."

"Tate Duncan," he replied coolly, hands tucked into his pants pockets. "I'm also Wesley Singleton, but that's a long, complicated story."

Hayden gaped at him before turning back to her grandmother.

"Never heard of you." Winnie's frown pulled the corners of her mouth lower.

Hayden looked up to tell Tate they could leave—no one should be subjected to her grandmother's abuse, but he chuckled good-naturedly.

"I'm not surprised," he said. "My reality show airs late at night, and I keep my celebrity appearances to a minimum."

"Smart-ass." But Winnie's mouth curled at the edge. Was it possible that Tate was winning over the world's biggest critic? It'd been a long while since Hayden's grandmother had regarded anyone with respect, so the experience was unique.

Patti, meanwhile, didn't catch the joke. "You have a reality television show?"

"Not yet," Tate's smile remained. Amazing.

Hayden gestured toward the hallway. "Can I talk to you in private, Mom?"

"What's wrong with in here?" Winnie demanded.

"Nothing's wrong, ma'am," Tate answered for them.

"Ma'am," Winnie barked, amused.

Had Hayden ever heard that sound come from her most embittered family member?

"I'll be right back, Mother," Patti told Winnie as she walked for the corridor. Winnie's call of "and bring me a cocktail on your way back!" followed her out and then the volume on the television skyrocketed.

"She's really very sweet," Hayden's mother explained to Tate once they were outside of the room.

Hayden barely banked an eye roll.

"No judgment from me," he said easily. When Hayden looked up at him she was surprised to see the sincerity on his face. He meant it. He wasn't standing in judgment of her or her family tonight.

Hand around her waist, he tucked her close, and Patti didn't miss it.

"You two seem close. Hayden and I used to be that

close." She sent a woe-is-me look at her only daughter. "I'm glad for her though."

Hayden hated that she was skeptical, but her mother had accused her of "flitting" to London instead of spending time with her family.

"Are you the one who took her to London?"

"Mom—"

"Yes. To meet my birth parents."

"Oh." Patti's ears pricked at the barest whiff of gossip. But then she faced Hayden, guns blazing. "You met his parents. And *this* is how you choose to introduce him to us?"

"That's not… We're not…" Hayden closed her eyes and pulled in another deep breath, staunching her knee-jerk reaction. She didn't owe Patti an explanation about why she did anything. "Why is she really here, Mom?"

"What's that supposed to mean?"

"It means you should look into rehab if Grandma Winnie's drinking so much she's blacking out."

"Blacking out? Who told you that?" Patti's eyes widened, flicking to Tate first as she offered a shaky smile of embarrassment. "This is hardly the place to air family grievances, Hayden. Your grandmother is ill."

"Yes, very." Hayden couldn't help agreeing. "She has been sick with this illness for as long as I can remember. You can't stop her. I can't stop her. I came as a courtesy…"

"A courtesy!" Patti let out a sharp, humorless laugh. "Well, my, my. Excuse us for interrupting your glamorous life. By all means, go and enjoy a *fabulous* night with your *celebrity* boyfriend. If you'll excuse me." She saved one last disingenuous smile for Tate before stomping back into the hospital room.

Drained and exhausted from that brief interaction, Hayden shook her head at Tate, at a loss for what to say.

He suffered no such loss.

"I don't remember if I told you…" His arm still looped

at her waist, he walked with her toward the exit. "You couldn't look more beautiful if you tried. I like you in red."

She shook her head. He was too much.

"Did you also know that your *celebrity boyfriend* knows the chef at the Brass Pony personally?"

"I did not." She was grinning, a feat in and of itself.

"It's true. Any special requests you have for your *glamorous* dinner are well within reach."

Warm browns, golds, and greens made up the décor at the Brass Pony, along with gilded frames holding mirrors and paintings of horses and landscapes. The tables were lit by low candles on crisp, white tablecloths, the silverware was gold and the glassware copious.

Upon entering, Hayden took her first full breath in hours, embarrassed more by her own behavior than her family's. What must Tate think of her? That she's completely intolerant?

"Mr. Duncan." A man in a smart blue suit, his hair dusky blond, regarded Tate with both surprise what could've been a borderline nervous smile. "I haven't seen you in a while."

"Jared." Tate's hand on her back, he ushered her forward, then offered that hand in greeting to the manager of the Pony. "Apologies for my behavior last time I was in here. You caught me on one of my worst days. This is Hayden Green, she owns the yoga studio down the street."

"A pleasure, Hayden." Jared nodded his greeting then said to Tate, "Glad to have you back. Your usual table?"

"If it's available."

"Right this way."

Hayden had been to the Brass Pony once since she moved here. The food was exquisite; the atmosphere on the stuffy side, but it had its merits. For one, it was quiet. It was also tidy. Bussers, waitstaff and hosts were dressed in black pants, long black aprons and white shirts with the restaurant's green logo on them.

Tate's "usual table" was located in a back corner, the C-shaped booth tall and private. From her spot in the center of the C, the restaurant's patrons were visible, but Hayden and Tate were shielded from prying eyes.

In short order they were served a bottle of wine, goblets of water and a special made by the chef that Tate requested.

All part of dating a billionaire, Hayden thought with a wry smile.

Fiddling with her gold fork, Hayden tried to think of a way to explain her behavior tonight. Explain that she'd endured years and years of neglect and verbal abuse from her grandmother and mother. Explain that while Hayden loved them, they were complicated to know and even more complicated to like.

Before she could arrive at any arrangement of those words, though, Tate spoke.

"My parents—the Duncans—aren't perfect, either, you know." His blue eyes sparkled in the candlelight.

"Yes, but are they manipulative?"

"They can be." He lifted his wine. "They're parents."

"I don't want you think that I'm this uncaring, selfish—"

He reached for her hand, shaking his head to stay her words. "Don't. You already know what I think about you."

Did she? He must've seen the question on her face.

"Giving. Caring. Selfless. Beautiful. Strong. Patient. Enduring. Really, *really* amazing in bed." He grinned and she pulled her hand away to shove his arm.

"Do you see where we are? Behave yourself."

"I'm tired of behaving myself. You should know that better than anyone."

"Are you a rule breaker now?" she teased.

"More like the rules I put stock into were broken for me. I'm enjoying not heeding them. And so should you."

She sipped her wine, both rich and complex, like the man who ordered it. "I'm not heeding any rules."

Not her mother's rule that Hayden should be involved in every family emergency. Not her own warning her not to get serious with a guy, or allow herself to be spoiled unnecessarily. And dining "off" the menu and letting her date treat her to a trip to another country definitely counted as her being spoiled.

No, she wasn't following any rules, which she knew damn well could lead to breaking even more of them. But as she met Tate's eyes over their appetizer of crisp calamari, she couldn't dredge up any motivation to change.

Although…maybe he'd changed her already.

Twenty

Hayden had dreamed of attending the swanky New Year's Eve party in SWC since she moved here.

As a business owner, she'd received a coveted vellum invitation to the event last year. Knee-deep in doing two million things business owners *without personal assistants* did during the week of Christmas, she hadn't been able to attend. By the time last year's party rolled around, she was full-on Cinderella minus the Fairy Godmother. She'd been overworked, exhausted, and in need of a mani, pedi, haircut *and* eyebrow wax. Readying herself for a fancy party where she'd be expected to present her best self was as far-off a fantasy as waiting for a prince to knock on her door with a glass slipper on a silk pillow.

So. She'd stayed home.

The FOMO had been epic.

This year, though, she was going. She had an invitation in hand, a gorgeous date chauffeuring her to the event, and a dress she'd picked up on the clearance rack of Basic Black Boutique in town. The dress was black and low-cut in the front, formfitting to show her curves, and sparkled no matter which way she turned thanks to a zillion small silver "diamonds" sewn into the fabric. She'd swept her hair up for the night and pulled on a silver cuff bracelet and chandelier earrings, forgoing the necklace. The plunging neckline drew enough attention without one.

Tate had offered to buy her a gown for tonight, but she'd declined. After the night of the hospital drama, he'd been everything she needed, and she didn't feel right expecting more. He'd taken her to the Brass Pony—where they ate an incredible gourmet meal that wasn't on the menu—and he didn't ask her to explain or talk about it. She'd opted to do neither. For too long her mother and grandmother had dictated her moods. Being in that hospital had cemented the reason she'd left Seattle in the first place: She wanted be her own woman—independent and self-reliant. And yes, that, too, was part of the driving force that led her to buying her own dress.

Excited, she waited in her yoga studio rather than outside, watching out the wide windows for Tate's Mercedes to show. She'd insisted on meeting him there, but he wouldn't allow it, even though the event was closer to his house than hers. It seemed no matter how much distance she tried to put between them he closed the gap.

She fingered the lacy material of her shoulder wrap as she paced along the scuffed studio floor. She'd shown up for him in London, and he'd shown up for her at the hospital. Originally she'd believed it was tit for tat, a simple exchange of favors. But that wasn't all this was, was it?

She'd erected that independence wall, building it as tall as she could. Ever since she'd said yes to Tate, he'd been chipping away at it and now that wall was crumbling. Through the holes she was seeing a future she'd never imagined.

Tate was in that future.

Not temporarily, not as means to goods and services, or favors. He was there, bold and exciting, for one simple reason.

She'd fallen for him.

Like Buttercup for Westley in *The Princess Bride*, Hayden had tumbled ass over teakettle down the hill, with her heart bouncing ahead of her.

Not her brightest move to date, but what was she supposed to do about it? Tate was giving, and kind, and great in bed and hot—*don't forget hot*. Puttying in the holes in that crumbling wall of hers was no longer an option. What used to be her protection was now starting to resemble a prison. She didn't *want* to hide behind a wall any longer.

Her ride pulled to the curb, and she drew her wrap over her shoulders and stepped outside. Gripping her clutch, she shuddered as sharp, icy wind cut through the thin garment. Nevertheless, she'd worn a sleeveless dress and had slipped her feet into sparkly peep-toe black heels to show off her new pedicure. No detail went unnoticed when she readied herself for tonight.

It wasn't every day she told the man of her dreams she'd fallen for him.

Stupid? Maybe. She had no idea how he'd react. But she couldn't think of a better time than midnight on New Year's Eve to tell him. That would blow up her wall completely.

Tate stepped out of the car in a black tuxedo and bow tie that weakened her knees. How...*how* could this man look good in literally any style of clothing?

He stopped short of opening her door for her, his eyes roaming over her dress, his mouth slightly open like he was going to say something but forgot what it was.

"I guess you can 'buy your own damn dress,'" he joked, throwing her words back to her. She hadn't been angry when she said it, just exasperated. She wouldn't allow him to cater to her *constantly*.

"I couldn't figure out how else to make you stop offering." She grinned.

"Fair enough." He opened her door and she walked to

him, tall enough in her heels to place a cold kiss on his warm mouth. He swatted her ass, reminding her that as gentlemanly as he was, he couldn't be defined him by only that word.

He was much more layered, and meant more to her than she'd previously imagined. All because she'd met him outside in the rain and offered him a cup of tea.

The Common, a rentable space for parties and where SWC held most of their meetings and sponsored parties, was a sea of Edison lights dangling from the ceiling.

Hayden couldn't suppress a gasp when she stepped through the double doors and was met with those glowing bulbs hanging from black wires and tied with a lush black bow at the base.

"Tate." She clutched the arm of his tuxedo, admiring the many guests in their finery. The black tie affair was dripping with luxury, from the gold and black and white decorations to the five-piece jazz band playing softly onstage.

The fairy tale, it seemed, was real.

"I like that smile." He brushed her lips with his. "Don't want to ruin your lipstick."

"Ruin away. I have more."

As they walked through the room, the guests parted like the Red Sea for Moses. All eyes were on Tate. In this community, he really was a celebrity.

He shook a few hands and introduced her to a few new people, though she spotted a lot of people she knew, too. She might not be as iconic as the *great and powerful Tate Duncan*, but seeing so many familiar faces reminded her that she'd built a life here as well.

She released Tate's arm to accept the glass of champagne, and he raised his own.

"To your first NYE at SWC." They *cheersed* and sipped,

and wow, even the champagne was expensive. Tate wouldn't have had it any other way.

"This is incredible. I feel like Cinderella."

"Good." Arm locked around her waist, he leaned in to kiss her, pausing a breath from her lips to mutter a very unromantic *"Son of a bitch."*

"Duncan." The gruff voice belonged to guy nearly seven feet tall, with arms the size of 55-gallon drums. His hair was buzzed close to his head, his mustache thick and walrus-like. He turned stony eyes to Hayden for a brief moment before glaring at Tate.

"Hayden Green," Tate said after a long, and awkward, pause. "Casey Huxley. I've mentioned him before. The contractor partnering with me to build a group of houses on the eastern side of the island."

"Oh. *Oh.*" The top-secret project that wasn't really secret, she remembered. Also, she'd learned at their dinner at the Brass Pony, the same contractor who Tate had argued with over taking down quite a few trees in SWC.

She hadn't wanted to talk about her drama, but she'd needled Tate about his. He'd shared, and she let him, until it was obvious from his copious swearing she shouldn't have pried.

She had hoped Tate and Casey would work out their differences. Since they stood positioned like they were about to have Wild West style shoot-out, it was safe to assume that hadn't happened yet.

Casey took a champagne flute, delicate in his wide, meaty palm, and with a final eye slice to Tate, stalked off in the opposite direction.

"That was intense," she told Tate after Casey was out of earshot. "The way you made it sound, you two nearly went to fisticuffs the other day."

"Nearly," he grated, then, "Don't look so concerned. I can take him."

"I wasn't thinking that." She palmed the front of his tux and smoothed her hands over his built chest. He wasn't a slouch by anyone's definition. "I was hoping you two would have worked things out."

"He cares about control, I care about my island. We're nowhere near being on the same page."

"Tate!" A cheery man with dark olive skin, dark hair approached.

"Terry Guerrero." Tate pumped the other man's hand and then introduced Hayden.

"Nice to meet you." Terry's accent hinted at Spanish descent. He was so friendly it was almost jarring after the tense run-in with Casey.

"I promised Terry I'd talk to him about the development tonight, but that was before I made plans with you." Tate narrowed his eyes jovially at Terry. "I'm guessing you're holding me to it."

"Much as I hate to sully your evening with business, I'm going to on vacation tomorrow for two weeks. I'm not working from the Bahamas—Ana would kill me."

"Good man," Tate said.

"I'll have to introduce you to my wife," Terry told Hayden, "when she's finished chatting up the interior designer—the woman who designed this party. What is her name? No doubt Ana wants to hit her up to do our daughter's engagement party."

"Lois Sherwood," Tate answered. "And congratulations."

Hayden knew Lois. The chatty gray-haired woman was waving her arms in the air, excitement reigning supreme as she spoke with Terry's wife. She was an energetic, busy little thing. And flexible. Lois attended yoga classes three times a week.

Tate and Terry spoke for another minute before Terry excused himself. "I'll be at the bar. Hayden, a pleasure."

Once he was gone, Tate let out a sigh.

"Go. I should probably be hobnobbing with business folk, too. This event is meant to bring business owners together after all, right?" She smiled, quoting the wording on the invitation.

"I guess." His mouth quirked playfully before he leaned in to kiss her. He didn't make it this time, either. Sherry interrupted next.

"Look at you two! You two are the cutest ever!" Sherry shuffled in place like she couldn't contain her joy, but lowered her voice conspiratorially when she spoke again. "I knew it! I knew it! Even in that class we took together, I *knew* Tate had a thing for you."

Hayden stole a glance up at Tate to find him wearing a patient smile.

"Your timing is perfect," Hayden told the other woman. "Tate was about to talk business at the bar and leave me standing here alone. Should we grab you a refill?"

Sherry glanced down at her empty glass. "Oh, goodness. Must be a hole in my glass. I'll grab another and meet you right back here." She pointed at Tate and then Hayden before moving to the nearest waiter to pluck a flute from a tray.

"I see her caffeine addiction hasn't gone anywhere," he muttered.

"*You're welcome* for letting you off the hook."

"I'll be brief," he promised.

"You'd better." Hayden gripped his lapels and kissed him solidly before someone else came along to interrupt.

After he met with Terry to discuss the new SWC neighborhood, Tate spotted Hayden in a conversation with a cluster of women. He decided to hang back and give her time to work her magic. By the delighted smile on her face he could tell she was enjoying her first SWC New Year's gala.

He watched her a beat longer, wondering if he'd have no-

ticed her if she'd come to last year's soiree. Yes. He would
have. Even if she hadn't worn the sparkling black dress—
an absolute showstopper. Her lethal curves and dark hair,
full mouth and elegant way she handled herself in a pair of
tall shoes would have been impossible to overlook.

She *glowed* with life.

Then again, he'd had a girlfriend last year at this time,
so noticing Hayden would have been moot. He couldn't
have acted on any passing attraction no matter how tempting she would've been.

He polished off his drink and relinquished the empty
glass to the bar. Shoving his hands in his pockets, he
strolled along the back of the room only to freeze in place
a moment later when he spotted a familiar golden-haired,
slim woman on the arm of Casey Huxley.

What the hell? Had he summoned her with his mind?
And what was she doing attached to Casey, of all people?
Especially now that the bigger man had cemented himself
into the role of Tate's nemesis.

How had Claire and Casey ended up in the same *room*
together let alone found anything in common once they
were there?

It was definitely his ex-fiancée, though. There was no
mistaking her slightly upturned nose and the rigid way she
held her shoulders. As if she felt eyes on her, she turned to
face Tate fully, giving him a demure finger wave before
standing on tiptoes to whisper into Casey's ear.

Casey murmured something to her, his coal black eyes
on Tate. And then they parted, Claire heading unmistak-
ably in Tate's direction.

Son of a bitch.

Twenty-One

Tate, with no other choice than to acknowledge Claire, crossed the distance to meet her halfway. Casey continued staring, but he wasn't Tate's problem tonight, or ever after Tate ended this deal.

"Hi, Tate." Claire stood before him, poised, wearing a no-nonsense black dress. No glitter, no shine, no light. Nothing like Hayden. The only sparkles on Claire were coming from the ring on her—

What the hell?

"Is that…" He hadn't meant to react, but there was no ignoring the giant diamond ring…on her left hand. She'd returned his engagement ring and, then what, run out to get engaged? *To Casey?*

She glanced down at her finger, almost like she'd forgotten the ring was there. "Oh, yes. I'm engaged."

"To Casey Huxley?"

"What? No. God, no. We're business partners, Casey and I. He invited me as his plus-one to introduce me around. *We're* not engaged. I'm engaged to…someone else."

That was a lot to ingest. Tate didn't know what to ask about first. He'd offered to introduce Claire around plenty when they'd dated, but she never would come with him anywhere. He'd start there.

"You hate Spright Island."

"As a residence, yes. As a business opportunity, no."

"Since when are you interested in land development?"

"Guess you rubbed off on me." She tipped her head. "It's my new side gig."

Tate's livelihood—no, *life's purpose*—was Claire's *side gig*? He was certain anger was turning his face a deep shade of pink.

"Are you getting back at me for something?" It was the only explanation that made sense. That or he was having his own private *Twilight Zone* moment.

"Always about you, isn't it Tate?" She rolled her eyes. "You're not the only one who knows what people want."

He had to let out a dry laugh at that. "And you do?"

"Casey and I do. People want wide open spaces. Room for lawns and yards. Fences."

"Suburbia." Tate's lip curled.

"People want lawns to mow, Tate."

The neighborhoods at SWC were designed to look as if they were tucked into the trees. There were no "lawns." Each plot fostered native vegetation—low growing plants interspersed with rocks and mulch. "I'd never compromise SWC's unique design. You know that. After our last meeting, Casey sure as hell knows that."

"People don't want to be buried in the woods."

"What the hell would you know about mowing a lawn or the woods? Aren't you a self-proclaimed city girl?"

"I like my space."

"No kidding." She'd taken plenty of it when it came to him. "You made it clear you didn't want to be married," he said through clenched teeth. Hayden hadn't noticed him missing yet. Maybe he could get her out of here before she laid eyes on Claire. He didn't want Hayden's evening to be ruined, too.

"Your family…confusion wasn't what I signed up for." Tate opened his mouth to say it wasn't what he'd signed up for, either, but before he could, Claire added, "I saw you with her earlier. Your date. She's—"

"Amazing," he interrupted, unwilling to let his ex-fiancée fill in the adjective. "*Amazing* is the word you're looking for, and even if it isn't, you can spare me your opinion."

His voice was hollow.

Like his chest.

Running into Claire had stolen the oxygen from his lungs and robbed him of reason. Probably there were some unexamined emotions revolving around their breakup he hadn't dealt with, but when would he have had the time?

Between winter holidays, and recovering from being in a couple, to trying to reacquaint himself with his brother and then Hayden… There hadn't been time to process much of anything. His head felt like a knotted ball of Christmas lights.

"Did you meet *him*—" Tate gestured to her engagement ring "—before or after ending it with me?"

Her mouth opened, then closed, but she didn't answer. At least she had the decency not to lie to him.

"Jesus, Claire."

"Don't judge me."

He took a deep breath and willed himself to stay calm. The last thing he needed was to make a scene and have this unfortunate run-in with his ex go down in the annals of Spright Wellness Community history.

"When you know you know." She offered a shrug.

More platitudes.

"Listen, I don't want to fight." She held up a hand, calling a stop to the conversation he should've called quits to first. "I came over to say hello, and I wanted to come clean about my involvement in the new project. Personally, and before someone else told you."

"How magnanimous of you."

Her expression was sharp, unfriendly. "I'll keep my distance for the rest of the party. Casey's not interested in talking business tonight, anyway."

"What business? Casey's fired. Especially if you're involved in the design." So much for being the better person, but he couldn't help himself. He'd been ready to throw Casey off his island after that last meeting, but learning of Claire's involvement had sealed the other man's fate.

"Don't make threats. He won't refund your *very* large deposit, some of which was my seed money."

"Keep it," he grated, hating that he'd unknowingly accepted money from Claire. Hating that he'd thought Casey might eventually come around to Tate's way of thinking.

With a shake of her blond head, she started back to the party.

"Who's the lucky guy?" he called after her.

"You don't know him." She blew him a kiss on her way out.

Thank God for small favors.

A blur of black caught Hayden's attention as she was resting her empty glass on a nearby tray. Tate's shoulders were beneath his ears, his fists balled at his sides.

He looked furious. Until she caught his eye and then he smiled, though it was a touch disingenuous.

"There you are." A few beads of sweat had broken out on his forehead.

"What happened to you?" She turned her head in the direction he'd come from but he pulled her close, one hand pressing her lower back, his other hand cradling her jaw. He gave her a lengthy kiss and she wobbled from the force of it, practically melting into him. Tate was an exceptional kisser.

"Wow, thank you," she said when he pulled away. He brushed her cheek with his thumb. "Was it that Neanderthal, Casey?"

He gave her a jerky nod.

"What did he do?" She searched the party, having half a mind to walk over to the idiot and give him a piece of her mind.

"He left." Tate turned Hayden's chin to face him. "Can we get out of here?"

She understood he was angry and processing an obviously loaded conversation, but... "Before midnight? I wanted to stay for the countdown."

She'd planned for a kiss at midnight under the chandelier in her beautiful dress. She'd planned on telling him she loved him.

"It's a lot to ask, I know." His frown faded, his lips softening some. "I have something better to do tonight."

Anticipation like warm honey trickled down her spine.

"You." He nuzzled her nose, charm dialed to eleven. "Ever since I saw you wearing that dress, I've been preoccupied with the idea of taking you out of it." His voice was a low murmur of appreciation, the flattery gaining him a lot of ground. She'd never been able to resist him when he couldn't resist her.

"Champagne at midnight here is special, but I have champagne at my house." He leaned close, his warm breath tickling her ear, his voice wickedly sexy. "When the clock strikes midnight, I'll drench you in champagne and kiss you everywhere the bubbles touch. Come home with me, Hayden, you won't regret it."

"That...is a compelling argument, Mr. Duncan," she practically purred. Tate offering private kisses at the stroke of midnight was more tempting than champagne toasts on New Year's, but she'd dreamed of counting down, kissing him, and offering up an *I love you.* "Can't we go home after? Midnight is a little over an hour away and—"

Blue eyes drilled into her. "It would mean *the world* to me if you and I could ring in the New Year alone."

Tonight she had very special plans for announcing how she felt about Tate, and by the look in his eyes, he had a similar announcement in mind. That was worth skipping the toast at the party. That was worth skipping a lifetime of toasts.

"Okay."

"Yeah?" He looked relieved as he cast another quick, maybe even nervous glance around.

"Yes. I'd love to go home with you."

His grin was heady and gorgeous, the attractive smile lines around his mouth and at the corners of his eyes in full force. She loved seeing him happy. She loved making him happy. Who cared about a silly toast when they had memories to make?

"Shall we?" He offered his arm, his relaxed features showing no signs of the turmoil she thought she'd seen earlier. Business rarely mixed with pleasure, but she was glad he hadn't allowed it to put a damper on the evening ahead of them. Not when he had so many delicious things in store for her.

"We shall," she said and then threaded her arm into his.

Twenty-Two

Flames in the gas fireplace bloomed to life and Tate tossed the remote onto the coffee table. Exactly how quickly he could turn her on, Hayden thought, eyeing her handsome date.

She admired the broad set of his shoulders in the tuxedo jacket, his perfectly even bow tie. His hair, playfully falling over his forehead, and his enviably thick eyelashes shielding those gemstone eyes from view.

She still wore her dress and shoes, the wrap covering her bare shoulders, but she'd discarded her purse on the kitchen counter.

A golden glow came from a floor lamp, the only other illumination in the room from the flickering fire. The woods beyond the living room windows were dark and quiet, no wildlife peeking through the trees tonight.

"You're right. Your house is a much better venue for a New Year's Eve party."

Tate approached her with the slow, intentional steps of a predator hunting its prey. "Sorry, I'm only available for private parties."

He lifted one of her hands and with his palm cupped

her hip, moving close to rest his cheek on hers. Then he began to sway.

"Are you dancing with me? To no music at all?" she asked, moving with him.

He continued the steps and smoothly spun with her in a slow circle before bringing her flush with his chest. "How's my driving?"

"You're doing great," she whispered into his ear, pleased when a shake ran down his arms. It was nice to know she affected him the same way he affected her—to the *marrow*.

"I owe you for leaving. It wasn't fair of me to ask."

She stopped their silent dance and pulled her cheek from his. "I had to talk to a few people I don't particularly like. I can imagine it'd be upsetting to deal with someone you loathe."

His eyebrows jumped. "You have no idea."

"As long as you reserved plenty of energy for me—" she smoothed the crease above the bridge of his nose "—then I'll overlook you whisking me out of there."

A hint of challenge tightened his jaw. "Are you questioning if I'd keep my word about the champagne kisses and fireside romance?"

"Of course not." She feigned innocence. "I'm simply reminding you that you made promises and that there's no room for waning energy."

He tilted his hips, a hardening part of his anatomy nestling gently into her belly. "Does that feel *waning* to you, Ms. Green?"

She rested her top teeth on her bottom lip, going for her most demure and sex kitten–ish expression.

Then she decided, *screw* demure.

She stroked his erection over his tuxedo pants. He grunted, and she rubbed him again. "Feels positively *mouthwatering* to me," she said against his lips. "But there's only one way to truly test that theory."

He crushed his mouth into hers, pulling away after she was breathless.

"Then test it," he commanded.

Fisting her wrap, he yanked it from her shoulders, sending chills along her back as the lacy material tickled its way down her arms. His grin was slow and sensual and enough to make her drop to her knees right then and there. He stopped her from sinking to the floor, though, his hands cupping her elbows. "Hang on."

On the other side of the room he opened a trunk, pulling from it a rug of faux deer pelts. He spread the blanket in front of the fireplace—large enough that if it *had been* a real deer, it'd have been the size of an elephant—and then threw a few pillows on top of their makeshift bed.

"I don't want you to be cold or uncomfortable." He returned to her embrace.

"Such a gentleman," she cooed.

"Not always."

"Do show me, Mr. Duncan, how ungentlemanly you can be." She loved the take-charge part of him whenever it came out, and tonight she wanted to play.

He reached into her hair and felt for the pins holding it back, and one by one tossed them to the floor. One, two, three… Her hair spilled from its updo, and then he swept it off her face and gathered it into a ponytail at the back of her head. Tightening his hold, he pulled her head back and lowered his lips to her neck. Teasing and suckling, he worked his way from her throat to her jaw to the sensitive skin behind her ear. "On your knees, gorgeous."

But when he backed away, there was a tickle of a smile on his lips and a question in his eyes, asking if she was okay with this. And since she was very much okay with him being in charge of her—heart and body—she replied, "Yes, sir," and then did as she was told.

Against Tate's chest, Hayden let out a satisfied hum, her breath coasting over his body as she snuggled against him.

After she'd blown his mind and he'd in return happily blown hers, he discarded the condom in the nearest bathroom and grabbed a shearling throw off the couch to cover them. They'd been lying here ever since, the fire warming them—as if they'd needed any help after the amazing sex they'd had.

"Ten point oh" were the first words out of her mouth.

"What's that?"

"The score on your stellar performance." She grinned up at him with sheer sexual satisfaction.

He put an arm behind his head, proud. "You were keeping score?"

"Not really, but I can't deny you any less than perfect, considering it's all I've thought about since we stopped."

He loved satisfying her. Loved more that she was open and forthright about complimenting him.

After the night he'd had, the unpleasant run-ins with both Casey—*the prick*—and Claire, Tate hadn't wanted to ruin Hayden's night, too. Bringing her back to his place was the best decision he could've made.

"What about me?" she asked, raising her eyebrows. "What's my score?"

He pretended to think about it, turning his eyes up to the ceiling. "Eleven million." Her husky laughter drifted over him and he added, "Point eleven."

Her eyes were soft, dreamy.

"Happy new year, Hayden." He was about to apologize for missing the countdown...and forgetting his own promise of champagne, but what she said next stole the remaining oxygen from his lungs.

"I love you, Tate."

He blinked, stunned to his core.

Love.

She loved him. That took living dangerously to an entirely new level.

"I've been in love with you since London. I think." Her nose scrunched in a cute look of consideration. "Probably sooner."

The throw, Hayden's body heat and the fire were suddenly making him overly warm. He threw the blanket off himself, but she only snuggled closer.

"It's hard to know how to tell you've *completely* fallen for someone," she said conversationally as sweat pricked Tate's armpits. "I wasn't planning on falling for you. But I did. So, here we are."

Here we are.

Her tone was playful and light and questioning at the same time. For good reason. When someone told you they loved you, the expected response was to say it back. That was the deal.

That's how it'd been with his and Claire's relationship. Hell, he didn't even remember who'd said it first, only that one of them had and the other had followed suit. Tate had been the one to propose. At a fancy restaurant while wearing a suit, with a ring in a velvet box. He'd done everything by the letter, exactly the way tradition insisted he should, and she'd walked away anyway. Walked away and become someone else's fiancée, before finding an interest in the very part of his life she'd been ambivalent about the entire time she and Tate were together.

In life he'd assumed the next step would naturally appear above the last. That he'd climb one and then ascend to the next. One step up after the last was how he'd built this community on Spright Island, how he'd handled his business dealings. How he'd acted every day of his life…up until the day he bumped into Reid Singleton at that coffee shop.

Life had no rulebook.

What he'd thought was firm footing leading to the next step up had instead been a chute spiraling him down into the darkness, where he'd felt as lost as if he'd worn a permanent blindfold.

Discovering his twin brother.

Finding out he was kidnapped.

Learning about his biological parents in London.

Realizing that his adoptive parents had been wary of the agency from which he was adopted…

Then there was Hayden.

Beautiful, strong, trusting, giving Hayden.

She'd been his confidante and true friend, the woman of his sexual fantasies come true.

And now she loves me.

In what might be the worst timing in the world, Hayden Green had fallen for him, and he had nothing to offer her except metaphors for what he thought life was…and wasn't.

Given enough space he could easily fall in love with Hayden. Hell, if he did a deep-dive into his emotions, he might find he already had. But in no way was he ready for a next step—not with anyone. Claire had reminded him of that tonight.

Hayden deserved a man who knew he loved her without pause or breaking into a cold-hot sweat. After meeting the family who'd put her second her entire life, Tate knew Hayden deserved a man who could put her first.

He wasn't that man.

Not with a hundred other things fighting for first place. His community. Two sets of parents and extended family. His own sense of identity.

Tate had a loose idea about where he was headed and a

truckload of physical affection to shower upon her. But an engagement ring and a future?

He swiped the sweat now beading on his brow. He wasn't ready. Not yet.

At the start of this evening, he'd been sure how tonight would go. He'd planned on kissing Hayden at midnight, drinking champagne as gold and silver confetti fluttered to the floor, and then bringing her back here and having sex in front of the fireplace. But only half that plan had come to fruition. He hadn't prepared for bumping into Casey or Claire, or learning that the two of them were business partners.

He'd been building a mountain out of surprise molehills lately, so it shouldn't come as a shock that Hayden had blindsided him with a proclamation of love.

His heart sank.

This was his fault. He'd leaned on her and let her take on his emotional baggage—he'd lavished her with physical love and flew her first-class. Tonight was a Cinderella story right down to the clock striking midnight.

He moved her gently from his chest, ignoring her when she asked where he was going. He reached for his pants and checked his phone. 12:15 a.m. Close enough.

He turned to face Hayden. Beautiful Hayden, with her mussed hair, holding the blanket over her naked body. She was ethereal and perfect and the most sensually attractive woman he'd ever spent time with.

And Tate?

He was the asshole about to break her heart.

Twenty-Three

It didn't take long for Hayden realize that the "I love you" she'd thrown out after Tate's innocent "Happy new year" hadn't gone over well. She didn't know what she expected, but she knew what she'd hoped for.

She'd hoped for one of his easy smiles. She'd hoped he'd thread his fingers into her hair and look deeply into her eyes. She'd hoped for those coveted words—"I love you, too."

She wouldn't have minded if his "I love you" had also included a lengthy explanation of how gobsmacked he was by her announcement.

But this…he looked like he'd witnessed an accident. Panic had surfaced on his features, and he'd become instantly fidgety.

So, yeah, it hadn't gone over well.

"Oh-kay, so that was awkward," she said with an uneasy laugh. "What I *meant* to say was 'Happy new year to you, too!'"

Her heart beat out a clumsy, erratic rhythm. She hadn't fallen in love with someone in a really, really freaking long time. And this time felt more real, more grounded. She knew who she was and what she wanted. She knew who she loved.

"Claire was at the party tonight." He stood and stuffed his legs into his tuxedo pants.

"Pardon?" Surely she hadn't heard that correctly.

"Claire Waterson. My ex-fiancée."

"I know who Claire is." What she hadn't wrapped her head around yet was that Claire was…at the party?

"She's engaged. And for some reason in a business partnership with Casey." Tate's teeth were all but gnashing.

If Hayden understood what he was saying, his evening had gone south not because of a run-in with Casey, but a visit from Claire…who was *engaged*.

"You didn't tell me she was there," Hayden said.

Hands on his hips, Tate looked down at where she sat on the blanket. "I didn't want to ruin your evening."

"But we left," she reminded him. "*She's* why we didn't stay?"

"It doesn't matter why we left."

But oh, it so did. She'd said I love you and instead of "I love you, too," Tate had told her that his ex-fiancée was engaged to someone else. As if that was the takeaway for the evening. The highlight of tonight!

"We had a special night planned," he explained. "I knew if you saw her it would derail those plans."

Wow.

So Claire had been at the party, had walked over to tell him she was engaged and instead of Tate coming to Hayden and telling her his screwy ex-fiancée was in the building and had apparently moved way, *way* on, he hadn't told Hayden anything. He let her believe that he'd been rankled by that Casey guy, then Tate had swept her up with his handsome smile and wooed her with promises of champagne and making love…

He'd lied by omission. And Hayden was the most honest she'd ever been.

"Let me get this straight…" Hayden heard the shake in

her voice. "You thought if I saw Claire tonight, that your chances of getting laid would go way down."

"What? No."

Hayden didn't wait for another of his explanations. She riffled through her discarded clothes and clumsily pulled on her bra and panties.

"Hayden, wait. Don't get dressed."

"I'm not arguing with you naked." She jerked on her sparkly dress, angry that she had nothing else to wear. This was hardly a time for celebrating.

"We're not arguing." When he noticed she was fumbling with her zipper, he offered to help, but she swung away from him.

She raced into the kitchen for her purse, but only when she lifted her coat off the chair did she realize she was stranded. She didn't drive herself tonight.

"Can we talk about this, please?" He snatched his shirt off the couch and pulled it over his shoulders, leaving it open in the front. She admired him, dammit, even while angry with him. He was handsome with his hair a disaster and his shirt open, revealing flat washboard abs, the legs of his pants falling to bare feet that were as attractive as the rest of him.

"There's nothing to talk about. You're still clearly in love with Claire if the news of her engagement hit you so hard you had to leave the party. I'm the moron who thought your heart would be as available as the rest of your body parts!"

"That's not true!" Tate actually shouted, the sound bouncing off the high ceilings and ringing off the light fixture over the dining room table where they stood on opposite sides in a faceoff. "Can we please talk about this?"

"There's nothing to say. I shouldn't have told you...what I told you." She couldn't say those three words to him—even in reference. She should've known better. "I'd been planning on telling you this evening and I thought—"

"You'd been planning this?" But he didn't sound flattered or even appreciative. He sounded *distraught*. "For how long?"

"It doesn't matter. It's clear you don't feel the same way about me." Try as she might, she wasn't able to keep her chin from trembling. This was a nightmare. A waking, living, breathing nightmare. She was in love with him, and not only didn't he know how to tell her he didn't feel the same way, but he'd sort of lied to her tonight, too.

"It's not that. I could… Given enough time. I think." His eyebrows arched sympathetically. Meanwhile, she'd be over here dying of humiliation.

Never had she been this hurt. This disappointed. Not even when her parents had skipped her high school graduation to rescue her grandmother from yet another midday bender.

"The timing is off," Tate said. "That's all this is."

"Oh, is that *all*?" She bit down hard and willed the tears currently tingling behind her eyes not to come. "Tell me, Tate, when is the perfect time for your girlfriend to tell you she loves you? For that matter, when's the perfect time for you to find out you have a secret brother? Or an entire family, for that matter!"

Anger brought forth the tears she'd been swallowing down. Angry at herself for so many reasons, she swept them away with her fingers.

"We can still—"

"Sleep together?" she interrupted before letting out a humorless laugh. "I bet you'd love that. Oh, sorry. I bet you'd *enjoy* that. Let's not use the L-word."

He stalked toward her, his face reddening with anger of his own. A muscle in his jaw ticked, and she felt that win all the way down to her toes. She'd rather him be mad at her than frozen with panic like he'd been earlier.

"I'm not saying the timing has to be perfect," he said. "I just need things to slow down for one goddamn second!"

He pulled his hands over his face like he was startled that he'd yelled, and then calmer, tried again. "I tried to live dangerously. I tried my life being in complete disarray. It didn't work."

Disarray? Danger? Was he referring to their relationship, or was he blaming Hayden for bringing disorder to his life? Was he longing for Claire? The perfect Stepford wife?

"I've worked hard my entire life to keep things steady," he said. "To achieve incrementally and move my life toward the finish line. The...*situation* with my family has made me question everything I thought I knew about myself. Learning that Claire was engaged threw me, but not because I want her for myself. She was another in a line of failures I couldn't prevent."

Hayden blinked, finally understanding. "And you don't want to be responsible for failing where I'm concerned. So you're not taking the chance? You tried to live dangerously, to give yourself over to the experience that was me, and now I'm not worth the risk."

"You don't understand."

"I understand perfectly. You're too scared to take the chance to love me. I thought you were lost. I didn't know you were a coward."

It was like his blue eyes went up in flames. His complexion darkened, his voice the low warning of a lion.

"I can't meditate and make my problems go away! I *am* Spright Wellness Community." He jabbed his breastbone with one finger. "I'm responsible for an entire community of people. I have to focus. I have to implement actual decisions and strategies that affect others. Even when my life was falling down around me, I kept this place going. Everything I do is in service to the legacy I built. This place will house generations to come. Throughout every bit of adversity I've faced, SWC has thrived. Casey Huxley was a warning that my island could be on shaky ground. I have to be responsible, Hayden. I have to live up to the unbelievable pressures of being the perfect environmental oasis for the families who live here. I'm not a coward. I'm a goddamn saint."

"A saint who is putting work before me!" Hayden shouted, her exposed heart burning with the realization. Another person she loved putting her in second place.

"Yes, exactly!" Tate threw his arms wide before ramming his hands into his hair. "I *can't* put you first! You deserve it and I can't do it."

"It's not like you're housing the homeless, Tate. This is a luxury community. You dwell in a mansion on top of a hill! And who cares what others expect from you? Your 'community' doesn't need you to survive. It can go on without you, you know. You're the asshole with a god complex."

His upper lip curled, the silence stretching between them like a band about to snap. Had she pushed him too far?

"Tell me, Hayden, all the ways you've sacrificed your own needs to take care of the people who need you."

Her ears rang like an explosion had gone off next to her. The words were like a sharp, stinging slap to the cheek. More tears fell, but she didn't feel them. She only knew they were there when they splashed onto her folded arms.

Realization dawned on his face so fast it was dizzying.

"I'm sorry." He stepped closer, and she skirted him and collected her shoes. "I didn't mean—"

"Take me home. *Now*." She slipped on her shoes and pulled her wrap over her shoulders protectively. If only it were an invisible cape.

"Hayden, give me a chance to…" He followed her to the front door. "That was… I'm angry, okay? I spoke without thinking."

"Now, please." She wouldn't allow Tate to make her

feel guilty over a situation he'd never understand. She'd worked hard to untangle herself from her family's codependent strings.

Besides, she was beginning to believe that she and Tate weren't good together. This argument had proven that they had a knack for exposing the other's soft underbelly.

She'd been open and honest with him. Now he was using that honesty against her, which made her feel as if she were slowly suffocating.

"Hayden—"

"I have some meditating to do, and I'd prefer to be at home when I do it." Their gazes locked, and she tried not to see the human part of him. Tried to hate him for being cruel and elusive. But she couldn't. She loved him too damn much.

She couldn't stay and continue loving him, not when he didn't love her. With sex in the mix, it would border masochism.

And she refused to linger and hope that one day the timing would be right. That he'd return her feelings when life settled down. Life didn't settle down. Life *was* change—it was a series of bumps and hills, not flat, even plains.

With a tight nod of acquiescence, Tate finished dressing and put on his coat. He shut off the fireplace and scraped his keys from the kitchen counter, walking past Hayden without a second look.

"I'll warm up the car. Come out when you're ready," he said over his shoulder.

Once the door was shut, she looked out the wide picture window into the dark woods beyond.

Like the cold, still landscape, she was empty and alone. As if she'd traded places with that earlier version of Tate who'd stood outside her studio lost, and soaking in the rain.

Twenty-Four

At her front door, her hand resting on the knob, Hayden read the black-and-silver frosting on the sheet cake. "'Happy retirement, Roger'?"

"A mistake," Arlene said, her normally huge blond waves pulled neatly into a ponytail at the back of her head. "Rodger's name is actually spelled with a *D*, or so the lady at Blossom Bakery told me. This was the only cake available on such short notice."

"Why are you bringing me cake?" Hayden stepped aside and Arlene bustled in, a tote and her purse slung over her shoulder.

She'd called Arlene the morning after the New Year's Eve debacle at Tate's house, and Arlene had promised to be right over with "reinforcements."

"I assumed you'd show up with Emily and a few tubs of ice cream." Hayden shut her front door.

"Emily is with *Josh*," Arlene paused for a meaningful eyebrow waggle. "And ice cream is cliché." She pulled a bottle of sparkling wine out of the tote. "I also have hummus, pretzel chips, brie, salmon and lots of those really fattening buttery crackers we love but know are bad for us."

Hayden offered a wan, though grateful, smile. "Don't ruin your resolutions on my account."

"Pfft. Please. It's not too early to crack this open, right?" Arlene asked rhetorically as she tore the foil from the neck of the wine.

"Three o'clock is well within the day-drinking window."

"I'm so sorry I wasn't closer, or I'd have been here sooner." Arlene had been in Seattle when Hayden called her and had promised to come ASAP.

"It's fine. What were you doing, anyway?"

"I was doing a *very* fine younger bodybuilder type named Mike."

Hayden's eyebrows rose.

"I snapped a pic in the shower when he wasn't looking. Want to see?" But her friend's smile fell when Hayden's eyes filled with tears. Arlene quickly put down the bottle and ran to hug her. "I'm sorry. Sorry, sorry," she soothed as she rubbed Hayden's back. "It's too soon for me to be bragging about my hot hookup. And forget about Emily and Josh."

Hayden let out a watery laugh. "It's not too soon. I want you both to be happy."

Arlene leveled her with a look. "I wore my yoga gear so you could torture me in the studio. Whatever makes you feel better."

That did make Hayden laugh. "Yoga's about being kind to yourself, not about torture."

"Whatever you say. Cake first, though. I insist."

Half a sheet cake later, Hayden and Arlene sagged on the sofa, their champagne glasses in hand.

"After that much sugar, you'd think I'd have more energy." Hayden stabbed her plastic fork into the remaining cake. They hadn't bothered with plates. Arlene found two plastic forks left over from takeout and brought them to the couch with the wine and the cake.

It'd been therapeutic to eat her way through half of Rodger's retirement cake, but Hayden still felt the hum of loss in her bones. Arlene knew, though, and like any good best friend did, offered practical advice.

"In Tate's defense, I can imagine his life feels like it's been shaken vigorously and then tumbled out like Yahtzee dice. Can you imagine the combination of joy and disappointment and terror and… I don't know, weirdly, probably peace, he must feel at knowing he has a brother and an entirely new family?"

"His whole life changed. In a blink." Like hers. She hadn't expected to ring in the new year with a breakup *or* a relationship. A few months ago she assumed she'd be working round the clock to accommodate January visitors who'd made resolutions to get fit for the new year.

"Regardless—" Arlene pulled her chin down and gave Hayden a stern stare "—you can't keep your love on ice and wait for Tate to come around. If he has stuff to work through, that's on him. Nobody puts Baby in a corner." She smiled at the *Dirty Dancing* reference, but Hayden couldn't smile just yet. She'd already used up her one for the day.

"I made a commitment before I moved here that I wasn't going to accept half measures in any relationship—from my family, friends or whoever I happened to date."

"I commend you on that." Arlene raised her glass.

"I also committed to listening to my gut. Which is why I called the woman I leased this building from right after I called you."

"*Why* did you do that?" Arlene winced. "Don't say you're leaving me!"

"I'm not going far. I don't think. I might get a job at a gym rather than have the overhead of a new studio right away. I need to not be *here*. Where I'll run into Tate or read about him in the *Spright Times*," she said of the local printed newsletter that was in the café every month.

"But this is your refuge!" Arlene argued, throwing Hayden's words back at her. "I know you're upset, but are you sure you want to give this place up? We love it here. It's peaceful."

"Not if I'm walking through town panicking over the possibility of running into him."

Arlene nodded in what looked like reluctant agreement. "What did the woman say? About your lease?"

"I don't know. I left her a voice mail. The problem is it's a five-year lease. I can't commit to that any longer. I need to cut that tie first. And figure out the rest as I go. I have a nest egg. I'll be fine." Even though Hayden knew that was true—she would be fine—she didn't want to start over. She didn't want to move. She didn't want to look for a job. But with her heart filleted and lying on a cutting board, she didn't see another option.

"You might feel differently in a few days. Don't do anything rash. What if he calls to talk—"

"I don't want to talk to him."

"Do you think he's in love with that Claire chick?"

"No. I don't. That was the spark that started an argument, not the reason for the argument. The only part that matters is that I love him and he can't love me back. His work means more to him than me, and while I want to tell him that's a crock, there was also a time that I put my work before my family, too."

"That's different and you know it." Arlene leveled her with a firm look. "Your family is detrimental, and you're nothing but good for Tate."

Hayden agreed, but… "I don't want to be here. I wish I could… I don't know. Just disappear for a while."

Arlene sat up. She set down her flute of sparkling wine—they hadn't drunk even half a glass apiece since they'd been eagerly wolfing down sheet cake—and stood from the sofa. "Let's go then."

"Let's?"

"Yes! I have frequent flyer miles and some vouchers from work for a free stay at Caesars Palace. You want to get away, and lucky for you, since I went in for the last holiday, my boss owes me. She even said, 'You can have a few extra days off whenever you need. Just let me know.'"

"Caesars Palace? In Vegas?"

Arlene was already tapping the screen of her iPhone. "Well, I ain't talking about going to Rome, honey." Then into the speaker she said, "Amy, hi. It's Arlene…"

While Arlene paced the width of Hayden's living room explaining to her boss that she'd be out for a few days, a smile Hayden didn't know she had hidden away pulled her cheeks.

Maybe this was what she needed in order to think straight. A few days of being somewhere that was the total antithesis to Spright Island. A loud, smoky, hectic environment where she couldn't sit still and lick her wounds. What had Tate said? That he'd tried living dangerously for a while? Well maybe it was time for her to do the same.

Leaving for a few days was only a matter of packing a bag and rescheduling a few classes. Tate might've convinced himself that this community couldn't survive without him, but she knew they could live without yoga classes for a couple of days.

She was in no shape to be teaching anyone this week, anyway—especially if she spotted Tate walking by or, heaven forbid, if he came in. No one needed to witness her screaming at him, or worse, *blubbering* in the middle of king dancer pose.

"Done." Arlene swiped her phone's screen. "Now for the flight. How soon do you want to leave?"

Hayden crushed Arlene into a hug. A vacation was exactly what she needed. Time to recoup and think about her choices. Maybe Arlene was right and a few days later she wouldn't leave her beloved home. Only time would tell. "Thank you."

"Oh, honey. You know I have your back." All business, Arlene disentangled Hayden from her neck and tapped her phone again. "How soon?"

"As soon as humanly possible."

"That's my girl," Arlene said with a grin.

Tate had promised to entertain his adoptive parents when they came in on January 2, so in spite of not being up to having company, he was resigned to keep his word. Especially since he had skipped Christmas with them to fly to London and spend it with the Singletons.

His mother, Marion, hadn't acted as if it'd bothered her but his father, William, mentioned she'd been sad over the holidays without their normal traditions. Tate loved his parents, and he hadn't been the most receptive son since finding out the news that he was *someone else's* son, too, so he decided to keep his chin up for their sakes—regardless of his tumultuous emotional state.

Which he was determined to compartmentalize.

After dinner at Brass Pony, Tate drove by Hayden's yoga studio, taking note of the closed sign. Her upstairs windows were dark, but it was after nine, so maybe she'd turned in early.

After their argument on New Year's Eve, he'd given her space the next day. It'd nearly killed him not to text or call and apologize or ask that she forgive him—though *begging* might not be out of the question. But he'd been where she was before—angry, bewildered, confused. She had expectations and he'd failed her miserably.

This morning he'd keyed in two texts. One: I'm sorry and another: Let's talk. Both had gone unanswered, and he supposed he deserved that. She was angry. She had a right to be. She'd professed her love for him, and he'd sat there like a dope.

After Claire's pop-up appearance, his only thought was to get Hayden the hell out of there. His ex showing up at the café had nearly ruined his and Hayden's beginning, and he'd be damned if she'd trumpet in the end.

As much as he wanted to blame his ex for ruining his relationship, though, he couldn't. The fault lay squarely on him. The problem was his inability to be honest with himself, or Hayden. He'd been trying to compartmentalize and control different facets of his life. His head over here in this box, his heart in that one. He was beginning to see it wasn't working. There were no "compartments." There was only him—the whole him.

Marion chattered away about how stuffed she was and how delicious dinner was. "The cheesecake wasn't necessary, Tate." She cradled a plastic takeaway box on her lap in the front seat of his car.

"You mentioned that turtle cheesecake was on the menu fourteen times, Mom." From the corner of his eye, he watched her smile.

"Yes, but my diet…"

"You're beautiful," William said to his wife, squeezing her shoulder. "I tell her that every day," he explained to Tate. "She doesn't believe me. I don't know how many times I have to say 'I love you' and 'you're beautiful' for her believe me."

"Only about a million more times," she answered, patting William's hand.

Dread settled over Tate like a dark cloud. The five-star cuisine in his stomach churned. He reached into his pocket for a red-and-white-striped peppermint candy, unwrapped one end using his teeth and popped the candy into his mouth.

"Are you okay?" his mother asked.

"Ate too much," he told her, but it wasn't true. His throat was full like there was a lump in it and it wasn't from the ahi tuna bowl he'd enjoyed for dinner. He hadn't even had a cocktail, choosing water with a slice of lemon instead. No, he wasn't okay. He was negotiating with grief...or maybe worry was more accurate. He reminded himself for the millionth time that just because they'd argued didn't mean Hayden was gone forever. She was just unreachable at the moment.

In his driveway, he slowed to open the garage door and parked inside. Once his family was in the house, his mother stowed her cheesecake in the fridge "for later," and his father went for the whiskey cabinet to see what was available.

Tate watched them interact with easy smiles and the playful elbow to the ribs he'd often seen his mother give his father. They were in love. It was painfully obvious and not exactly the sort of behavior he'd welcomed as a teenager. He remembered when he was a teenager, rushing his friends off to another part of the house when William and Marion started making out in the kitchen.

"Here you go, son." His dad handed over Tate's drink. "I'm going to watch football. You coming?"

"Yeah. Let me just... In a minute."

William bypassed the dining room and the fireplace where Tate had laid Hayden down two nights ago. In the attached family room, the television clicked on, the sounds of cheering and announcers infiltrating the space.

"Okay." Marion climbed onto one of the bar stools at the breakfast bar and folded her hands. "Why don't you pour me a glass of wine to go with your cocktail and we'll talk about it."

Marion and William Duncan were well into their fifties. Both shorter than Tate, he remembered noting how obvious it was that he was adopted when he'd shot up to six two at age seventeen. Marion's dark hair was cut medium and circling her face. Her cheeks were rosy and round and, despite her suggestion that she needed to lose ten pounds, was on the slim side.

William had a belly, suggesting he liked to eat, and was losing his hair, something that Tate wouldn't have to worry about given George Singleton's full head of hair. But that was a simple matter of DNA and genes passed down—scientific markers of who he was.

Whether or not he was taller than Marion and William, or didn't share their body types didn't matter. Marion and William knew her son. Tate had been living with them from age three and a half until he flew the nest.

In short, they were his parents. They loved him. And his mother could help him through this if he would let her.

"Her name is Hayden" was where he started the story. And since it was a long one, he rounded the bar and sat down before sharing the whole sordid tale.

Twenty-Five

Tate's parents stayed for breakfast and then they were off to catch their plane to San Francisco. The second they were out the door, Tate told himself he needed coffee, but he knew once he left his house and pointed in the direction of the café, he'd drive by Hayden's once more.

Damn.

The closed sign was still hanging on the door of the yoga studio. This was the third day in a row.

At the risk of being accused of being a stalker, or at the very least a heartsick moron, he decided to park and try knocking on her front door.

Last night he'd told Marion everything about Claire. About Hayden. About the trip to London. As the old black-and-white gangster movies his dad liked to watch were known for saying, Tate had sung like a canary.

It bubbled out of him in one messy, winding story, and by the end he was mortified to find himself hunkered over his drink, his eyes burning with unshed tears and his liquor untouched.

But his mother had never expected him to ignore his emotions, so he didn't.

"It's too much to handle. I just need time," he'd said in

frustration, finally taking a burning swallow of the whiskey his father had poured for him.

His mother's hand rubbed his back as she hummed thoughtfully to herself.

"That's what you've got for me?" he asked. "A thoughtful hum?"

Knowing he was teasing her, Marion's mouth curved at the edge. "I'm not sure if you want me to tell you you're wrong or not. Should I agree instead?"

He'd had to admit he could use some female insight, so he answered his mother's question with one of his own.

"How am I wrong?" The question came out with a frustrated edge, so he took another swallow from his glass. "What the hell was I supposed to do when everything was thrown at me in rapid succession?"

Another thoughtful hum came from Marion. "Be honest with yourself, and then be honest with Hayden."

"I was!"

"You *weren't*. You acted as if you don't know how to feel." Marion shook her head. "That's bull, Tate. You know. You're afraid to admit it, but you know."

He'd opened his mouth to argue, but he couldn't.

She was right.

Last night he'd gone to bed and had slept three, maybe four hours on and off. He'd tossed and turned and rationalized and thought through, around and over everything he and his mother had talked about.

He was in love with Hayden. Of course he was. She'd taken as much of him as she'd given of herself, and when she'd been vulnerable, he'd offered a lame excuse about *timing*.

He woke with a panicky feeling, an unease unlike any he'd felt before. He knew what he had to do, and for once, making the decision to confess how badly he'd fucked up seemed easy.

Upstairs, at Hayden's apartment door, Tate ignored the fullness of his heart, now lodged in his throat, and knocked. He waited. Knocked again. No answer.

"Hayden? If you're in there, I just need a few seconds." He braced his palms on the doorframe and waited. Nothing. "I have something to say and it has to be in person. Sixty seconds, tops."

He needed her to listen to what he had to say. He couldn't let another moment pass with her believing that he'd prioritized everyone and everything in his life over her—over the woman he loved.

"How about thirty seconds?" He could work with thirty. He just needed her to open the damn door.

Pulling his phone from his pocket, he called her and heard the distinct jingle of her ringtone inside the apartment about one second before he heard the outside door close and the sound of someone coming up the stairs.

"She left her phone at home. She's not here." One of Hayden's friends, the one with the short hair, not the bawdy blonde one, regarded him coolly. "I'm here to water her plants."

"Where is she?" He stepped aside so she could unlock the door and let herself in.

"I'm sure if she wanted you to know that, she would have told you."

She started to shut the door but he stopped it with one hand. "Is she safe?"

"She's safe." Her eyes warmed slightly. "She's with Arlene."

"Arlene. The blonde one." Tate offered a smile, but the brunette only scowled. "Thank you…"

"Emily." She sighed.

"Emily. Thank you. Can you tell me when she'll be back?"

She pressed her lips together.

"Ballpark?" he tried.

"Tomorrow, unless they decide to stay in...*wherever* they went."

"You know though. Where they went."

"Of course I know where they went." She frowned. "I also know that she's seriously considering buying herself out of the lease and leaving Spright Island because of *you*. Do you know how much she loves it here? Can you even fathom what she did to move here? What she gave up? She doesn't own a car, Tate. Not because she's trying to save the planet but because she sunk every dollar she had into her yoga studio. When Hayden goes in, she goes *all in*. Her friends are lifers."

Her lips twisted in consideration as she considered him, and his position in Hayden's life.

"I know I screwed up," he said, still wrapping his head around the idea that Hayden might leave Spright Island because of him.

"You think?" Emily propped her fist on her hip, not ready to let him off the hook.

"I *know*. I'll do whatever it takes for her to stay."

"Like what? Buy the building?" she snapped.

He smiled, not denying that buying the building was his first instinct. But he wouldn't trap her into staying. He wouldn't trick her into sticking around. She deserved to have the life she built, and he'd honor that.

"No. I'm not going to buy the building. But I promise, I won't be the reason she leaves."

Some of Emily's skepticism fled from her face, compassion replacing it. "This community is better because of her."

Emily was right. He'd seen residents interact with Hayden, the smiles at the café or the restaurant whenever she was around. She was contagious and beautiful. Incredible, really. How had been so obtuse not to see what was right in front of him. Of course Spright Wellness Community was better because of Hayden.

"We all are," he told Emily. And then he turned to leave.

Twenty-Six

Vegas was exactly what Hayden needed, which was surprising to say the least. Normally she focused on being quiet and listening to her inner voice to clear her mind.

In this case a few days of drinks, gambling and a male strip show had cleared her mind just fine.

Arlene dropped Hayden off at her studio, a large pair of dark sunglasses hiding the evidence of a killer hangover. Hayden, while she'd enjoyed a few cocktails, hadn't abused her liver while she was in Vegas. Her drug of choice had been the craps table. She left up forty dollars, which she considered a win since she'd been down over two hundred bucks before that. She knew when to cut and run.

Apparently.

"I'm going to go home and die," Arlene said, droll.

"I have detox tea upstairs if you think it would help."

"Not sure anything would help except maybe a time machine. Then I could undrink those last four margaritas."

Hayden had been swamped with regret during the flight home to Washington, which made Arlene's next question easy to answer.

"Are you seriously moving off Spright Island?" Arlene

looked sad to ask it, which warmed Hayden's heart. She truly loved her friends.

"Of course not."

"Yes!" Arlene shouted before clutching her head with both hands. "Ow, my skull."

"Go home. Get some sleep. And thank you for a fantastic trip."

She stepped out of the car and Arlene drove away. It was cool, but sunny, and Hayden paused to take in the market across the street, waving at Sherry who'd just pulled open the door to walk in.

All around her there were smiling faces, and beautiful trees. Homes and retail establishments that were cared for and well-loved.

Spright Island and the people who lived here were Hayden's salvation. No matter what happened between her and Tate in the future, she wouldn't rob herself of the joy of living here. She was a better person here and this community—a place that Tate had envisioned into all its glory—was special. She sucked in a lungful of crisp air and turned, alarmed to see the man of her thoughts standing on the sidewalk outside her studio.

That speech had sounded fine inside her head. Faced with him, however, her instincts told her to protect herself. Build that wall as high and strong as she could.

"Hayden."

That voice.

Tate had said her name in every way imaginable. During the throes of heated sexual contact, in jest, when he was angry or happy. She heard compassion in his voice now; saw it on his face, too. He regretted their argument, that much was clear. But if he didn't love her—when she still loved him with everything she was—then nothing had changed except the date.

"Hi."

"Can I talk to you?" he asked.

She didn't want to talk to him. Not yet. Not until… Until what? Until she fell out of love with him? Who knew how long that would take.

Willing herself to be brave, she called up the very strength of character that brought her to Spright Wellness Community in the first place. "Sure."

"May I?" He gestured to her carry-on and she nodded, letting him take the luggage as she unlocked her studio door. She tried to ignore the brush of his hand on hers and the soft scent of leather coming off his coat. She tried, but failed.

Mere days ago she could've greeted him with a kiss. A hug. Maybe more. It was hard to believe after all they'd experienced together—with his family and hers—that this was over.

Stepping into her yoga studio, she focused instead on its pale wood floors and salt lamps. The padded blocks and yoga mats and water bottles for sale.

No way would she abandon her dream any more than Tate would abandon his. She hadn't run away from her family or her responsibility when she left Seattle. She'd run *toward* a dream—a vision that burned in her heart. There was a difference.

"I heard you were considering leaving," he said, flipping the lock behind him.

So they were doing this here.

"Where'd you hear that?"

"Emily. But don't be upset with her. She told me that so I'd know where her loyalty lies. With you. She doesn't want you to leave." He took a long, slow look around her studio. "No one at Spright Island wants you to leave. *I* don't want you to leave."

It was great to hear that. She wanted to shout with joy!

But just because he didn't want her to leave didn't mean he was suddenly and madly in love with her, did it?

"I'm not leaving," she said cautiously.

"Good." His smile caused an ache in her heart she was sure would drop her to her knees. So she flexed her core to keep her standing and folded her arms to protect herself. It wasn't a wall, but it was all she had. She wanted to believe that everything had changed. That he'd recalled their fight with the regret she felt whenever she thought about it. That he wished as much as she did that they had stopped and put their egos on hold long enough to have a conversation about what it meant to be together—and just how much they meant to each other.

It might not have salvaged what they had—she wasn't accepting less than she deserved from anyone—but they could've ended things amicably.

He stepped deeper into the room and came as close as he could without touching her. So close she had to tilt her head back to look up at him.

"I love you, Hayden. I fell in love with you probably before you fell for me, but I was too busy compartmentalizing and trying to sort out everything to realize it. I *should've* realized it. Nothing has ever been clearer than the fact that you belong with me and I already belong to you. I handled that night by the fireplace so badly. I messed up."

She felt her mouth drop open and she stood there in stunned silence combing over everything he'd said. He'd... fallen in love with her?

"I'm sorry," he continued. "For everything I said that night that was unfair and untrue. For making you think for one second you mattered less to me than anything on this planet."

She still couldn't speak so she stood there, mute as a mime as Tate reached into his jacket pocket and came out with his phone.

"You were thinking of leaving so that you didn't have to run into me, weren't you? So we could avoid each other at the market. Not cross paths while dining in the same restaurant." He tilted his head. "Not bump into each other in the park in the spring."

Yes to all of those things, but that was juvenile, wasn't it? Trying to avoid him. Tate Duncan *was* Spright Island.

"We'll work it out," she said carefully, still unraveling what he'd said to her. Her heart was grasping to his "I love you," desperate to be healed, but her mind… Her mind was more skeptical.

"I have a proposition for you. If you still love me, I want to be with you without barriers. Without compartments. Without playing it safe. Safe is for pussies."

Half her mouth lifted, hope filling her heart against her will.

He swiped the screen of his phone. "But if you've stopped loving me, or you can't trust me to make good on my promise to love you back, well…"

He offered the cell phone and she took it with shaking hands.

"It's a deed," he explained. "To my new house in San Francisco." He tapped the screen of the phone and brought up a text message with a timestamp from yesterday. "Which means I can sell my house here."

It was from Sherry, the real estate agent. Hayden read it, her eyes heating with tears. *I'm sure we can find the perfect buyer for your house, and fast!*

"You're…leaving?" Spright Island without Tate was as wrong as Hayden's life without Tate. "You love that house."

"I do," he admitted.

"You love it here," she said, emotion tightening her throat.

"I do." He put a hand on her arm and gave her a gentle squeeze. "But not more than I love you. I won't put anything before that."

He plucked the phone from her trembling fingers and pocketed it. "I know you can't see it, but I'm falling apart, Hayden. I miss you every moment you're not here, and hearing that you were considering uprooting what you've built because of—because I was too afraid to be honest with you… It's not right for you to compromise. So I will. For you. You deserve everything you've worked so hard to gain."

He waited while she stared, tears trembling on the edges of her eyelids. His every word had sealed up the crack he'd put in her heart.

He loved her. He *loved* her.

And he wanted her to stay. He was willing to walk away from his legacy and move back to California. He was giving her the community that needed him as much as he'd originally stated.

Silly billionaire.

"If I could rewind that night, we'd stay at the party, and drink champagne at midnight, and I'd kiss you so that everyone there would know what you meant to me. We'd still make love at my house by the fire—" he blew out a breath "—I don't see how that could get any better."

She bit her lip to hide a smile. Neither did she. It'd been everything.

"But you wouldn't have had the chance to tell me you love me, Hayden. Not before I said I loved you first." His eyes shimmered, as if the emotions he'd refused to share with her had pushed their way past his defenses.

"I followed rules my entire life. None of them kept me safe from drama or a broken relationship. When I broke those rules with you, though, I was more whole than I've ever been. My identity was mixed up in parents I'd never met and a twin brother I was getting to know. What I didn't know was that with you, I was becoming someone else. Someone better. I hope…the right man for you." His smile broke through, but nervous like he had no idea how she'd react. She knew, though. She knew. "I love you so much. I don't know where you went, but I know why, and I deserved it. I deserve whatever it is you say next."

He swallowed thickly, straightening his shoulders for the blows that would come. Ready to accept whatever she had to say—ready, if she said the word, to walk away from everything he cared about.

But she loved him. She'd never ask him to do that.

"When I left Seattle behind, when I parted ways from my family, it was to become a better version of myself. The reason I'm not leaving Spright Island isn't because of my yoga studio, or my apartment, or even this amazing community. I'm staying because of who I am when I'm here. I'm better. More caring. More giving. And that has a lot to do with you, Tate Duncan. You're more than this community. You're more than a legacy for generations to come. You're the man I love more than anything." A tear tumbled from her eye. "I'm better when I'm with *you*."

Before she finished speaking, Tate was crushing her against him.

"Thank God," he said into her hair, before lifting her face and seeking her lips with his. One kiss, perfect and sweet, and then he looked down at her with sheer awe.

"You, Hayden, are my legacy. Not this community. I'll never let work, or exes, or family come between us again. Whatever comes up we'll handle it. Together. Forever."

"I like the sound of forever." She wrapped her fingers around his and stood on her tiptoes. "But first, you have to make up for the last few days."

He smiled against her lips. "Name your price."

"Well, there was this strip show I saw…shirtless guys covered in oil…" She ran her hands over his button-down shirt. "How do you look in a g-string?"

He laughed, but frowned when he saw that she was serious. "Really?"

"Maybe. But I definitely will need you to call Sherry and tell her you're not selling your house in the woods."

"Done."

She brushed a lock of dark hair from his forehead. "I see no harm in keeping the house in San Francisco, though. We have to stay somewhere when we visit your parents in California."

He scooped her up against him and kissed away her grin, his mouth exploring hers in a movie-worthy, happy-ever-after kiss before setting her on her feet.

"I love you, Hayden Green."

"I love you, too, Tate Duncan." She tapped her chin. "Or is it Wesley Singleton?"

"Something else for you to decide."

"Me? Why me?"

"I'd like to give you one of those last names soon, along with a wedding ring. And a coveted house in the woods on an island."

Her head spun with possibility, with a future she hadn't dared imagine before this moment.

"What do you think?" he asked.

"I think...that fairy tales do come true."

"Except in this case, you're the one who saved me." Tate gestured to the sidewalk outside her studio. "You pulled me out of the rain, and then you kissed me. And I was never the same."

"Me neither."

"Well, then maybe we saved each other."

"Yeah." She smiled. "Maybe we did."

Epilogue

3 years later

The Duncan-Green wedding had happened last summer. The Commons were transformed for the lavish ceremony, decorated in, lavender and cream.

Hayden's family—the Greens—had attended, on their best behavior without Grandma Winnie in tow. She'd passed away eight months ago now, her suffering meeting its end. Quite a bit of Hayden's and her mother's had died along with Winnie. Both of Tate's families had shown as well—the Duncans and the Singletons—and as a result the Singletons hadn't returned to Spright Island that winter for Christmas.

This year, they had. Christmas dinner had been served in their home—Hayden and Tate's mansion in the woods. They'd proudly stepped Marion and William through the tradition of Christmas crackers, and Jane and George had gotten their first taste of American holiday cuisine.

Reid and Drew had come to celebrate with them as well and were currently sitting on the floor with their two-year-old son, Roland. Drew cooed over her baby boy, who was tearing apart a box—a box that had previously contained an outfit that Roland was ignoring.

Aunt Hayden understood his lack of excitement.

Tate came into the room with a tray of mugs as Jane followed with their family's specialty: bread pudding. Hayden had thought she was too stuffed for another bite, but now that she saw the rich dessert she knew she wouldn't be able to deny herself a taste.

"We have one more gift," Tate said after everyone had settled into the sofas and chairs with their desserts.

"A surprise actually," Hayden said, pulling one last paper-wrapped Christmas cracker from its hiding place on the tree.

"Another cracker?" Jane asked.

"A *very special* cracker." Tate took the wrapped gift from Hayden and handed it to Jane, then gestured to his Marion. "Mom, why don't you take the other end and give it a tug."

"Okay, but I'm not reading another silly joke." Marion warned. Her Christmas cracker contained a dirty joke about Rudolph and his "sleigh balls." Hayden wasn't sure how it got there, but she thought Reid might have had something to do with it.

"I promise there is no joke." Hayden tucked her palms around her protruding belly, excited for the grandparents to learn what she and Tate now knew.

The pair of moms tugged and the cracker popped, spraying out paper confetti and a rolled photo. Jane reached for it first, gasping as she studied the blurry black-and-white ultrasound.

"You know the sex!" Jane exclaimed, squinting at the blurs and bumps on the photo.

"Let me see!" Marion sat close to Jane and leaned in also.

It took only a few seconds for Jane to recognize what had so obviously been there all along.

"Twins!" Jane exclaimed.

"Twins?" Marion repeated and both women burst into tears.

William and George shook hands and then claimed it was time for celebrating with cigars. Drew left Roland in Reid's arms to see the photo for herself.

"Twins?" Reid frowned at his own son and then to Tate. "Show-off."

Soon after, the bread pudding and coffee were gone. The men went to light cigars in celebration of twin baby boys coming soon to a wellness community near them.

Before Tate went outside with his brother and fathers he made sure to stop and place a kiss on Hayden's lips.

"Merry Christmas, Tate."

"Merry Christmas, Hayden." He bent to press his lips to her tummy then stood and gave her a wink. "And family."

* * * * *

COMING SOON!

We really hope you enjoyed reading this book.
If you're looking for more romance
be sure to head to the shops when
new books are available on

Thursday 19th December

To see which titles are coming soon, please visit
millsandboon.co.uk/nextmonth

MILLS & BOON

LET'S TALK
Romance

For exclusive extracts, competitions and special offers, find us online:

f MillsandBoon

X @MillsandBoon

⊙ @MillsandBoonUK

♪ @MillsandBoonUK

Get in touch on 01413 063 232

OUT NOW!

Available at
millsandboon.co.uk

MILLS & BOON

 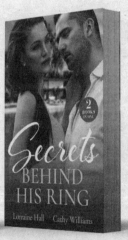 

MILLS & BOON

THE HEART OF ROMANCE

A ROMANCE FOR EVERY READER

MODERN
Prepare to be swept off your feet by sophisticated, sexy and seductive heroes, in some of the world's most glamourous and romantic locations, where power and passion collide.

HISTORICAL
Escape with historical heroes from time gone by. Whether your passion is for wicked Regency Rakes, muscled Vikings or rugged Highlanders, awaken the romance of the past.

MEDICAL
Set your pulse racing with dedicated, delectable doctors in the high-pressure world of medicine, where emotions run high and passion, comfort and love are the best medicine.

True Love
Celebrate true love with tender stories of heartfelt romance, from the rush of falling in love to the joy a new baby can bring, and a focus on the emotional heart of a relationship.

HEROES
The excitement of a gripping thriller, with intense romance at its heart. Resourceful, true-to-life women and strong, fearless men face danger and desire - a killer combination!

From showing up to glowing up, these characters are on the path to leading their best lives and finding romance along the way – with plenty of sizzling spice!

To see which titles are coming soon, please visit

millsandboon.co.uk/nextmonth